Praise for the So

THE SONG OF SEARE

C. E. LAUREANO

THE SWORD

and

THE SONG

a novel

A NAVPRESS RESOURCE PUBLISHED IN ALLIANCE
WITH TYNDALE HOUSE PUBLISHERS, INC.

NAVPRESS●.

NavPress is the publishing ministry of The Navigators, an international Christian organization and leader in personal spiritual development. NavPress is committed to helping people grow spiritually and enjoy lives of meaning and hope through personal and group resources that are biblically rooted, culturally relevant, and highly practical.

For more information, go to www.NavPress.com.

For Reagen: editor, ringmaster, and plotter extraordinaire.
Thanks for helping me bring order to the chaos.
I couldn't have done it without you.

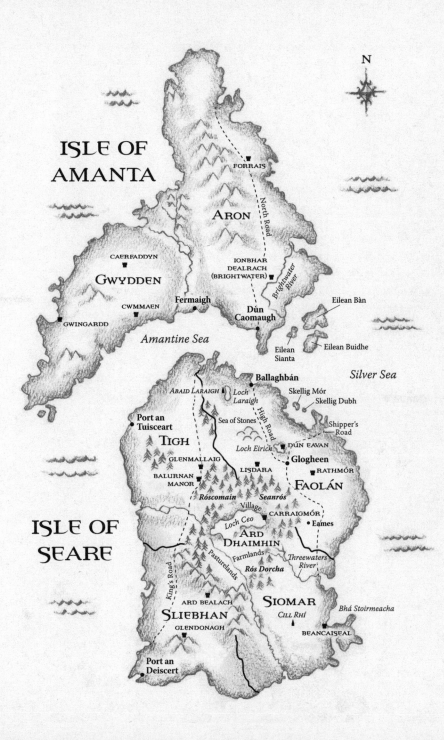

CHAPTER
ONE

The sword came close enough for him to feel the breath of wind in its passing. Conor jumped back, meeting the edge of the blade too late with his own, and groaned as the impact shuddered into his arms and shoulders.

"You've gotten slow." Eoghan backed off a fraction, just enough that Conor would know he was letting him rest. "This is what happens when you get lazy."

"I wasn't lazy," Conor said through gritted teeth. "I was in captivity." He used the momentary distraction to launch his attack, harrying his friend with a flurry of strikes. Eoghan brushed them aside in the same way one would swat at a gnat.

Eoghan was right: Conor was slow. And lazy.

The idea burned like fire in his gut. Three months. He had left Ard Dhaimhin for the war in the kingdoms three months ago at the pinnacle of his skills, besting both his friend and Master Liam, former Ceannaire of the Fíréin brotherhood, before he left. And now he could barely keep up in a simple practice match, his arms and shoulders shaking with the exertion of holding the lightweight wooden sword.

Never mind that what he'd said to Eoghan was true. He'd been captured by the Sofarende and fed survival rations for a month, then been entrapped in a sidhe's glamour at the keep of a Gwynn prince for another. The last of his bruises had just faded, and he'd barely returned to his sword work. His victory over the prince's guard captain in Gwydden hinted that perhaps it wasn't his skills that were subpar, but it still rankled to have fallen so far behind his friend, his mentor—his king.

He sprang forward on a surge of energy and irritation, directing one flawless strike after another. Eoghan blocked each of them, but he couldn't counter under the speed. Then Conor closed too much of the gap between them, and Eoghan's sword connected with his right wrist. Involuntarily, Conor's hand opened and the sword fell to the soft sand.

"Yield?" Eoghan asked.

Conor's answer was a shoulder into Eoghan's midsection as he drove him to the ground. Eoghan let out a surprised laugh along with the air in his body as they hit the sand. They grappled for a minute before Conor realized his mistake. He might have several inches on the other man, but Eoghan packed dozens more pounds of muscle, especially considering the weight Conor had lost off his already-lean frame. Half a dozen moves, and Eoghan had Conor in an inescapable clinch, his face pressed into the dirt, sand grinding into his mouth.

"Yield?"

"Yield." Conor drew a deep breath when Eoghan released him and the weight shifted off him. He pounded his fist into the sand in frustration, only to look up and find his friend regarding him sympathetically. "Don't say it."

"You need to get back into drills with the other men—"

"I said, don't say it."

"I know you're distracted by your reunion with Aine—"

4

"Aine is not a distraction." Conor shook the sand out of his tunic and retrieved his practice sword. He weighed it in his hand for a minute before tossing it back into the pile. "Unlike the reason you brought up this topic. When are you going to announce it?"

"You're the ones who insist that I'm meant to be the High King." Eoghan deflated, his conflict plain in his stance. "I don't want this."

"Just as I don't want to be responsible for the city, but it seems that Carraigmór has chosen me as clearly as the prophecies have named you. Speaking of which, the prefects are probably waiting for me. Don't forget the Conclave meeting this morning." Conor picked up his sword—his real sword—and shrugged it on. Ever since the attack on Ard Dhaimhin, not a warrior went about unarmed. They could not lose a minute should their enemy decide to finish the job he started.

Conor trudged up the path from the private practice yard, noting the change in light from dawn to full day as he moved into the village proper. Wood smoke carried the scent of food on the breeze, and the faint noises from the craftsmen's cottages said that the day's work at Ard Dhaimhin had already begun. Thousands of people, many of them fleeing the druid's violent anti-Balian actions in the kingdoms, and no way to provide for them. In the days after the druid had laid waste to the city, they'd made an assessment of their resources. Three-quarters of their crops burned, half of the livestock killed, the forest animals and bees gone. The fish in the lake dead, and so many of them that the Fíréin hadn't been able to salvage them. Who knew how long the city would be feeling the effects of that habitat's destruction?

And he was responsible for it. Not just because he should have been here to intervene sooner but because he had inherited responsibility for the city when the password of Ard Dhaimhin's secret places passed to him.

He combed his fingers through his hair in frustration. Running the city required authority, but he couldn't help but feel his was merely borrowed. Ever since he had announced to the Conclave his belief that Eoghan, not he, was destined to become the new High King, there had been an uncomfortable power shift. They still obeyed Conor's orders, but now their obedience came with a sideways look, a held breath, to see if this was the moment Eoghan would finally step up and take leadership. That he held back didn't change the fact Conor was filling a position that was not rightfully his.

Men nodded to him as he passed, but in his current mood, he wondered if their acknowledgment weren't a shade less deferential than it would be toward Eoghan.

This isn't about me, Conor told himself firmly. *This is about the future of Ard Dhaimhin, the future of Seare. And the men need to know who will be leading them when the time comes.*

The men needed the assurance that Comdiu had once again sent them their High King.

Conor changed his plans midstride. Rather than make his usual rounds through the village, he turned toward Carraigmór, the great keep on the edge of Loch Ceo, carved with forgotten technology from the massive granite rock face. He'd have just enough time to clean up and head to the Ceannaire's office before the prefects arrived with their reports. And thus would begin another long day in Ard Dhaimhin. The only bright spot was the possibility of seeing his wife for a few minutes before he started into the day's tasks. Knowing her, she'd be dressed and ready to start her work at the healers' cottage in the village below.

But when he reached their small, sparse chamber in the upper reaches of the keep, his wife still lay beneath the heavy coverings of wool and fur, her eyes closed. A frown creased his forehead. This was unusual for her. But then, she had been working harder than anyone expected of her, putting in long hours in the village below during the daylight and then again in the keep with her stacks of books after dark.

Quietly, he poured tepid water in the basin and washed the worst of the sand and sweat from his body. As he was reaching for a clean tunic, a rustle from the bed caught his attention. Aine was watching him, a sleepy smile on her face.

"I was beginning to worry." He sank down on the edge of the bed and propped himself on one elbow beside her.

"What time is it?"

"An hour past dawn. I just came back to change after my match with Eoghan."

"So late?" Alarm lit her eyes, and she sat up abruptly. "What happened to your arm?"

Conor glanced down at the long red abrasion that stretched from his elbow to his wrist. He hadn't noticed it through his annoyance. "The bout turned into something of a wrestling match, I'm afraid."

"It might be easier if you could just talk things out."

"Eoghan isn't ready to talk about anything that matters." Not about the kingship. Not about the fact the other man harbored feelings for Conor's wife.

Maybe it was good that Eoghan's skills surpassed his own at the moment. The mere thought made Conor want to grind him into the sand, something that was wholly inadvisable when thinking about his uncrowned king.

Conor shifted his attention instead to the book on the chair beside the bed, one he'd had to pry from her fingers when he'd returned to the chamber the night before. "Did you find anything?"

"Nothing helpful. King Daimhin didn't even bother to date this one, though from some of the entries, I'm guessing it's from the fourth or fifth year of his reign."

"But nothing about the sword?"

Aine pushed back the covers and retrieved her dress from the peg beside the bed. "No, mostly just his musings about clan disputes. Thoughts on how to get his chiefs to stop squabbling and start working together against a common enemy."

"What enemy?"

"He doesn't say."

Conor's momentary hopes deflated. When they'd found the cache of journals written in Daimhin's own hand, they'd been sure it would contain something useful about those mysteries of the kingship that still remained locked away: the sword, the Rune Throne, the wards. But in the month in which Aine had pored over the books while Conor had read through those writ-ten in foreign languages, she'd found absolutely nothing of help.

"Maybe he purposely left the details out," Aine said. "He had no reason to think his line would die with him. Magic is typi-cally something passed down from one generation to another."

"And yet he rambled on about grain tallies and livestock breeding."

"He works through his thoughts on paper, as you do with music or in the practice yard."

Conor paused to look at her—really look at her. Not for the first time, he thought what an excellent queen she'd make. Intelligent. Insightful. More patient than any man had a right to expect. More hardworking than she had a right to expect of herself.

The shadows beneath her eyes had deepened sometime in the last few weeks, and he hadn't even noticed. "Aine, maybe you should take some time to rest."

"Nonsense. I'm fine." She pulled her dress over her head and began lacing the front with brusque movements, as if he might forcibly prevent her from preparing for the day.

He remained seated and just watched her. After a few moments, she stopped and sighed. "I have to do something, Conor. I hate feeling useless, and that's what I would be if I sat here and did nothing but read old books all day."

He couldn't argue with that when he felt the same way. "Just promise me you won't work yourself to exhaustion."

She hesitated, but at last she nodded. He kissed her lightly on the lips, donned his tunic, and steeled himself for whatever awaited him in the Ceannaire's office.

He strode down the corridors to the other side of the keep, where Master Liam's old study lay. The thought still brought on a pang of grief. He might have disagreed with the old Ceannaire, who had also happened to be Aine's half brother, but Liam had helped Conor develop the skills that saved his and his wife's life more than once. Not to mention access to knowledge that had helped him reinstate the protective wards that kept the city safe from magical incursion. The city still reeled from the loss of its leader.

When he entered the small chamber, Brother Riordan waited for him. Conor's father had temporarily taken on leadership in the city, only to cede it to his son when he returned—just another way the chain of command in Ard Dhaimhin had been tangled since Liam's death. "There you are. Someone said they'd seen you below before daybreak."

"Practice match with Eoghan."

"How'd it go?"

The look Conor gave Riordan must have said it all, because the older man chuckled. "Give yourself some time. After the treatment your body has received, some rest isn't out of order."

"And if the druid decides to attack again, I'll be less than useless."

"Losing to one of the brotherhood's most talented swordsmen hardly qualifies you as useless. You haven't noticed that Eoghan is spending all of his time in the training yards these days?"

Conor hadn't, but it explained much. Maybe he wasn't as out of shape as he thought after all. Before he could say anything, a rap sounded at the door and two men entered.

"Sir," the first one said, bowing to Conor.

Riordan made a move toward the door, but Conor gestured to an empty chair. "Please, stay. I'd like your opinion."

Riordan lowered himself into the seat, while the two prefects remained standing.

Conor accepted a wax tablet from the first man and scanned the notations there. "What's the latest tally, Arlyn?"

"We're nearly back to four thousand," Arlyn said. "Two thousand of them warriors, the rest mainly women and children."

Conor nodded, though his heart sank. Four thousand. That was close to the city's population before it had been attacked, but now more than half of their food was gone. He glanced at the second man. "Your report?"

The man handed over his tablet. "Fewer incidents this week. The guards have helped, but some of the kingdom men have not taken well to the restrictions."

"I'm sure they haven't." That was the problem with introducing outsiders into Ard Dhaimhin. Those men were used to a measure of freedom that was simply untenable here. The tension between the former brothers who were used to obeying without complaint and the newcomers, who by Fíréin standards did nothing but complain, was only bound to escalate as their situation became more difficult.

Conor dismissed the men with a nod and leaned back in his chair. He focused on his father. "What do you think?"

"I think that you can't expect kingdom men to uphold the same standards as the Fíréin when they haven't had the benefit of our training or our ways of life."

"I don't see how we have a choice. This arrangement works only if everyone pulls their own weight. Aine has even the women and children organized to maintain the cottage gardens to supplement our supplies. If we can't get the newcomers to work with the brothers, we'll most certainly starve."

"It is that dire?"

"It's that dire." Conor sifted through the stacks of tablets on his desk and pushed one toward Riordan. "I was going to present an updated tally to the Conclave this afternoon. We'll run out of food before midwinter unless we find an outside source of trade. And Niall still has a stranglehold on the kingdom. Anyone found to be trading with Ard Dhaimhin is to be summarily executed."

"If he starves us out, he doesn't need to fight us."

"Exactly."

"Comdiu will provide," Riordan said quietly, but doubt colored his tone. They both knew that being beloved of Comdiu did not exempt them from tragedy. Their Lord's view was wide. In the scope of the entire world, who was to say He wouldn't sacrifice the small sliver that was Seare for a greater purpose?

+ + +

"Sir? They're ready for you."

Conor glanced up at the young brother who had poked his head into the office. It took a moment to register the honorific and a moment longer to realize what he meant. The Conclave. The meeting. He'd been so absorbed in his tallies that for a moment he'd forgotten the reason he was compiling the information. He shrugged on his sword and gathered up several wax tablets that contained the basic information he needed to convey. With the evidence before them, the Conclave could not fail to agree with his conclusions.

The men were already gathered in Carraigmór's great hall, just barely illuminated by a single man-sized candle, another of their conservation measures. A quick glance showed that only Eoghan was missing.

They stood and bowed when Conor approached, another show of honor that rested uneasily with him. He nodded, and they all took their seats. "We're just waiting for—"

"I'm here." Eoghan entered the room and took his seat without fanfare, his placid expression hinting nothing of their argument this morning.

"Good. Brothers, you asked me for a report on the situation outside the city, and I'm afraid it's not nearly as definitive as I'd hoped." Conor sat and spread his tablets out in front of him. "It's been nearly impossible to get an accurate read on the number of men that Niall commands currently because they're spread throughout the countryside. I can only assume he is using some thread of sorcery to keep them under control and be able to summon them at a moment's notice."

"That's promising, though." Gradaigh might be the youngest member of the Conclave, but he nonetheless brought a calm, balanced perspective to their discussions. "It means that, at present, he is not marshaling his forces against us."

"We don't know that," Conor said. "Just because he doesn't have them gathered in one place doesn't mean he's not planning to attack."

"I don't see how he could." Dal, the exact opposite of Gradaigh in temperament and tone, spoke next. "Either he's commanding his men by sorcery, which means he can't enter the city because of your shield, or he doesn't have enough nonsorcery-controlled men to be able to move against us."

"He doesn't need to," Conor said. "He's already dealt Ard Dhaimhin a deathblow."

All eyes settled on him.

Conor tugged one of the tablets nearer to him. "Our population has topped four thousand, two thousand of whom are warriors. The rest are women and children who have sought sanctuary here. At these current rates of consumption, we have about three months' worth of food stored. We still have some fall and winter crops to be harvested, and there is hunting to be had in the forests and mountains to the south of the city, but it's not nearly enough. At this rate, I'd estimate that our food stores will run out somewhere in midwinter."

"Ration," Gradaigh said immediately. "Cut the men to half."

"Which will get us to spring. And then what? Do you expect they'll be able to live on bean sprouts until summer harvest?"

"What do you suggest?" Dal shot back, his tone irritated.

Conor cleared his throat. "I'm suggesting that we look further afield."

"Leave Ard Dhaimhin, you mean. That's exactly what the druid wants—to force us out of our city, to where we are defenseless."

"Better to fight now, while the men are still strong, than to wait for an attack when they're weak from a winter of half rations. How successful do you think we'll be in defending the city, including the women and children, if the men are unable to fight?"

The men shifted uncomfortably at the table—all but Riordan, who stared at him with clear and understanding eyes. He understood the difficulty of what Conor proposed, and he understood that only desperation would drive him to the suggestion.

"What do you think the druid wants with the city anyway?" Gradaigh asked. "It's not as if there's much left."

"What he wanted in the first place, I'd think. He still wants the oath-binding sword. He still wants to eliminate Balus's gifts. Attacking us in our weakness would go a long way to accomplishing that."

"You're asking us to abandon a city to which our brotherhood has pledged defense for half a millennium." Dal's flat tone held a distinct note of accusation.

"We've already changed our ways by allowing brothers to leave and opening the city to refugees," Riordan said. "It seems to me that mere tradition is no longer an adequate argument for inaction."

"And it seems to me that you're awfully anxious for war." Dal turned his scowl on Riordan. "Did you enjoy your taste of the fight so much that you're anxious to return us to it?"

"I've seen enough bloodshed and destruction for a lifetime. Yet pretending that dangers don't exist outside our borders will win us nothing."

Conor softened his tone and tried a different tactic. "Brothers, I'm no more anxious for war than any of you. That's why I believe we must be slow and strategic. Attack from a position of strength, without exposing our weaknesses. If you think Niall's desire for battle with Ard Dhaimhin was sated in a single attack, you're wrong. He will come at us again."

"What say you, Eoghan?" Gradaigh asked. "You've been quiet."

A hush fell over the table as all eyes rested on Eoghan. Conor tensed, waiting for his response, trying not to show his irritation. Eoghan had not been involved in the gathering of this information, yet Conor instinctively knew that their uncrowned king's opinion would hold far more weight than his own. When Eoghan finally spoke, his tone was low and measured. "I don't want outright war."

A few triumphant glances passed around the table.

"But you're wrong if you believe we can stay like this

indefinitely. You chose Conor—Ard Dhaimhin chose Conor—for a reason. He speaks the truth of our situation."

"So you think that we, too, must conquer the kingdoms?" Dal asked stiffly.

"I believe we must venture outside our city. But not now."

The group erupted into conversation, shocked by Eoghan's stance, but for different reasons. Conor rapped the hilt of his dagger against the table to gain their attention. Then he directed his question to Eoghan. "When, then, do you suggest we make our move? In the dead of winter, when we'll be hampered by weather? If you understand the situation as you say you do, you know that we haven't the food or the supplies to bide our time through another season."

"And I know that when the time is right, Comdiu will speak."

Conor's breath hissed out from his teeth and he sank into the chair. He didn't need to take a vote to know what the Conclave would decide. Conor might be the one with responsibility for the day-to-day operations of the city, but Eoghan heard the very voice of Comdiu. How could anyone argue with that?

Yet Conor was not wholly convinced Eoghan was speaking on behalf of their God. "Tell me, then. What has Comdiu said about the fact that you refuse the call to leadership?"

Eoghan's dark gaze fixed on him, hard, dangerous even. "You question my honesty? I have said that I did not feel it was time."

"You've said plenty more than that. You wish to exercise your influence as king without taking the responsibility."

"Conor," Riordan said softly.

Conor shook his head, aware this was a fight he could never win, despite the righteous anger boiling in his chest. Why had he expected anything different? Eoghan had been raised in Ard Dhaimhin, among men who spoke and debated and supposedly prayed for Comdiu's will but never did anything. They stood by and watched while Seare lost its magic, while the kingdoms were slowly overrun by an evil man, and they did nothing. Had Liam not been so stubborn, had he let them fight, perhaps Niall wouldn't even be in power now.

"I take it you're all in favor of waiting?" Conor asked.

"Let's put it to a vote," Daigh said. "In favor of revisiting the situation in another month, say aye."

"Aye."

"Opposed?"

"Opposed," Conor and Riordan said simultaneously. He met his father's eyes and gave him a swift nod.

"The ayes have it. Master Conor, if you would present any new information in one month—"

Conor pushed away from the table and gathered his tablets, not waiting to hear the rest of the conversation. He stalked from the room, fury trembling in his limbs. He was halfway back to the Ceannaire's study when Eoghan's voice rang out behind him. "Conor, please wait."

He stopped and turned. Eoghan walked toward him, his palms turned forward in a gesture of truce. "I don't want this to turn into a battle between us."

"That's the problem, Eoghan. This has nothing to do with us. This has to do with the well-being of four thousand people for whom we, as leaders, are responsible."

"What would you have me do? Do you think I have not begged Comdiu for the answer to this very question? He has not spoken to me. I take that to mean we wait. Comdiu's timing is not always our timing."

"I'm sure the mothers in the village will find that to be a comfort as they watch their children starve to death," Conor said. "Because that's what this decision means. A failure to act means death, just as the brotherhood's failure to act in the war meant the death of countless of our countrymen, including Aine's family."

Eoghan studied him closely. "Is this what this is really about? Revenge? Aine would not want men to die in vengeance for her family."

"I thought you knew me better than that, Eoghan. When you can bring yourself to embrace your calling, then we can talk. Until then, I have work to do."

Conor kept his pace deliberate, measured, willing Eoghan to stay behind. Should he follow him, Conor couldn't guarantee it wouldn't come to blows. Besides, he didn't have time for futile arguments. He had mere weeks to put together a more compelling case for action, one that even Eoghan and his claim to know Comdiu's will couldn't sink.

Conor might have been rejected as king, but he had been chosen as leader of Ard Dhaimhin. He would not fail them.

CHAPTER
TWO

A dozen sword forms, and Eoghan still felt like punching something.

He lowered his sword and sucked air into his lungs, wishing for the quiet of the mind that came only from pushing his body to its absolute limits. But he felt nothing. For the last two months, he'd spent nearly all day every day with the men in the training yard. It would take much more than a few sword forms to reach that point of blissful exhaustion, yet he dared not return to Carraigmór with this roiling anger burning in his gut.

When you can bring yourself to embrace your calling, then we can talk.

He adjusted his grip on the sword and launched into yet another form, the memory of Conor's scorn churning inside him. There were perhaps three men that he respected, three men he had loved in this world. One of them was dead, sacrificed for Ard Dhaimhin. The other two—Conor and Conor's father, Riordan—stood opposed to him. They thought he was shirking his duty, avoiding Comdiu's calling.

They were right.

Conor, Aine, and Riordan—the entire Conclave, in fact—accepted that Eoghan was meant to be High King. Daimhin's own writing stated that the man who would sit the Rune Throne would hear the voice of Comdiu, and he was the only one who fit that description.

So why could he not bring himself to embrace it?

He broke off the form and lowered his sword. It was no use. A dozen forms or a thousand—they would still not exorcise this feeling of failure or bring the peace he sought.

You're seeking peace where there is none to be found.

Comdiu's piercing presence stopped the thoughts in their tracks. "What shall I do, then? What do You want from me?"

Your obedience.

"I've done everything You've asked of me."

Have you?

"Aye."

That was a lie, though, and it didn't take word from Comdiu to tell him. His entire life, he had been raised to do his duty, groomed to take leadership from Liam. But when Conor had beaten the Ceannaire in a challenge match to earn freedom from his oaths, he'd dared to hope that perhaps his duty was done, that he could be free.

You worry about losing a life that did not belong to you. Why do you doubt Me?

I don't doubt You. I'm not needed here. Liam's plans for me failed. Conor was doing a fine job in the position of Ceannaire, and the city ran as smoothly as it ever had under Liam's command, even considering the presence of the kingdoms' subjects. Few people would question Conor should he decide to step forward and claim the kingship.

Men's most foolish decisions are made from fear.

I am not afraid.

Are you not? Then you are *foolish.*

What do You want from me, Comdiu? Do You want me to be afraid, or do You want me to be courageous? Even in his mind, Eoghan's voice took on a petulant tone that made him cringe.

Comdiu's next words came with a tinge of amusement. *You are afraid because you believe you are alone. Do I not walk with you? Do I not speak to you? Why do you think you have been chosen? My leaders must be of My heart, My mind. Why do you rely on your own strength when you have Me?*

The chastisement, kind as it was, filled him with shame. Eoghan bowed his head.

Which do you think better achieves My glory: your pride or My strength?

The shame only intensified, raising a lump in his throat. He had been focusing on his own shortcomings, his own desires. Did he think Comdiu wasn't aware of his weaknesses?

I have not given this gift since Daimhin's time. I have given it to you for a purpose. Will you obey?

What choice did he have? There was no way to outrun Comdiu's plans, even if he wanted to. And hadn't he learned long ago that he was far better off within Comdiu's will than outside it?

Yet the fear grew in his chest, squeezing out the kernel of assurance that Comdiu's words had placed in him. *Tell me what I must do. Give me a sign.*

Eoghan expected Comdiu to chastise him for his lack of faith. Instead, He merely said, *Return to Carraigmór.*

"Carraigmór? I had planned on—" He cut himself off. One would think that a lifetime of discipline and service would have left him more prepared to obey.

Instead of turning toward the practice yard where he had been spending his days, he turned toward Carraigmór. "Very well, Lord. Direct all my steps. I will obey."

He climbed the long flight of slick steps to Carraigmór, nodded to the brother on guard as he passed, and entered the great hall. Even having been raised here, the technology that had managed to carve an entire fortress from a granite cliff still awed him. Each room was like a cavern, the corridors that connected them rounded like tunnels and smoothed and polished by hundreds of years of feet and hands. What kind of knowledge must Daimhin have possessed to accomplish such a thing in an age where hardened steel had just been discovered?

Eoghan turned into an intersecting corridor that led to his chamber on the south side of the fortress, his mind fixed so firmly on the past that he nearly collided with a figure coming from the opposite direction. He reached out to steady his victim before he realized it was Aine.

Abruptly, he dropped his hands from her shoulders, his face burning. "I'm sorry. I didn't see you."

"Clearly." Her wry tone set an uncomfortable squirming in his gut. He swallowed and struggled for something noncommittal to say but only managed an awkward silence.

Aine's smile faded, making him think she was all too aware of his thoughts. But that only made him focus on the concern tracing her pretty face, the way her braided hair fell over her shoulder and tangled in the chain of her ivory charm. His hand was on its way to pull the braid free before he realized what he was doing and jerked his hand back.

Her gray gaze collided with his, and her eyes widened. Then her shock gave way to determination. "Eoghan, we need to talk."

"Not necessary, my lady." If he could melt into the stone wall behind him and save them this embarrassment, he would. He had tried to suppress his feelings for her to no avail. Each time he managed to convince himself it was just a passing infatuation, one look at her would make him feel like pledging his undying devotion. Even more humiliating, both Conor and Aine were fully aware of it.

Truly, he was the worst sort of man.

"You are not the worst sort of man," she said softly.

Their eyes snapped together once more, and this time she flushed at being caught using her mind powers on him.

"If you'll excuse me, my lady." He gave a stiff bow and brushed past her before he could embarrass himself further.

He barely made it a few steps down the corridor before he caught a glimmer from the corner of his eye. He stopped and scanned his surroundings. What had he seen? Maybe it had been a trick of the light, a torch reflecting off a patch of minerals in the stone. Or perhaps his sword forms had brought him closer to exhaustion than he'd thought. He shook his head and continued down the corridor.

But once more, that tiny spark caught his eye, clearly coming from the wall this time. He squinted at the stone and spread his hands over the span of granite. "Aine?" He retrieved a torch from its stand and held it close to the rock while Aine stretched up on tiptoes beside him.

"A rune," she breathed.

His breath seized in his chest. It was unmistakably a rune, barely visible in the speckled gray stone, a finely etched circle with several intersecting lines.

"What does it mean?" she asked.

The answer came with a swiftness that could only be attributed to Comdiu. "Soft."

Their gazes met again, an unspoken question in her eyes. He looked away, uncomfortable. She and Conor had spent months poring over texts from the Hall of Prophecies, and he had just deciphered a rune at first sight.

So why this? Why now? The only other time Comdiu had

revealed the runes' meanings to him was when they'd reassembled the pins in Conor's harp. And those had been objects of power, needed to reinstate the wards around Ard Dhaimhin. This was just a random scrawling of ancient symbols on the inside of a corridor. And soft? Why soft?

Eoghan traced the pattern with his fingertip again. His nail caught the edge of a curve. A sliver of rock fell to the ground.

No, that's impossible. He squinted at the gouge in the granite. He scratched his nail over another part of it and came away with his fingers covered in powder.

"The rune made the rock soft," he murmured.

Again, Aine pressed in beside him, stretching to see the gouge in the rock. "So that's how they carved out the hill. I've always suspected it was magic."

The wonder in her voice echoed his own. They'd known Daimhin had relied on old, forgotten magic to secure his kingdom, and they'd suspected it had something to do with runes. But to find evidence of the practical uses—this went far beyond anything they'd ever imagined.

"Why this? Why now?" Aine said, echoing his musings of moments before.

But Eoghan knew this small revelation would be the key to something important. And it seemed he was the first to bear this knowledge since Daimhin, the first and only High King of Seare.

Like it or not, Eoghan had his sign.

CHAPTER THREE

Aine climbed down the steps to the village, her mind tumbling around the recent revelation. All these weeks, looking for something—anything—related to the runes, and the evidence had been under their noses the whole time. Comdiu simply hadn't seen fit to reveal it until this moment.

Even worse, Eoghan had asked her to hold off telling Conor until he could consult Comdiu on the matter. He didn't want to reveal the news to the Conclave without understanding what it might mean, but she couldn't help feeling uncomfortable that he had asked her to keep something from Conor, considering the rift between the two men—considering the feelings that Eoghan struggled against.

Guilt wound through her. She could end his conflict with a handful of words, had been moments away from doing just that, and still she had held back. What she needed to tell him about her abilities, no one knew, including Conor.

So many secrets, and she still didn't know which ones were necessary and which were just plain foolish.

Thoughts tickled the edge of her consciousness as she

approached the village, and she forced her attention to the barriers that protected her from the press of so many thoughts. Worries, complaints, small joys—they flooded around her like rainwater poured into muddy footprints, filling any crevice of consciousness she did not deliberately seal. The growth in her powers might mean she had to exert less effort to pick out individual thoughts, but it also meant she had to expend more to keep them out.

Aine kept her steps brisk and determined, avoiding eye contact that might encourage conversation. Instead of the usual glut of people wanting her attention, though, there was just a trickle. Only the women and children were at the cookhouse for the midday meal, the men long gone to their work assignments.

When she burst through the door of the first cottage in the healers' quarter, a gray-haired man was already bent over the workbench, the tendons and muscles in his trim arms straining as he ground something with the heavy granite pestle. "Good morning, Brother Murchadh."

He looked up immediately and set the stone into the bowl. "Good morning, Lady Aine. You're tardy."

"Late evening," she said, without offense. Murchadh was blunt with everyone.

He grunted a response and gestured to a bundle of herbs hanging from the wire hooks over his head. "I'm making agrimony powder. We're running low."

"We're running low on a lot of things." Aine moved along the wall of shelving that housed the prepared remedies in vials and jars, much like the workroom she had temporarily established at Forrais. "Bitterroot, heart's ease—I'm not sure where we're going to find any of these things in winter."

"Not that it's so essential with your presence, my lady."

"I won't always be available. And it won't be long before the city's needs outstrip my abilities."

Aine dragged the bucket of tallow from its spot on the bottom shelf to an empty space at the workbench and selected several dark glass bottles of essences. She would start with one of her most useful concoctions, a healing salve for blisters and abrasions, something of which there was no shortage in Ard Dhaimhin these days. Some of the new laborers had been craftsmen and scholars, their hands more used to delicate tools and pens than shovels and picks.

She measured out a scoop of tallow into a wooden bowl and then carefully added the lavender, chamomile, and geranium extract to the fat. After she finished several batches of skin salve, she moved on to preparing newly harvested herbs. Hot water from the pot over the peat-burning hearth was poured into jars containing herbs for tinctures. Other jars were filled with the clear grain alcohol that the brothers distilled under close supervision for medicinal purposes on the opposite end of the city. Drunkenness traditionally had little traction in Ard Dhaimhin, considering the high degree of discipline, but the kingdom's men had changed that.

The kingdom's men had changed much.

"You seem troubled," Murchadh said after they'd worked silently for nearly two hours.

Aine lifted her head. "I do?"

He gave a single nod.

"I suppose I'm concerned. More refugees arrive every day, and our stores grow more depleted."

"I'm sure the Ceannaire and the Conclave are taking steps to ensure that doesn't happen."

Aine nodded, not bothering to argue the point. Murchadh shared the attitude of many of the elder brethren. They trusted their leadership wholeheartedly and devoted themselves to their own duties. Those in charge surely had a plan for all contingencies. Aine wished she didn't know how far from the truth that actually was.

By the time afternoon sunlight changed to the bluish tint of dusk, Aine had filled one of the long, empty shelves with new tinctures and salves, all of which would need to cure before they could be used. She put the last jar on the board and pressed a hand against the sudden ache in her lower back.

Murchadh shot her a knowing smile. "Have you told your husband yet?"

Aine lifted her gaze in surprise. At least one of her secrets was not as secret as she thought. "No, not yet."

"See that you do." His smile softened, the lines of his face gentling. "And see that you don't exhaust yourself."

"Aye. Tomorrow?"

"Tomorrow. Heed my advice, my lady. Rest."

Aine nodded and slipped from the healer's cottage, a flutter of nervousness in her middle. Tonight she would broach several long-overdue topics with Conor. And then she would find Eoghan.

Engrossed in her own thoughts, she forgot to shore up the barriers in her mind. The thoughts and emotions of the villagers slammed into her like a tidal wave, driving her to one knee. She doubled over and gasped for breath.

"Lady Aine, are you well?" A feminine voice broke through the background noise in her head. She stared at the speaker, searching her memory for the woman's name while she forced the intruding thoughts outside the barrier. Sorcha. One of the kingdom's refugees, kind-natured if a bit of a busybody.

"I'm fine, Sorcha, thank you. Just became a little light-headed."

The woman helped her to her feet. "Perhaps I should walk with you a bit to make sure you're feeling well."

"You're very kind." Aine started back toward Carraigmór

again, and Sorcha stayed by her side. She didn't need to delve deep into her mind to know she had motives other than simple kindness.

Still, it took her several minutes to broach the subject. "The rumor is that a High King has been named in secret."

Aine's heart lurched. "Who said that?"

"So it's true? The High King really has returned?"

How could she possibly answer that question? She hated lying outright, but anything other than a categorical denial would send rumors flying. The last thing Ard Dhaimhin's leadership wanted was to force Eoghan's hand.

In the end, she dodged the question. "Why would you think I know anything about the High King?"

Sorcha leveled a reproving glance. "My lady, I've been married for almost as long as you've been alive. The woman nearest the man in charge always has the most complete perspective on what is actually happening."

Aine chuckled. It wasn't far from the truth. Aine might not be queen, but she was the nearest Seare had. Idly, she wondered if Queen Shanna had been plied with questions and flattered by Daimhin's courtiers in the hope of gaining inside information.

And then it struck her what they had been overlooking all this time. "Excuse me, Mistress Sorcha. I just remembered an urgent task at Carraigmór." Aine hurried away, barely registering Sorcha's baffled and disappointed expression. How had she never considered this possibility?

All this time, they'd focused on King Daimhin's writings when they should have been looking at the volumes penned by the woman responsible for the Fíréin brotherhood in the first place: Daimhin's warrior-queen, Shanna.

Aine searched the Ceannaire's office first, which turned up one of Shanna's journals that Conor had brought up from the Hall of Prophecies. Her husband, on the other hand, was nowhere to be found—not in his study, their chamber, or Carraigmór's great hall. Finally, she went back down to the cookhouse, where she stood in line for her bowl of venison soup and a small chunk of bread.

"Join me?"

Aine turned to find herself the object of Riordan's sympathetic stare. She hesitated, but he gestured to a cluster of boulders away from the crush of villagers. "A few minutes of quiet conversation before duty calls again?"

She relented and took her seat on top of the flattest one, balancing her bowl on her lap. She liked Conor's father, but the structure of Ard Dhaimhin was such that they rarely saw each other.

"You've been working yourself hard," he said quietly.

"Did Conor ask you to speak with me?"

Riordan chuckled. "No. But I'm not surprised he's concerned."

"Well, when Conor stops working himself to exhaustion, then he can lecture me on my habits." She softened her words with a slight smile. "Can I ask you a question?"

Riordan nodded.

"Can we win this fight? Or are we just holding off the darkness for as long as we can?"

He didn't answer right away, a sign that he was actually considering the question rather than giving her the reassuring answer he thought she wanted to hear. "I have to believe we can. I don't think Comdiu has brought us this far just to have us give up."

No empty reassurances or platitudes, but there was a quiet confidence in the words that somehow buoyed her spirit. When Comdiu had sent his son, Balus, to visit her in that place between life and death when she'd nearly drowned in Loch

Eirich, He had told her it would not be easy. He had told her there would be a price to be paid. But He had also told her not to despair.

"I think I'll rest now," she said, standing with her bowl. "Thank you."

"Of course." Riordan rose with her and gave her a warm smile. "Sleep well, daughter."

The use of the word put a warm glow in her chest. Both her parents were dead, her brothers and sister likely murdered at the taking of Lisdara. She'd begun to think that Conor was all she had left, and Riordan knew it. But he had reminded her that he was her family too, as strange and strained as his relationship with his son might be.

She retreated to their chamber and undressed automatically, then sank down into the cushioned chair by the window with Shanna's journal. Unlike Daimhin, the queen had dated her entries. That alone gave Aine hope that Shanna had recorded information for posterity rather than to work through her own thoughts.

The first several entries contained much of the same information as Daimhin's, though she had some interesting insights into the feuding clans, just nothing about runes or wards or anything beyond common statecraft. Had she been overconfident about this solution to their dilemmas?

Hours passed without any sign of Conor, and Aine's eyelids slowly drooped. She closed the journal and blew out the candle. But once in bed, her mind refused to settle. Maybe it was her conscience bumping up against all the things she wanted to communicate but hadn't yet spoken aloud.

She threw off her blanket in frustration and wrapped her shawl around her. Then she slid her feet into the soft silk slippers she had brought back with her from Forrais. This late,

Carraigmór's halls were deserted but for the occasional man on watch, half the torches extinguished until morning.

Inside the Ceannaire's office, a single lamp burned, illuminating Conor's familiar form bent over a book spread across the desk. "I've been waiting for you," she said quietly. "Were you planning on coming to bed tonight, or should I just bring your blanket down here?"

Conor looked up from his book, and his shoulders fell in defeat. "I'm sorry, love. I got wrapped up in this and lost track of the time." When she circled the desk, he pulled her down on his lap and nuzzled his head into the space between her neck and shoulder.

"And what is so interesting that it could keep you from my bed?"

Conor pulled back to smile at her. "Nothing that interesting, I assure you. Just my own . . . distraction."

She twisted around to catch a glimpse of the old-fashioned script in the book and realized it wasn't in the common tongue. His education shouldn't surprise her—after all, her own had been relatively extensive—but this language she didn't even recognize.

"Ciraean?"

"Hesperidian. It's an account of the Hundred Years' War between the city states of the southern peninsula. Have you heard the story?"

Aine shook her head.

"Well, it's bloody and depressing, hardly a bedtime tale. But there are certain battles that were won against incredible odds."

"And you're looking for ideas."

"I'm looking for something to show the Conclave that victory is possible with a series of small-scale battles like these."

Aine craned her neck, even though it didn't help her decipher the foreign script. "How did they do it?"

"Massive casualties and dramatic sacrifices. And they didn't even have magic with which to contend."

Aine heard the despair in his voice and wrapped her arms around him. "Trust Comdiu will find a way."

"Aye, Comdiu will find a way. But Comdiu's way doesn't always guarantee survival for the largest number."

"And you think you can do better?"

He chuckled. "No. I just mean that knowing we will prevail in the end doesn't mean we won't do it with some terrible costs. It's my responsibility to minimize those."

She looked back at the book, with its geometric writing that looked so much like a child's scrawling, marveling again that he could make anything of it, let alone translate what he learned into something useful for their situation now. "Did you ever think you would be here? Ceannaire of Ard Dhaimhin, responsible for the survival of an entire city?"

"No." This laugh lacked any trace of humor. "I most certainly did not."

"When we met, what did you want most?"

He cocked his head. "You're in an introspective mood tonight."

"I suppose I am."

He lifted her hand to his lips and trailed kisses along her palm to the inside of her wrist. "I wanted a quiet life, filled with music and study and books. And I wanted you most of all."

She met his eyes, those beautiful eyes that never seemed to lose their intensity no matter how much he changed, and saw the truth. He would make a great king, a just king. He already made an admirable commander. And yet all he really wanted was a quiet life with her. She wrapped her arms around his neck and kissed his temple, just enjoying his nearness for a long moment.

"I have something to tell you," she whispered.

His expression turned alarmed. "Is something wrong?"

"No. Nothing's wrong. In fact, I'm surprised you haven't noticed." She took his hand and placed it on the slight swell of her abdomen.

His eyes widened. "It's true? You're . . . we're . . . having a child?"

She nodded, her heart thudding in her throat. She'd suspected for months, but only now, feeling the first flutter of movement in her womb, was she convinced she wasn't simply imagining things.

Conor's expression remained frozen in disbelief. She drew an unsteady breath. "You're not happy?"

A smile broke over his face and he kissed her fiercely. "Of course I'm happy. Just surprised. When? How long?"

"By my calculations, I'm about four months along."

"But that means . . . when we left Seare?"

"I suspected while I was in Aron, but now I'm sure. You're going to be a father."

His expression turned to one of wonder, and he returned his hand to her abdomen. "Will I be able to feel it move soon?"

She nodded.

Then he was kissing her again, leaving no doubt as to his feelings on the topic. She eased against him, her arms returning to his neck, losing herself in the few stolen moments they had found together in the necessities of Ard Dhaimhin.

"I love you, Aine," he whispered. "When this is all over, I promise I will give you that simple, happy life. No matter what I have to do to get it."

She understood then what he wouldn't say. He might be struggling for their survival, for the well-being of the future of Ard Dhaimhin and the endurance of their way of life, but deep down, he was fighting for their future together. She kissed him one more time, a long, languorous kiss meant to change his mind about his evening's activities, but before she could get very far on her plan, the door to the Ceannaire's office banged open. Aine practically leapt off Conor's lap, her cheeks burning.

Daigh's eyes flicked between them, the slight tightening of his mouth communicating disapproval. When he finally focused on Conor, his voice was hard.

"You're needed in the hall. The fortress has been breached."

CHAPTER
FOUR

Conor followed Daigh at a near run, aware of Aine a step behind him. His thoughts bounced between the shocking revelation Aine had just given him—he was going to be a father!—and his inability to comprehend how someone had breached the fortress. Who would dare? How was that even possible?

When they reached Carraigmór's great hall, the area that had been empty less than an hour before now hummed with activity, candles and torches lighting up the space. A small circle of warriors concealed what he assumed was the intruder. As Conor approached, the circle opened, revealing the kneeling, unmoving figure of a young man. His dark hair hung loose around his shoulders, and his stained and tattered clothes spoke of a long journey. Conor strained to get a glimpse of the man's face, but he kept his eyes trained firmly on the floor, his hair concealing his features.

Eoghan stood at the front of the group, his own sword drawn, the tension in his body at odds with the relaxed position of the blade, tip to floor. Conor paused, wondering if Eoghan had taken command of the situation, but the other man stepped aside and held out a hand.

Conor stepped up into the gap between two guards and crossed his arms over his chest, making his voice quiet but stern. "What's your name, boy?"

The intruder lifted his head, and Conor's eyes widened. This was no boy.

"Sir, she slipped the perimeter guard and managed to reach Carraigmór without raising the alarm. She says she knows you."

Conor barely heard the words, focused on the familiar face of the woman in front of him. Dark brown eyes, the color of rich spring earth, just a shade lighter than her hair, pale skin spattered with freckles. Even the trickle of blood from a cut on her scalp and the faint shadow of a bruise could not hide her beauty.

"What are you doing here?" Shock made Conor's voice harsher than he intended.

"Sir? You know her? She was telling the truth?"

"Aye, she was telling the truth." He finally dragged his eyes away from her to the confused expressions of the bystanders. "This is Lady Morrigan. My foster sister."

"Lady?" One of the brothers lowered his weapon.

"Aye, though she's currently not acting like one, for reasons I'm most anxious to hear. Bind her and check for weapons."

Morrigan's eyes met his, startled. Apparently, she had thought their shared history would earn her a different sort of reception. But the young woman he remembered didn't have the skills to dodge a highly trained perimeter guard nor give the scowling brother beside him what would become a most impressive black eye.

One of the guards brought out a length of rope and secured her wrists behind her back. Conor stepped back and turned to Aine, his chin tilted down so his voice wouldn't carry. "What do you sense?"

"Very little." Aine's dismay seemed to prove out his caution. What exactly was going on here?

When the brothers had checked Morrigan for other weapons with uncomfortable thoroughness, Conor inclined his head back toward the corridor from whence they had come. "Daigh, Riordan, Eoghan, with me, please." He nodded to the brothers currently holding her at sword point. "Bring her."

Morrigan's expression never changed, but when she struggled to her feet, he caught the hint of a smile playing on her lips. She thought this was amusing, did she? She obviously had no idea of the seriousness of the offense, nor the way the Fíréin dealt with such matters.

Conor hung back behind the others, gesturing for Aine to stay with him as they proceeded to the Ceannaire's office. "You sense nothing?"

"Not a single thought. Her mind is completely closed to me."

"How is that possible? Magic?"

"I have no idea. If it's magic, it's strong. I'm not sure this has ever happened to me."

Unease crept into him. There was certainly more at work here than just the appearance of someone from his past. And yet, despite all his justified suspicions, he couldn't help the rush of relief that spread through his limbs. He'd assumed she was dead. Could that mean other members of his foster family were still alive?

Aine squeezed his hand in a gesture of silent understanding, though her expression still urged caution.

The group filed into the Ceannaire's office, and the guards lowered Morrigan into a chair far more gently than she deserved. Something in her calculating expression said she knew it too. What had happened to the sweet, delicate young woman he had known back at Balurnan?

A warning glance from Aine said she knew his resolve was waning. He straightened his shoulders and circled around.

"Leave us," Conor said to the escort. Daigh and Riordan took up posts by the door, hands on their daggers.

"Am I such of a threat that I require five warriors to guard me?" Morrigan asked, a coquettish lilt to her words. When they continued to stare, she turned pleading eyes to Conor. "Was I wrong to hope you'd be at least a little happy to see me, Conor? When I learned you were still alive and here of all places. I had given you up for dead!"

Conor softened as a glimmer of the girl he remembered surfaced. "Of course I'm pleased to find you alive. But what are you doing here, Morrigan? Breaching the fortress like a spy?"

"I couldn't be sure that if I asked to be taken to you directly, they would comply. I knew if I made a dramatic entrance and demanded to see you, it would at least gain me an audience."

"Well, you've gotten your wish. Why are you here? I don't believe you risked so much for a family reunion."

"No. Not merely for that." She shifted in her chair and winced. "If you'll take these bonds off me, I'll tell you anything you want to know. The rope is cutting off the blood to my hands."

Conor drew his dagger and took a step toward her, but Eoghan stopped him. "Not so fast. You may have convinced Conor that you have no ill intentions toward us, but that still doesn't explain why you had this in your possession." Eoghan withdrew a small glass vial from his belt pouch and held it in front of her nose. "Care to explain?"

"That depends. Who exactly is in charge here? I'd hate to waste my time convincing the wrong man of my innocence just to have the other throw me in the dungeon."

Conor looked at Eoghan, trying to keep his irritation from

showing on his face. Within a single minute, the other man had managed to undermine Conor's authority in the situation. If Eoghan didn't step up now, they would lose their only chance to get the truth from Morrigan.

Finally, Eoghan cleared his throat. "I am."

Something resembling a smirk touched Morrigan's lips. "Are you sure about that? Your companions seem surprised."

Eoghan perched on the edge of the desk and crossed his arms over his chest, now looking completely unruffled. "You're not helping your case, Lady Morrigan. We're here to determine whether you're a threat to the safety of Ard Dhaimhin, and your first action is to cause division among my advisors."

His advisors? Conor had to visibly force himself not to stiffen at the flush of anger that surged through him. But the slight lift of the eyebrows Morrigan directed his way said she'd picked it up anyway. Curse both of them. What about Morrigan's arrival had suddenly convinced Eoghan of the need to seize command?

Morrigan bowed her head as if to acknowledge Eoghan's authority. "You asked me what I was doing with poison, my lord. Your healers can confirm it is merely a sleeping powder I slipped into one of the sentries' food. Surely you realize that had I truly wanted to harm someone, I had the opportunity and ability to do so."

"We will indeed confirm that before we determine your fate." He studied her closely and then crouched down before her. "Let us dispense with the games, Lady Morrigan. I would like to believe for Conor's sake that you are trustworthy, even if I suspect you are no longer the girl he remembers from Balurnan. So if you have any regard for your safety, you will deal with me plainly."

For a moment, Morrigan looked like she might spit in Eoghan's face. Then she smiled. "Let us also dispense with the threats, *my lord*. What I know is far more important than any little show of authority you're trying to make here."

"And what is that?"

"The bard Meallachán is alive. And I can tell you where to find him."

+ + +

Eoghan kept his expression blank, even as his heart jolted at the revelation. Meallachán was alive? What were the chances that a stranger would arrive with something that could be the answer to their problems?

Just as quickly, caution quashed his surge of excitement. It was convenient—too convenient, especially considering that Morrigan had been in control of the situation since she breached the fortress. Every bit of this performance had been calculated to elicit a particular response, and they had played right into her hand.

It was that warning in his chest, the sudden conviction that this woman was dangerous, that had made him seize command. Especially when it looked as though Conor was about to be taken in by the act.

Eoghan stood and walked away from her. "That's a bold statement. What makes you think we care about Meallachán's whereabouts?"

"Because you need the runes, and he's one of the few men who understand them."

"Why do you say that?"

"He told me." Morrigan flicked a glace behind her toward her bound hands. "Untie me and I will tell you everything I know."

For a moment, Eoghan considered throwing her into one of the rarely used cells beneath Carraigmór. But that same something—call it intuition or Comdiu's prompting—said she was both hardened and stubborn enough to wait them out. And if Meallachán were indeed alive . . .

"Fine. As long as you understand that any wrong move means you will not leave this room alive. Do you believe I'm being truthful about that?"

No hint of mockery traced her face. "I believe you."

She shifted so he could reach around her and sever the ropes. Before he could move away, she turned her face toward his. Her breath brushed his skin, her eyes lifting to his with something he could describe only as invitation.

Eoghan backed away to a safe distance and let out a long, careful breath. Morrigan was still playing them as skillfully as Conor played his harp.

"Meallachán is being held prisoner at Ard Bealach."

Once more, she caught him off guard. Why would she give up her most important information freely? "You've been there."

"Aye."

"As a prisoner?"

"It depends on what you consider imprisonment. Was I locked in a cell or chained? No. But neither was I allowed to leave."

"Are you telling me you managed to escape a fortress that is nearly as secure as Ard Dhaimhin?" Eoghan realized the irony in the words the moment they left his lips, and the sudden spark of laughter in Morrigan's deep brown eyes said she did as well.

"I escaped, aye. But it was more a matter of bribery and good timing than any feats of daring. All men can be bought, Brother Eoghan. The trick is knowing their particular price."

"Tell us how you came to be at Ard Bealach in the first place."

"From the beginning? This might take a while."

"Do we look as though we have somewhere else to be in the dead of night?"

"Besides bed?" Her eyes were innocent, her tone free of innuendo, but Eoghan felt it all the same. Comdiu have mercy.

"You know what happened to my father, I presume." Both Eoghan and Conor nodded. "As soon as he received word that King Galbraith had been slain, he sent my mother, my sisters, and me into the passages beneath the manor that had been built to smuggle priests in and out after the Balian faith was outlawed. My father surrendered and told them we weren't in the manor, which I suppose was true.

"Lord Riocárd didn't believe him. His men found the tunnels. When it looked as though we would be discovered, Mother sent us through with Captain Tadhg and stayed behind as a diversion."

"She was killed?" Eoghan asked.

"Aye. Riocárd's men were waiting for us though. Half our guards fell in battle, and Tadhg was wounded. But we still escaped.

"Tadgh didn't last the night. We made our way to Sliebhan, where I got a job as a serving girl. I managed that until the girls started drawing male attention. When I had to beat a man off my youngest sister Liadan one night, they threw us into the street."

Eoghan watched Conor's reaction to the story. He had been raised alongside these girls. It would take a truly heartless person not to feel sympathy for their plight, something on which Morrigan was likely counting. But other than the flex of his jaw, Conor's expression gave away nothing of his thoughts.

Morrigan pressed on, her eyes focused on the floor as if she were alone in the room, telling the story to herself. "The war was already in Sliebhan and Siomar by then. Food was becoming scarce in the villages and we lacked the skills to survive off the land, so I decided that we must go where the food was. I thought I could sign on as a cook or a washerwoman with

Fergus's army, but at that point, the only organized soldiers were mercenaries. I realized my mistake when one of the men took a liking to Liadan again."

A ten-year-old girl targeted by mercenaries? Eoghan couldn't repress the ill feeling that crept into him.

"I did everything I could to protect her, but I was too weak. That's when Bersi stepped in."

"Who in the blazes is Bersi?" Conor burst out.

She glanced over her shoulder at her foster brother, her voice hard. "My lover."

Now it was Conor's turn to look ill, and Eoghan gave him a slight shake of the head. "Go on," he said to Morrigan.

"At the time, he was the leader of the group of mercenaries who had been called to Sliebhan. I don't know why he stopped them, but he did.

"He made me an offer: if I served him in whatever way he wished, he would take us under his protection and teach me how to fight. There was nothing else I could do. It was either starve or be at the mercy of men, so I agreed. But it was not washing and cleaning that he wished from me."

Small spots of color bloomed on Morrigan's cheeks, but she lifted her chin and stared at Eoghan. "Bersi was not a kind man, but he was true to his word. He kept the girls from harm and began to teach me the basics of defense: sword work, knife fighting, archery. Before long, he and his men were called to Ard Bealach.

"Bersi was one of the captains there, below only the commander in charge of the fortress, a man named Somhairle. Bersi may have had a code of honor, twisted as it was, but Somhairle had no such scruples. When he learned of the agreement I had made, he thought to use it against me. Wouldn't impose on another man's rights, but he implied that he would allow his men to do whatever they wished to Etaoin and Liadan. I had no choice but to agree. Their protection for my cooperation. Bersi was sent away after that, and I belonged to Somhairle." Her cheeks burned redder, and Eoghan fought the urge to comfort her. Either she was a talented actress, or she had endured some truly horrific events. He didn't have a wife or sister of his own, but when he thought of Aine being put in such a situation, how could he not feel sympathy?

"Where are the girls now?" he asked softly.

"Conditions were almost as bad at Ard Bealach as they were on the outside. Within half a year, they sickened and died. That's when I escaped. Without them, there was no reason to stay."

And there it was again: the warning that something didn't ring true, doubt that kept him from fully extending his sympathy. *What am I sensing, Comdiu? Should I believe her? Does it even matter?*

I brought her here for a reason.

Well, that was comforting at least, but it still didn't answer his question. He focused on Morrigan again. "How did you come in contact with Meallachán?"

A wry smile surfaced. "Somhairle's mercenaries were not particularly quick. They knew they got paid only if they followed orders. After Meallachán was brought to the keep, I passed around a rumor that Somhairle was secretly using me to extract information from the prisoner. After that, it was easy enough to convince the guards to let me into Meallachán's cell."

Conor dragged a chair up to her and sat so he could look her in the eye. "This is important. You said Meallachán was brought to Ard Bealach. Brought from where?"

"I'm not sure. Somewhere in Siomar, I think."

Conor looked to Eoghan, no doubt thinking the same thing. Eoghan had found eight of the pins from Meallachán's harp in the burned-out ruins of Cill Rhí in southern Siomar. They had assumed he had been murdered at the time the harp was destroyed, but it was plausible he could have been taken to Ard Bealach instead.

"Why take him there? What did Somhairle want from him?"

"That I don't know. But I knew he was Fíréin, so I thought he could help me somehow. Perhaps provide information I could use."

"And did he?" Eoghan asked.

She looked between them and nodded slowly. "He told me to come here."

CHAPTER
FIVE

Eoghan ordered that Morrigan be taken to a chamber on the
upper floor and guarded at all times by two men. Daigh and
Riordan took him at his word and escorted her from the room
themselves. As soon as she was gone, Aine collapsed into a chair,
exhausted by the story.

She would never have thought one woman could cause so
much trouble in such a short period of time.

"So what does this mean?" Conor burst out as soon as they
were alone.

Eoghan wiped a hand over his face. "We'll have to present
her before the Conclave—"

"No, I meant this. You. Taking command. Are you finally
doing it, then?"

Eoghan actually looked startled. "I hadn't thought about it."

"You just undermined me in front of two Conclave members
and Morrigan on a whim?" Conor's voice lowered, became more
measured, a sure sign his anger was reaching the boiling point.

Aine rose and put up both hands. The sudden crackle
of tension between the two made her nauseous, and even

concentrating on her barriers against their thoughts didn't dampen the fog of animosity. "Gentlemen, please."

Conor glanced her way, and the emotion pouring off him eased a little. When he spoke again, his tone was far less danger-ous. "Whether you like it or not, Eoghan, you just made a pub-lic declaration. Riordan and Daigh will be telling others as we speak. They will expect me to formally cede my authority."

"And that's not something you're ready to give," Eoghan said.

"That's not my decision. I just hope you understand the responsibility this entails."

Anger flashed in Eoghan's eyes, and Aine stepped in before the tension could escalate again. Right now, they were merely bickering, but she didn't need to search very far to know the depths of hard feelings between the two. Their animosity wasn't their biggest problem now.

"She's manipulating you," Aine said flatly.

"I know," Eoghan said.

"You know?" Conor glanced at Aine. "I thought you couldn't read her."

"Not with my gift. But a woman knows these things."

"So does a man," Eoghan said with a grimace. "The minute Conor stepped back, she turned her focus on me. Manipulation aside, though, I think she's mostly telling the truth. Her story is plausible, and it fits with what we already know."

"She clearly has her own agenda," Aine said. "The only ques-tion is how closely it aligns with ours. I don't think we need to care if she has her own reasons as long as they're not at cross-purposes with ours."

Eoghan nodded, his expression verging on admiring. Conor merely scowled. She couldn't delay the discussion much longer.

"What concerns me more," Aine continued, "is the fact I can't read her at all."

"You think she might be ensorcelled?" Eoghan asked.

"Doubtful," Conor said. "She wouldn't have been able to breach the wards if she were possessed by sorcery."

"She could be spelled," Aine said. "The druid took your memories of your mother's death. He used Keondric's weaknesses to make him open to suggestion. Both of you were able to cross wards, and I couldn't pick up on it until I purposely looked for it."

"So you think she might be a spy?" Eoghan asked. "Working for the druid?"

"It's a possibility we can't ignore."

After a moment of quiet consideration, Conor turned his gaze on Eoghan, the challenge clear. "What do you want to do, then?"

"Nothing." Eoghan held up a hand to forestall protest. "Comdiu told me she's here for a reason. Regardless of her motives, she can't cause much harm while under guard. Even if she is spying, she'll have no way of passing information out of the city."

"There is one possibility we haven't discussed," Aine said softly. "Maybe she really is seeking safety, and Meallachán's message was her way in. You heard what I did. She has to harbor plenty of shame and anger over what she's had to do to survive."

"Then maybe you're the best chance we have to learn the truth," Conor said to her. "She might tell you things she wouldn't say to us."

It was a sound theory, though Aine wondered if they had any chance of getting the truth from Morrigan before she was ready. "I can speak with her in the morning. I'll also see if I can sense Meallachán's presence at Ard Bealach. It might be challenging, but at least we'd be able to verify that part of her story."

"You can do that?" Eoghan asked, surprised.

"I can do my best. But not here. I can't sense anything past the animosity in the room."

The men actually looked penitent then, especially Eoghan. She had to confess her abilities soon. Even if he were angry over the deception, it had to be better than the guilt he felt around her now. But not yet. One woman with troublesome secrets at a time.

✦ ✦ ✦

Conor and Aine returned silently to their chamber, their thoughts held close—at least Aine's were. Tonight had reminded him that she could reach his deepest thoughts at any time, should she choose to.

The things he hid from her couldn't remain buried forever.

But that wasn't tonight's concern. He was still too stunned by the dual shocks of Aine's pregnancy and Morrigan's arrival. As soon as they reached their chamber, he said, "I thought she was dead."

Aine's sympathetic look said she immediately followed his thoughts. "It was a reasonable assumption. You couldn't have known."

"I could have tried, though. Calhoun had spies. He could have found out."

"But he wouldn't have been able to act, even if he'd wanted to. And she seems to have made an effort to keep their identity secret." Aine slid her arms around his waist.

"About that. Does it seem strange to you that she escaped the druid's grasp only to seek out his army again? Three girls by those names . . . mercenaries or not, someone would have started to question them."

Aine considered for a moment. "Perhaps it no longer mattered after several years. Or perhaps she was too much of a prize for a mercenary to give up, even to Niall. Regardless, Conor, she made her own choices. She did what she must to survive. That's what one does in war."

Conor's heartbeat sped. Had something happened to her while in Aron, something she'd kept from him? Dread spread through his insides like ice.

Aine pulled away from him and loosened her hair from its plait. "I haven't been completely honest about what happened in Aron."

So he was right. He latched the door and leaned against it, telling himself he was giving her space, even though he held back from fear. "How so?"

"When I arrived, no one believed that you and I were married. My aunt claimed my story was a way to explain a bastard child. I feared that if I were indeed pregnant, we would be shunned and my inheritance would be somehow denied to me. Lady Macha pushed me to marry one of her lords."

"You didn't—"

"No!" Aine took a few steps toward him and stopped. "I considered it, though. Especially when it looked as though Lord Uallas was my only chance for survival."

A laugh escaped from Conor, carried on a wave of relief. This explained the image that Briallu, the sidhe posing as Talfryn's daughter, had shown him in the scrying bowl. It also explained why she had so quickly cut off the vision. He took Aine's face in his hands and kissed her. "My love, you don't need to apologize for what you almost did. You were faithful to me. Of that I have no doubt."

She softened against him, returning the kiss for a moment before she pulled back again. "There's more."

"Whatever it is, I'm sure it's not as great a sin as you think. You have an overdeveloped conscience, love." He dipped his head to kiss her neck.

"Stop, Conor. This is important." She hesitated. "I can influence people with my presence. Men especially are drawn to me."

"You, my dear, are an incredibly beautiful woman."

Aine huffed and slipped out of his reach before he could make good on his next thoughts. "Be serious, please. I don't mean I can influence them that way. I mean I could command the loyalty of the men around me if I wished. And I have. To the death."

Conor just stared at her. "How long have you had this ability?"

"I don't know. At least since I came to Seare. Probably earlier. Conor, men have died to protect me. Ruarc. Lorcan. Diocail. What if their loyalty was all compelled?" Tears shimmered in her eyes.

Immediately, he put his arms around her. "Aine, that was not your fault. You couldn't have known. And I suspect they would have done their duty regardless." Then the more obvious implication slammed into him. "Wait. Eoghan?"

A tear slid down her face. "Not just Eoghan."

He pulled back from her, horrified. "Surely you can't believe that you and I . . . that this . . ."

"What if this is all a lie, Conor? You said yourself that you were determined to do all Comdiu asked of you until you saw me again. What if what you feel for me is all just a result of my gift?"

He considered the possibility within a rush of agony for the space of a second and then shook his head. "No. Impossible. I don't believe that." He took her hands and looked directly into her eyes. "If that were true, I wouldn't have worked so hard to come back to you. You were what kept me going during my years at Ard Dhaimhin. You were what kept me alive while I was a prisoner of the Sofarende. If I were merely compelled by your presence, surely that would have worn off while we were apart."

He brushed a stray lock of hair from her face and pressed his lips to her temple, then her mouth. "I'm afraid you're not going to get rid of me that easily, especially now that I finally have you back."

She sighed, some of the tension seeping out of her body. He held her close, hesitating over his next words. "But, Aine, you have to tell Eoghan. It's not fair to him. Or to us. Will that break the compulsion?"

"I think so. I'm sorry, Conor. I know I should have told you sooner, but I was afraid of what it might mean."

He supposed he couldn't blame her. Yet she'd let him stew over Eoghan's interest when she knew it was out of his control. There was only a small difference between what she had done to Eoghan—even unintentionally—and what the sidhe had done to him.

Except, unlike Conor, Eoghan hadn't acted on that compulsion.

Then the bigger danger occurred to him. If Aine had some secret influence over the High King, she was a liability. What might someone be willing to do to use her influence against them?

"You have to tell him tomorrow," he said.

"I will. I promise."

"Good." He smiled mischievously. "In the meantime, perhaps I should remind you that I'm legitimately mad about you."

Lying on his pillow later that night, though, sleep eluded him. Aine had kept secrets of her own. If he came clean about his moment of indiscretion with Briallu, would she understand?

No. She was carrying his child. If Aine ever caught a glimpse of that passionate scene—even accounting for the fact he'd recovered his wits in time—she would never trust him again.

He could lose the thing that meant the most to him.

Gingerly, he eased his arm from beneath her and slid from

the bed. He took a few moments to dress, but he didn't bother to put on his boots before stealing out into the hallway.

Without realizing where he had been heading, he found himself before the door of his father's chamber. It took him several attempts to work up the courage to knock.

Rustling inside led to the scrape of a bolt, and then the door swung open. Riordan stood aside for Conor to enter and shut the door behind him. "How are you feeling about all this?"

"Guilty."

Riordan misunderstood his comment. "I know it must be hard hearing about what happened to your foster family, but you can't blame yourself. If anyone is to blame, it's me. I made Labhrás's faith known to Galbraith when I arranged your foster-age with him. I put him in the druid's path."

"But if you hadn't—"

"I didn't say I regretted my actions, just that I bear some responsibility in the outcome." Riordan sat on the edge of the bed and gestured for Conor to take the chair opposite it. "That's a hard lesson to learn but one we'll be faced with sooner than you know."

"We are going to have to make a move on the kingdoms, whether it's Ard Bealach or another target," Conor said.

Riordan gave a single nod. "You've said it yourself. We're cut off from outside sources of food, and we can no longer support the needs of the city. For all Eoghan urges caution, he has known that for a while. He's far more strategic than he lets on."

"As a good king should be." The words fell with finality between them.

"Liam was so sure it was you," Riordan said. "Right up until the end, when he came across Daimhin's journal saying the High King should hear the voice of Comdiu."

"You don't have to spare my feelings. I never wanted to be

king. I never wanted to lead at all. If Eoghan is to rule, what has
been the point of all of this?"

Riordan arched an eyebrow. "Are you forgetting how you rein-
stated the wards around the city? How you're meant to recall the
men with Daimhin's sword? Eoghan cannot win this war without
you, Conor; that I know. Sometimes I wonder if Liam acted as he
did to bind you two together, give you a common enemy."

"Liam wasn't an enemy."

"An obstacle to overcome, then."

Conor sighed and raked his hands through his hair. "And
now we two are here, leading a starving kingdom on the brink
of war."

Riordan's brow furrowed. "I don't believe this is just concern
about Ard Dhaimhin's future. What exactly is troubling you?"

His father always was too perceptive. No harm in telling him.
He'd find out soon enough anyway. "Aine is pregnant."

Riordan merely smiled.

"You knew? How?"

"I'd noticed something different about her magic when she
arrived, but I thought perhaps it was related to her multiple
gifts. Since then, it's grown. Changed."

"You're not saying our child is gifted? You can tell that already?"

"Enormously so, if I can sense its magic in the womb."

Conor flopped back against the chair, stunned. Somehow
it just made the whole situation that much more real. He was
going to be a father to a child whose gifts would likely surpass
his own. A spike of fear shot straight through his heart and
into his stomach. He was only one and twenty years old. True,
Riordan hadn't been much older when he'd sired Conor, but that
hadn't turned out so well, had it?

"I will be here for this baby," he murmured, almost to himself. "I know what it's like to grow up without a real father."

Riordan flinched. Too late, Conor realized it must have sounded like criticism. "I just meant—"

"No, you're right. I wasn't there for you. Galbraith hated the fact he had to pretend my son was his, and as good a man as Labhrás was, he had his own agenda. But, Conor, you understand now why it had to be done. There are some things greater than just a single person's happiness. Or a single person's safety. If we fail here, if we divert from our course even for the best reasons, we could be dooming the world to a darkness it has never known. Could you live with that sacrifice?"

Conor didn't answer. He rose and placed a hand on his father's shoulder, a silent gesture of gratitude, and then slipped out the door.

Riordan was right. He couldn't let personal concerns sway him from his duty. If they were going to take on the full thrust of Niall's might and magic, they needed help.

Eoghan might finally have seen the need to leave Ard Dhaimhin's protections, but Conor's task was at least as daunting. With or without Meallachán's help, he had to figure out the secret of Daimhin's sword.

CHAPTER
SIX

"Aine."

Her eyes snapped open in the dim morning light. She reached for Conor beside her, but her fingertips touched only the cold bedcovering. He was long gone, probably to morning devotions in the amphitheater below. But, then, what had woken her?

Aine pushed back the covers and pulled her dress from the hook beside the bed. Dreams, she decided. Scarcely a night passed undisturbed by memories and fears, all tangled together in a jumble that left a lingering sense of dread long after the recollections faded. Or maybe she simply dreaded her conversation with Eoghan. How could she justify letting him drown in his infatuation when she could have ended it with a word? Put that way, it was unforgivable.

She had laced up her dress and thrust her feet into her boots before she noticed the stack of books on the chair beside the bed. Flipping open the cover of one, she smiled. Conor had somehow noticed that she had moved on to Shanna's journals and brought up the remaining stack from the Hall of

Prophecies. If she didn't know better, she would say he was the one with mind-reading abilities.

The sooner she found Eoghan and made her promised trip to Morrigan's chamber, the sooner she could get back to her reading and see if Shanna's writings actually contained anything that could help them. But Eoghan wasn't in his chamber, the Ceannaire's office, or the hall. She stretched out her awareness through the city, searching for Eoghan's thoughts. She finally found him below in the private practice yard used by the Conclave—with Conor. Even from a distance, the mood seemed easier than it had the night before, a good sign. Dare she hope that with this matter settled they could come to an understanding about command in the city?

No point in interrupting their newfound peace with unpleasant news, then. She made her usual trek down to the cookhouse for a bowl of porridge and then stopped by the laundry on her way back to Morrigan's borrowed chamber.

"Lady Aine." The guards at the door gave her a deferential bow, which she returned with a polite nod.

"Has she left at all since she arrived?"

"We took over the post at sunrise," one of the men said. "She hasn't so much as opened the door."

Probably because there was no point. She would accomplish nothing while they suspected her. Aine shifted her burden. "Knock, please," she instructed the guards.

Moments later, the door opened. Morrigan's wary expression changed to one of puzzlement. "My lady?"

"I brought breakfast." Aine indicated the bowls in her hands. "The men said you hadn't ventured out this morning."

"Considering my reception last night, it didn't seem prudent." Morrigan stood aside for her to pass. One of the guards attempted to follow her in, but Aine stopped him with a sharp look.

"I think I'm safe enough, thank you. I will call if I need you."

Aine set the bowls on the table and shifted the bundle of cloth from beneath her arm to her hands. "We haven't been formally introduced. I am Aine Nic Tamhais, Conor's wife."

Surprise flickered on the other woman's face. "King Calhoun's sister?"

Aine dipped her head in acknowledgment. "The same." She offered the bundle in her hands. "This is for you in case you want to change clothes."

Morrigan shook out the dress, her brow furrowing. "I don't understand."

"I thought you might like to appear in front of the Conclave in something other than bloodstained trousers." Aine took a seat at the small table across from Morrigan's breakfast tray and gestured. "But first let's eat. I'm famished."

"I expect you would be, in your condition." Morrigan sat across from Aine and pulled her bowl toward herself.

A smile twitched on Aine's lips, but she suppressed it. So the game had begun. "My condition?"

"Naturally. The men might be too blind to notice, but you're clearly with child. I would guess four or five months. Am I right?"

"Very good. You're correct."

"Does my brother know?"

"Aye, he knows. Please eat. I suspect times have been lean, and you'll need your strength."

Now it was Morrigan's turn to smile. "Does Conor know how skilled you are at this?"

At least that proved Morrigan wouldn't be manipulated. She'd get further playing it straight. "Of course he does. That's why he sent me."

Morrigan broke into a full-fledged smile. "Then tell me, my lady: what do you want from me? We both know the plan

to coax out my secrets woman to woman was doomed from
the start."

"Tell me about Ard Bealach."

A flash of disquiet crossed Morrigan's face and disappeared
just as swiftly. "Compared to Lisdara or Carraigmór, it's a relatively small fortress, but it's deep. Three stories of stone with
catacombs and passages beneath. Meallachán was imprisoned
in the cells on the lowest level, though they're really more like
bolt-holes with grates across them. Not even enough room
to stand."

Aine studied Morrigan closely as she spoke. There was no
hesitation, no wavering, no shifting of her eyes that would indicate she was fabricating this story. "So given that the fortress is
so small and isolated, how did you escape? Why didn't Somhairle
send men after you?"

Morrigan stared, a tinge of sickness coloring her skin, a sign
that she hadn't expected that question from Aine. Then it was
gone behind her cool, controlled facade.

"You're a beautiful woman, Lady Aine. Surely you've discovered the advantage that gives you. You were alone in Aron, as I
understand it. It must have been useful."

Aine recoiled a bit, the comment hitting too close for comfort, even if Morrigan couldn't know her current turmoil. "Aye.
But you were a prisoner."

Morrigan studied her for a moment. "You really are an innocent, aren't you? I wouldn't have thought that still possible." Her
tone gentled, almost as if she didn't wish to shock her. "All men
have their price, my lady. And all women have their weapons.
You'd be surprised what you can accomplish when you're willing
to use them."

Innocent as Morrigan believed she was, Aine received the
message clearly. Rather than shocking her, it set a deep pity in

her chest. That could have been her situation, had she not been born with her gifts.

"I think you've told me everything I need to know for now, Lady Morrigan. You'll wish to dress for the Conclave. I imagine the summons will come shortly." Aine pushed herself up from her chair and then swayed on her feet as if dizzy. Morrigan's hand shot out, and she clamped her own over it.

In that instant, she thrust out her awareness into the other woman, searching for anything that would indicate a spell, a gift, *something* to explain why she had not been able to pick up a single thought from her the entire time they had been speaking. Morrigan's eyes widened, and she let go of her hand abruptly.

"Lady Aine," she said shakily, "I do believe that you are far less innocent than you let on."

"Perhaps so, Lady Morrigan." Aine nodded politely and turned toward the door. "I do have one last question. How did you know I had spent time in Aron?"

"I think you're far better known that you realize, my lady. Have a care you don't reveal too much."

It felt like a warning, an acknowledgment that Aine had tipped her hand. But at least she had found out something very important in return.

Morrigan was indeed spelled.

✦ ✦ ✦

Somehow, in the course of half a day, everything had changed.

When Eoghan passed through the hall on his way to the practice yard for his morning workout with Conor, Gradaigh and Dal stopped their conversation to stare at him. So Conor had been right. Rumors of the way he had seized control from Conor had gotten out, and now they were waiting for him to make an official statement.

Was this what you had in mind, Comdiu? Was this Your plan all along?

But that implied that Comdiu had tricked Eoghan into doing something he didn't want to do. Like it or not, he had taken command of the situation voluntarily. The weight of responsibility fell on him suddenly. Heavy. Suffocating. Aye, he had been trained for this, but trained to take over the brotherhood, not this blend of kingdom men and Fíréin that the city had become.

Yet when faced with the potential threat that their newcomer posed, he'd been absolutely convinced of his path. That could only be due to Comdiu's guidance.

Aine had said she would seek Meallachán's presence to confirm Morrigan's story, and she was probably preparing to visit Morrigan at this very moment. If anyone could get to the truth, it would be her. He somehow didn't think she would need her mind powers to determine whether Morrigan was being honest or not.

Unfortunately, that thought brought with it warm feelings that were better left unexplored. No wonder Conor was angry with him. Not only had he just usurped Conor's role in the city—one that Eoghan had insisted he didn't want—he also had feelings for his wife, never mind the fact that he would never steal her away, could not even if he tried. It was just a miracle that Aine wasn't perpetually angry with him too.

When he reached the private practice yard, Conor was waiting. For a change, he didn't greet him with a scowl, just tossed him a practice sword and began his own warm-ups. Perhaps it was the easing up of their animosity, or perhaps it was a result of the late night, but they both held back their usual aggression as they started into the bout. Eoghan knew Conor well enough to see he was testing his own weaknesses, looking for flaws in his technique, probably trying to figure out how he had lost the last time.

Finally, Conor stepped back and swiped a sleeve across his forehead. "You're right. I'm just slow. And lazy."

Eoghan felt a pang of guilt over his earlier taunt. "No. Not lazy." The fact was Eoghan had put more time into his sword work this fall than ever before. If he were honest, he'd needed to prove to himself that there was one area in which Conor couldn't overshadow him.

Now it seemed their roles were reversed.

He put up his sword. "Conor, I'm sorry."

"For what? For telling the truth?"

"For what's happened here. We are friends. Brothers. We shouldn't be at each other's throats."

"It's not your fault," Conor muttered, but he didn't elaborate. "Shall we go up and see if Aine has any news for us?"

Eoghan nodded and gathered the practice weapons, puzzled by Conor's sudden change of attitude. "We need to bring Lady Morrigan and this matter before the Conclave as soon as Aine can give us some more insight into the situation. I think you should be the one to call the meeting."

"Oh? You've clearly taken command here."

"You are still the Ceannaire, and the Conclave are technically your advisors. I have yet to make a formal announcement."

"But you will."

"Aye, I will."

Conor still didn't look convinced, but it wasn't as if Eoghan had any choice in the matter. No doubt word had already spread through the brotherhood that he was taking leadership as the High King, and that's what he must do no matter how ill the title fit.

When they reached the Ceannaire's office, Aine already waited for them, perched on a chair while she perused a book spread open on the Ceannaire's desk. She rose when they entered.

"Did you speak with her?" Conor asked immediately. "Did you learn anything?"

Aine gestured for them to take seats, giving Eoghan the impression they were about to get lectured for their impatience. He barely repressed a laugh at the thought, but his mirth faded with the first words.

"Morrigan is spelled."

Conor spoke first, his voice heavy. "So she's a spy."

Aine hesitated. "I don't know what to think. Between the spell and the fact she mentioned Lisdara as though she'd been there, it's very suspicious. Yet the spell feels odd. Like it's . . . inert, for lack of a better word."

"How is that possible?" Conor asked.

"I don't know. Maybe the city's wards are interfering with it? Either way, her story about Meallachán rings true. I still can't read her, but after I left, I was able to locate him where she said he would be."

"Is he alive?" Eoghan asked immediately. "Were you able to contact him?"

"Aye, alive. But I wasn't able to speak to him. I think he was unconscious."

Eoghan's mind flew through the possibilities. If Meallachán were unconscious, that didn't give them many options. Ard Bealach was weeks away. "We'll need to bring her before the Conclave immediately to choose a course of action."

Conor seemed surprised there was any question. "If Meallachán's alive, we have to rescue him. He has the information we need about the runes."

"And if he's bait?" They had far too much to lose to trust Morrigan so easily. Niall knew the Fírein well enough to realize that nothing short of a solution to their problems would tempt them from Ard Dhaimhin's security. Who better to deliver the message than someone Conor had once trusted?

"Of course he's bait," Aine said. "Knowing that gives us the advantage, doesn't it?"

Eoghan's attention shifted to Aine at the same time Conor's did. Once again, they had underestimated her. "We'll get the Conclave's opinion," Eoghan said finally, rising. "You'll call the meeting, Conor?"

"Wait." Aine shifted, looking suddenly uncomfortable. Truth be told, she looked downright ill. His heart sank. From the way her eyes refused to meet his, he knew he wouldn't like this.

"Eoghan, while I was in Aron, I discovered a gift that I had been unaware of."

"What kind of gift? Something that could help us?"

Aine chewed her bottom lip. "I can influence people around me."

"So, this is helpful to us. Right?"

"Eoghan," she said gently, finally looking at him directly. "What you feel toward me? That's simply a result of my gift. I'm so sorry. I know how you've wrestled with this."

Eoghan felt as if someone had struck him in the chest with a sling stone, hard enough to pierce him through. It felt suspiciously like betrayal. He looked to Conor. "You knew about this?"

"Only since last night," Aine said. "I'm sorry. I should have told you sooner, but I feared if Conor knew the truth—"

"You might learn he was being influenced by you too," Eoghan said. All this time he'd spent berating himself for his weakness, all the guilt he'd suffered because he felt that he was betraying his best friend, all unnecessary, yet he found it hard to hold on to his anger when he saw how miserable she looked.

Could he really blame her for fearing what might happen should they find out?

Eoghan sighed. "I take it that once the person learns of your ability, they're no longer susceptible to it?"

"That seems to be the case with other gifts of the mind," Conor said.

"Well, that's some consolation. I can't say I'm not relieved."

"You forgive me, then?" The hope in her expression was heartbreaking.

"Of course. I have no reason not to."

Aine let out a relieved breath, and she and Conor rose simultaneously.

"I'll call the Conclave this afternoon," Conor said.

Eoghan acknowledged the words with a decisive nod. "I'll be along in a moment." But when the door closed, he stayed in his chair, fingers clamped on the wooden arms. Conor and Aine assumed the matter was over. He had forgiven her, and now that he knew the truth, his feelings would vanish.

They were right about the first part at least. He would forgive her anything, especially when he suspected there was nothing to forgive. The uncomfortable pang of truth seeped into the place hope had just occupied.

He really was in love with his best friend's wife.

CHAPTER
SEVEN

Conor called the Conclave together, and as usual, Eoghan was the last to arrive, a fact that was not lost on the group. The anticipation crackled in the air as they waited, no doubt due in part to the dramatic arrival of their "guest," but more likely because of the rumors that had been rippling through Carraigmór all morning. Still, when Eoghan finally showed, he took a seat at the center of the table and wordlessly turned his attention to Conor at the head.

"Brothers, we have matters of importance to discuss," Conor began. "By now, you all know there was a breach of the fortress last night."

"Why is Brother Eoghan not speaking to the matter?" Dal's eyes glittered with something that could have been anticipation or malice.

That was quick. Conor had thought he would at least get through his introduction without having his authority questioned. He raised his eyebrows at Eoghan.

"Conor is most qualified to speak on this particular matter, given the identity of the intruder."

Heads swiveled back toward Conor, and he wasn't sure whether to be grateful or irritated. "Indeed. The intruder in question is my foster sister, Lady Morrigan. I was raised alongside her by her father, Lord Labhrás, who was executed by King Fergus at the beginning of the war."

"What is she doing here? Why arrive in such a fashion?"

Conor acknowledged Gradaigh with a nod. "She claims her dramatic entrance was a way to guarantee an audience with me. She has potentially crucial information."

"A traitor's daughter," Fechin said flatly. "What do you suggest we do with her?"

"Lord Labhrás was no traitor. He was a victim of political assassination. And regardless, her father's actions have no bearing on her honesty."

"Yet you yourself doubted her story," Daigh shot back.

Conor let that comment pass. Sometimes the Conclave acted more like squabbling children than grown men. "Morrigan has brought us news that Brother Meallachán lives and is being held prisoner at Ard Bealach. Lady Aine has confirmed this."

This got their attention, and all eyes moved to Aine. "This is true?" Daigh asked. "You spoke with him?"

"No. But he is alive and where Lady Morrigan claims he is." She hesitated. "He is not in the best of health. I suspect illtreatment, most likely torture."

"The question I put to the Conclave today is whether we launch a rescue attempt," Conor said. "Meallachán is one of the few men living who understand the harp's full capability and how the runes work with it. We need him on our side and, if possible, before he gives up that information to our enemy."

"And why are *you* putting this question to us when Eoghan has stepped forward to take leadership?" Dal asked, a little smile on his face. The man truly did not like Conor.

The entire table fell silent, looking between Conor and Eoghan in anticipation. Conor's stomach tightened. This was the moment of truth.

Eoghan met his eyes and gave him a solemn nod before rising. Conor sank to his seat, feeling as if the air had gone out of him. At last Eoghan had given in to his badgering. So why didn't he feel relieved?

"Conor is correct in his assessment. Meallachán is too great an asset to be left in the hands of our enemies. I propose that we launch a rescue mission to retrieve him from Ard Bealach."

The room erupted into a babble of voices: questions about his leadership, the mission, what this meant to Ard Dhaimhin. Eoghan held up his hands for silence and nodded to Riordan, who was waiting to speak.

"Does this mean you are claiming the kingship?"

"It means I am taking the leadership of Ard Dhaimhin's fighting men and our military actions," Eoghan said. Unease once more rippled through the gathering. "As of yet, there is no throne to claim. Our land remains divided and on the brink of extinction. Only when the threat of war is gone and this evil is put to rest is it proper for any man to don a crown."

Conor didn't think he misread the undercurrent of disappointment. So Eoghan would seize leadership but not the crown?

"Conor needs to remain at the head of the city, overseeing our supplies and the integration of the kingdom's citizens. He is best suited to lead Ard Dhaimhin. But I know our men. With proper planning and strategy, we can succeed at Ard Bealach."

"Yet you will not take the title of High King," Gradaigh said, clearly disappointed.

"As is right."

All men swept their attention toward Aine, shocked by her statement. "Daimhin did not declare himself king and demand

fealty," she said. "He earned the respect of the clans and delivered Seare from the threat they too faced. Only when his job
was complete did he accept the High Kingship. Would you ask
Eoghan to seize an honor for himself that even our first High
King dared not?"

That halted everyone mid-grumble. Eoghan nodded to Aine
and then looked around the table. "What say you? Will you
accept my leadership in military matters and continue to recognize Conor as Ceannaire of Ard Dhaimhin?"

Slowly, heads dipped around the table, followed by "ayes"
in varying degrees of enthusiasm. Eoghan seemed to relax, even
though the tension built in Conor with every voice that added
itself to the fray. Eoghan seemed to think he had come up with
a solution, a compromise, when all he had done was complicate
matters. As if the chain of command weren't muddied enough,
he'd just divided their authority without recognizing that military plans directly affected the operation of the city.

"Good," Eoghan said. "Now, Ard Bealach. Conor?"

Conor quashed his feelings and unrolled two large sheets of
parchment across the table. "This is a map of the Sliebhanaigh
mountains and passes. Below it, the most recent map of Ard
Bealach."

"How did you get these?" Aine burst out.

Eoghan answered before Conor could. "We have maps and
plans of every fortress in Seare. Most of them were built during Daimhin's time. The ones that weren't—let's just say that
hostages weren't the only reason Queen Shanna demanded the
firstborn son from each clan be sent to Ard Dhaimhin."

Conor bent over the map. Its precision was astounding,
detailing everything from the height of the mountain peaks to
the exact dimensions of each chamber and corridor in the fortress. "The very things that make it so defensible are the things

that will make it easy to hold. We wouldn't need but a few dozen men to secure it, once we'd taken it."

"Ard Bealach was constructed to withstand a full frontal assault," Riordan said. "A handful of archers could hold off an army."

"That's why we won't launch a full frontal assault." Eoghan circled to the other side of the table, and Conor stepped back to make room. "If Lady Morrigan's entry to Ard Dhaimhin showed us anything, it's that a few men may succeed where an army would fail. So we won't attack from the outside; we'll attack from within." He tapped a set of broken lines on the map. "We enter through the tunnels."

"These have been sealed for years." At the surprise directed his way, Conor said, "Surely you know this story. Mad King Ragallach was convinced the Fíréin were conspiring with Tigh against him and holed up in Ard Bealach with his personal guard, two hundred strong. He had the tunnels sealed and the iron gates melted shut."

"What happened?" Aine asked.

Conor shot her a rueful smile. "He was killed at the hands of a Timhaigh assassin among his personal guard. He may have had reason for concern, even if the Fíréin weren't actually involved."

"Even so," Gradaigh said, "walls can be broken."

"Rumor was that they were sealed not with stone and mortar but with magic. Solid, seamless rock."

"So perhaps Fíréin were involved," Aine said. "Just on the other side."

They mulled that thought for a moment, until Dal finally spoke up. "We'll never bore through without attracting attention. The Sliebhanaigh range is mostly granite, just like Ard Dhaimhin."

"We don't need to bore; we just need to dig." Eoghan left the room without explanation, leaving more confusion in his wake.

When he returned, he plunked a chunk of stone in front of Daigh. "Please confirm this is just an ordinary piece of stone."

Daigh tapped it on the table with a solid thud. "It appears to be."

Eoghan took it back and used a lump of charcoal to draw an unfamiliar symbol on its surface. A rune? He handed the stone back to Daigh. "Break it."

Daigh's brow furrowed, but he took it in both hands as one might attempt to snap a twig. The rock crumbled between his fingers. He jumped from his seat, knocking the chair backward onto the stone floor. "Magic!"

"Aye," Eoghan said calmly. "A rune."

Expressions ranging from amazement to shock played over the council members' faces. Aine just watched Eoghan with a little smile. Had she known about this and failed to tell him?

"Did you decipher it from the Rune Throne?" Conor asked. Was that why Eoghan had suddenly taken leadership? Had the runes that always just looked like squiggles to him suddenly become meaningful?

"No." Eoghan's smile faded, as if the reminder had tempered his enthusiasm. "Comdiu revealed it to me in the corridor, right before Morrigan arrived. To me, that can be no coincidence. The rune means 'soft.' I believe this is how Daimhin carved the fortress out of this cliff, and it's how we will reopen Ard Bealach's tunnels. They won't be expecting attack through an entrance that's supposed to be permanently sealed."

"If we rely on stealth, it could work," Riordan said. "There's still the matter of moving the men unnoticed. Even if they think it's impregnable, they'll be watching the passes."

"We can move them in groups, disguised as Clanless," Conor said. "They have hunted those passes for generations."

"Aye, that could work." Eoghan nodded thoughtfully. "We'll

want to hear from Lady Morrigan about the numbers and their discipline."

"I'll retrieve her." Conor jumped at the chance to leave the room before he said or did something stupid.

"Wait." Daigh's terse word stopped him. "There is one thing left to resolve. You and Eoghan are both involved in this plan to some degree. Who has the final say in the event of a dispute?"

Conor froze and looked back at Eoghan. This was his decision—the turning point. Eoghan's pained expression said he knew it too. He straightened and cleared his throat. "I do."

Conor swallowed, aware of the men waiting for his reaction while blood thrummed in his ears. Then at last, he dipped his head and left the room without a word.

✦ ✦ ✦

Aine excused herself and followed her husband from the hall. "Wait, Conor, please."

He threw a glance over his shoulder, expression composed, but kept walking. "Are you coming back to the hall? They'll want you to testify to her truthfulness. What you can determine, at least."

"I will. But, Conor, why are you upset? I thought Eoghan handled that as diplomatically as possible. Isn't this what you wanted? Your hard work to keep the city running won't go to waste, and Eoghan finally took command of the men. It seems like the best possible solution."

"It does seem that way, doesn't it?" Conor started up the stairs that led to Morrigan's chamber.

Aine frowned. This wasn't like Conor. She knew he wasn't pleased by the shift of authority, even though he knew it had to happen, but this was something else. The attitude pouring from him could freeze a kettle on the boil. She hurried after him, resisting the temptation to pull it from his mind.

"Then what's wrong?" she asked softly. "Tell me, please."

He stopped short and at last turned to face her. Anger flashed in his eyes, even while his voice remained quiet. "Why didn't you tell me about the rune?"

The look in his eyes gave her a jolt. She'd never seen that emotion directed toward her. "I don't understand."

"Of all the people in the room, you were the only one unsurprised by the revelation. At first I thought you read it in his mind, but he looked at you as if you'd already discussed it. So why didn't you tell me?"

Her heart slammed into her rib cage, bringing with it the sick feeling of guilt. "I was there when he discovered it. He asked me not to say anything. It was only yesterday—"

"I see."

Those simple words chilled her even more than his anger. "Conor, I swear, I didn't think it mattered. Besides, what was I supposed to do? He asked me to give him time to consult Comdiu! He is supposed to be my king."

It was the wrong thing to say. Conor's manner grew even icier. "So that's what it takes to earn your loyalty? A throne? What else would you do if he asked you to?"

In a flash, Aine's guilt turned to fury. "That is unworthy of you. I'll wait for you and Morrigan in the hall."

"Aine, wait . . ."

But she kept walking, her boot heels sharp and echoing on the stone floor, nearly as loud as the beat of her pulse in her ears. Of all the things she expected from her husband, cruelty was not one of them. She blinked away tears before they could do more than dampen her lashes. All this because of her gift. Some gift it turned out to be. It might have saved her life, but it also put her husband and his best friend at odds and made Conor distrust her. And none of it was within her control.

CHAPTER
EIGHT

He was in an impossible situation.

After his actions last night—and the hope it had subsequently raised—Eoghan had to make some sort of declaration. Yet for all the conviction he had felt in taking control the night before, he had the equally strong feeling he couldn't declare himself High King. Not now. Maybe not ever. Even if he were ready, he was not qualified to take command of the city, didn't know where to start.

That in itself should give them pause.

It certainly did Conor. He was too shrewd to express his concerns before the Conclave now that Eoghan had finally taken command, but they were evident in his manner. Eoghan was beginning to think nothing he did would satisfy him.

While Conor retrieved Morrigan, Eoghan looked over the map with Riordan and Daigh, considering both the shortest and least-exposed routes through the mountains to Ard Bealach and debating which would be least likely to bring them into contact with actual tribes of the Clanless. These Seareanns—unsworn to clan or country—hated all outsiders, but they seemed to have a particular dislike for the Fíréin. All it would take was a band of hunters to raise the alarm, and they'd have enemies pouring over them like ants from an anthill.

Aine came back into the hall alone, and it took only a glance to see she was upset. Had she and Conor quarreled in the corridor? He had to resist the urge to comfort her. It wasn't his place, especially when he was supposed to be hiding his feelings. Besides, if they'd argued, it most likely had something to do with him.

Eoghan hesitated as conversation continued around them, but it somehow didn't seem right to ignore her when she looked so forlorn. He sat across the table from her and leaned over his folded hands. "Tell me what you think about Morrigan."

"As I said before, I think she's being truthful about her information, but she's hiding her true motivations."

"Do you think she's a threat?"

"You'd be better asking that of Conor."

"I'm asking you."

"Potentially? Aye. If our actions conflict with her goals."

"Which we don't know."

Aine cracked a smile. "Exactly."

Not all that helpful in choosing a direction, but at least it confirmed his own uneasy feelings. Morrigan was a manipulator, and he'd feel far better if he knew what she was trying to accomplish.

The sound of footsteps preceded Conor's return with the prisoner. Eoghan blinked in surprise when he saw her. Morrigan's title had seemed laughable last night when Conor introduced her. Now, in a blue wool dress that hugged every womanly curve, with her dark hair secured in a modest braid, she looked every inch the lady.

From the look on the other men's faces, he wasn't the only one who thought so. He could almost feel the softening of their attitudes toward her.

All except Daigh, who continued to scowl at her as though she were a viper near a baby's cradle. "She's an intruder, not a guest. Why is she not in bonds?"

"Because one woman is hardly a threat against the might of the Fíréin brotherhood in this stronghold." Morrigan's voice, pleasant and well modulated, almost demure, seemed calculated to calm the situation. Oh, she was far more dangerous than she appeared.

Eoghan rose and gestured to a seat beside him. "Lady Morrigan, please join us. We would like to ask you some questions."

She gathered her skirts and settled into the chair he indicated. "What would you like to know?"

Eoghan sat beside her. "Who is in command at Ard Bealach now?"

"As I told you last night, a man named Somhairle, a Sliebhanaigh warrior loyal to Keondric."

"Is he being commanded by magic?"

"I don't know. Would that be evident?"

Eoghan moved on without answering. "How many men under his command?"

"About a hundred, supplemented by mercenaries. Anywhere between ten and sixty additional men, depending on season."

"You seem well-informed, Lady Morrigan."

Morrigan met his gaze, unflinching. He could swear he saw a hint of amusement in her expression. "It doesn't take much intelligence or imagination to know what I would be asked when I arrived. I made it my business to know."

"How well trained are the men?" Now Riordan interjected himself into the questioning.

"Very. These are no farmers and craftsmen. Professional warriors, the lot of them, and the fact that some of them are from the other kingdoms tell me they were selected for their skills, not merely proximity."

"You seem very knowledgeable on the subject," Riordan said.

"And you're surprised because I'm a woman? I'm Timhaigh, my lord. There are few things we do better than wage war. So, aye, I know how to size up a man's skills, just as I know there is something at Ard Bealach worth protecting with experienced men."

It felt like both defiance and a warning, and Eoghan couldn't help but feel the slightest glimmer of admiration for her nerve. From the smile playing at Riordan's mouth, he seemed to feel the same way. In fact, she reminded him a little of Conor. Perhaps they were truer siblings than their blood would lead them to believe.

"Very well, Lady Morrigan. Thank you for your cooperation."

"That's it?"

"What were you expecting? Do you have something else to add?"

"No, it's simply that . . . are you going to rescue Master Meallachán?"

"We haven't decided."

Morrigan blinked, but Eoghan said nothing more on the subject. "Conor, would you call the guard to escort her back to her chamber? You are needed here."

Conor left the room and appeared with two men in tow. Aine still hadn't made eye contact with her husband, but perhaps it was more apparent to Eoghan than anyone else. As soon as Morrigan departed with the guards, he looked to her. "What do you think?"

"I believe you can be confident about the numbers and her assessment of the men. Beyond that, I've already said I can't read her."

Surprise flared from the Conclave members, who apparently hadn't put the suspicion of magic together with the blocking of Aine's gift.

"What does this mean for us, then?" Dal asked finally, more subdued than usual. "A hundred well-trained men in an impenetrable fortress."

"Which we will secretly enter and take before anyone is the wiser," Conor said. "Or do you forget that we have both our fading abilities and the runes on our side?"

"*A* rune," Daigh corrected. "And if we're talking two dozen men against more than a hundred, we have to be prepared for casualties. We are not invincible. Mistakes happen."

It was a far more humble attitude toward the Fíréin than Daigh had ever exhibited before. Was the man's reticence to break tradition actually born from fear?

"What are the chances this could be a trap?" Gradaigh asked.

"High." Eoghan didn't mince words. "We can't discount the idea that Lady Morrigan set up this situation on Niall's behalf to draw Conor or me out."

"Then why take the risk?" Daigh asked.

"Because if one of our own is being imprisoned and tortured, it's the right thing to do."

"That's certainly a reversal of your position since yesterday. What's changed?" Conor's tone remained quiet and measured, but the challenge was clear.

"What's changed is the urgency and the goal," Eoghan said. "This is a call I believe we must answer, regardless of whether Meallachán is in any condition to assist us. If we accomplish secondary goals, all the better."

"Moral obligations aside," Conor said, "we are in the middle of a war. Taking an enemy fortress is hardly a secondary goal."

"I'm on your side of this argument, Conor."

Conor shut his mouth and gave Eoghan a tense nod.

Eoghan appealed to the Conclave. "I believe we can mitigate the risk. For one, we should bring Lady Morrigan. She's clearly shown a talent for self-preservation, so I don't believe she'll willingly put herself in harm's way."

"Unless she was lying about her escape and she's leading us into a trap," Daigh said.

"Be that as it may, I'd rather have her where I can keep an eye on her. We won't share our plans, simply bring her along for the trip. Think of her as a hostage."

Eoghan felt Conor flinch at the word, but he didn't acknowledge him. "Shall we put it to a vote?"

"I think we've passed the point of voting," Conor said. "You're in command. You have spoken."

A quick look around the table proved the truth of Conor's words. Slowly, nods circled through the men. "A week to prepare, then," Eoghan said. "I'll select the party. You and I will need to discuss provisions."

"You're suggesting we both go?" Conor asked. "That leaves the city without a leader in the event we fail."

"I'm not sure we have a choice. It's only right I lead the campaign, and you're needed to erect a shield around the fortress after we've taken it."

"As you command." Conor's voice was hard, but he delivered the words without a trace of irony.

In that moment, Eoghan realized that the brotherhood—and the way of life to which he had devoted himself—was well and truly broken.

CHAPTER
NINE

Conor avoided Carraigmór—or rather Eoghan and Aine—
while his temper cooled. He'd been unfair to his wife. He didn't
need time or distance to know she'd been put in an impossible
situation, torn between her loyalty to Conor and the man that
he himself insisted was their High King.

His feelings about Eoghan, on the other hand, didn't soften
a bit. He should not be seeking private audiences with Aine,
shouldn't be asking her to keep his secrets. The fact that Eoghan
had always been so circumspect in the past made Conor wonder
if he'd deliberately tried to drive a wedge between them because
he wanted Aine for himself.

Conor wandered the practice yards, watching matches with a
jaw clenched so hard it ached. Men bowed to him deferentially,
though he knew that would change. He was no longer a leader
of warriors but a bureaucrat. His worth had been reduced to
tallying tablets and counting bushels. Wasn't that what Eoghan
had meant when he'd said Conor's expertise was too valuable
to lose?

"Master Conor, care to step in?" One of the younger men, an

apprentice whose face he recognized but whose name he couldn't remember, stepped back from his opponent.

"I'll just watch." Conor couldn't guarantee his irritation with the situation wouldn't spill over into his fighting. The last thing he wanted to do was injure an apprentice because he couldn't take out his feelings on his real target.

By the time he felt reasonably in control of his emotions, the sun had set and most of the villagers had already made their way to the cookhouses for supper. Conor bypassed the line and slunk upward into Carraigmór, determined to avoid contact until he could manage some semblance of civility.

Instead, the first person he spotted in the hall was Eoghan.

"Conor. I've been looking for you. I've asked Riordan, Daigh, and Aine to meet us in your study. Will you come?"

Conor nodded stiffly and followed Eoghan to the Ceannaire's office, where the other men and Aine already waited. His wife raised pained, regretful eyes to him, but she said nothing, for which he was grateful. Now was not the time to air their private issues.

Eoghan hesitated just inside, and Conor swept a hand toward the heavy chair behind the table. He had claimed the honors of leadership, so it was only logical that he take Conor's place in the office as well. As Eoghan sat behind the desk, looking far more comfortable behind it than Conor had ever felt, the truth hit him full force.

"Eoghan cannot lead this mission."

All heads swiveled toward him. He found a seat, his conviction growing. "He's too important to the city, too important to Seare, to be risked. I have to go anyway to erect the shield. I can see the rune, so I imagine I can reproduce it."

The room remained silent for a moment, and Conor focused on Eoghan's face so he didn't have to see the betrayed look in

Aine's eyes. Finally, Eoghan gave a small nod. "Whom do you propose to leave in command after the fortress is taken?"

"Surely we have a Conclave member of Sliebhanaigh descent who will do nicely. Daigh, perhaps?"

Daigh's eyebrows rose, but before the man could object, Aine interrupted.

"Then I'm going with you."

"No."

"Why not? You need a way to communicate with Ard Dhaimhin—"

"Which you can do from here."

"—and having a healer on hand is an undeniable advantage—"

"Which I can't take away from the city."

She stared at him, eyes glimmering with hurt and anger. She thought he didn't want her around, which was not remotely the truth.

"Aine," he said evenly. "You must think of our child."

Heads whipped toward them, shock on Daigh's and Eoghan's faces.

"You're expecting?" Eoghan asked, his voice rough. Aine nodded.

"Congratulations," Daigh said. "Conor's right. We'll be traveling on foot for weeks. You would put yourself and us at risk."

"What say you, Eoghan?" Conor asked. "The final decision is yours."

"I don't like it. I feel like I'm shirking my duty."

"What says Comdiu on the matter?"

Eoghan sighed. "Nothing specific. But I have been asking Him whether this endeavor is the right one. Not if I must go."

"This is what must happen," Conor said. "You know it as well as I do."

Eoghan at last nodded his agreement, and Aine stood. "If you'll excuse me, I'm going to go rest now."

The men rose with her and she escaped the room, leaving an echo of silence in her absence. Or maybe it just felt that way to Conor, knowing she was hurt and angry.

When they were all seated again, Eoghan looked to Conor. "What of Lady Morrigan? Does she stay as well?"

"Aye, she stays. I don't trust her yet, and I don't want to be responsible for her safety. If we're to be successful, I need experienced, disciplined men. I need to be assured of their reliability."

It took several hours to choose the members of the parties, a dozen each to be led by Conor and Daigh. It took nearly as long to make the list of supplies and weapons they would bring with them, balancing the need for self-sufficiency with the desire to travel light and fast. All the while, Conor wondered how furious Aine would be when he returned to their chamber.

But when he at last entered the room, she seemed merely sad. Perched on her chair with a shawl wrapped around her shoulders and a book open on her lap, she watched him undress in silence.

Conor waited until he could no longer stand the quiet. "This is the way it must be, Aine."

"Must it? Or is this just your way of proving you're capable of more than the administrative tasks to which you've been reduced?"

Her quiet words pierced to his heart, even knowing she'd likely picked the unacknowledged thought from his mind. He knelt by the chair and buried his head in her side, breathing deeply her familiar scent of sage and lavender and mint. After a moment, she softened and combed her fingers through his hair in acceptance of his unspoken apology.

"I love only you, Conor," she murmured. "I'm loyal to you. What must I do to prove it?"

"Nothing, love. I'm sorry. Forgive me for being cruel."

"Of course I forgive you. I'm sorry for not telling you about the rune. I didn't know what to do."

"I know. I blame Eoghan, not you."

She pulled away from him, her face creased into a frown. "Conor, whatever is between you and Eoghan has to end. The two of you are responsible for the well-being of this city, of this kingdom. Our enemy would like nothing more than to have you divided and ineffectual."

He straightened and took a seat on the bed, embarrassed to be scolded by his wife like a child. "He does not make it easy."

"Nor do you make it easy for him. You once had a family. Now you have a wife and child. Do you think you're the only one who feels envy? This cannot be about the three of us. If it were, you would not be leaving me again on a mission from which you might not return."

"Aine—"

"I know why you must go. Just don't act as if you and Eoghan are the only ones who make sacrifices."

Conor set aside the book and drew her to her feet, then pulled her into his arms. "There are times when I think Seare might benefit from a High Queen instead."

Her expression softened and a smile quivered on her lips. "Since that's not going to happen, Seare will have to muddle through with you two."

"Comdiu help us," he murmured.

"He always does." She stretched up and planted a light kiss on his lips, her way of telling him that for the moment at least, all was forgiven.

✦ ✦ ✦

Eoghan didn't wait for morning to knock on Morrigan's door. With more time came more of a chance she would hear the news on her own, and he wanted to see her reaction. Still, the men on guard looked at his arrival with curiosity. He ignored them.

Morrigan, however, seemed completely unsurprised. "I wondered how long it would take for you to come see me. Would you like to come inside?"

Eoghan stepped through the door, but he left it cracked open. He would not be the one responsible for discarding the last tatters of her respectability. He didn't wait for her question. "You're not going to Ard Bealach."

"I don't understand. I'm the only one who has been there. I'd think you'd want my memory of the layout."

"We don't need your memory of the layout. Conor is more than capable of leading this mission on his own."

Dismay surfaced in her expression. "Conor is going to lead the assault?"

"Is there some reason why you're concerned for him?"

"Of course there is. Whatever you might think of me, I'm not completely heartless. Nor am I foolish enough to think this mission is without its risks. I don't want to see him get hurt. Especially not with a pregnant wife."

Now he was taken off guard. "How on earth did you know that?"

"Women know these things." She pulled out a chair from the table and sat. "Where men look for the obvious, women look for the nuance."

"Nuance is certainly not a problem for you, my lady. But considering you like so well to style yourself as a man, perhaps you could state the obvious."

"Fine. I will. Conor was not raised as a warrior, and you most certainly were. He's going to get himself killed."

"And what makes you so certain of that? If you're truly worried about his safety, you should come clean now."

"I have told you everything I know." She spread her hands wide. "But it would be foolish to think that after I leave, they wouldn't be looking for some sort of attack and laying traps. Isn't that what you would do if someone who was privy to sensitive information disappeared mysteriously?"

She was right; it was exactly what they would do. "What information do you have that could be so damaging?"

"I've told you already. Their numbers. Their training. The fact they hold Master Meallachán."

"All of which could be common knowledge."

"I think you overestimate the interest of the people in the region. They're busy trying not to starve. They don't care who's taken over the fortress."

Eoghan cast a quizzical look at her.

"Where do you think Keondric's forces have gotten their supplies? They've stolen—excuse me, *commandeered*—them from the surrounding villages. The livestock, the autumn harvests, everything."

"Be that as it may, I can assure you that Conor is most certainly capable of taking care of himself."

"I shall take your word on it. Just take mine. Don't underestimate what you might face at Ard Bealach."

Eoghan gave her a terse nod and then moved toward the door. Perhaps her concern for Conor was real, but he didn't believe for a moment that she had told them everything she knew.

CHAPTER
TEN

The week that preceded Conor's departure from Ard Bealach sped by in a blur, during which Aine was lucky to capture a handful of minutes with her husband. Conor rose long before she did and crawled into bed hours after she went to sleep. There was work to be done in the village below, of course: endless rounds of patients to be seen and the regular decoctions and salves to be made. She also spent hours at the workbench, putting together a kit of every possible remedy Conor and his party might need. Just because she wasn't permitted to come along didn't mean she would send them into the dark reaches of the Sliebhanaigh mountains unprepared.

When she wasn't in the healer's cottage, she was reading through Shanna's journals—a slow process, considering the queen's tiny, old-fashioned handwriting.

"You're working too hard," Conor murmured, slipping his arms around her from behind as she read. It was late on the night before his departure, and she had almost given up on his appearing to spend their last few hours together.

She twisted around and kissed him in greeting. "Not as hard as you. Have you left the Ceannaire's study in the past two days?"

"Two? Three? I've lost count." He moved around her to perch on the bed and nodded toward her book. "Anything yet?"

"The same. I feel we're missing a volume somewhere. She refers to a pervasive darkness on the land and the troubles that came out of it, but she doesn't give any details."

"That's interesting. We know that Daimhin took power because he solved a problem, and we know it had something to do with the wards."

"Perhaps I haven't gotten there yet. I thought this was from the early years of his reign, but Carraigmór hasn't even been built yet." Aine sat back in her chair. "Does it strike you as peculiar that the last time the runes were discovered, it was when the High King was needed to face down a massive threat?"

Conor's brow furrowed. "You think Comdiu purposely brings the runes back to attention when they're needed by the High King?"

"It makes sense, doesn't it? Where did they go for the last five hundred years? Aye, they've been on the throne all this time, but no one alive knows what they mean. Meallachán has carried them on his harp, but we're not sure if he was actually aware of what they could do individually."

"That's why we need to ask Meallachán. For all we know, that's why he's being held in the first place." Their eyes met, and Aine could see him putting together the pieces without even touching his mind. "We need to know as much as we can about the events of Daimhin's kingship."

"I'll keep reading, and I'll keep you apprised of what I find." Aine paused. "Conor, what if Meallachán really doesn't know anything? What if he, like you, just happened to be born with a gift and access to an object of power?"

"Then we've simply done what I've been trying to accomplish. Once we secure Ard Bealach and the passes, we have a direct conduit to bring men into Sliebhan, as well as a base of operations for expansion."

Aine stared at her husband, understanding dawning along with a glimmer of admiration. "This was never about Meallachán for you. You just knew they needed a legitimate reason to break them out of their apathy."

Conor said nothing, but if she weren't mistaken, he looked a little smug. Could he be that calculated, to hide his intentions even from her? His gentle spirit and kind nature sometimes made it difficult to remember that he had been educated as a prince, with all the understandings of political machinations and strategy that entailed.

Just like Morrigan.

"What do you think your sister's game is?" Aine asked suddenly.

"I don't know. That's what I need you to find out. We have to know why you can't read her and why she's really here. You may be able to gain her confidence more easily than I could."

"Not likely. She already knows I suspect her."

"And if I know Morrigan at all, she'll still think she can get the best of you. I used to play King and Conqueror with her. For all her feminine trappings, she was the most audacious strategist I've ever seen."

"You were matched, then?"

"Evenly, if differently. I always tried to win while preserving every piece I could. You never know what you might need until the end."

"And Morrigan?"

"She would risk anything. Down to her last piece."

✦ ✦ ✦

It shouldn't have surprised Aine that her sleep was disturbed in the days before the departure. However confident Conor was in the selection of his companions and the soundness of his plan, she couldn't forget that he could very well be walking into a trap. Perhaps that explained the sensation of watching eyes and grasping hands that clawed at her in her sleep. Clearly, her helpless feelings in her waking hours carried over to her resting ones as well.

Worse yet was when Aine learned that what she assumed to be a short trek on horseback was actually weeks on foot, with only ponies to carry their belongings.

"The Clanless don't have access to riding horses," Conor explained. "For our disguise to be convincing, we must travel exactly as they would."

"Then perhaps you should have picked a closer fortress to besiege."

"Sadly, we're fresh out of nearby fortresses. But we'll be in enemy territory for only a short time."

"That's a comfort." Aine took Conor's hand and held it to her abdomen, the swell of which was beginning to grow more pronounced. "You do realize you may miss the birth of your child."

From the startled look on Conor's face, he'd not considered that possibility. "I will do everything in my power to keep that from happening."

"If only everything were within your power." Five months seemed like a long time, but it wasn't. Not really. The thought of Conor's being gone when she gave birth made her shiver with fear—not because of the actual birth, as there were midwives in the village and she had attended dozens of births herself, but the idea of becoming a mother alone, without his quiet, reassuring presence. She would be responsible for a new life, one she was bringing into a nation at war, where their very survival was horribly uncertain. A tear slid down her cheek.

Conor slipped an arm around her shoulder and buried his face in her hair. "I love you, Aine. And I love our child. Being here or there will not affect that."

Aine swiped the tear away. "I'm sorry. The baby makes me terribly emotional. I'm told it gets worse before it gets better."

"I wish I could stay. I wish it were safe for you to be with me. But the sooner I leave, the sooner I'll be back. And by that time, perhaps you will have learned how the sword and the runes and the kingship all fit together."

"With Comdiu's provision, I will have. To think I believed we wouldn't be parted again."

Conor flinched, and she knew he was remembering his promise not to leave her side again. It was cruel to act as if he were letting her down when he was merely doing his duty.

"Enough of this talk," she said. "Let's go to bed. It's an early day tomorrow."

The next morning, she rose early to help Conor prepare for departure, even though he didn't need assistance. The actions—adjusting the buckles on his sword baldric, handing him the blades that went into sheaths on various parts of his person, draping him in the furs that were part of the traveler disguise—all felt like a mystical barrier against the dangers to come. She knew it was pure superstition, yet the accompanying prayers in her heart were anything but. *Comdiu protect him. Let him prevail against his enemies. Let him come back to me safely.*

Let my child have the chance to know his father.

Only when she removed the rune charm, the ivory one he had given her before he left to join the Fíréin brotherhood years ago, did her composure break. She chewed her bottom lip to keep her tears from flowing and draped it over his head, then tucked it beneath his tunic.

"None of this, now." Conor brushed away the single escaped

teardrop on its descent down her face. He kissed her deeply, a reassurance, a promise. "We will be successful. And I will be back in plenty of time to see the birth of our child."

Aine smiled as he caught her around the waist and gave her a little spin, the playfulness of the gesture at odds with her dark thoughts. She trusted Comdiu to watch over Conor, to protect this endeavor, but the little nagging fears still nibbled away at her faith. Each time they parted, she wondered if they'd used up all their allotted reunions.

"I can't delay any longer," he said finally, regret heavy in his voice. "Contact me each night, and I'll update you on our position. You can have Eoghan mark it on the map so the leadership knows our progress."

"Of course." She put on a cheerful attitude and let him take her hand as they proceeded to the clearing below Carraigmór. The party had staged themselves at the bottom of the steps beside four pack ponies loaded with food, supplies, and wicker cages containing gray and white rock doves to be housed in Ard Bealach's dovecotes.

Warriors milled around the horses, dressed similarly to Conor and fully armed with sling staves, swords, and bows. Some Aine recognized as being from the ranks of older and more experienced brothers. Others looked barely old enough to shave. They all, however, shared the confident quality of men born and reared in Ard Dhaimhin, at once fearless and cautious. Aine felt a twinge of appreciation in her chest and realized that somewhere over the course of the past two months, living and working alongside Ard Dhaimhin's brothers, she'd come to care about them.

"You ready?"

Eoghan's deep voice behind them startled her, but he was directing his question to Conor, who simply nodded. "As ready as we can be. I will be contacting Aine regularly as we go, and we'll send back a dove as soon as we've taken the fortress."

Conor's certainty that they would be successful unknotted the tension in her stomach by a degree. He wasn't given to bravado. If he thought they would succeed, she believed him.

"You've the coin that we set aside for you?" Eoghan asked.

"Aye, though I don't expect to need it."

Eoghan had insisted that Conor take a good amount of gold from Ard Dhaimhin's coffers for bribes and quiet purchases. Aine had been horrified at the hoard of gold and silver, considering the city's dire struggles, until Conor reminded her that the true problem was the scarcity of supplies.

Conor drew Eoghan off a few paces, and from the speculative glance that Eoghan cast in her direction, she knew she was the topic of conversation. She barely resisted the urge to pick out the details from Conor's mind.

"You asked him to watch over me, didn't you?" she murmured when he came back.

He slipped his arms around her and pressed his lips to the top of her head, heedless of their audience. "Of course I did. No matter how I feel toward him at the moment, he will see that you're safe. Promise me you won't work yourself too hard. Not just for you, but for the baby."

"I promise I will not do anything to harm our child," Aine said. From the look on his face, it wasn't the assurance he wanted. She sighed. "Conor, the needs of the city are great. I can't simply lock myself inside Carraigmór until you return. But I promise I will not do anything foolish. That will have to be enough."

"It will have to be," he said with a hint of humor. "Let it never be said you don't have a mind of your own." He kissed her then, sweetly and much too briefly for her liking, and then shouldered his staff. "Contact me tonight. Don't forget."

"How could I?" she shot back, plastering on a teasing smile that she didn't feel. "Go with Comdiu, my love."

He bowed his head as if to receive the blessing and then clasped forearms with Riordan and Eoghan one more time before taking his place at the front of the group. He raised his voice loud enough to be heard through the clearing and raised a hand. "Forward."

Aine's heart rose into her throat as she watched her husband walk away, her eyes locked onto his familiar figure until he disappeared into the small sea of warriors. The crowd around her began to dissipate, but she didn't turn away until the last man was merely a speck on the edge of her vision, swallowed by the trees and structures of the village.

Only Eoghan remained by the time she turned back to Carraigmór's steps. Except he wasn't watching the departing party; he was watching her. And the equal measures of determination and darkness on his face started her anxiety all over again.

CHAPTER
ELEVEN

Conor had never ventured south of the city into the farthest
fields, so over the next week, he found himself surprised by
the expanse of the Fíréin domain. Farmland and pastureland stretched as far as he could see to the near peaks of the
Sliebhanaigh mountains. It would have been beautiful if not for
the char that scarred the patchwork of arable land, almost as if
the damage had been random, indiscriminate. But nothing the
druid did was random. He'd targeted the crops they depended
on to get them through the winter—the grains, the alfalfa fields
where the beehives were located, the hay used to feed the animals. Somehow the destruction only brought home the urgency
of their mission.

Daigh found his way up to his side, which surprised Conor.
The man had never sought him out unless he absolutely had to.
He simply walked alongside him without speaking, until Conor
finally said, "It's bad, but not as bad as I expected."

"It gets worse," Daigh said grimly. "Some areas aren't
touched. Others are wiped out for acres."

"Have you seen it yourself?"

"Aye. Went out after the attack to evaluate the situation for myself. Someone from the Conclave needed to have firsthand knowledge of the damage."

As bad as the destruction was, Conor thought they were lucky it hadn't been worse. He changed his mind when they entered into the pasturelands, which had once been wide green swaths of grazing land, and found only charred and blackened earth.

"There were animals here," Conor said to Daigh, hoping he was wrong.

Daigh just gave him a tense nod. "We lost over half of our herds, which you already know. Looks like the druid reserved a group of men to circle around south and do as much damage as they could before they retreated. Even if we were able to rebuild the herds, there's no grazing left. Regrowth should have begun months ago."

"Unnatural fire." Cold dismay started in Conor's chest and crept through his body. "This could affect Ard Dhaimhin for generations."

"Unless we find a way to reverse it, aye."

Over that first week, Conor's estimation of his fellow leader rose. Regardless of his attitude or his feelings about Conor, Daigh was committed to Ard Dhaimhin. And it seemed as though Conor's willingness to undertake leadership of what was a potentially dangerous mission had endeared him to Daigh in return. As Conor began to learn exactly how badly his stamina had suffered from both imprisonment and inactivity at Carraigmór, he appreciated when Daigh took on the job of camp marshal. It allowed him to rest, study maps, and pretend that he had better things to do than reveal the truth: he was just too tired to do anything besides sit by the fire.

His nightly check-in with Aine was the single bright spot of his day, particularly as their time within the protective circle of Ard Dhaimhin's wards drew to a close.

Things are as they always are, Aine reassured him, an oddly disembodied voice in his mind. *Eoghan is in command of the men and presides over the Conclave as if he were born to it. Riordan has stepped into your place as Ceannaire without a hitch. You needn't worry how things are going in your absence.*

I'm not sure if that makes me feel better or worse. Couldn't you at least pretend that things have fallen apart in my absence?

Then you would be fretting about how the brotherhood should have been better trained than that and how you're not living up to your role as Liam's successor. I know you, Conor. Concentrate on your mission.

She did know him, and she was right, at least about his expectations for the brotherhood. His smile quickly faded. *We've reached the furthest edge of the Fíréin's domain now. We should clear our border and the shield by mid-morning tomorrow.*

We will be petitioning Comdiu on your behalf. Be careful. I love you.

And I love you.

When he looked up, he saw that Daigh had come near enough to speak to him.

"News?"

"The same. Letting her know we'll be entering the pass tomorrow."

Daigh looked past him to the shadow of the mountains. Conor knew what he was thinking. Considering the dizzying drop to the plains of Sliebhan below, one would expect the road to rise steeply. But Ard Dhaimhin was located on a high plain, and the pass was actually a dark corridor, little more than a crevasse that sloped downward. Somehow that was even more disconcerting than a climb.

"We'll separate at the first fork in Little Neck?" Daigh verified, referring to the point where the road bottlenecked and then
split into two passes, one that moved around the north side of
the fortress and the other to the south.

"Aye. Our cover will work better that way."

"Assuming they haven't seen us and made us for Fíréin
already."

"Which is why we stick to the story." Conor patted the
pouch of coins at his belt. If they were questioned about why
they were returning from Ard Dhaimhin, he planned on saying
they'd traded meat for coin to the brotherhood, who were in
desperate need of supplies. In the event they were questioned
why they would trade away such precious commodity for something that couldn't warm them or fill their bellies, Conor had
ordered the men to say they were planning on hopping a ship
to Gwydden as soon as they could secure passage. The Clanless
should have little enough experience with travel outside Seare
that they wouldn't question the feasibility of the plan.

Daigh fell silent again, and Conor could almost see the
orderly march of thought through the other man's head. "You
realize that once we set foot outside of Ard Dhaimhin's domain,
we also step outside the protection of our wards."

Conor nodded. He'd thought of little else for the past day
or two, trying to devise some way to safeguard his men against
the influence of the sidhe. "If I play a ward through the pass, we
will lose the element of surprise. Plus, our fiction about being
Clanless will be less than convincing. If you can think of a way
to do it with subtlety, I am all ears."

"The sidhe tend to be subtle and target just a few men at a
time," Daigh said slowly. "Before we leave the city's wardings, we
should arrange the men into groups of twos and threes. Make
them responsible for monitoring each other's behavior. The

likelihood of all three men in a group being corrupted or misled at once is small."

"That's a good idea," Conor said. "Do it."

Inwardly, though, he wondered if it would be enough. When discussing the matter back at Ard Dhaimhin, they had determined that the Sliebhanaigh mountains were unpopulated enough that the sidhe's influence would be light. Unlike the cities and villages, there were not enough souls to lead astray, not enough misery from which to feed. But Conor knew all too well the havoc that one spirit alone could wreak when it had a mission and a plan.

The uneasiness dogged him through the night and lingered when he woke in the cool gray morning. As if in defiance of their hope for good weather, a fine mist settled over them, dampening their clothes and supplies. Still, it was a natural kind of mist, not an unearthly cold that indicated the presence of the sidhe.

"Fifteen minutes to break camp," Conor called, and the men sprang into action. Fires were doused, bedrolls tied and stowed on the packhorses, weapons checked and double-checked. The men possessed an extra measure of gravity today, and once more, Conor was grateful for Ard Dhaimhin's unceasing training and discipline. Not a word was uttered that hinted an unwillingness to face what might lie ahead of them. Not a movement of a hand toward a weapon betrayed the nervousness that they must feel.

"Delay your party an hour," Conor told Daigh. "It will look less conspicuous when we divide at the Neck."

"Aye, I will." He held out a hand to Conor, who clasped his arm without hesitation. "Go with Comdiu. And use caution. Ard Dhaimhin needs you."

Surprised, Conor nodded for a second. "Aye. And you. We enter on the first night of the full moon. I'll see you inside."

Daigh clapped Conor on the shoulder. "See you inside."

"All right," Conor called. "My group, forward. Daigh's group, stay put."

A dozen men fell into the rough jumble that ran contrary to their training but would help them sell the impression that they were Clanless traders. Conor signaled to the man directly behind him to move forward. "Tomey."

"Aye, sir?"

Conor leveled a reproving look at him. No one but warriors responded so respectfully or with such alacrity. The man grinned at him. "Whatcher want?"

Conor repressed a laugh. "Better."

"My people were lowborn Faolanaigh. Early memories don't easily leave." But neither did the precise, educated way of speaking that he had acquired from a life mostly lived in Ard Dhaimhin.

"Good. I'm counting on that. Do you know any of the old folk prayers?"

"Aye, of course I do. Why?"

"I want you to see which the men know and teach those who have never heard them. I remember my wife saying they had banished the sidhe through their prayers."

"Wouldn't any prayer do? Does it have to be by rote?"

"No, but it will make it easier when the men are scared shiftless. If you've never been in the sidhe's presence, you don't know the kind of fear they can incite."

"Aye, sir. Er, yeah, I'll do that, Conor."

"Good lad." Conor clapped Tomey on the shoulder much as Daigh had done to him. It was all they could do.

CHAPTER
TWELVE

Aine sped down the corridor after the young boy who had been sent to retrieve her from her chamber, twisting her messy hair into a knot as she went. Considering that it was barely past dawn, only something dire could cause Riordan to call her to the Ceannaire's office before she was even dressed.

When she burst into the office, both Riordan and Eoghan waited for her, a steaming pot of tea and a plate of oatcakes on the table between them. She blinked at the scene, taking in their calm demeanors and the three place settings.

"Lady Aine. Tea?" Riordan lifted the pot questioningly and hovered over an empty cup.

"Aye, please, but . . . I don't understand. You called me here for tea?"

"No, of course not." Eoghan's voice was calm, but his dark eyes held something sorrowful that unnerved her more than the early-morning summons. "Given the early hour and your . . . condition . . . I ordered it be brought so you could eat while we talked."

"Oh. Thank you. I think." She took the chair Eoghan

indicated and accepted the cup of tea from Riordan, still confused. "What's happened that requires my attendance so urgently?"

Riordan and Eoghan exchanged another look, and Riordan nodded, a show of deference toward his leader. Eoghan drummed his fingertips on the table. "We've word from Faolán. Niall has taken a small fortress not far from Lisdara."

Aine's heart rose into her throat. It was bad news that the druid was on the move, especially if he were stirring from his stronghold and turning his eye to other conquests. "But there's more, isn't there? You wouldn't have called me here if there weren't."

"Aine," Eoghan said gently, "the lord of the fortress was already dead. The crofters had holed up there for more protection. They stood no chance against Niall's men. The ones who did survive the initial battle, if you can even call it that, were given the choice to renounce their Balian beliefs or die."

"And did they renounce?" She feared the answer even as she asked the question.

"No. They were slaughtered. Every last man, woman, and child."

Aine pressed her hands to her mouth and wrestled down her emotions. She could not afford to think of those individuals as people—as fathers, sons, mothers, daughters. Could not think of what kind of evil could justify killing innocent children. This was war, and the event had significance beyond the human cost. "Do we know his objective? Is this a strategic holding?"

"We don't know," Riordan said. "The location is puzzling, near the coast without any nearby cities, towns, or targets. It's an old stronghold from Daimhin's time that has been seized and abandoned numerous times over the centuries as newer and more comfortable structures were built along trade routes. It makes no sense that he would have targeted such an unstrategic location."

"Trying a new weapon, perhaps?" The idea that the druid might have other unknown resources chilled her.

"We don't think so," Eoghan said. "Used a simple battering ram to take down the doors."

"Then why am I here? I have no particular strategic insight."

"I beg to differ," Eoghan said quietly. "You asked the exact same questions as Riordan and I did. But we called you here for another reason. Since word has circulated that the fortress fell and Niall killed the villagers, Ard Dhaimhin has seen an influx of refugees. Some of them came from Bánduran itself."

"And you need me to heal them?"

Riordan shook his head. "By all means, heal those who cannot be healed by mere medicine, but that's not why we called you. We need you to read them. We need to know exactly what was said, what the druid might have revealed of his plans."

"You want me to mine their memories." What they were asking was far more difficult than merely picking thoughts from someone's mind. It required her to dig around, search for trauma they might have already purposely buried to protect themselves. She'd never used her gift in such a deliberate way before. She wasn't even sure it was possible. She did know from experience that it would take far more focus than she typically had available in the midst of the crowd.

Eoghan reached out and took her hand, looking into her eyes, before he realized what he was doing. He released her as if he had been scalded. "My lady, I know this will be both taxing and unpleasant. But if we are to be able to do anything about it, we need to know as much of what they observed as we can. We need to see through their eyes. And you are the only one who has that ability."

Will you do anything? she wanted to ask, but she kept the challenge to herself. The teacup in her hand was a useful diversion while she considered her answer, even if she didn't notice the hot liquid scalding her lips and tongue until it was too late. "Very well. I'll do it. But not in the village, and not more than one or two a day. If you find the most reliable witnesses and bring them to Carraigmór, I'll see what I can do."

"Thank you, Aine," Eoghan murmured. "We know what we ask of you."

"I don't think you do." She set her cup firmly on the table and left the study without further comment. Once she reached the corridor, however, she paused on the steps and let silent tears slide down her cheeks. Maybe it was just the new life growing inside her that made her so much more sensitive to the slaughter of innocents. Maybe it was just how out of control her emotions were, between the child's effect on her body and the fact that her husband was away on a dangerous mission.

Or maybe you just feel Comdiu's pain at seeing His people persecuted and killed for their beliefs.

She pressed a hand against her abdomen and tried to get control of her shaky breathing. She would do what they asked. But she knew one thing: once she saw what the refugees had endured and what awaited the rest of her land, she would not be able to stay silent and do nothing.

✦ ✦ ✦

"I'm concerned," Riordan said when they were once again alone.

Eoghan poured his own cup of tea and drank half of it in one gulp. It seared his tongue and most of his throat on the way down. "About Aine? She's the only chance we have to discover the druid's plan early enough to do something about it."

"I'm not talking about Aine. I'm talking about you."

Eoghan jerked his gaze to the older man's face. "What do you mean?"

"Don't lie to me, Eoghan. I know you have feelings for her. It's written all over your face anytime you're within five steps of her. You're in love with her."

"Doesn't matter if I am or not. She's another man's wife."

"It matters because you're the king and you have the potential to hurt many people with your decisions."

"You think I would do something immoral? That I would pressure her?" He'd known Riordan his whole life, and the man dared to question his integrity?

Riordan cut him off with a laugh. "Son, you know very little about women if you think you can make them do anything they don't want to do, especially where matters of the heart are concerned. Aine loves Conor. But your feelings toward her, and your guilt over it, will lead you to make bad decisions. Have you even stopped to think about what it will be like for her to bear the memories of those refugees, many times over? Do you have any idea how hard she has to work to control her gift in a city of four thousand people?"

Guilt washed over him immediately, but he steeled himself against it. "What other choice do we have? No, I do not want to cause her any pain. But if I'm to be the leader this city—this country—deserves, shouldn't I be able to put aside my own feelings? Shouldn't I be able to weigh what's best for Seare against what's best for one person?"

"I don't know the full answer to that, Eoghan. But I do know that you have to weigh the cost of using your resources for small things when you might need them for larger acts later."

"You're saying I shouldn't push Aine now because she will be needed later."

Riordan rose, but his expression didn't waver. "I'm saying that if you ask her to do this for us, you'd better be ready to make hard choices."

Eoghan nodded, but inside he felt sick. He understood the subtext of what Riordan was saying, no matter how much he cringed at the idea of calling Aine an asset. If he were going to put her through enough trauma that it put her sanity and health at risk, he needed to be ready to act on that information.

He needed to be ready to take Ard Dhaimhin to war.

✦ ✦ ✦

The first refugee was brought up from the village the following day and situated in the hall with a pot of tea and oatcakes, a luxury considering their dwindling resources. But Aine's initial surprise at the spread was quickly replaced by shock when she saw the witness they had brought her.

"He's little more than a child!" she whispered to Eoghan near the edge of the hall. "This was your most reliable witness?"

Eoghan merely shook his head. "Listen to his story and then make your decision."

Aine circled the room and approached the young man slowly, aware that she was treating him much like a skittish foal—which, she supposed, was an apt comparison. He had the gangly look of a boy who had just started growing upward but had not yet filled out, perhaps a dozen years old. She instantly recognized that beneath his look of defiance lay fear.

"May I join you?" Aine asked.

He dragged his eyes away from the untouched plate of oat-cakes and then shrugged. Aine pulled up the chair next to him. "My name is Aine. What is yours?"

For a second, she thought he wouldn't answer. Then he said sullenly, "Roark."

Unexpected tears blinded her, but she managed to keep her voice calm. "I like that name. Someone very special to me had a similar name."

"What happened to him?" the boy asked. "Did he die?"

Aine swallowed. "Aye. Only a few months ago, killed by Lord Keondric. I'm not sure I've spoken his name aloud since."

"I was named after my grandfather," Roark said. "He was killed by Lord Keondric too."

Aine breathed a prayer heavenward for guidance. It wasn't hard to read the layers of grief and shock beneath his words, the conflicting desire to keep the pain close and to share it with her. She might know his thoughts, but she also knew she had to tread carefully lest he withdraw back behind his sullen shell. "I'm sorry, Roark. I've lost too much of my family so far in this war. I'd like to see it end as quickly as possible."

"They said you wanted to ask me questions. I guess you can ask."

She wasn't going to waste Roark's approval, but she didn't rush him. Instead she poured a cup of tea and pushed the plate of oatcakes toward him. "Eat first. Questions will wait, but that growling in your stomach will not. I could scarce hear your answers over that noise anyhow."

He flashed her a surprised smile that made him look at once younger and more vulnerable. The expression tugged at her heart. She could already read from his unguarded thoughts that he had lost not only his grandfather but also both his parents and his younger siblings. He had escaped with an uncle only by the slightest thread of fortune, the breath of Comdiu's providence. Aine poured herself a cup of tea and waited while the boy wolfed down the plateful of oatcakes with scarcely a breath in between each bite.

In the meantime, she gathered the loose threads of thoughts, the scattered images that flitted through his mind: having to share a single slice of bread with his brothers and sisters because food had become so scarce; cold nights huddled together when the firewood ran out; hushed, worried voices in the hall, the words indistinguishable but the meaning understood all the same. This was no great fortress that had fallen to the druid; this was a village full of poor crofters with no food, no weapons, little defense against the might of Niall's army. There was no reason for him to have attacked if the location held no strategic purpose. So why had he?

Finally, Roark drained his cup and turned a much friendlier face in Aine's direction. "What do you wish to know, my lady?"

"What happened when Lord Keondric laid siege to the fortress?"

"It was no siege, my lady. No terms for surrender sent in. They just came to the gates and battered them down with a ram. He gathered all the people together in the courtyard and said who he was. Said he was there to take our fortress, and if we wished to live, we would denounce our Balian ways. Everyone refused." Roark swallowed hard, his chin quivering, but he continued bravely. "I don't know if they didn't think he would really do it or if they were truly that devoted. But when they refused, he killed them all in a rush of blue fire. One moment they were standing there, and the next, they were a pile of ash on the stones."

Aine nodded calmly, though inwardly she was sickened by the description. Niall had used sorcery to kill them, rather than using some horrifying, bloody display to force their conversion. That meant the people were irrelevant to his plan. He wanted the fortress—or something inside the fortress.

"And how did you escape?"

"My uncle and I had been spreading rushes in the hall. We climbed into the cart and pulled them over top of us. I thought for sure they knew we were there, but they walked right by us."

"This is very important, Roark. Did N—Lord Keondric say

anything when he entered? Did he give any clue as to why he was there?"

Roark shook his head. "I was too scared. I couldn't make much out. I would swear he said something about standing on stone. Only the hall of Bánduran is stone. The upstairs corridors are all wood."

Aine reached out and squeezed the boy's shoulder. "You did well, Roark. Thank you. I'll have one of the brothers take you back to your uncle."

"Did that help?"

"Very much so."

"I'm glad. Are there any more oatcakes?"

Aine chuckled. Even tragedy didn't take a growing boy's focus off food, especially after the scarcity he had experienced. What she told him was only partially true. He had helped, but she was still no closer to understanding what Niall was doing at Bánduran. When she related her findings to Eoghan and Riordan, they looked as perplexed as she felt.

"So they didn't even try to conscript them?" Eoghan asked. "Simply killed them? I'm surprised."

"Clearly he didn't want anyone knowing what he was doing there. He eliminated the witnesses. Perhaps the conversion would have given him a foothold to be able to spell them into compliance."

"Perhaps," Eoghan said, but he sounded unconvinced.

That night, she contacted Conor at the designated hour and related the day's events to him. He sounded as puzzled as she felt.

He killed everyone and took a fortress with no apparent strategic advantage? That's unlike Niall. He has no conscience, but he doesn't seem to kill for fun, either.

I'm going to interview the uncle tomorrow. Perhaps he can shed more light on what actually happened.

But the next morning, Aine waited at the table in the hall as the minutes slipped by. Finally, Riordan entered the room, his expression hinting at the bad news that was coming.

"He refused, didn't he." She'd feared as much. If the boy had gone back and told his uncle her line of questioning, the man might have decided it was something better left unspoken. Adults had the tendency to push painful memories down and try to move on as if they hadn't happened.

"Worse, I'm afraid. They're gone."

"Gone? Gone where?"

"No one knows. They must have left in the night, because the other men in the barracks don't recall having seen them today at all. Their few belongings are gone."

Aine just sat, stunned, trying to think through the implications. Had they gone because they were afraid of what she would find out? Or afraid they knew something that put them in danger?

No. I'm not going to let them go without a fight. She had connected with the boy's mind. They couldn't be far away. If she could find him, maybe they could learn why they had fled in the first place.

But when she cast her awareness through Ard Dhaimhin and beyond its borders, she could find nothing. Roark was gone as thoroughly as if he had never existed.

CHAPTER
THIRTEEN

Conor sensed the exact moment he stepped across the borders of Ard Dhaimhin's wards. He had spent so much time in that protective enclosure of magic that its absence momentarily felt as though the air had been sucked out of a room. Was it because it was somehow tied to him, because it had come from the music of his harp? Or had he just become so attuned to the feeling of the runic magic that it had become a part of him?

"Remember what I said," he reminded the men, and they nodded soberly. They were not to discuss the arrangements outside of the protective magical enclosure; they couldn't take the chance that the sidhe would use that knowledge to their advantage. Still, he felt they were plunging blindly into the unknown, relying on the most rudimentary of protections against the greatest of threats.

They had barely begun their second day into the pass when the first fight broke out. It started as an argument between two men at the rear of the group, following the pack ponies. Blair and Larkin didn't particularly like one another, but they'd never shown an inclination to drop discipline to explore that dislike.

When shouts went up, Conor pushed back through the

column to find the two men wrestling on the rocky ground. Blood already seeped from one's nose, and the other had a cut over his eyebrow. Thankfully, they'd relied on their fists and not their weapons. Two other men were already intervening, Ferus hauling the aggressor off while Tomey lifted the supine brother to his feet.

"What's this about?" Conor asked. The two men just glared at each other. He sighed and looked to the witnesses. "What started it?"

"I have no idea," Ferus said. "They weren't even speaking to each other when Larkin just attacked Blair. No warning, no argument."

Conor furrowed his brow while he considered the two men, then rubbed his arms against a sudden chill. It was autumn in the mountains, but this felt more like winter on the highest peaks. There could be no doubt that this was the doing of the sidhe. He couldn't even exact discipline for this breach, because he knew well that it was out of their control.

"Larkin, up front with me. Blair, remain at the back with Ferus. Men, now would be a good time for a recitation."

Uncertainty rippled through the group, though they were no strangers to liturgy, given the way the brotherhood structured their worship. Even Conor felt a little odd doing it while trudging through a pass to a fortress they planned to infiltrate, but once he began, the other men slowly joined with him.

Slowly, the pressure of the sidhe's presence eased and the unnatural chill faded. The Holy Canon stated that Comdiu was present when they prayed and that no evil could stand before His presence. This seemed to bear out the truth of that statement. Just because they'd been prepared for this eventuality didn't make it any less disturbing, though. It had scarcely taken a day for them to be targeted and, Conor assumed, to be marked as a threat.

Even more disturbing was if the spirits had identified them, did that mean the druid knew they were coming?

They continued their slow progress through the pass, Conor mentally marking off the map's landmarks as they crept by. The terrain here was similar to that surrounding Ard Dhaimhin: craggy mountains covered in a combination of evergreens and deciduous trees interspersed with outcroppings of granite so rugged that only the tenacious scrub clung to their sides. In some places, the trail ran through the mountains so deep that the sun never touched them. At other times, they found themselves at the highest point for miles. The sidhe didn't try to attack again, but Conor had no doubt they were merely biding their time.

That night, the Fíréin camped beneath an outcropping of rock tucked back from the main pass, a small fire crackling beneath the overhang. The men had been even more restrained since their short encounter with the sidhe, so very little conversation circulated while they ate provisions from their packs. Once more, Conor was grateful for the Fíréin's unrelenting training. Knowing that their will could be compromised by the dark spirits would send less-disciplined men running for home. Instead, the experience stoked their determination to reach their destination quickly.

An autumn breeze rustled the trees outside and sent the turning leaves skittering across the hills. Chills rose on Conor's skin, for which he quickly chided himself. The temperature drop simply indicated the changing season, nothing unnerving or otherworldly. Still, when the horses shuffled uneasily outside, he found himself on his feet, his sword drawn.

"Sir—uh, Conor?" Larkin asked quietly, crouching by the fire, his hand on his own weapon.

"With me," he murmured and then nodded toward the opening of the indentation.

With Larkin at his back, Conor crept into the pass. The waxing moon shed a little light from behind the thin layers of clouds overhead, but it only served to cast ordinary objects—trees, rocks, their horses—in hair-raising shadows. Still, his instincts told him there was something out there waiting, watching.

From the corner of his eye, he sensed movement. Every nerve ending sprang to alertness, but he worked to keep his stance easy and unconcerned. "Nothing out here," he said, turning back as if to return to the fire. Instead, as soon as he reached another pool of darkness, he faded into the background. Larkin quickly discerned his intentions and did the same.

Slowly, the shadows around them morphed from pools of darkness into the figures of men. Conor clenched his jaw and held down his apprehension. For all their mysterious appearance, the glint of moon and firelight on weapons told them they were dealing with men, not spirits. He replaced his Gwynn sword in its sheath, grateful for the sheepskin lining that dampened the sound of the blade, and eased his dagger out instead. Soundlessly, he crept up behind the nearest man.

The man sensed Conor's presence and spun, his sword at the ready, but not fast enough. Conor swept his legs out from beneath him and twisted the man's sword arm back until the weapon clattered to the ground. He then pressed his knife to the artery in his opponent's neck. Instantly, the scene erupted into activity as the Fírein realized the threat and jumped to meet it, swords ready.

"Tell them to stand down or you die," Conor said in a low voice.

His prisoner stared up at him, unafraid. "Why should I? We have you outnumbered."

"That's what you think." Conor took in the men facing off against his warriors: tattered clothing draped in furs, long hair and beards. Clanless, the very group they were attempting to impersonate. Now that he saw them up close, Conor realized that their own disguise would never stand up to close scrutiny. These men looked far more like Sofarende than Seareanns, with their furs and beads and numerous baubles. Plus, every one of the men was simultaneously brawny and covered with a prodigious layer of fat, about as opposite from the whip-lean Fíréin as one could get.

"What do you want from us?" Conor demanded.

"I would ask you the same question. You pass through our lands, armed and pretending to be one of us." The more he talked, the more clearly Conor picked up a peculiar cadence and pronunciation that didn't quite fit into any of the Seareann accents to which he had become accustomed.

"You're Clanless. By definition, that means you have no land."

"And you're Fíréin. By definition, that means you should not be here at all."

Conor couldn't catch the surprised laugh that burst out of him. "Perhaps we're both right, then. Will you agree to a truce until we sort this matter out?"

"Aye, you have it. Men, stand down."

Conor signaled his men, and they lowered weapons. He rocked back on his heels and withdrew the blade, though he didn't sheath it. He offered his other hand to the Clanless warrior and hauled him to his feet.

"You're the leader," the man said, looking Conor over curiously. "You're young. Was the battle so fierce that it took all your experienced men from you?"

"Not so fierce. Are all Clanless so fat? Looking at you now, I think perhaps the stories of scarcity in the mountain have just been tales."

The man let out a booming laugh and clapped his hands to the paunch of his belly. "No, the tales are true. We simply eat what we kill, and there's no better hunter than Old Oenghus."

"Then come. I can't offer you much food, but there is still tea."

"Ah. That we have not had in some time. I'd thank you for it."

They ordered themselves around the fire, Oenghus taking a seat beside Conor, two of their men joining them. The rest of the warriors stood uneasily around them, hands on weapons, ready for any sign of aggression. Conor poured tea into a tin cup and handed it to his guest. Oenghus said nothing, just sat and sipped the hot liquid.

Finally, when he had drained the cup, he turned to Conor and asked, "Why did you leave Ard Dhaimhin? And what do you want in Sliebhan?"

Conor refilled Oenghus's cup, suddenly wishing that Aine had come with them. It would be helpful to know what Oenghus was thinking and how far they could trust him before he answered that question. "I suppose my answer depends on why you want to know."

"We're not spies for Keondric or any of his ilk, if that's what you're asking. We're simply attempting to decide if you're any threat to us and if we will let you live."

"I respect that. Unfortunately, regardless of the answer, I'm afraid we won't let you kill us today."

"That confident in your skills, are you? Want to put the Fíréin's reputation to the test?"

"Not particularly. I'd rather be on our way as quickly as possible, and bodies left behind raise questions."

Oenghus stared at him from beneath bushy eyebrows for a long moment. Conor held his gaze, unmoving. Then the big man started to laugh again. "I believe you. The fact is, there's only one reason you'd be coming through *this* pass, and that's because of the fortress at the end of it."

"That's a pretty big assumption."

"Not when I consider the young woman who passed this way

not two months ago, headed *from* the fortress to Ard Dhaimhin. Seemed to be in a right hurry, too. Makes one think she might have had information of importance to pass along."

Morrigan had come into contact with these men? Why hadn't she said anything? "If it's the same woman, that was my sister."

"Sister, eh? You look nothing alike."

"We don't share blood, if that's what you are asking."

"I'm not asking anything, merely observing." Oenghus stroked his beard for a moment. "Looked pretty beat-up, she did. I've seen enough of the men at Ard Bealach to know that they're cowardly enough to abuse women and steal food from the mouths of babes. A fair number of new arrivals we've had since they took command there."

"You mean there are more of you?" Conor rethought the question the moment it left his mouth. Of course there were more of them. It was preposterous to think otherwise. "I mean, you have some sort of organization?"

Oenghus said nothing for another long stretch, savoring his tea this time. "I imagine if you were headed to the fortress—not that you are, mind—you would probably already know that the gates are unbreachable."

"Aye, I imagine I would know that."

"So I would assume that you have another way in."

"Aye, that would be reasonable."

"Then I imagine you would want to know that there are sentries posted in the mountains above and around for miles. A rather impressive perimeter, as a matter of fact."

Conor felt a slight smile start to form. "For someone who planned on heading to Ard Bealach, aye, that would be helpful information. As would current counts of the men inside. If one was to be heading that way, that is."

"Hmmm." Oenghus stroked his beard again. "That would

require the help of other parties who would be keeping an eye on such things."

Now they got to the heart of the matter. "How would an interested party acquire the help of such individuals?"

"Such individuals are fond of hard-to-come-by items like tea." Oenghus's eyes glittered avariciously. "And gold."

"Tea is easy. Gold is more difficult."

"I don't believe that."

"Let's speak plainly, then. Aye, I have some gold. I have more tea. Both can be yours. But you will guide us through the passes. You will send men back to our other party to help them as well. And you will find out the numbers of men in the fortress and the positions of the sentries."

Oenghus took so long to consider the proposal that Conor began to fear the answer. "Aye," he said finally. "We have an agreement. On one condition: when you have taken the region, you will find a permanent place for us. Ours by right, without claim by any clan."

Conor certainly couldn't blame the man for seizing every advantage he could. He would do the same. "I'm afraid I can't do that. I do not take the fortress under my name or under my own authority."

"Then in whose name do you take it? We will petition him directly."

"In the name of the rightful High King of Seare."

Oenghus's eyes widened, and his voice lowered to a whisper. "He has returned? Truly?"

Conor nodded.

The man seemed to straighten then. "As a representative of the High King, you will have our help. And we will trust that you will remember your friends when the time comes."

CHAPTER
FOURTEEN

"I need something to do."

At the first strains of a feminine voice, Eoghan looked up from the tallies he was reviewing. Morrigan stood in the doorway in her borrowed gown, her demure posture at odds with the irritation in her voice. He nodded to the two guards behind her, who promptly stepped outside and closed the door.

"I'm sorry that you're finding our hospitality lacking," Eoghan said, careful to keep any hint of sarcasm from his tone. "I'm afraid we don't have many things of interest to the feminine mind. Perhaps one of the launderers would send up their mending."

"You know very well that's not what I mean." Morrigan circled the chair opposite him and plopped herself down without waiting for an invitation. "And feminine pursuits were hardly what I had in mind."

"You must forgive my confusion. After all, you seem determined to convince us that you are a lady and no threat. And don't ladies like such things as embroidery and music?"

He waited for a caustic comeback, knowing that he was

intentionally baiting her, but she just stared at him unblinkingly. Then her manner changed. "Very well. What do you want from me?"

"The truth."

"I've already given you the truth."

"Only bits of it, and only the parts you want us to know. Which I'm afraid still leaves your intentions suspect."

"If Conor were here—"

"Who do you think ordered you kept in your chambers having minimal contact with others? If Conor, who you seem to think knows you so well, thinks you're a threat, then so do I."

"What do you need from me to convince you that I'm telling the truth?"

"Let Aine read you."

"Are we past pretending she's merely the wife of my foster brother, then?"

Eoghan simply stared at her.

Morrigan shrugged. "She's already tried. Unsuccessfully it seems, given your dismay over my supposedly nefarious intentions. What makes you think that she'd have any better luck this time around?"

"I think you know exactly why she can't read you, and I think you can let her around whatever that protection is."

"I would if I could," Morrigan said. "But I'm afraid I'm not conscious of doing anything."

Even urging himself caution, Eoghan found himself stretching to believe her. She was an appallingly good liar. Every single thing she said so far had been true. Aine had tried reading her, unsuccessfully. And everything in him believed her when she said she was not consciously doing anything to block Aine's ability.

Which meant that she was using some sort of object, spell, or passive trick to prevent them from gaining access to the truth.

"I'm sorry to hear that," he said finally. "I'll have a book of devotional readings sent to your room for entertainment. Brothers?"

"Wait." Morrigan thrust her hand out to stop him just as the door opened. Eoghan gave a slight shake of the head and they retreated again. "If I tell you the truth about why she can't read my thoughts, you must promise me that you won't try to strip me of it."

"Why would I promise that?"

She chewed her bottom lip, a gesture he was sure she used to convey vulnerability even when she felt quite the opposite. "Because the thing that prevents Aine from reading me also prevents Keondric from locating me."

The air in Eoghan's lungs momentarily turned to mortar; he couldn't relax his muscles enough to draw a breath. When he finally did regain full function, he couldn't figure out which question to ask first. Inquire what could block Keondric's notice of her, or ask why the druid would be looking for her in the first place? He finally settled for an order. "Tell me."

"I am not spying for him. I told you the truth about that. But I know enough about his movements, his interest in Ard Bealach, for him to take an interest in my whereabouts once it's reported that I'm missing. Do you think that even behind Ard Dhaimhin's wards he couldn't locate me?"

"What is this thing of which you speak? An object? An amulet?" She met his eyes. "A rune."

"A rune," he repeated faintly. "Where? How? Show me."

"Are you sure? It requires a more intimate view than I would normally offer." At his confused look, she explained, "It was placed over my heart."

"Oh? Oh." He called for the guards again. "Bring Lady Aine, please. She's needed immediately."

Morrigan looked amused by his cautiousness, so he swiftly changed the subject. "Where did you learn about this rune? Meallachán?"

"I cannot say. I made a vow to keep that a secret, and it must remain so. But if this is the price of trust, then I will show you— or Aine—and you can do with the knowledge as you will."

She threw the offer out so casually, much as she had with Meallachán's whereabouts, that he was tempted to believe her. But he also knew this was probably just a strategy. Give them the information that seemed most important but was easiest for them to learn on their own. Hold back the details for her own purposes, all the while seeming as if she were cooperating. Maybe he was giving her too much credit, but he didn't think so. Every instinct told him not to underestimate her.

Just when the silence began to stretch to awkwardness, the door opened again and Aine walked into the room. She stopped short when she saw Morrigan. "You called for me?"

"Morrigan has shared a very important piece of information with me. She's in possession of something that might be of particular interest to you."

"My lord?"

"A rune."

Aine's eyebrows flew up. "Really? In what form?"

"That's what I've called you here to determine. Since it is positioned in a rather delicate location . . ." He crossed his arms and deliberately turned his back.

From the rustle of fabric, he assumed Aine was helping her unlace her dress, a bit of knowledge he would rather not have at the moment. Maybe he should have stepped out of the room. Then Aine stifled a cry, and he spun automatically, his hand on his dagger.

Morrigan clutched her bodice, but not before he caught sight of the angry red marks emblazoned at the top of her breast. "You were branded?" The words spilled out before he realized he was still staring. Blood rushed to his face in a humiliated flush, and he turned his back to her once more. "You said we had to promise not to take it from you? If it's burned into your skin, how do you think we'd manage that?"

"The usual way, my lord. Knives and fire." Morrigan kept her tone wry, but he sensed the tremor beneath it. Did she actually believe they would torture her for the sake of the information she might carry?

Aye, he decided, especially considering she'd spent years among men who wouldn't hesitate to do that very thing.

"You should let me find you some salve for that," Aine murmured. He sensed movement, assumed she was helping Morrigan back into the dress. "It's healing, but it could still become infected. This was done very recently."

"Aye, it was."

"There are easier ways to do such a thing with ink."

"Runes are very particular. They must be done quickly and accurately. Drawing it on makes it potentially ineffective, and tattooing takes too long."

"So instead you mutilated yourself," Eoghan said.

"I'm so sorry, *my lord*, that you don't approve of my choices. Once you've experienced life outside of your precious High City, perhaps then you'll have earned the right to comment on what I have found it necessary to do."

Eoghan spun to face Morrigan, who looked angry enough to spit fire, but he couldn't voice his irritated reply. He deflated. "You're right. I'm sorry. It was a difficult choice, I'm sure."

"Why, my lord? Because I'll never find a husband now that I'm branded like a common whore?"

"No," he said quietly. "Because you will bear it for the rest of your life, whether you want it or not. You may find it needful to be without it someday, and that can't happen. Now, tell us what it means."

"I don't know, exactly. It was given to me to make me invisible to magic. That's how it was explained."

"Any magic?"

"If Aine can't read me and she possesses what I assume is a gift of Balus and the sorcerer can't use his ability on me, then aye, I would assume any magic."

Eoghan's mind reeled with the possibilities. This might be exactly what they were looking for. "Aine, can you reproduce it so I can see it?"

"Aye." She moved to his table and found a blank wax tablet and stylus, then carefully sketched the mark: a circle with several intersecting and oblique lines. Instantly, a word came to mind.

"Shield."

"What?" Aine and Morrigan asked simultaneously.

"The rune means 'shield.' That's why it blocks magic. You've essentially made yourself immune to magic." He shook his head while he tried to work through the implications. "That's incredible. Do you have any gifts yourself? I wonder if it would block *you* using magic as well."

"I don't think so. None of my blood has ever shown any inclination toward Balus's gifts."

"Why didn't you tell us this sooner, Morrigan?" Aine asked.

"I find it's better to give out one's information sparingly," Morrigan replied. "Especially not knowing what you suspected about runic magic."

"I must understand where you learned this," Eoghan said. "The questions that could be answered . . ."

"No. I promised I would not tell anyone, and I keep my promises." She focused a hard look on Eoghan. "Do you?"

It was a clear challenge, a test. Did he want information on the runes enough to break his word? Somehow he felt there was no good answer: be thought untrustworthy or weak; break her confidence or reveal his vulnerabilities.

"Aye. I keep my promises. All of them." He seated himself behind the desk again. "That's also why I'm not going to promise you can leave your chamber. I told you I expected the complete truth from you, and what you've told us is only what you have seen fit to share. But I'm true to my word. We won't force you."

Despite the fact she had to be angry with his decision, she bowed her head graciously. "I appreciate knowing that you are a man of your word at least."

Eoghan gave her a crisp nod. "You may leave. Your guards will take you back. Lady Aine, a word?" He waited until Morrigan left the room and counted to ten to make sure they could not be overheard. "Your impressions."

"Not very helpful, I'm afraid. She's either skilled at lying or skilled at telling her way around the truth so she doesn't look as though she's lying. And this rune . . . With some study, this could prove to be very useful indeed. I don't understand why she would have given up something this important without earning anything in return."

"I agree." Eoghan tented his fingers against his lips. "Something tells me she's playing a long game, and this was a sacrifice she had planned all along."

"Every piece down to her last one," Aine murmured. "Conor warned me she was strategic."

"What else did he warn you about?"

"That she was arrogant enough to believe she could always win."

Eoghan stared at the door Morrigan had just walked through. Considering how well she had been playing them all this time, Conor just might be right.

CHAPTER
FIFTEEN

Oenghus and the men stayed the night in their camp, and after everyone was adequately assured the Clanless wouldn't slaughter them in their sleep, they were glad for the extra numbers.

The next morning, however, Oenghus issued several quiet orders, and half the party disappeared back into the canyon. "Spreading the word," he said. Conor could only hope the message was to stand down attacks on his and Daigh's parties.

But Oenghus seemed to be sincere in his promise to help. "You don't look like our people, and no one will be fooled by those disguises. Here." He pulled the fur mantle from his shoulders and swapped it for Conor's cloak, taking the fine piece of wool for himself.

"Are you sure you don't just want my cloak?" Conor asked with an arched eyebrow.

"Oh, aye, I want your cloak. But that doesn't negate the fact that it shows you as Fíréin as surely as your weaponry does."

"You're not going to try to take those, I'd assume."

"No, your weapons you keep. We're generous in that way."

"So very generous," Conor replied with a snort. "You also aren't confident you could actually accomplish it."

"That as well."

The sparkle in Oenghus's eyes made Conor think he simply enjoyed his bluster. Despite his doubts, he found himself liking the man. When they started back down the canyon, he waited for the Clanless party's leader to fall in beside him.

"Most people think the Clanless are merely bedtime stories to scare children into obeying. 'If you don't behave, you'll be thrown out of the keep, and you'll have to go live with the Clanless.'"

"Aye, and they say we eat children with our pointed monster's teeth as well." Oenghus grinned. "Either way, the rumors are good for us. Those who believe are too frightened to come look for us, and the rest don't bother us."

"Like the Fíréin."

"Like the Fíréin." He looked Conor over appraisingly. "But those rumors are mostly true, now, aren't they?"

"Mostly. But you, Oenghus, you can't tell me you are not an educated man. So how did you come to be Clanless in the first place?"

"Like most of us do, I suppose. Anyone who challenges his clan, particularly in Sliebhan, finds himself cast off. For me, I wouldn't bow to the old gods. Our mam raised us to believe in Balus and the One True God Comdiu, but our da was loyal to the warrior gods until the day he died. He made it so I couldn't inherit his title, couldn't marry, couldn't find a profession. So I left. Wandered a bit. Fell in with the Clanless here in the mountains."

"How many of you are there?"

Oenghus cast another appraising look at Conor. "More than you probably think."

Fair enough. The man didn't want to reveal too much, and Conor couldn't blame him. He probably believed that the Fíréin would think of them as threats, even though Conor was really feeling out whether or not they could be potential allies.

"What about the sidhe?" Conor asked finally. "If you dwell in these passes, surely they are attracted to your presence. Don't you have problems with them causing disturbances among your people?"

"The Fíréin know of the sidhe?"

"Firsthand."

"Then you know there are ways to block their influence."

Conor thought of the charm beneath his tunic. "Aye, I do."

"So do we."

So the sharing would go only so far. That, too, he could understand. But Conor didn't see any evidence that the Clanless warriors were wearing amulets of any sort. Were there other ways to defend against the spirits?

Conor thought they had seen the last of the party that had split off that morning, but when they made camp around a small fire again after nightfall, one of the men—Oscar, Conor thought—reappeared with a brace of rabbits over his shoulder. He tossed them to Conor, who passed them off to Larkin and Ferus to skin.

"You're our guests," Oenghus explained. "We show hospitality to our guests."

"And if we attempted to hunt in *your* territory?"

Oenghus just shrugged, but Conor had the feeling these Clanless men were every bit as territorial as the Fíréin when it came to their livelihood.

They were just finishing the last greasy pieces of rabbit meat cooked over a spit and sharing around the last bit of tea when a familiar voice broke into Conor's consciousness. He excused himself and stepped into the shadows.

Aine? I'm here.

Thank Comdiu.

Why, is something wrong?

Her long pause made his heart stutter. *No, not wrong,* she said at last. *Just puzzling. Morrigan is branded. With a rune.*

Conor frowned into the darkness. If anyone were watching him, they'd likely think him insane. *I don't understand. What kind of rune?*

One that means "shield." Once she showed it to us, Eoghan identified it. This is why I haven't been able to read her. This rune blocks magic completely.

Where did she get it?

She wouldn't tell us. Said she had made a solemn vow not to reveal its source.

Aine, how recent is the brand?

Weeks, perhaps. It's still not healed. Why?

What he was thinking was completely impossible and yet the only logical explanation. He looked back at Oenghus and his four men. Could they have been the ones who gave her the rune? And how would they have come across such a thing?

We've made contact with the Clanless, Conor said. *They seem to have some way to keep the sidhe from affecting them. Perhaps they branded her.*

The Clanless? How is that possible?

I don't know, but I'm going to find out. Tomorrow night I'll tell you what I've learned. And, Aine?

Aye?

Be careful. Just because she shared that fact with you doesn't make her less dangerous.

Aye, I know. I love you, Conor.

And I love you. He felt it the moment she disconnected from his mind, registered the loss. It wasn't like being physically present with her, but after so many separations, the fact they could speak in their minds was a comfort. It was also a concern. He could feel her worry and her wariness through her words, even if she didn't realize she was transmitting it. He returned to the fire and lowered himself to his spot atop his bedroll.

"Everything all right?" Larkin asked in a low voice.

"Aye, it's fine." He directed his attention to Oenghus, sitting across the fire. "Where is it?"

"Where is what?"

"The rune."

When Oenghus simply stared at him, Conor sighed. "The one you branded my sister with. The one you use to keep the sidhe from affecting your people."

For a moment, Conor thought he wouldn't answer. Then Oenghus smiled. "So you figured it out, did you? Took you long enough. Aye, I gave her the rune."

"Why?"

"Because she was afraid she would be tracked. And anyone coming from Ard Bealach would not want to be tracked."

"So you do know something about the fortress. Tell me."

"There have been whispers. People who have heard screaming. Rumors of experiments."

"What kind of experiments?"

"The kind that people think if they don't talk about never really happened."

Conor heaved a sigh. So things were as bad as they thought. "Tell me this, then. She was afraid she would be tracked. Does that mean that Lord Keondric has been here with the druid?"

Oenghus smiled. "Aye, both of them. And you know why."

So he knew that Keondric *was* the druid. How did someone supposedly out of touch with the matters of the kingdoms know so much? It sounded as though the Clanless kept a better eye on the situation than the Fíréin. "Show me this rune."

Oenghus nodded toward Oscar, who immediately unlaced his shirt and pulled down the neckline to show a pale white scar directly over his heart. Conor studied it for a moment. It was old and puckered, a sign that this was not a recent discovery.

"Where did you learn it?"

The Clanless men exchanged a glance and remained silent.

"This is a magic that no one has known for half a millennium, and you're wearing it casually on your body. I want to know where you learned it."

"The Fíréin do not have an exclusive right to magic," Oenghus said. "Nor do they have a right to make demands in my territory. We have answered your questions out of courtesy. Don't mistake our willingness for cowardice."

Conor bowed his head slightly and tempered his tone. "Forgive me. But you must understand, this is an old magic, one that we believe predates even Balus's gifts in Seare. It may be our best chance of stopping the druid and once more binding the sidhe. It's important that we learn all we can about it."

"That may be, but you will not learn it from us. You have your secrets; we have ours."

But they had shared this secret, and it was one they could use. He picked up a stick and sketched the rune in the dirt at his feet. "What effect does it have on a person? Does it work only if it's branded?"

Oenghus and the other Clanless stared at him openmouthed.

"What?" Conor asked.

"You can remember it."

"Of course I can remember it."

The other men exchanged a glance. So this rune was like the throne, not universally recognized for what it was. Perhaps to many people, it looked like a scar or a tribal marking. "What would happen if I drew it on?"

"The rune depends on its precision," Oenghus finally answered. "You could draw the marking, but if it became blurred, there is no telling what could happen. It could kill the wearer. It could simply stop working. We don't know enough about it to risk the impermanence."

"Hence the brand."

"Aye."

Conor stared silently into the fire as he considered. This could be a solution to the problem of the sidhe, but it was also risky. He couldn't ask his men to take the chance that a smudged marking would kill them, and he wasn't about to have them brand it permanently into their skin until he understood exactly how it worked.

Now their mission at Ard Bealach—to retrieve the bard Meallachán alive and whole—was more important than ever.

CHAPTER SIXTEEN

After Morrigan's revelation, Aine redoubled her efforts searching Queen Shanna's journals. There was no guarantee she would find what she was looking for there, yet something—whether it be intuition or Comdiu's leading—kept her reading until her vision blurred and her head ached.

Instead of passages about the runes, however, Aine stumbled across something unexpected. She shoved a piece of ribbon into the book and marched down to the Ceannaire's office, where Eoghan sat alone, bent over a similar-looking book.

"You have to read this." She shoved the volume under his nose and flipped it open to the marked page.

He frowned but he didn't argue. When he finished reading the passage indicated, he blinked. "I don't understand. That can't be right."

"What reason would she have to lie?" Aine turned the book around toward herself. "'The druid Struthair claims that the spirits can be bound so they cannot harm humans, but it requires a language that has long since been forbidden in the nemetons. Few are able to even read it. Fewer still know where to locate the keys so it can be deciphered.' They have to be talking about the runes, don't they?"

"I can't imagine what else. We already knew that the druids were the ones who bound the sidhe in the first place. But we'd assumed it happened prior to Daimhin's time, prior to the coming of the Way."

"This means that at one point, the druids weren't in opposition to the Balians."

"Or the sidhe were a big enough threat for them to put their differences aside," Eoghan said.

Aine circled around the table to where she could perch on the chair opposite him. "What do they mean by keys, as in the meanings for the runes? They knew they existed but they didn't have access to them?"

"I don't know. I've never heard anything of the sort. Either no one read this journal or no one thought this fact was significant. After all, the sidhe had been bound for some time, and despite the fact they were growing stronger, their influence was confined to places where faith was weak."

Aine remained silent, thinking. It all had to fit together somehow: the sidhe, the runes, the druids. But the answer remained just beyond her reach.

"I'll keep reading. If you come across anything—"

"I'll let you know. This is good work, Aine." He met her eyes fully for the first time in days and gave her a warm smile.

Her heart hiccupped at what she read there in that unguarded moment, clear indication that his feelings toward her really hadn't changed. She managed a nod and scooped up her book, then fled the study as quickly as possible. Either telling him about her gift hadn't broken its effect on him, or his feelings—like her husband's—had nothing to do with magic after all.

Either way, until Conor came back, she needed to stay as far from Eoghan as possible.

But the isolation in her chamber with the journal didn't last long. Refugees continued to stream in and stretch Ard Dhaimhin even further to its limits. As soon as word came of another siege on another small fortress and the resulting flood of escapees from the battle arrived, Murchadh called Aine back to the healers' cottages.

"There's not much I can do for malnutrition," Aine whispered to the healer when she saw the line of skeletal-looking people in front of the cottage.

"It's worse than that," Murchadh said. "They're fleeing an outbreak of disease because they had too many people crammed in behind the walls without proper sanitation, and they were kind enough to bring it with them."

So that was the real danger, and not just to the new arrivals' health but to Ard Dhaimhin itself. The city's excellent sanitation, skilled healers, and strict discipline kept any influx of disease from sweeping unchecked through the population, but that continued to work only if the newcomers were healthy.

Ard Dhaimhin had no space for quarantine, so she couldn't wait for the medicines to do their work. At the same time, she wasn't about to spread the word that she could heal by touch. Instead, she gave her patients a dose of foul-tasting herbs mixed with oil—most people believed that for medicine to be effective, it had to taste awful—and healed them while she was making a show of her examination. Most were too distracted by the terrible aftertaste to immediately notice that their symptoms had gone, and by the time they did, they just assumed Ard Dhaimhin had knowledge of exceptionally effective medications.

She'd never thought she would find herself lying to so many so frequently.

"Are you sure you can keep this up, my lady?" Murchadh whispered to her when they were halfway through the day's patients.

"I'm fine. A little tired and thirsty, but not nearly as exhausted as I'd expected to be."

Murchadh looked as if he didn't quite believe her, but he said nothing, just continued to dose the patients with the foul-tasting medicine before Aine set to her examinations.

She also took the opportunity to scan their thoughts for information of interest, but for the most part, she found nothing but mindless fear. They had been fleeing for their lives, often ahead of the actual siege. It seemed that word of the other attack—and the fate of the inhabitants—had now gone before the druid and his men, to the point that all the women and children were sent out before the fighting began. Aine had to give the villagers credit for their bravery. They were not professional warriors; they were merely farmers with mostly rudimentary implements, defending castles that were not their own simply because they felt they had to oppose the evil that Keondric represented.

"My lady," Murchadh said, "you should take a break. Why don't you get some fresh air while you check on the herbs? I think the burdock fruit in the hedgerow is overripe, but we might be able to salvage some of it."

The stern look on his face said he wasn't going to be dissuaded, so she removed her apron and slipped out the door. She kept her head down as she trudged the well-worn path through the cottages to the walled garden, hoping the city's inhabitants would take a clue from her posture and keep their distance.

She let herself into the small garden and raised her face to the thin rays of sunlight filtering down from the overcast sky. She had once spent hours in the garden, digging in the earth, drawing strength and peace from the landscape, cataloguing each healing herb, pulling the weeds that threatened to choke out the useful plants in her garden. Mistress Bearrach's garden at Lisdara felt far away now. Who tended it now? Had it been razed by Keondric's men? Did anyone see the value of her hard work in the midst of war?

She sank down on the wall, once more feeling the weight of what they faced. *Can we even win this fight, Comdiu? It feels as though every time we make progress, the next wave is worse and harder to endure. What is Niall doing? How can we stop him?*

Aine sighed, tracing an aimless pattern in the dirt with her toe. She resisted the urge to call out to Conor. They'd agreed on nighttime communications so she wouldn't risk distracting him in a moment of attack, when his attention needed to be on his opponent.

"What is that?"

Murchadh's trembling voice interrupted her thoughts. She straightened at the note of alarm. "What is what?"

"That." He pointed at the design at her feet, and with a shock, she realized she had been tracing the shield rune over and over with her foot. How had she managed to do that without noticing? She'd been praying for wisdom and direction—was this her answer?

Murchadh's leather-shod foot shot out and smeared the rune into oblivion. "You mustn't, my lady. I don't know where you learned that, but it is not for you to know."

"I don't understand. The runes are part of the foundation for Ard Dhaimhin. They exist on the objects of power we still possess, not to mention the Rune Throne itself. There isn't anything evil about them."

"No, my lady, not evil. But powerful beyond measure. There

is so little we know about their origins that those who use them without understanding could bring us to ruin."

She studied the healer, taking in the sudden authority of his speech. "This is no idle belief. You've seen them before. You know something about them."

Murchadh looked around and then gripped her arm. "Come, this is not something of which we should speak in public."

"Then come to Carraigmór and tell us what you know."

"No, my lady. What I know is not for anyone else to learn. You will not convince me otherwise."

She softened her voice, even though frustration was welling up inside. "You understand that once I tell Eoghan about this, he will summon you."

"Aye. And if he summons, I will come. But I will not do it voluntarily." Murchadh gave her a funny little bow, turned on his heel, and marched back to his cottage.

Uneasiness swelled inside her as she studied the obliterated design in the dirt. The healer was not given to hyperbole. What did he know that frightened him so much that it required a direct order to divulge?

The passage from this morning came back to her instantly. Knowledge of the runes had been forbidden once before. It couldn't be a mere coincidence that this had happened on the same day, right after she had asked Comdiu for direction. An idea began to form in her mind. Could it be true? She had to look at the rolls of the brotherhood.

When she burst into the Ceannaire's office, it was not Eoghan sitting at the desk but Riordan. "Aine? What's wrong?"

"I need to see the brotherhood's roster. The most recent volume."

He didn't question her, just pulled the heavy tome from a shelf and laid it on the desk. She had to guess where to look based on Murchadh's age, but after several minutes of scanning the membership, she came to the healer's entry: *Murchadh (age 30)*. She frowned. She'd always assumed he had come to Ard Dhaimhin as a youth, raised in his healing vocation. Then she saw the notation at the end of the line, the spot reserved for the city or kingdom of origin: *Sliebhan, Banndara N.* She flipped the book closed. She didn't need a translation to know that *Banndara N.* referred to the White Oak nemetons.

Murchadh had been a druid.

CHAPTER
SEVENTEEN

As Aine had expected, Eoghan summoned Murchadh before the Conclave as soon as he heard what the old healer had told her. The man halted before the nine men and Aine, his wrinkled skin turning the color of faded, bleached linen.

"Thank you for coming, Brother Murchadh." With a warm smile, Eoghan gestured to an empty seat. Murchadh cast an uneasy glance around the table before settling into it. "We've called you here because—"

"You want to know about the runes."

Aine exchanged a glance with Eoghan. They'd thought they would to have to pull the information from him bit by bit. She'd never expected him to come right out and acknowledge it.

"Aye. We want to know about the runes."

The healer heaved a sigh and dropped his chin forward to his chest, his hands clasped in his lap. For several moments, Aine thought he wouldn't answer or perhaps he had fallen asleep. When he raised his head, he wore a look of resignation. But instead of addressing Eoghan, he looked to Aine. "Ask your questions, my lady. I will answer you truly."

Aine considered her questions carefully before speaking. "Were you a druid before you came to Ard Dhaimhin?"

Surprise flared in the healer's pale gold eyes, but he nodded. "Aye. I was raised from infancy at Banndara."

"What made you leave the nemetons? What made you leave the Old Ways in favor of the brotherhood?"

Murchadh licked his lips, a tremor shooting through his body. "What do you know about the history of the druids?"

"Very little." Aine glanced around at the Conclave members, who all looked as perplexed as she felt. "I know there are those who stay with the Old Ways—devoted to nature and the unity of all life. And I know there are those who delve into blood magic."

"Like Niall."

"You knew Niall?"

"I knew *of* Niall. You see, the druidic religion is not so far removed from the brotherhood as most believe."

Murmurs erupted around the table. Eoghan held up a hand, and the whispers stilled. "Go on."

"I am not saying that we believe in the same god. I'm not saying that those who serve the gods and goddesses of the Old Ways accept the truth as we know it. But our lives are similar: humility, devotion to our rites, self-sufficiency. At least that's how the nemetons have operated since the druids were confined to them in Daimhin's age. But just like here, just like in the kingdom, there are those who are seduced by the promise of power, who are tempted to reach into things forbidden."

"The Red Druids," Riordan said from the opposite end of the table.

"Aye. You see, the Red Druids understand the power of blood. This is not so far from what the Balians believe in, the power of the blood of Lord Balus. But the druids of the nemetons also understand the power of the word."

"The power of the word," Eoghan said. "I don't understand. What does that mean?"

Understanding dawned within Aine. "The power of written language."

"But the druidic magic is of the oral tradition, is it not?" Gradaigh asked.

"Aye. It is now. Because . . ." Murchadh hesitated. "The runes were given to us first."

"That's preposterous!" Dal thundered, jumping to his feet. "The runes were brought to Seare by King Daimhin."

Eoghan stared at Dal and gave him a barely perceptible shake of his head. The older man visibly drew his composure around himself and sat down in a huff.

"That's not entirely true," Eoghan said quietly. "Lady Aine has recently found some writings that implied King Daimhin and Queen Shanna rediscovered them—with the help of the druids."

"Have you never wondered why the magic of the isle predates the coming of Lord Balus?" Murchadh asked. "Why some of the wards seemed so old? Why the druids' influence was so feared?"

"Speak plainly," Dal said. But now his tone was far more frightened than angry.

"Very well. But I warn you, you may not like what I tell you."

Murchadh looked at every single one of them in turn, his gaze lingering on Aine. "The meanings of the runes were given to a few who existed here on the isle. They were not given to our order. Our order was formed from those to whom Comdiu granted the understanding of His divine language."

Angry voices erupted around the table, but Aine barely heard them over the whoosh of blood in her ears. Aye. It made sense, considering how the shield rune on Morrigan's body had blocked her power. The only thing that could overcome the gifts of Balus would have to be other gifts of Comdiu. That would explain how the shield rune had also warded off the dark spirits of the isle. "They were given to the druids to bind the sidhe, to stop their power. But the sidhe corrupted your order."

Murchadh's shoulders slumped, this time with relief. "There were still those who had the clarity of mind and purpose to put them to their intended use. With the runes, they bound the sidhe to a sort of half realm, to the forests surrounding the nemetons. And then they scattered the runes across the land. They recognized that even though it was too much power to be contained in the hands of one man or group of men, there still might be need of it later."

"I don't understand. Scattered how?"

"They etched them on the standing stones, spread across the whole of Seare. The secret was to die with those who knew, all but a select few. When the bindings faded and the sidhe were loosed, it was those druids who worked with Daimhin to reclaim them."

"Why did the bindings fade in the first place?" Eoghan asked, his expression intent.

"I don't know. That's not something I was ever told."

"Go on," Eoghan said. "Why has no one revealed this until now?"

"It is our greatest secret. Those who still belong to the order would bear the secret to their deaths. The tattoos we take are a reminder of our responsibility as guardians of those runes, even if most of us no longer possess the ability to read them ourselves."

Murchadh drew down his tunic to reveal the spiral of faded black ink on his chest. "Only by the grace of Comdiu did I reject the teachings of my order and turn to Lord Balus."

"What I don't understand is why you reacted so violently to the rune," Aine said. "From what I understand, it was not the runes themselves that you found to be evil but rather the fact that men were corrupted by their thirst for power."

"Good men," Murchadh said softly. "Ones who believed, at one time, in the only True God. And the thirst for power slowly twisted them, made them susceptible to the sidhe's lies. If we, the ones chosen to bear that power, were corrupted by it, what makes you think you're any different?"

Silence fell around the table. Aine had to concentrate on drawing her breath evenly in and out of her lungs. "If Comdiu erased the understanding of the runes from human knowledge, why would He allow some of us to read them again? Are you saying that He made a mistake in giving that power to man the first time? Are you saying He's making a mistake again?"

"I am not qualified to judge the wisdom of Comdiu," Murchadh said. "I only tell you what I know of the druidic tradition and how we came to be what we are now. And I offer a warning: using the runes for your own ends, being too dependent on them, may be your downfall, just as it was ours."

Aine nodded slowly. "Thank you for sharing your knowledge with us, Brother Murchadh."

The healer rose and gave them a little bow. Just before Murchadh reached the door, Eoghan stood and called after him, "Brother? You referred to the druidic order as 'we.' Do you still consider yourself one of them even now that you've accepted the salvation that Lord Balus offers?"

Murchadh thought for a long moment. "Do you still consider yourself a brother of Ard Dhaimhin even though you may someday be king?" With that cryptic question, the healer turned and slipped out the door, leaving stunned silence in his wake.

Aine's mind whirred, trying to organize all the bits of information he had given them with what she already knew. Shanna had said the language had been scattered. That was most surely the runic language that had been distributed across the standing stones of Seare, those old places of worship that predated the coming of Balianism. Shanna and Daimhin had likely collected them and compiled them in one place for their use. But where? The Hall of Prophecies held no such volume.

She looked up to find Eoghan watching her, a peculiar look of curiosity on his face. When she averted her eyes from his, they landed on a point behind his shoulder. The Rune Throne.

She broke into laughter, aware it was tinged with a bit of hysteria. Of course. It was so obvious that they'd continually overlooked it. She clamped her hands over her pregnant belly as stitches stabbed into her sides and she tried to catch her breath. "Truly, we are among the most foolish of people, or it has powers of concealment that we never dreamed of."

All attention landed on her, some faces betraying worry, others outright bewilderment.

"The Rune Throne. It's the key. It's the object that contains all the runic knowledge of the kingdom, and it's been right under our noses. It has to have some sort of concealment for us to have continually overlooked it. An added layer of protection in case Ard Dhaimhin was ever sacked."

Full understanding hit her like an avalanche. The look on Eoghan's face said he'd made the connection at the same time she did.

"The boy," he said.

"Aye," Aine said. "Not standing on stone. The standing stones."

"Once Niall failed to take Ard Dhaimhin, he decided to compile his own key."

Riordan looked between them, his brow furrowed. "I don't understand. What does this have to do with his taking of the fortresses?"

"Old Balian fortresses," Eoghan explained. "Some of them used the old standing stones as foundations or cornerstones. There are only a few intact circles left out of the hundreds that were once scattered across the country. Most of the original stones are now inside, part of, or beneath the oldest structures in Seare."

"Which have the weakest defenses," Aine murmured. "Convenient."

"Not so convenient," Riordan said. "No one really knows where all the stones are, where they were used, or how many existed. He's taken two fortresses this month, but it could take him years to locate them all."

"Then we have time to stop him," Eoghan said.

"How?" Dal asked.

But Eoghan had no answer for that. As they exchanged glances around the table, Aine's exhilaration at having solved the puzzle gave way to a heavy dread. They might know the druid's plans, but without a way to fight him on his own territory, they were no closer to stopping him than they were before.

CHAPTER EIGHTEEN

They continued the slow trek down through the pass for the next three days, but Conor struggled to keep his mind on the terrain in light of what Aine had told him. The druids had once been followers of Comdiu? It wasn't so much that Conor had thought them evil, exactly. His interactions with the ones who occasionally came to Balurnan from the Timhaigh nemetons had been pleasant, if a bit confusing. But being raised a Balian in a country that was hostile to his faith, he'd begun to think of all those who held opposing viewpoints as the enemy. In some cases, like his uncle, he had been right. But it sounded as though the druids weren't necessarily one of those cases.

What else might they have been wrong about?

Aine had promised to continue to dig through Shanna's journals to see if she could find anything that shed light on the runes, but that still didn't solve the more pressing problem: the druid was collecting them, and they had no way to stop him. Facing him and his ten-thousand-strong army was no more advisable now than it had been when they were trying to protect their countrymen.

That made taking Ard Bealach all the more important. It was too new to contain any standing stones, but it would be a valuable stronghold from which to deploy men, another location to which they could recall their sworn brothers. Assuming they ever figured out how to use the sword to do that.

Oenghus moved up beside Conor, his hand resting on his sword. "This would be Esras coming."

Conor followed the man's gaze, but he didn't see anything but trees and granite. "Where?"

"There." As Conor watched, what he thought was part of the forest clarified into the shape of a man dressed in dark brown and green, his only visible weapon a short sword at his waist. He descended the granite rock face with the gravity-defying balance of a mountain goat and then came to rest in front of them.

"What did you find?" Oenghus asked.

"Four only. No difficulties."

Oenghus glanced at Conor and explained, "Four sentries in the pass ahead of us. Esras has taken care of them."

"Won't they notice that they're missing men?"

"Our men have replaced them. We've been watching them long enough to know their signals. As usual, overconfidence will be their downfall."

"We're indebted to you."

"We're counting on that." There was a touch of humor in the words though. Oenghus nodded a dismissal at Esras, who disappeared back up the cliff face as quickly as he had appeared.

"And how far does your assistance reach?"

"Will we fight with you, you're asking?" Oenghus's humor faded. "We will clear the passes and perimeter of sentries. We can give you information, but we don't involve ourselves in matters that don't concern us. How do you think we've lived peacefully for so long?"

"That sounds exactly like the Fíréin's policy," Conor said. "And look where we are now."

"You're alive, which is more than I can say about most of those who oppose Keondric. No, I will not send men to die in your battle. But our offer of hospitality continues."

Conor understood. It would have to be enough. The less effort they had to extend on hunting and reconnaissance, the better. And the mountain dwellers certainly knew the region much better than the Fíréin did.

Besides, with any luck, it would not be much of a battle.

They reached the rendezvous point almost exactly three weeks after leaving Carraigmór, two days prior to the full moon on which they had agreed to attack. Oenghus's men sited their camp up a small, rocky path cut into the side of the canyon, where they could watch for the Clanless below and bide their time until the attack. While the other men prepared cold food and checked their weapons, Conor removed the leather harp case from the pack pony and checked the instrument's frame for any damage that had come about from the pony's jostling gait. Finding none, he looked to the strings instead and tuned them as quietly as possible.

"You're going to play this close to the fortress?" Oenghus asked, his tone doubtful.

"No. Just preparing." Conor didn't elaborate, and the Clanless leader didn't press, though he must have been confused by the response. When Conor was sure, even through his light touch, that the notes were tuned true, he carefully laid it back in the case and settled down to check his own weapons.

The rest of the day passed slowly and stretched into night. Despite the men's discipline, Conor could feel their edginess at being stationary and exposed. Oenghus's men came and went with offerings of food that could be eaten cold, even if he didn't know exactly where they had come by it. The Clanless community seemed to be even larger and more widespread than anyone had ever dreamed. Did they owe it all to the use of the runes?

The moon wasn't even fully up yet when Conor felt the first touch of unnatural cold. "The sidhe are here," he murmured to Oenghus.

"Aye," the man agreed in a low voice. "They carry with them the chill of the grave."

He should have expected it. The sidhe had been watching, waiting for their moment to strike. And now they must know that within earshot of the fortress's sentries, Conor's men had little chance to guard against them. Conor had the charm to help keep his mind clear, but his men were still susceptible while the order of silence was in effect. For a moment, he considered drawing the rune on them anyway—consequences be hanged— but something held him back. What if that was the very thing the sidhe wanted them to do? What if the consequences of tak- ing the mark—or smearing or miswriting the mark—were even worse than they thought?

"I need your men," he said in a low voice to Oenghus. "All of them, on guard duty tonight. Is that something you're willing to do?"

The answering light in the man's eyes said he followed his thoughts. "Aye. To keep them from disappearing." Oenghus raised his hand toward one of his men, who immediately approached, and they conversed in low voices before the sentry disappeared. Less than an hour later, eight more men had arrived and stationed themselves at various points around the perimeter. Conor gave Oenghus a nod of thanks.

The night passed quietly without any incursions from the sidhe. Conor took the first watch and then curled beneath his blanket by the fire. His hand remained on his sword while he fell into a state of half slumber, still too edgy to sleep deeply. Every sound took on an ominous cast, starting him awake. Then sometime near morning, the sound of a scuffle in the brush woke him. He was on his feet, blade in hand, before he'd completely shaken off sleep.

One of his men—Lachtna, judging from the flash of white-blond hair—struggled beneath two of Oenghus's warriors. Instantly, Conor rushed to their side, realizing as he did that the men were only restraining him.

"What's happening?" Conor whispered fiercely.

"Trying to leave the camp." Oenghus arrived beside him. It was clear from Lachtna's wild-eyed look that he was under the influence of the sidhe. "What do you want done with him? Restrain him until the sidhe decide to release him?"

If they ever decided to release him. Conor had firsthand knowledge of how hard their influence could be to overcome without something to break that hold. And with the way Lachtna was thrashing and moaning, he would bring the sentries down on them.

There was only one option left to him. Conor dragged the ivory charm over his head and pressed its rune-carved surface against the back of Lachtna's neck, the first bit of exposed skin he could find. The warrior thrashed for a moment longer, then went still. When Oenghus's men released their grip to roll him over, his eyes at last looked clear.

"What happened?" Lachtna asked, his eyes darting around their grim circle.

"Deceived by the sidhe," Conor murmured. "Do you recall what happened?"

Lachtna shook his head. "No. I was on watch. Then I woke up here on the ground."

"Back to your post, then," Conor said. "We've only a few hours until sunrise. Their influence will be diminished then."

The men sorted themselves back into their previous posts, but Oenghus held back, his attention still directed toward the charm. "You know something of the runes?"

"Aye, a little." Conor returned the necklace to its place beneath his tunic and furs.

"Yet you don't protect your men?"

"We don't have enough information about them. You may be willing to brand them, but I'm not. And these objects are hard to come by."

Oenghus said nothing, but as he trudged away, Conor felt that he had somehow disappointed him, like he was being careless with his men's lives. Given the nature of the threat, maybe he was. But there was far too much at stake here if he were wrong.

Morning arrived, and the day passed at a rate akin to slow torture. Men came and went from the traveler party, replacing the ones who had spent the night on watch and once more making Conor wonder how many skilled warriors Oenghus had at his disposal. The Fíréin grew restless, as did the animals, who had been hobbled in the clearing with little fresh grazing for nearly two days now. Conor expected an alarm to be raised at any moment, but the Clanless warriors were true to their assurance that they had effectively replaced the sentries. By now, surely someone would be aware of their presence.

Unless they were being set up.

No. He had no reason to believe that Oenghus was going to betray them. The fact they bore runes didn't automatically make them trustworthy, of course; it just meant they probably weren't working directly with the druid. Still, he trusted Oenghus's motivations: they were on the side of the future High King, and they expected to benefit in thanks for their help in the siege on Ard Bealach.

At last the sun dipped behind the hills and the light slid from white to blue to black. Conor kept a close eye on the moon as it rose from its spot near the edge of the horizon, trying to time how long it would take to reach its zenith, that point when Daigh would make entry from the other tunnel. When he thought it was only perhaps three hours away, Conor signaled for the men to ready themselves.

Conor turned to Oenghus and grasped his forearm. "Thank you for your help. We are indebted."

"Aye, I know. We'll keep your passage clear while you make your entry, but as soon as you're in, you're on your own."

"Understood. Thank you. We're only going as far as Throne Rock, so if you can keep that area open until morning, we'll be safe."

"Aye. Go with Comdiu."

They painstakingly made their way back to the pass below, where they proceeded down the rocky path with only moonlight guiding their steps. Conor squinted at their surroundings in the dark, looking for the landmarks that would signal the tunnel's opening was close and wishing he'd been able to scout ahead. It had been deemed too dangerous, but now he wondered if they wouldn't be simply wandering around for hours in the dark.

Then Larkin nudged him in the back and pointed to the dim shape of the rock face ahead and to their left. Indeed, even barely outlined against the night sky, the outcropping appeared to be chair shaped, a throne sized for a giant. According to the map, that meant they were close. The cliff, however, seemed to be a solid chunk of rock without any distinguishing marks. Conor retrieved a wax cloth-wrapped torch from the packhorse and lit the pitch with his knife and flint. When at last the torch flared to life, he walked slowly along the wall of the canyon, illuminating patches of rock in the hope of finding the entrance.

Then he stopped short as something caught his eye. Not a variation in the stone, exactly—just something different, like the hidden panel that led to the Hall of Prophecies back at Carraigmór. He ran his hand over the area, indistinguishable from the rest of the rock. It was here, he was sure of it. He gestured for them to bring the packhorse near.

"Are you sure?" Larkin whispered. "If you're wrong, we could be digging into a solid mountain of stone."

"I'm sure." He handed off the torch, removed a chisel and a small mallet from one of the packs, and began to painstakingly chip the softening rune into the jagged rock wall. He purposely kept it small, the entire thing near the ground and barely wide enough for a man's shoulders. Even though he trusted Oenghus to keep the area clear, there was no reason to draw attention to the tunnel's location.

It took him nearly two hours to carve the rune into the rock wall, only a finger width's deep, checking against the small scrap of parchment onto which he had copied it. Then he took a different chisel and began to carve it deeper. To his surprise, the rock crumbled away like sand, the marks growing deeper and deeper with almost no effort.

Finally, he stepped back and looked around at his party, the men's faces alight with anticipation. "Ready?"

Slowly, they drew their weapons. Conor took that as an affirmation. He hefted the shovel, drew back the haft, and rammed the blade end through the center of the rune. It bit into the rock as easily as the shifting surface of a sandy beach. A single twist and the whole area crumbled into powder.

Conor knelt at the opening. It was a tunnel, all right, even if he could only see into blackness, the rock wall a mere eight inches thick. "All right, men. I want you to enter, wait until we have a count, and then fade into shadow." He hoisted the harp case through the opening first. The bulky instrument would hamper his movements, but it was too integral to the security of the fortress to leave on the outside. Cautiously, he climbed through the hole.

Spider webs clung to his face, and he swiped them away. Larkin passed him the torch, which he swept in front of him to illuminate the space. If the layers of dust and cobwebs were any indication, these tunnels must have been closed up centuries ago. Gravel crunched beneath his feet. At least he hoped it was gravel. He didn't look too closely.

Beside him, quiet footfalls indicated that his men followed. Conor drew his sword, even the hiss of the oiled blade against the sheepskin lining loud in the dense, deep silence. They were far below the mountain here, and if the scale of the map had been accurate, the tunnels wound for miles before they met the catacombs beneath the fortress.

He paused a few dozen steps in and, no louder than a whisper, said, "Count off."

Eleven voices answered, but when he glanced behind him, he saw nothing. Unlike the others, he didn't fade. The men needed someone to follow, and the torch prevented the illusion from working anyway. He was all too aware that made him the obvious target for the fortress guards' blades and arrows.

Conor counted off his paces as he walked, estimating the distance in his head. At map scale, the tunnel hadn't seemed particularly long. But in person, they might as well have been journeying downward into the center of the earth. As it was, he could feel the weight of the mountain like a physical force, his pulse speeding the closer they got to their destination, his instincts heightened for potential battle.

They passed the single mile mark without a sign of opposition, then two. He made himself draw in deep breaths and shake off his apprehension. Adrenaline was the enemy in battle. It made one slow, sluggish, uncoordinated. And they needed every sense at its best.

Too late, those senses prickled at the danger behind him. He whirled just as something slammed into his hand. The torch skittered across the gravel floor, but it didn't go out. It left just enough light to see the face of the man who threw himself at him and bore him to the ground. Conor's head banged the earth hard enough to make him see white sparks.

"Larkin," Conor wheezed. He raised his forearm to block a strike before it could connect with his face. "What are you doing? Stop. It's me."

But the other man's fingers closed around his throat, pressing down with a force he hadn't even known the other man possessed. As he gasped for air, he aimed strikes to Larkin's throat— what should have been disabling blows—but the man didn't even flinch, as if he were dreaming . . . or possessed.

The sidhe. "Help me," he cried, appealing to the other men, but his voice came from his constricted windpipe weaker than a whisper. Nothing he did even made an impact; Larkin merely absorbed the strikes to the ribs, groin, and head and kept pressing. Conor's movements grew weaker as his oxygen-depleted body lost strength, and the white sparks in his vision became a snowstorm, blanking out everything but the knowledge of impending death.

Comdiu, help me. It was his last thought before he disappeared into oblivion.

CHAPTER
NINETEEN

Water dripped somewhere in the distance. Drip. Drip. Drip, drip, drip. Conor focused on the sound as consciousness came back in layers, his head pounding with every splash as if it were a gong. From the way his entire body ached, he knew something had happened, but recalling it was as impossible as opening his eyes.

Or moving his body.

His heart jumped into his throat before it picked up a furious hammering that only intensified the ache. Why couldn't he move? Had he been injured? Drugged? Restrained?

No, it couldn't be. Not again. His imprisonment with the Sofarende had been enough. He couldn't bear another round.

Then he was hit with a more horrifying thought: what if he had never escaped in the first place? What if he were still locked in the goat pen, paralyzed by the herbs he'd been given, while his mind concocted his return to Seare and all that had come after?

No, that was ridiculous. He forced himself to stay calm, drawing in deep, pained breaths until his heartbeat returned to a slightly more normal rate. He couldn't move or see, but that didn't mean

he was completely without resources. The damp, cold silence
meant he was still beneath Ard Bealach, perhaps somewhere in the
catacombs; keeps, no matter how secure, were drafty when above
ground. He forced himself to move through his pain and take
stock of every sensation. His fingers brushed something rough.
Wood, a table perhaps. At least that meant he wasn't paralyzed. He
was merely bound tightly, ropes lashing down his entire body.

His pulse raced once more. Any way he thought of it, bound
to a table in a chamber beneath Ard Bealach could mean only
one thing.

Before panic could make his thinking cloudy again, he forced
himself to recall every detail of what had happened before he
passed out. He remembered leading the way down the tunnel
. . . and after that, nothing. Had they been ambushed or, worse
yet, betrayed? Right now, his men could be dead, dying, captured. He couldn't afford to hope for a rescue.

Conor flexed his muscles against the ropes, attempting to
work some slack into them. It was a futile effort, but when he
thought of what Oenghus implied happened in the fortress, it
was the only way to keep himself from succumbing to terror.

Metal scraped somewhere to his right—a key in a lock. The
door swung open on creaking hinges, spilling light into the room.
He could make out the backlit figure of a man, but no features.

"Conor Mac Nir. I've been looking forward to our reunion."

A chill slid over Conor's skin, a clammy sense of recognition.
He knew that voice.

"Ah, you see your predicament now." The speaker retrieved
a torch from the corridor, which illuminated Conor's surroundings. Even knowing what was coming, Conor recoiled inwardly.

Niall. Or rather, Niall wearing Keondric's body like an ill-
fitting disguise. Conor blinked to clear that impression. His
thoughts felt sloppy, muddled, maybe by whatever had knocked

him out and stolen his memory. His skull didn't feel cracked, despite the pounding headache, but he also didn't feel right. Poison? If they were going to give him a draught, the least they could do was give him something to take away the pain.

He reeled in his speculations before they could run away from him. Focus. He needed to focus.

The torch illuminated enough of the room to show it was not a dungeon, nor were there the usual implements of torture laid out beside him. In fact, it seemed he was tied to a trestle table amid stacks of crates and boxes.

"What do you want from me?" Conor's throat ached for a reason he couldn't fathom. Had he been screaming while he was unconscious?

"I'm not going to torture you for information, if that's what worries you." Niall stopped and looked down at him impassively, as if he were having a conversation with a slightly dense stranger. "I can learn that anytime I want."

Just keep him talking. "What do you mean?"

"I mean I have my sources of information inside Ard Dhaimhin already."

Morrigan? Was he talking about his sister? The mention of Ard Dhaimhin made him remember what should have occurred to him earlier. *Aine! Can you hear me? I need help!*

"She can't hear you." Niall took his knife from his belt and nudged the opening of Conor's shirt aside. "Can you see that?"

He managed to lift his head enough to see a blistered red rune branded into his skin. "The shield. I don't understand. That makes me immune to your magic. Why would you give that to me?"

Niall dragged a stool over to Conor's side, his movements matter-of-fact. "You and I are going to perform some experiments together. I've already determined that the rune blocks my powers from working on you and interferes with your ability to communicate with the lovely Lady Aine. But frankly, I'm not sure what else it does or does not allow."

Conor's gorge rose at the implication. Somewhere he had the presence of mind to force it back down. Tied as he was, it would be an undignified way to die, drowning in his own vomit. Somehow the thought managed to be both horrifying and hilarious at the same time.

"Interesting. Hysteria already? I didn't take you for the type. Or is it some new effect of the rune?"

Conor wrestled his emotions back under control. There was nothing funny about his situation. If Niall meant to torture him for information, he'd eventually break, and then the sorcerer would either stop or put him out of his misery. If he was merely testing the rune's properties, there was no reason to quit until Conor was mutilated beyond all recognition.

So this was how it all ended for him. Taken apart piece by piece in some Sliebhanaigh fortress, never to see his wife again, never to lay eyes on his child. At least Aine was safe in Ard Dhaimhin. Eoghan would see that she and the child were cared for. That was the only advantage to the fact that his best friend loved his wife.

How long would it take for her to grow to love him back? Conor had already said Aine would make a fine queen. It would only make sense for her eventually to marry the High King.

The thought of Aine in Eoghan's arms, his hands on her, made Conor's stomach twist. Of course Eoghan would bed her. Of course she would bear him children. It wouldn't even be a hardship, considering what Eoghan could offer. And Conor's sacrifice would be forgotten.

His failure, on the other hand, would be immortalized by his absence.

A tear trickled from the corner of his eye. Niall caught it on the tip of his knife and gave the blade a twist, nicking the skin of his cheekbone. "I'm disappointed. Tears already, and we haven't even begun." Niall waved a hand, and a blue flame danced on his palm.

Conor swallowed and kept his eyes fixed firmly on the curved stone ceiling. He knew now that he wouldn't be leaving this room. Nothing he said would change that. The only thing he could control was how he conducted himself in the minutes or hours or days before his death.

But when the first flicker of unnatural fire licked his skin, he screamed.

✦ ✦ ✦

Drip. Drip. Drip, drip, drip.

He woke to a stinging slap across the face and the sound of more water dripping onto the floor. Pain seared every nerve ending, surprising him with its intensity, surprising him that it didn't dull the other sensations: the cold breeze against his face, the sticky wetness on his skin.

Only then did he realize that the drip coincided with the hammering of his pulse. Not water. Blood. His blood.

Footsteps scuffed along the stone floor. "This has been quite enlightening, don't you think? It seems that the shield rune, as you call it, is effective against direct incursions of the mind and at blocking innate magic. But it is shockingly useless against physical attacks brought by magic. As, of course, you know."

Conor struggled to focus on the voice, struggled to hang on to consciousness, though he didn't know why. It would be so much easier to embrace the cool comfort of darkness.

"No, not yet. We're not finished. And you need to be awake for this to work. Do you want to see what's been done so far?"

Conor shook his head with all the strength he could muster. Niall laughed. "Fair enough. That might sever the last tether on your mind, and I still need that engaged. What I wonder now is if the rune works both ways. You can't contact your beloved Aine, but if she were told you were in trouble, could she contact you?"

"No." Conor moistened his cracked lips and tried to make his voice strong. "Better that she doesn't know. I don't want her to know."

"Then why don't we save that for last? I think you'll want to say good-bye in the end. In the meantime . . ."

Conor didn't hear the rest over the whoosh of blood in his ears. But when the pain again became too much, he stopped fighting and succumbed to the embrace of the dark.

✦   ✦   ✦

Flashes of light. The raspy sound of breathing. His own, he thought. Pain, but more distant now. Hard to grasp, slipping away.

"Not yet." Who was the other voice? He couldn't remember. "You've been very helpful. We're almost finished. And then you'll have your reward. You can say good-bye."

The sound of sobbing came to his ears. His voice. He didn't care. He was broken. There was nothing left of him to salvage. No pride. No purpose. He had failed in every way that mattered.

He eagerly raced to meet the blackness.

✦   ✦   ✦

Conor. Conor, it's me. Can you hear me?

He tried to pry his eyelids open, but they wouldn't move, sticky and encrusted with blood. At least the pain was less now. Or maybe there was so much of it he couldn't distinguish one sensation from the other. The dripping had slowed too, slowed with the barely perceptible beating of his heart. He trembled with cold and struggled to focus on the voice.

Tears seeped from beneath his eyelids. "I'm sorry, Aine. I failed. We failed. We were betrayed. I did my best, but—"

Conor, listen to me. It's not over. You have to be strong.

"I'm dying, Aine. I love you."

No. You are not dying.

"What's been done—"

Nothing's been done to you, Conor. Open your eyes!

"I can't!" He meant the words to come out as a shout, but they came out as a croak instead. "He took them. Don't you understand? I'm blind!"

You are not blind. You are not being tortured.

He turned his head away as if he could shut out her voice. What kind of cruelty was this? Did she think she could give him some comfort in his last moments? He had just one more thing to convey. "I love you, Aine. I always have."

He closed his eyes and drew what would surely be his last breath.

✦   ✦   ✦

"Conor!" Aine screamed his name aloud and pounded her fists against the stone floor. "Don't die! Don't give up! Do you hear me?"

Eoghan gripped her shoulders. "You can get through to him, Aine. You must. If you don't, he really will die."

She tried to still the beating of her heart, tried to regain their connection. It had to have been Comdiu's voice that roused her from a sound sleep, and that meant she could still save him. She found his consciousness again, barely a whisper in the tunnels of Ard Bealach.

Conor, listen to me. You are not dying. You are not being tor-tured. None of this is real. You're trapped in a glamour.

+ + +

Why could he not die? Was it Aine's fault? Was she the one holding him back from finding peace in the arms of his Maker?

"I love you," he mumbled. "Let me go."

Conor, listen to me. You are not dying. You are not being tortured. None of this is real. You're trapped in a glamour.

The words pierced the fog, even though they didn't make any sense. "Please, just let me go."

No. I will not let you go. The sidhe are deceiving you. This is all an illusion. Don't you remember Cwmmaen? Prince Talfryn?

It seemed familiar somehow, but he couldn't remember why. Cwmmaen was a Gwynn name. When had he been in Gwydden?

That's right. You were in Gwydden. The sidhe were keeping you there to prevent you from finishing your mission, just like now. Are you listening to me, Conor? You have to break free. You have to shake this off.

"I can't."

You can. You must. Otherwise, you fail. Isn't that what this is about? You're afraid that you will fail me? Seare? Now, think. Think about all the things that don't add up. If you have the shield rune, how are we talking now? It blocks magic.

That was true. It was supposed to block all magic of the mind. But how had Niall known what he was thinking, then? Unless he had spoken his thoughts aloud.

No. It's all a construct. You have to fight it. If you don't listen to me now, it's all for nothing. You're a failure.

A spark of anger ignited at the words. He was dying. How dare she.

But the pain. Where was the pain? He flexed his fingers and realized his hand was no longer bound.

That's right. You see? It was an illusion. Where's your harp?

By the tunnel entrance, wasn't it? But how could he escape?

Open your eyes now, Conor. Now! Do it! I promise you, you can see.

But he remembered the pain quite clearly. The screaming.

Just like he remembered the opulence of a destroyed Gwynn fortress. The kiss of a beautiful girl who wasn't a girl. None of it was real, at least not in the way he imagined it.

Aine's voice sounded tearful now. *Please, Conor, just open your eyes. If you love me, if you love your child, finish this mission and come home to me.*

Could it be true? Could she be right? Or was this all a hallucination born of blood loss and pain and madness?

He took a deep breath and opened his eyes.

A flame, little more than a flicker, guttered from the torch on the tunnel's gravel floor. His ivory charm—the one he'd counted on to protect him from the sidhe, the one he'd foolishly revealed—lay beside it. Slowly, he took inventory of his body. No blood, no pain except the throb of his neck where Larkin had throttled him. His eyes darted around the tunnel as the strength flooded back into his limbs.

His men lay sprawled out as far as he could see into the dark, lifeless, limp. A few twitched or moaned. Were they undergoing torture as he had, or were they experiencing their own private torment?

Embarrassment flooded him. All his worst fears had been laid out before him. Captivity and torture. Failure. Losing his wife and child—and losing them to Eoghan. All had been used to ensnare him and make him ineffectual. All used to cripple him so he couldn't do the things Comdiu had sent him to do. Shame joined embarrassment now. These things onto which he held so tightly he had let consume him until they nearly destroyed him.

Had he admitted the fears and given up and let go, they never would have been able to be used to deceive him. He couldn't even put it into words, the depth of his shame and sorrow. How many times did he have to learn the same lessons? Today his stubbornness could have cost twelve lives for which he was responsible, including his own.

Aine, I'm here. I'm going back for the harp.

He could feel her relief. *Thank Comdiu. Be careful, Conor. You have no idea how close we were to losing you.*

But he did.

✦ ✦ ✦

Aine let out her held breath before she realized it was the only thing keeping her upright. She would have collapsed had Eoghan not scooped her up beneath her arms and helped her to a chair. He hovered above her while he waited to see if she would stay there on her own.

"I'm fine. I am. I just . . ."

She became aware of the looks exchanged around the room. Somewhere in the minutes or hours that she had been linked with Conor's mind but unable to break through the illusion, more of the brothers had arrived to stand silent watch with her. Eoghan. Riordan. Dal. Even Fechin. For the first time, she understood the unbreakable strength in the brotherhood, why they had fought so hard to keep it intact. Their support for Conor, who was no longer really one of them, was plain in their support of her.

They remained quiet, leaving Eoghan to ask their question. He reached for her hand, then apparently thought better of it. "Is he free?"

"He's free." The words seemed to sap the last of her strength, and her body sagged forward toward the tabletop.

"Come, let's get you to your bed. Riordan?"

Gently, they slid an arm under each side and helped her to her feet. She would have protested, but she felt too weak to put one foot in front of the other. She'd never been linked so closely to another's mind, had underestimated the effect on her. She had felt every moment of the torture, so intense that she almost believed it was happening, even knowing it was an illusion. Even worse had been feeling his agony and hearing the thoughts that ran through his head as he tried to escape something that just continued to grow worse. Eoghan had repeatedly pulled her out of the trance, forced her to drink water, made her focus on the reality around her lest she get pulled too deeply into the illusion herself.

She felt a gratitude toward him that was altogether unsettling considering she understood what lay behind his concern.

"Sleep now, my lady. We'll have one of the women check on you in the morning."

She couldn't manage anything but a weak nod as she climbed into her bed and pulled the coverlet to her chin. Only when Eoghan blew out the candle and the room drained of its inhabitants did she let her tears fall.

Great, racking sobs for what Conor had experienced, for what she had experienced through him, and for the one thing she never thought possible, the one thing she wished she had never been able to see through his eyes.

While Conor was in Gwydden, there had been another woman.

CHAPTER
TWENTY

Conor retraced his steps toward the tunnel entrance, praying
that the harp was where he had left it. How long had he been
trapped in the glamour? How long had he lain there, unconscious and helpless? It was all too possible that the men of the
fortress were waiting for them, and if they weren't, the minute he
played the harp, they would be alerted to the Fíréin's presence.

The trip back took much less time than the approach, his
steps picking up speed until he was almost running. His body
was finally remembering that it was not dying, he had not
been carved up and tormented until he wished for death, even
if flashes of false memory still sent his heart racing. Later. He
could deal with that later. Right now his men needed him. He
still had to finish the mission.

The cold glimmer of moonlight shone through the tunnel's
entrance, illuminating the outline of his harp case. He let out a
breath of relief. A quick look outside revealed that the moon had
sunk toward the horizon again, an indication that a few hours
had passed. Given the time it had taken to traverse the passage,
he couldn't have been unconscious for long. He reached for

the case and then thought better of it and climbed through the opening to where the horse still waited. It tossed its head and huffed impatiently as if to ask where Conor had been.

"I know," he murmured. "But you're going to have a long wait." He retrieved a mallet, chisel, and shovel before climbing back through the tunnel opening and adding the harp to his burden. He hadn't thought to see if the dead end was part of the glamour or a reality, and he wouldn't have time to return for the tools if the passage really were blocked.

He reached his men in no time, though he suspected that might have more to do with the residual fogginess than the actual distance to the end of the tunnel. He let the tools fall and set the harp down as gently as he could manage, then held the torch out. No, it had been no illusion. The tunnel was seamless rock, just as the outer entrance had been. Whoever had sealed the tunnel had been taking no chances. That worked in their favor. The men above would never dream that it could be so easily reopened.

For a moment, he debated. If he had been so close to dying, the others might be as well. Playing away the illusion now would free them from the enchantment, but it would also alert the others above. What happened if they followed the sound and figured out they were being attacked?

No, he couldn't risk it. He picked up the chisel and mallet and began to carve the rune into the surface of the rock wall, just large enough for them to climb through. This time he only scratched the surface, relying on speed rather than thorough-ness. The basic shape came together quickly, and Conor used the chisel to deepen the lines and double-check his work. Little bits of granite began to crumble at his feet. It had worked. Two strong thrusts of the shovel, and there was a hole big enough to squeeze his shoulders through.

A light breeze ruffled his hair as he knelt beside the opening.

He had definitely broken through to a chamber of some sort. Carefully, he leaned in and looked around. The soft glow of a torch from somewhere in the recesses of the space gave just enough light to see that it was empty—for the time being.

Comdiu, please let this work, he prayed. He opened the harp case and drew out the instrument, the same plea circulating through the back of his mind like a litany. He could not fail. This had to work.

He didn't question the melody that came to him. If he trusted Comdiu to give him this gift, he had to trust Him to bring the right notes to mind as well. The music spread out around him, filling the dark spaces of the tunnel with sound, but the golden light he'd come to expect in his mind's eye was absent, as if he were blind. *Please, Comdiu*, he prayed again. *Let this work. Let this be successful. Bring them back.*

And then he heard the screaming.

It was the sound of men in agony, as if they were being torn limb from limb.

No, worse. It was the sound of souls being rent from their bodies.

Conor's fingers faltered on the strings, but the screaming continued, and he realized that it was not coming from his own warriors but somewhere in the keep itself. His stomach turned and his throat tightened, but he kept playing. It was only when he stopped, his eyes blurred with unshed tears, that he realized the shrieking had been silenced.

Larkin was the first to push himself to a sitting position, his eyes wild. He scrambled back on his hands and feet until he hit the tunnel wall. "Where am I? What's happening?"

Conor replaced the harp into the case and moved to his side, but Larkin recoiled. "It's all right," Conor said soothingly. "I don't know what you saw, but none of it was real. It was all an illusion."

"But you . . . you're dead. I killed you. I—" Larkin shook off the thought. "That was all an illusion?"

"Aye. Clearly, I'm alive." He didn't have the heart to tell Larkin he was remembering his own actions, that he had almost killed Conor. His eye once again caught a glimmer of white on the ground—the charm. The sidhe had used Larkin to remove the charm so Conor would be susceptible to their illusions. He palmed the necklace and surreptitiously slid it into his pouch.

"What happened?" A voice rang out from farther down the tunnel. Everyone seemed to be stirring now, murmurs of fear and confusion filling the cavernous space.

Conor held up his hands for attention and pitched his voice low. Now that the tunnel was open to the catacombs, they had to be especially careful not to be discovered. "I don't know what you saw or what you just experienced. I know that it was likely different for each one of you. But it was not real. The sidhe are trying to keep us from accomplishing our mission."

The dazed expressions were fading from their faces, a sign that they were shaking off the glamours' influence at last. He hoped that meant the others' experiences had been less dramatic than his. It would be a struggle to force enough strength into his still-trembling hands to hold a sword. As it was, he'd barely been able to make his fingers move on the harp strings.

"What are your orders?" Larkin asked.

Comdiu bless him. These were men who were used to following orders. Clear direction would give them enough structure to shake off the illusion. "Bar the front entrance. No one goes in or out. Secure each room of the keep from the bottom up. Anyone who resists dies. Anyone who surrenders loses his weapons. We don't have many men to accomplish this, and we don't know if Daigh's men even reached the tunnel."

He should have thought to ask Aine, but his mind was still

working at reduced capacity. He could only trust that Comdiu would be with them.

To his relief, the other eleven men seemed to come back to themselves more quickly than he had, sorting themselves into order and checking weapons. Maybe the harp's music had helped eradicate the memory of their mental captivity, whereas he'd not had that advantage. Recollections of torture still lurked around the edges of his mind like shadows seen from the corner of his eye.

"You ready?" he asked. "This only works if we're alert. No mistakes. If you think you haven't recovered, speak now. You can stay behind. After what you saw, there's no shame in needing time to pull yourself together."

They exchanged glances, but no one volunteered. Conor hoped they were showing wisdom and not bravado. "No? Then let's go."

Conor climbed through the opening first, sword at the ready, but the center chamber of the catacombs was deserted. As the others climbed through behind him, he stayed alert for the sounds of onrushing footsteps, the shadows from the connected tunnels that would indicate they had been discovered. Yet there was nothing but the sound of their own breathing and the faint scuff of their shoes against the stone floor. A quick inspection revealed a steep flight of stairs leading upward.

He gestured for them to follow and quickly climbed the stairs, pausing at the top before pushing the heavy wooden door open. Had no one heard the harp and been curious about its origin? He had been sure they would already be facing down dozens of men, but the corridor was as still and quiet as the catacombs below. Slowly, he moved into the great hall.

It was empty.

Conor lowered his sword. "I don't understand."

"Maybe they're elsewhere?" Larkin's expression was equally confused.

"All the corridors lead into the hall. If anyone heard us, they'd be here already. Blair, Ferus, stay here on guard. Bar the front doors. Men, the rest of this level now."

They spread out down the two corridors, dividing themselves evenly. As Conor passed the doorway to the catacombs again, it creaked open. He pressed himself against the wall, sword at the ready. The soft shuffle of feet on stone heightened every sense as he prepared to strike.

And then he let out his held breath. "You made it."

The other Fíréin party flooded the corridor, and he automatically counted each man as they entered. He frowned when he came up one short. "Where's Daigh?"

Ailill, a stocky young man with quick dark eyes, stepped forward. "He didn't make it. He's still below in the tunnels."

"What do you mean he didn't make it?"

"He didn't come out of . . . whatever that was . . . at the sound of the harp." Ailill cleared his throat. "He was already dead."

Guilt and sorrow crushed down on Conor. He had been too late. He just as swiftly pushed the emotion away. They had no time for sentiment. "My men are checking this floor. Secure the upper level. Those who surrender, take prisoner. Kill the rest."

"Aye, sir."

"And be cautious. We haven't encountered anyone yet, but that doesn't mean they couldn't be making an ambush."

"Aye, sir."

Conor gave a nod and they moved toward the stairway that led to the next floor up. Uneasiness washed over him. This was all too easy. They'd been expecting a fight, and instead all they found were empty rooms?

Yet in chamber after chamber, the only things Conor found were the remnants of personal belongings and weapons. "I don't understand this," Conor murmured to Larkin, who had accompanied him with two other men. "This doesn't make any sense."

Ailill's group met them back in the great hall several minutes later, looking as baffled as Conor felt. "It's empty," Ailill said. "There's no one here."

"Why set the sidhe on us if there's nothing to protect?" Larkin asked.

But Conor knew. The sidhe depended on human passions to sustain them and their strength. Starved for pain and fear on which to feed, they'd simply taken the opportunity that Conor and his group presented.

"My bigger question is where are the men? Ailill, Larkin, Seanán, and Tomey with me. The rest of you, secure the entrances. Check every last nook and bolt-hole to make sure we haven't missed anything. We're going to check the catacombs."

Ailill looked doubtful, but he followed Conor down the stairs without question. When they emerged into the heart of the catacombs, he took the torch he'd left burning and lit the others scattered around the space.

Five tunnels branched off from the main space, including the two they had broken through with the runes. That left three unexplored. Conor nodded toward the one from which he'd seen light coming, a sure sign of human presence. The sidhe hardly needed torches. He lifted a finger to his lips and gestured for the men to follow him.

Their footsteps crunched on a scattering of gravel over the hard stone floor as they entered the tunnel. The foul smell grew steadily stronger as they proceeded. It was the stench of living men, not dead. Did that mean that prisoners might still remain?

Just as Morrigan had described, the cells were tiny holes in the rock, barred by metal grates. He held the torch out to illuminate the interiors, looking for signs of life.

The prisoners might not have been dead before, but they were now.

Dirty hands curled around the bars, faces frozen in terror and agony as if they had died mid-scream. Some of the men had bloody gashes where they had thrown themselves against the bars in an effort to get out. This must have been the source of the screaming he heard when he had played the shield around the fortress. They had been ensorcelled.

Conor pushed aside the knowledge that he was responsible for these gruesome deaths and signaled the men to follow him past the cells. The tunnel widened slightly into an alcove housing a table and two stools—a guard station. The smell of recently burned pitch still hung in the air. He touched the torch set into the bracket in the wall. Still warm. He signaled a warning to keep alert for resistance. And then he stopped short.

Sweat broke out on his forehead as he saw the small room that lay ahead. He nudged the door open with his foot. His fingers trembled around the grip of his sword.

The storeroom where he had been tortured. He'd somehow hoped the sidhe had fabricated their illusion from nothing, but now he saw they had rendered every detail faithfully. Boxes and crates packed the perimeter of the room, leaving just enough space for the trestle table to which he had been tied—or, rather, not tied. Bloodstains darkened the wood and the stones below. It may not have happened to him, but it had happened to someone else.

He backed out of the room so fast he nearly knocked Larkin over. "Keep looking. Go."

Larkin gave him a concerned look, but he led the party onward. Conor hung back to mop the sweat from his face and wrestle his breathing back under control.

It never happened. It was all in your mind. Pull yourself together.

Conor flexed his fingers around the soaked leather wrapping of his sword and forced himself forward, just as Larkin pushed open a second door. The warrior stumbled back with a cry, holding his sleeve over his nose and mouth.

"Dear Comdiu, what happened here?"

CHAPTER
TWENTY-ONE

Conor pushed his way to the front of the group out of obligation, not curiosity. The stench hit him first, the horror of the sight soon afterward. He closed his nose and squeezed his eyes shut as he pulled the door closed again. Too late. He barely made it to the side of the corridor before he emptied his stomach on the stones. From the sounds around him, he wasn't the only one.

"That explains where the inhabitants of the fortress went," he said, wiping his mouth.

"Why did we not smell them before now?" Ailill asked.

"The druid must have sealed the room with some sort of magic," Conor said. That many bodies, rotting without proper preparation or burial, should have filled the fortress with a stench that would have been noticed for miles. With the seal broken, they'd have to deal with the bodies quickly. No doubt Niall had meant them to serve a double threat, considering they had most likely been ensorcelled. The wards had at least mitigated that danger. As they'd learned from the siege on the city, the magic didn't die with its victims.

Faint sounds drifted from elsewhere in the tunnels. He held up his hand for silence and listened. Probably just the scurrying of a rat. But a rat didn't explain the light they had seen earlier or the fact that some of the prisoners had been alive just hours ago. That suggested a caretaker, one they had not found. Yet there were no other doors in this corridor, and they reached the dead end without seeing any sign of life.

The second corridor yielded nothing more than more storerooms, thankfully only containing a scattering of crates, some old weaponry, and battered furniture. Thorough examinations of the spaces revealed no one. The third and final corridor, however, yielded much more interesting results: a series of tiny rooms packed with six narrow cots.

"Soldiers' quarters," Conor said. "Cheery place to bunk."

"Better than next to dungeons," Tomey said.

None of these rooms looked as if they had been occupied for some time. Conor ran a hand across a table and held up dust-covered fingers. "Either they're far stealthier than we think or there's no one here." He realized he should have posted a guard at the near end of the corridors to ensure that no one could slip into one of the areas they'd already checked. A stupid, novice mistake. Maybe his experience really had rattled him more than he'd thought.

"Ailill, Tomey, stay here in the central chamber. Raise the alert should you see or hear anything suspicious."

Neither of them looked pleased with the assignment, but they were too well disciplined to say anything other than "Aye, sir."

Conor leaned against the wall of the main chamber and pressed his fingertips to his temples. So far none of this had gone how he'd planned. There were no guards at the fortress, though the bodies appeared to match the numbers Morrigan had revealed. There were less than a dozen men in the dungeons. So where was Meallachán?

"I want to check the cells again," Conor said, indicating he wanted Larkin to accompany him.

"Are you sure that's a good idea? If they're ensorcelled . . ."

"The wards will have driven any sorcery out." He strode back down the corridor, his sword in hand, though at this point he didn't truly expect to encounter any resistance. He breathed through his mouth to avoid vomiting again while he looked through the bars of the cells. The expressions on the faces of these men would give him nightmares for weeks. Still, he checked each cell as thoroughly as he could, peering into their dark recesses.

Then he reached the last one, and his fears were confirmed. Meallachán.

The old man was dressed in only a shift over his dirty body, sprawled against the wall in a space not even large enough to stretch out in. His eyes were closed, his face peaceful as if sleeping, though dried blood and the uneven jut of his fingers suggested torture as well. At least it didn't appear he'd been ensorcelled. But that just raised the question of how he had died. A closer look gave Conor his answer: the freshly bloodstained shift said he'd been put to the sword. Recently.

A chill shuddered through Conor's body. He'd been killed when they breached the catacombs. That meant there was at least one man at large here.

"See if you can find the keys," he said when Larkin walked up behind him. Some prickle of danger, a sense of self-preservation, made him spin just in time to raise his weapon against an incoming thrust. Not Larkin. His attacker was bulky, blond, and well fed. His clear, determined expression didn't suggest the influence of sorcery.

Before Conor could even think of mounting a defense, the man crumpled to the ground. Conor blinked until he comprehended Larkin's holding his sheathed sword like a club. He looked down at the motionless attacker. "I figured he'd be more useful to us alive. I didn't kill him, did I?"

Conor knelt to check the attacker's pulse and found it strong. "He's alive. For now." He frowned and pulled aside the man's shirt. A pink scar lay there. The shield rune. And somehow, he knew. "I presume this is Somhairle. Help me move him."

"To where?"

"To the storeroom. Somehow I have a feeling he'll be familiar with it."

Larkin looked confused, but he didn't question Conor, merely helped him hoist the man and drag him down to the room from his illusion. Conor jerked his head toward the table. "Help me lift him."

For the first time, there was a spark of disquiet in Larkin's eyes. He stayed rooted in place.

Conor shot him a stern look. "On the table. That's an order."

Doubt written all over his face, Larkin complied and then backed to the door. "What are you planning on doing?"

Conor lashed the man to the table with several lengths of bloodstained rope. "Right now? Nothing. When he wakes up? I have some questions to ask."

Larkin recoiled and Conor didn't bother to explain his thinking. He expected he would have to do little other than invoke the memories of everything Somhairle had witnessed, perhaps assisted in. At least he hoped so. But what did it say about him that Larkin thought he was capable of torture?

And what will *you do if Somhairle doesn't tell you what you want to know?*

He squared his shoulders and stuffed a rag into the prisoner's mouth. He wouldn't need to answer that question. Somhairle was a mercenary. He would do whatever it took to save his own skin.

Conor just prayed that the man's sense of self-preservation was better than his ambush skills.

✦ ✦ ✦

Conor posted a guard on the storeroom while he and Larkin went upstairs to explain the situation to the other men. "I'm questioning one man downstairs. Keep your eyes and ears open in case there are more. In old fortresses like this, it's nearly impossible to check every secret passageway and room. We'll post guards on each opening of the tunnel as well while we wait for reinforcements from Ard Dhaimhin."

"And Meallachán?" asked Cairell, one of Daigh's men.

"Dead."

"So this whole mission was a failure," Ferus said, his disappointment reflecting that of the men around them.

"Not a failure. Once we secure this fortress for Ard Dhaimhin, it will be an excellent strategic outpost for us. For now, everyone is on guard. We'll set up watches as soon as the sun comes up. But for now, stay where you are. Anyone who isn't one of us is to be captured. If you must, kill before you let anyone escape."

"Aye, sir."

Satisfied that they knew their job, Conor returned to the catacombs. Larkin rushed to catch up with him. "I'm coming with you."

"Are you my conscience now?"

"Someone needs to be."

Conor rounded on him. "Let me make one thing clear to you, Larkin. *I* am in command here. What I choose to do for the safety of our party and the success of this mission is my business. If you interfere, you'll be watching a hole at the end of the tunnel for the next two weeks. Do you understand me?"

Larkin shrank back a little, as Conor expected. "With all due respect, sir, I'll do what my conscience demands."

"As will I. Now come and keep your mouth shut." He made his voice hard, but inwardly Conor was proud of the young man for standing his ground. Principled, if more than a little naive. He had saved Conor's life, though.

Conor moved brusquely into the room where Somhairle was still tied to the table. The tension in the ropes that bound his wrists said he was awake and trying not to show it. "Remember what I said," he told Larkin. "Keep out of my way. If you're going to stay, you're going to help. Wake him up."

Larkin just lifted an eyebrow.

Conor sighed. Nuance apparently wasn't Larkin's strong suit either.

"Fine," he said. "If you won't help, you can clean up when I'm done. Blood draws rats, and we can't afford vermin in our supplies."

Larkin looked sufficiently horrified, but Conor was gratified to see movement beneath the prisoner's closed lids and a slight increase in his breathing. Good. He was afraid.

Conor didn't give him long to contemplate his situation before he struck him soundly across the face. Somhairle jerked and his eyes opened, but he didn't cry out. Conor leaned over and smiled. "Hello."

The man's eyes wavered between Conor and Larkin, then settled on Conor again.

"You should know I don't particularly enjoy torture. I tend to believe that men who inflict pain on others for their own pleasure are the smallest kind of human beings. That said, I've been on the receiving end one too many times to not see its usefulness."

Confusion showed on the man's face. That worked in Conor's favor. He continued in a neutral tone, "I already know you are Somhairle, the commander of this fortress—that is, when there was still something to command."

A slight widening of the eyes. Confirmation. Conor had guessed right. "Now I'm going to ask you a question. For every truth you tell, you get to answer another question. For every lie . . . well, you'll see." Conor removed his knives from his belt and set them on the table beside him, placing each one with a deliberate click. "You should probably know that you're not the only one to benefit from Lord Keondric's tutelage. By the time he's done, he could make a man say day is night and believe it too. Isn't that right?"

The fear emanating from the captive was so powerful that Conor could practically taste it. Another right guess. Somhairle knew exactly how the blood had stained the table and floor in this room, exactly how the bodies piled in the other storeroom had gotten there. The recollection should have sapped Conor's will to continue, but instead he felt only a cold void around him. He needed answers, and Somhairle was the only one capable of giving them.

"Ready to begin? Good." Conor pulled the rag from Somhairle's mouth. "First question: how long ago was Lord Keondric here?"

Somhairle stared at Conor. So he was going to attempt to resist? Brave for a mercenary. He moved to Somhairle's feet and sliced the laces from one of his boots, then pulled it off. He rested the cold flat of the blade against his leg, a hint. The man's muscle twitched involuntarily. Conor waited.

"One month. A little more, perhaps."

"Was that before or after Lady Morrigan escaped?"

"After."

"Good. Next question: what was he doing here?"

The prisoner didn't answer again, but it took only the scrape of the edge against the sole of Somhairle's foot to compel words, even if Conor did let the blade slip enough to bring up a tiny bright line of red. "Experiments."

"What kind of experiments?"

"I don't know. I don't understand how his magic works."

Conor didn't completely believe him, but the details didn't matter. The sidhe had already let the secret slip when they used Niall's experiments for the basis of the glamour. Still, he couldn't let him get away with an evasion without penalty. He pressed the top of the knife into the joint of the prisoner's toe, hard enough to draw a trickle of blood, and left it there.

"All right! He was trying to see what the marks would do to someone under the influence of sorcery."

"Why?"

"I don't know."

"But you can guess."

"So can you," Somhairle choked out. "I'd think he was trying to enter Ard Dhaimhin."

"And what happened to the men when they took the mark?"

"They all died screaming. Just like when the harp was played."

Conor nodded and exchanged a look with Larkin. It was what they had already expected, since in the early battles the ensorcelled warriors had died on the wards made by Meallachán's harp. Niall was indeed trying to find a way to shield himself from the city's magic without destroying himself.

"What about you? Why do you have the rune? Why did he allow you to keep it?"

"He didn't know."

"Then where did you learn it?"

Somhairle averted his eyes. His voice was low, gravelly. Had Conor not known better, he would say it held shame. "The prisoner."

"Meallachán?"

A long hesitation, then a nod.

"So you're telling me that you gave him a knife, and rather than kill you with it, he protected you from Keondric's powers. And in the end, you still killed him."

Somhairle swallowed and nodded again, his muscles tensed. Then Conor realized what the mercenary felt was not remorse but fear of retribution. He wiped a hand over his own face, pushing down the rising feel of sickness, the slow burn of anger. He would be completely within his rights to kill the man for his crimes. No one would blame him; no one would question it. In fact, given that he bore the rune, he was too dangerous to be left alive.

Conor tested the edge of the blade with his thumb, considering. Somhairle's eyes followed the movement, resigned to his fate, his thoughts tracking with Conor's own.

Abruptly, he shoved the rag in Somhairle's mouth and strode from the room, leaving him tied to the table. Larkin followed, questions in his eyes, but Conor silenced him with a look. He didn't want to explain why he'd made the choice he had.

Because for a split second, in the mercenary's coldness and resignation, he had seen himself.

CHAPTER
TWENTY-TWO

"My lady."

Aine groaned into her pillow and pulled the coverlet over her head. Surely it couldn't be morning already. That meant this was simply another dream in a series of awful ones.

"My lady, you need to wake up and eat something. It's nearly supper."

The voice sounded vaguely familiar, but she couldn't bring to mind a name for the speaker. She squinted in the dim light that spilled through the window. "It's early yet. The sun is not even up."

"The sun is about to go down, my lady."

Morrigan stood at the edge of the bed, looking even more uncomfortable about her presence than Aine felt. "Master Eoghan has sent me up to check on you several times, but he insists you eat. If not for you, for your child."

Eoghan. Of course he would be checking on her. The fact that he sent Morrigan seemed to imply other intentions, though. She pushed herself up on one elbow and shoved her hair out of her eyes. "I've slept all day?"

"Aye, my lady."

She must have been more exhausted from last night's ordeal than she'd thought. Last night's ordeal. The siege on Ard Bealach. How could she have fallen asleep? Why hadn't Conor contacted her? She sat straight up, her heart leaping into action. "What news? Is it done? Have we heard?"

Morrigan's smile broke through her worried expression. "Aye, my lady. It's over. We won. The bird arrived a few hours ago."

Aine's relief whistled out with her sigh. "Thank Comdiu. Casualties? Conor?"

"Conor is fine, my lady. Only one man lost, none wounded. An answer to prayers."

"Indeed," she murmured, though she couldn't help but feel a pang of sorrow for whoever the lost man was. She had known much of the party only by sight, but they were still part of the city—still part of the brotherhood—and knowing Conor, he would feel responsible for that life.

"Brothers Eoghan and Riordan wish you to dine with them if you feel well enough. Should I tell them you'll join them, or will you take your supper here?" Morrigan's voice was perfectly polite and measured, but there was something underlying it that said she resented being sent to fetch and carry.

"Why are you here? There are a number of women they could have asked."

"I suspect this is Master Eoghan's way of giving me something to do while he still keeps an eye on me. And perhaps reminding me that I'm at your mercy."

"If you want to leave your chamber, aye, I suspect that's right." Aine nodded her head toward the table holding her toiletries. "I'll eat with them. While you're here, will you help me with my hair?"

"Aye, my lady." She didn't seem perturbed or insulted by the question, merely retrieved the brush and gestured for Aine to move to the chair. Morrigan drew the brush through her hair with surprising gentleness, but she didn't say anything.

"Tell me one thing, Morrigan. Why did you not warn the men about the sidhe?"

Morrigan's movements faltered. "The sidhe?"

"Aye. Surely you knew about them. You must have realized the influence they had at Ard Bealach and how the rune rendered them powerless. Why did you let Conor and the rest of the men go in without knowing what they would face?"

"I don't know what you mean."

"Don't lie to me, Morrigan. You have been holding back, if not telling complete fibs, and it almost cost Conor his life." She twisted around to stare into Morrigan's eyes, to impress on her the seriousness of her intentions. "If I tell Eoghan that you're a threat, you will be put in the dungeons. However soft you may think me, I will make it so you never see the light of day. So tell me the truth, and Comdiu help you if you lie to me."

"I do not think of you as soft, my lady," Morrigan said. She put down the brush and moved to the edge of the bed. "Anything but, in fact. Anyone can see—"

"And now you are attempting to manipulate me."

Morrigan's expression closed. "The truth doesn't help you, Lady Aine. The truth is, I have no idea how much of what happened there was real and how much was an illusion."

"So Meallachán might not even be there? That could have all been a fabrication of the sidhe?"

"It's possible, but not likely. Their glamour is one that steals your worst fears and amplifies them. At least that's what I believe now. What I endured at Somhairle's hands—I think that was real. But I have no way of knowing for sure."

Despite the fact Morrigan had not been completely honest

since she arrived, Aine wanted to believe she was finally telling the truth. "Why not just admit it? Why not just be honest from the start?"

Morrigan trembled—with anger, Aine thought. "Because what happened to me took something from me. My pride. My free will. It doesn't matter if my body experienced it. My mind still remembers."

She couldn't have said anything that would strike deeper to the heart. Aine had tried to tell herself that Conor would be okay, that because what he'd experienced had happened only in his mind, he'd be able to forget it. But the depth of the mental torture he'd experienced, so intense he had been on the brink of death—that could be something from which he might never fully recover. Even worse was the realization that he had lived out his greatest fears—and memories. How much of that had he actually experienced at the hands of the Sofarende? How much had he kept hidden from her?

Like the woman you saw in his mind?

She pulled that thought out ruthlessly, even though it had planted itself in the back of her mind like a weed. She had no way of knowing if that were real. Perhaps he only feared that weakness. She owed him the opportunity to tell her the truth in person.

Aine cleared her throat. "Finish my hair, if you would, please."

"Of course, my lady." Morrigan straightened herself quickly and picked up the brush before going back to work on a simple braid. When she was finished, she tied it with a ribbon and smoothed down the back of Aine's dress. "There. Neat and simple."

"Thank you for your help, Morrigan. And your honesty. I wish it had come sooner."

Morrigan just bowed her head to accept the chastisement. But when Aine rose to leave, her hand shot out and clamped around Aine's wrist. "My lady, just beware. You may think they have your best interests in mind, but they will use you until you are no more help to them. And then they will discard you."

Aine just stared, shocked by the vehemence of Morrigan's words. In contrast to her usual strategic, calculated speech, she sensed sincerity in the warning. "Why would you say that?"

"Because it's what men do."

Aine swallowed, unable to put together a response. Instead, she just nodded and continued past Morrigan's guards to the great hall to meet with Eoghan and Riordan.

But when she arrived, the entire Conclave waited. Gradaigh stood when he saw her. "Lady Aine, the heroine of the moment."

She looked around at the men's earnest expressions. "I don't understand."

"You broke the glamour, my lady," Eoghan said. "We owe you our success at Ard Bealach."

He pulled out the chair between him and Riordan, and she sat, still bewildered. "I broke nothing. I merely convinced Conor that what he was seeing was not real."

"Well, the service that you did for him is a service to us all." Gradaigh gave her a smile that made her vaguely uncomfortable, and she focused instead on serving herself a portion of the hot stew that sat on the table before her. "Have you heard anything from him yet?"

"No. And I wouldn't expect to until later tonight." She stared at her stew silently, willing him to leave her alone. She couldn't relive what had happened last night. Those memories would haunt her without giving them voice. But she could see that the men were disappointed she wouldn't tell them more.

They will use you until you are no more help to them.

No. She wouldn't let Morrigan's twisted outlook poison her mind.

When she looked up again, Eoghan was watching her with an uncomfortably piercing expression. Then he gave her a little nod and addressed the rest of the table. "We have a decision to make, brothers. The fortress needs a commander now that Daigh is gone, and Conor is needed back at Ard Dhaimhin right away."

"It was Daigh who died?" she blurted. "How?"

"He never woke from the glamour," Eoghan explained. "The fortress was deserted, so there were no other casualties."

She really needed to speak with Conor now. Why were the sidhe protecting an unmanned fortress? Where were all the men? And had Conor been even closer to death than she had thought?

She made it through the rest of supper without being pressed for information. After a lengthy debate, the Conclave selected a man Aine didn't know to take command of the fortress and then excused themselves. Aine lingered behind and Eoghan remained seated beside her. "Is there something wrong, my lady?"

That was a question she couldn't begin to answer. There was nothing right about this whole situation. "Lady Morrigan says she knew about the sidhe."

He let out a little sigh. "I was afraid of that. I trusted that you would understand why I sent her to you. Did she say anything else?"

"She's angry. Whether what she experienced at Ard Bealach was real or imagined, she holds all men responsible."

"I suppose I can't entirely blame her for that," Eoghan said. "Do you think you can get her to open up?"

"I don't know. I think she sees me as her jailer, in a way. And that makes me the enemy. Worse yet, a collaborator."

"Noted. I wish there were something we could do, but I simply don't trust her enough to give her access to the rest of Ard Dhaimhin, which is what I suspect she wants most of all.

Especially now that she's proven herself to be holding back important information." He hesitated. "Lady Aine, I know you don't want to talk about what happened last night. But is there anything else we need to know? Did Conor tell you anything you haven't mentioned to us?"

That he wanted to die? That he loved her? That he feared she would turn to Eoghan in his absence? No, she would never betray Conor's confidence by giving away what he had thought in pain and despair and weakness.

"Nothing," she said finally.

"Let us know when he contacts you tonight. We'll wait up in the Ceannaire's office. And if you need anything . . ."

"Aye. Thank you." She rose and then paused. "Eoghan?"

"Aye, my lady?" His expression was completely open, guileless, but the eagerness in his expression was almost painful to see.

"Nothing. I'll let you know what I learn."

She fled to her room, praying as she went. For wisdom, for favor, for Conor's swift return.

And that he would still be the person she remembered when he came back.

CHAPTER
TWENTY-THREE

Conor ordered Somhairle placed in a small, dank cell in the newly emptied dungeons with only the rats for company while he decided what to do with him. He had given up his secrets so freely that Conor didn't trust him not to have a bigger game in mind. He couldn't risk his attempting to sway or deceive the Fíréin should they be allowed to have contact with him.

After securing the fortress, the next order of business was to give Daigh and Meallachán the proper funeral rites in the fortress's courtyard. Conor had never liked the Conclave member, but his short eulogy reflected the respect he had come to bear him. What it didn't convey was his guilt. Had he worked faster on the rune, had he decided to play the wards into place first, Daigh might still be alive.

Meallachán was more difficult. He had been Conor's mentor once, the one who had helped him discover his musical gift. Yet there were indications that he had worked with the enemy to break the wards, an action that cost them the war in the kingdoms. What could Conor say about one of their own who may or may not have been a traitor?

In the end, he spoke noncommittal words of sorrow and regret and commended the old bard's spirit to its Maker, as he had with Daigh. They witnessed the bodies turned to ash and the fire burned to coals, numbness on Conor's part standing in for solemnity. When it was done at last, he retreated to an upper chamber overlooking the courtyard and sank onto the edge of the shelf bed.

By all accounts, the mission had been a success. They'd taken the fortress bloodlessly, with only one loss of their own. The wards he had erected around Ard Bealach would protect men from both the sidhe and the druid's ensorcelled men. Tomorrow they would assess the defenses and supplies and determine how many warriors to request from Ard Dhaimhin.

Tonight, though, he had to tell those back at Carraigmór that the druid had the shield rune and was looking for a way to use it to enter Ard Dhaimhin.

Aine, are you there?

Nearly immediately, her voice came back in his head. *I'm here. I was waiting. Is everything all right? Settled?*

For the time being.

Conor, what's wrong? He felt a tremor in her question.

Nothing's wrong. No, that's not true. Is Eoghan or my father with you?

No, I'm alone.

You might want to get them. I'll wait.

Minutes passed. Conor took the opportunity to explore his temporary chamber. He realized when he rummaged through the wardrobe that this must be Somhairle's chamber. Could there be anything useful here? His eye fell on a small, polished box of burled wood, secured with a brass lock. He took the dagger from his boot and worked the long, thin blade into the lock.

Conor?

The blade slipped from the metal and jabbed into a finger of his opposite hand. He shoved it into his mouth. *What?*

Is everything all right?

Aye, you simply startled me. Who's there with you?

Eoghan and Riordan. Conor, you're frightening me.

He couldn't figure out what she had to be frightened about, so he brushed off the comment. *Niall was here after Morrigan left, experimenting on ensorcelled men. With runes.*

How do you know?

Conor got the sense this was a question from one of the men. *We captured Somhairle and I . . . questioned him.*

What does that mean?

That question was all from Aine, once more tinged with fear. He ignored it. *Niall knows about the shield rune. I'm not clear if he learned it from Meallachán or vice versa. Either way, I think he's trying to figure out a way to negate the wards around Ard Dhaimhin. So far he hasn't had any luck because sorcery added to runic magic always ends badly.*

This isn't good, Aine replied after a few moments. *But as long as he still has the sorcery in his blood, he can't use it on himself.*

Aine, with the sorcery in his blood, he shouldn't be able to use it at all.

A long pause. *I'll contact you tomorrow when I've had a chance to converse with Eoghan and Riordan. I love you, Conor.*

Good. At least he didn't have to be part of the discussion that would ensue at Ard Dhaimhin. He could barely put two coherent sentences together at this point, let alone try to antici-pate what Niall would do next. He looked down at the smear of blood on his hands and tunic and shoved his cut finger back into his mouth as he returned to working the lock.

Blood flooded his mouth.

The blade slipped and scored the surface of the wooden box.

He screamed in agony as the druid began to pry another of his teeth loose.

Blood smeared the surface of the wooden box, making it hard to see what he was doing, making it hard to work the knife.

This wasn't about the magic anymore. Niall wanted to break him, to see if it was his will that was blocking the sorcery or if it was the rune itself.

Conor threw down the box and backed away in horror as he saw the cuts on his hands, the gouges on the wood he didn't remember making. *It's not real. Comdiu, please. It wasn't real. It was an illusion. It wasn't real.*

He poured water into the basin and washed the wounds, but his blood staining the water pink and smearing the earthenware pitcher started a trembling that he couldn't stop.

No. He had to stop thinking about it. He had to stop remembering.

His eyes traveled to the wooden box on the floor. The lid had broken off the hinges on its impact with the stone, spilling out its contents. He ripped the face cloth by the basin in half and wrapped the pieces around each hand and then knelt beside the box.

He'd been hoping for something helpful to his cause: a map, letters, something rune-etched. Instead, there was a tiny bubbled glass vial, sealed with paraffin, no larger than his thumb. He turned it over in his hand. Why would Somhairle keep something like this locked away? It had the feeling of a secret. A contingency plan.

Poison.

He stared at it for a long moment, fascinated. If Aine were here, she might be able to identify it by color or odor or consistency. She'd be able to tell him its effects. If Somhairle had been saving it for murder—to use against the druid, for example—Conor would bet on slow and painful. If he'd been saving it for himself, it would likely be far less traumatic. Either way, Conor had the suspicion it would get the job done.

He replaced the broken box on the table, intending to replace the vial as well. It wasn't until he went to remove his weapons that he realized his hand seemed to have taken on a will of its own and slipped the poison into his belt pouch.

He wavered for a moment, then left it where it lay.

✦ ✦ ✦

"I'm concerned about Conor." Aine twisted handfuls of wool cloth before she realized she was mangling her only skirt and dropped it abruptly.

Riordan leaned back against the table in the Ceannaire's office. "What makes you say that?"

She hesitated. How could she explain what she had felt from Conor without raising too much concern? His thoughts had a recklessness to them, a desperation, a confusion—all completely reasonable reactions considering what he'd experienced. It didn't matter that it hadn't actually happened in the flesh. "I think he's coping the best he can, but you need to send Daigh's replacement immediately."

"Do you question his judgment?" Eoghan asked quietly from his post against the wall.

"No, I question his safety." And that of the prisoner at Ard Bealach. She hadn't missed how he'd glossed over the method of questioning Somhairle, even if she didn't get the feeling he'd done anything particularly terrible to him. But the anger she sensed beneath the surface was altogether out of character.

"Why did I not go with them?" she murmured.

"For this very reason," Eoghan said firmly. "You are our only connection to Conor and Ard Bealach. What if you were compromised and we didn't know it? The damage you could do . . ."

Eoghan was right. Eoghan was always right, because he never let emotion cloud his judgment.

"Do you think what he said about the runes is accurate?"

"If Somhairle is truthful, aye. Conor is not lying. He would not lie about that."

"No one is implying that he would." Riordan placed a hand on her shoulder, but she shook it off. He studied her and then said, "You should rest, my lady. Conor isn't the only one who experienced something terrible."

"We still haven't decided a course of action," she said.

"And we won't tonight." Eoghan gentled his voice. "Sleep first. It will all be clearer after some rest and prayer."

She bowed her head in acknowledgement and exited the study, though with the way her mind was spinning, she doubted she could rest. Once more, they were at a disadvantage. If they were to win this fight, they needed to be a step ahead of Niall, not two steps behind. And they needed Conor to be clearheaded and stable.

Usually Aine made a conscious effort to block out the minds of those around her while she slept. Only those to whom she was closest—like Conor—ever managed to breach that barrier. But Conor was hundreds of miles away in a mountain fortress. She might not hear him if he called out for her, assuming he overcame his stubbornness. Even though she knew the risk, tonight she left those doors to her mind open.

She dozed more than slept that night, tossed in a relentless sea of other people's dreams until a single voice snapped her to attention.

Aine.

She sat straight up in bed, sleep fleeing. Moonlight still shone through the window.

Who's there? It was a futile effort, a thought cast into darkness, considering she had no idea whom she was addressing.

Aine, please help me. I don't understand what happened. I don't know where I am. Can you even hear me?

Gooseflesh broke out over her arms. It couldn't be. And yet somehow, she knew that voice. No, more than that, she recognized that soul.

Keondric.

Not Niall in Keondric's body, that unsettling mismatch of soul and flesh, but the man who had sacrificed himself to let Conor and Aine escape when she was being held captive at Glenmallaig.

Except that was impossible. No body could contain two souls. The druid had displaced Keondric when he took control. This had to be some trauma-induced hallucination.

If it's you, answer this question. The first day I saw you at Abban's camp, what was I doing? Whom was I healing?

The pause stretched so long Aine thought sure she had proved this was an imposter, perhaps the druid himself, trying to trap her. And then a slightly puzzled reply came back.

You healed no one that I saw, my lady. You had returned from Fíréin territory. I conveyed my respect for your bravery.

Aine sucked in a breath so quickly it stung her lungs. They had been in a warded camp, supposedly immune from magical eavesdropping. No one else could have been able to answer that question so specifically.

Keondric was still alive—or, rather, he was still present in some way. Did that mean he was still in his own body, alongside the druid's soul? How had he known to reach out to her in the first place?

Tell me where you are now. Do you know?

She waited, holding her breath for the answer. If he knew where he was, they would know where the druid was. She cast about her consciousness for Keondric's presence, but she could grasp nothing. It was as if he had ceased to exist.

But that couldn't be true either. Niall had to be suppressing his soul, his consciousness, so that he could control his body. If Keondric had contacted her once, he could do it again. In fact, now she felt sure this had not been his first attempt.

Aine jumped out of bed and darted from her room, grabbing her shawl as she went. Her feet seemed to carry her without conscious thought to Eoghan's chamber, where she pounded hard enough to wake the entire keep.

The door flung open. Eoghan stood there, wild-eyed and dressed in only a knee-length shirt, a bared sword in hand. He froze when he saw Aine. "What is it? What's wrong?"

"I need to speak with you." Aine averted her eyes from his half-dressed state.

"Just stay there. I'll be—just don't go anywhere."

She paced little circles in the corridor until the door opened again. Eoghan stepped out, now unarmed and stuffing his shirt into the waistband of his trousers, though like Aine he hadn't bothered with shoes. "What is it, my lady? Is it Conor?"

"No, nothing like that." She lowered her voice. "Keondric's alive."

"I don't understand."

"Keondric Mac Eirhinin, the man whose body Niall took. His soul. It's still here. It's still in his body."

Eoghan stared at her as though she'd come unhinged. "That's impossible."

"Aye, impossible, but true. Don't you see? If his soul is still there, that's why Niall can use the runes. Keondric was—is—a Balian. He was gifted. He had abilities similar to the Fíréin."

"But Balians can't be possessed."

Aine huffed in frustration. "I know that. But this is different somehow. Don't ask me how it happened. Keondric is still there, and he managed to take control long enough to contact me. More than once, I think. Maybe he's getting stronger."

"If he is, perhaps he could push the druid down." Eoghan grabbed her shoulders, his face alight with excitement. "Do you have any idea what this means? If we—you—can get to him, we could end this completely. Let's find Riordan and wake the others."

"Wait." She didn't want to dampen his enthusiasm, but he hadn't thought this through. "There's another possibility. I don't think the druid knows that Keondric is still present. I don't think he realizes why he can use the runes or the extent of what he can do while he's sharing the body with a Balian soul."

A horrified look crossed Eoghan's face. "What are you saying?"

"If he learns he can use the runes because of Keondric, he'll realize he can take the shield rune without risking death. And there will be nothing stopping him from just walking into Ard Dhaimhin."

✦ ✦ ✦

"What you are saying shouldn't be possible." Riordan's words were disbelieving, but they held more wonder than skepticism.

"I understand that. But I verified that it was him. He knew things that even Niall couldn't know." Aine looked around the table to see how the others were taking the news. For the second time in a handful of hours, she found herself surrounded by the entire Conclave, though this time she didn't mind being the focus of attention.

"Surely this doesn't change anything," Fechin said. "He is still infected with the sorcery. That alone would keep him from crossing the city's wards."

"Except the presence of Keondric's soul has already proven to be a buffer between sorcery and the runes. That's why he's been able to use them on others. Add the shield rune and he would be impervious to any magic, including the city's wards."

"Here's what we know," Eoghan said. "Niall has been experimenting with the shield rune on ensorcelled men to see if he could move them into Ard Dhaimhin, but they died in the process. He won't be anxious to try it on himself. As long as he doesn't know of Keondric's presence, he won't take the risk. But he can use the runes individually, which is why he's attempting to collect them from the old fortresses."

"So Keondric is the key," Gradaigh said.

Eoghan nodded. "The way I see it, we can use this information in two ways. We can try to prevent him from getting the runes and assume he won't attempt to enter the city. But that's a temporary plan at best. Or we can have Aine contact Keondric and try to seize control of his body from Niall. But if he's unsuccessful, we risk hastening the very scenario we are trying to prevent."

"Realistically, what is the danger he could do if he himself could enter Ard Dhaimhin?" Dal asked.

"He was once the Ceannaire. He could conceivably still be able to open the Hall of Prophecies. And once he did, he would have access to everything, including the Oath-Binding Sword." Eoghan dragged his hands through his hair, loosening strands from his braid without noticing. "Remember, the runic magic is dangerous enough that it's been removed from our grasp twice in the last thousand years. What could a man with truly evil intent accomplish with that knowledge?"

They fell silent, mulling the possibilities. Each way involved its own risks, and not just to them. For the first time, Aine truly understood why Balus had said that the storm of darkness must be stopped in Seare before it spread over the face of the earth. The runic magic was nearly limitless. Niall could become the emperor of the known world with a combination of magic, sorcery, and the sidhe to enforce his unholy will.

He could usher in a true age of darkness.

"There is one possibility we're not considering," Aine said. "Keondric should not still be here. He should have moved on to his eternal rest. Without his presence, the druid has nothing."

"You're suggesting we figure out how to get Keondric's soul out of his body and give it completely over to Niall?" Gradaigh asked incredulously.

"No, I'm suggesting we let him know he can enter Ard Dhaimhin's wards and *then* we help Keondric's soul go to its eternal rest. And then let the wards do what the wards will do."

The men's faces showed their doubt, but Riordan and Eoghan wore expressions of admiration. Eoghan began to smile. "It's bold, Lady Aine, I'll give you that."

"It's a last resort," she said. "But one we can't afford to ignore."

"Conor won't be happy with the idea of Aine's putting herself at risk," Riordan said.

Aine shook her head. "Conor can't know—at least not yet. I won't have him distracted from his other tasks when we aren't even certain it's necessary or possible."

"Aine's right," Eoghan said. "I'd like to know if she can get through to Keondric at all. If Niall becomes aware of what she's doing, then we move on to . . . the desperate options."

"You realize that if we fail, if the druid wins, we all die." Fechin looked around the table seriously. "Seare will be gone and a good portion of the world with us."

"That's always been the case," Eoghan murmured. "But now we finally have a plan to stop it."

+ + +

Eoghan remained behind, staring into the shadowy recesses of Carraigmór's great hall, after the others returned to their chambers. As many times as he was awakened or surprised from sleep, he should simply make his bed in the hall and save himself some time. Not that he'd be sleeping anytime soon. The new revelations, problems, and challenges pouring in every day ensured that every minute of his sleep was plagued with concern or guilt.

They'd thought the fact Niall was mounting an army was the worst part, but the collection of the runes was far more dangerous. The fact he'd slaughtered dozens of his own men experimenting with the runes only highlighted how brutal and ruthless he would be were he ever to get the opportunity to rule. And Eoghan was asking the people he loved most in the world to face this man, while he stayed safe and protected inside. He had no family, no one to miss him if he died. It should be him out there risking his life.

Do you see My plan so clearly that you can make that statement? Do you presume to be the Creator so that you can decide who should live or die?

Why is it terrible to want to save my friends from harm? Is it not Lord Balus's teaching to risk one's life for one's friends?

You act not out of love but out of pride. You would sacrifice to be seen sacrificing. You wish to be the savior. But sometimes to lead is to sacrifice glory.

Comdiu was rarely so blunt with him. He bowed his head and took the weight of the correction. *What do I do, then?*

Obey. Act when you must act, and wait when you must wait. Comdiu's tone softened. *Have faith that you were chosen for this task at this moment for a purpose.*

Eoghan propped his head in his hands. Comdiu could not

have been any clearer. Eoghan was to rule, whether that meant coordinating mundane tasks or making decisions about the lives of his men.

Except he knew what else needed to be done, and he didn't want to do it.

He pushed himself away from the table and walked to the Rune Throne, cast in shadow in the dim light. Even now, he had a hard time focusing on all the runes at once. They swam together, joining and separating in his vision. Here and there he could pick out the ones he knew: the three-spoked wheel, the symbol of Comdiu; the sword, which translated to "protection"; the softening rune, which could crumble rock and yet somehow did not affect the Rune Throne. Clearly, there was much they didn't understand about this magic. There was so much out there, littered across Seare, that had the potential to cause harm.

There was no question what had to be done. And as much as Aine would hate him for the decision, there was no question who had to do it.

CHAPTER
TWENTY-FOUR

Sleep did not come. Or rather, Conor fled from it each time his eyes closed and the memories crowded back in. Instead, he spent the night pacing, working sword forms, examining every item in the room. He thought perhaps he could learn something about Somhairle from his possessions, but they were straightforward and nonspecific. Seareann-style clothing. A straight razor and shaving bowl with a tiny brass mirror. A leather saddlebag. In fact, the only thing of interest was the poison.

Conor spent a fair amount of time turning the vial over in his hands, wondering what it meant. It had been locked away, which meant that it was not meant to be a swift end in the event of a capture. If he'd planned to use it for himself, which Conor suspected he had, that meant he was afraid, and for good reason. Somhairle had seen an entire fortress annihilated by the druid's experiments, yet he survived. What about him had caused Niall to leave him alone?

Conor dropped the vial back into his belt pouch, shrugged on his sword, and strode out of the chamber. He didn't stop when he hit the great hall but instead proceeded to the dungeons.

The smell hit him immediately, bad enough in small doses as it drifted throughout the upper floors of the keep, but so strong up close it made him gag. He went to the last tiny cell—the one in which Meallachán had been kept—and squatted down beside the bars.

Somhairle didn't open his eyes, but he obviously sensed Conor's presence. "Are you going to threaten me again?"

"Not this time. What I want to know has no strategic importance."

Somhairle turned his head and looked him in the eye. Conor expected malice, but all he saw was a cold, deep emptiness.

"Couldn't sleep, could you?"

Conor lowered himself to the ground beside the cell and leaned against the stone wall. "No."

"This place does that to a man. The screaming." He gave Conor a chilling smile. "Even when it's silent, it's there. In the stones. Waiting."

"You supervised the experiments."

"Some of them."

"Why?"

"The most capable man is the last to die."

Conor's skin prickled. There was something unearthly about the conversation—a lack of emotion in words that should be fraught with it. Somhairle could feel emotion, Conor knew, because he had seen fear. He fished out the vial and held it up. "What is this?"

Conor was sure he wouldn't answer, but he only smiled. "Hemlock."

"For yourself?"

"For myself. For others. Poison does not differentiate. It's fair. Unlike the human heart and mind."

"The most capable man may be the last to die, but he still dies. So why are you here?"

Somhairle didn't answer. He just stared at the ceiling of the cell. "The funny thing about torture is that it can make a man admit to anything, say up is down and believe it. You said that, didn't you? But it's purifying, those thoughts that come right before death. The things men say when they want pain to stop, they're telling. They appeal to your humanity, your compassion, all the things they still want to believe exist in the world, as if that's their last chance to prove it." He turned his head. "Pain is a mirror."

"What did you see, then? What do you want to believe still exists in the world?"

"Self-interest. I don't need to believe. I know." Somhairle sent him a knowing smile. "Your kind doesn't believe in torture. It's your weakness. It always has been. Expedience, aye, but in duty to the greater good."

"Then why did you tell me what I wanted to know?"

Somhairle's grin widened to show a row of crooked teeth. "I already told you. Because you wanted revenge for what was done to you. Information was just an excuse." The smile turned feral. "Sometimes the mirror goes both ways, doesn't it?"

Conor stood abruptly and dropped the vial back into his pouch. He wanted to believe that the man was mad, but in reality he was simply amoral. He'd said it himself. He did what he needed to do to save his own skin, to achieve his own ends.

That wasn't what Conor had done. Not at all. The information he gained from him was vital, but there was only so far he would have taken things.

He tried to shut out Somhairle's laughter, but it followed him all the way up the stairs.

✦ ✦ ✦

As soon as day broke, Conor gathered the men together in the great hall, twenty-two warriors who looked only slightly more rested than he felt.

"Our goal today is to clear the chamber of the bodies before they can cause disease."

"Or permanently foul the fortress with the stench," Ailill muttered, looking less than pleased by the job.

"Indeed. Ailill, you can be in charge of finding the handcarts to transport them. Our best bet is to wheel them down the tunnels and burn the bodies in the canyon. Best to confine any potential . . . mess . . . to the lower levels."

The looks passed around showed exactly how the men felt about those prospects. Larkin spoke up. "If we're going back into the pass, won't we be vulnerable to the sidhe again?"

"I have an idea for that. In the meantime, I need six men on watch, and the rest in teams of five to clear the chamber."

Conor sorted them out quickly—those on watch far more pleased than the others—and then retreated to his chamber. Larkin's question highlighted the bigger concern he'd been mulling. If his men had been susceptible to the sidhe in the passes, the reinforcements from Ard Dhaimhin would be in even more danger now that the spirits had been deprived of their victims.

Conor took the stairs to the upper floor two at a time and staggered as the corridor swayed around him, the effects of little food and no sleep. Once they cleaned the storerooms, they could assess their supplies. He was counting on the hope that the fortress had stored up food for the cold seasons.

Up in his borrowed chamber, he retrieved his harp case and then returned to the hall, where he pulled up a chair. *Let this work*, he thought, partly a plea to Comdiu and partly a reminder to him to focus through his exhaustion. He sat, adjusted the strings that had already gotten out of tune again, and then closed his eyes to visualize the passes that connected the High City and Ard Bealach.

Blue fire danced along his skin, searing but not consuming.

Conor jolted upright with a gasp. It had taken that little, just closing his eyes, to doze off and be drawn back into the nightmare. He wiped his sweaty palms on his trousers and laid his hands against the strings. He couldn't sleep. He couldn't be drawn back in. He would be of no use here, and there was far too much for him to do to crumble.

The pass. The long stretch of road that connected the edge of Ard Dhaimhin's domain to the downward slope of the mountain range. What they needed was a corridor, a tunnel of magic. When the notes rang from the harp, they took similar form to the song he had played before, now so natural that he didn't think about anything but his need. In his mind's eye, he used the notes to bend the magic through space, sending it rolling like a flood through the canyon to where it met the edge of Ard Dhaimhin's domain. It felt like a sigh when the edges of the ward met and melded together into one large, misshapen carpet of golden light. He opened his eyes, satisfied. It was done. And even more surprising, it had been easy.

He returned the harp to its case and the case to his chamber, looking longingly at the bed before he returned to the catacombs where the men continued to work. They had almost completely finished relocating the bodies outside, where they would incinerate them upon the pyre. It would be like a smoke signal to anyone in the area, but there was nothing to be done about that. The craggy topography made digging a mass grave difficult, not to mention the manpower it would consume from their limited resources.

When he encountered Larkin returning with an empty hand-cart, the man stared at him with a slight air of awe. "You did something again. I felt it."

"Aye. The men coming to join us should have nothing to fear from the sidhe."

"That easy?"

"That easy."

Larkin seemed to be thinking, debating. "Why haven't you done this elsewhere? Gone around the towns and played wards around them?"

It was a legitimate question. It wasn't as if the idea hadn't occurred to Conor, but the risks had as well. "I'm the only one left who can play the wards, especially now that Meallachán is dead. The only reason I dare do it here is because we're secure behind walls and the druid can't pass through our defenses. Out in the open, though, it would take only a well-paid assassin to kill me—or a well-aimed arrow."

Larkin nodded slowly. "You're too valuable to our efforts to lose. It's a shame we can't protect the entire island."

It was. Niggling guilt started to creep in, but Conor shut it out. Leadership may bring the privilege of delegating the most unpleasant tasks, but it also brought the necessity of making hard decisions. It made no sense for him to risk everything to help individuals when his larger responsibility was to end the threat all of them faced. Wasn't it?

By the end of the day, the unpleasant task had been completed: the bodies burned on a great pyre, the putrescence scrubbed from the chamber with lye and water. The faint smell of corruption lingered, but it was at least bearable on the lower level again. In the root cellar, they even managed to find vegetables and salted meat, which two brothers turned into a nourishing stew for supper. They ate in shifts with the change of the watch, Conor offering what encouragement he could muster. Then he retreated to his chamber once more.

When Conor called out to Aine, she was waiting for him. *Conor. Thank Comdiu. It's late. What's wrong?*

Nothing's wrong. The fortress is secured, bodies disposed of. He struggled to form the words in his head. The weariness was too deep, his sorrow over all that had happened too great. He was swiftly sliding into numbness and exhaustion.

Conor, try to rest. I know it's not pleasant—

Pleasant? Try torturous. Literally. He gave a harsh laugh. The fact that the dreams weren't real—that the torture had never been real—made it no less vivid in his mind.

They have selected Nuada to command the fortress. He commanded a céad of archers here at Ard Dhaimhin.

I know him. He's capable.

Aye. He and another fifty men will be there in a fortnight, and then you can come home.

Right. Home. He rubbed his temples with his fingers and flopped back on the bed. *They shouldn't have the problems that we had on the way.* He filled her in on what he had done with the harp earlier that day. It felt so distant and unimportant now.

That's incredible! We will be able to move freely. Do you think you could do it—

In other places? No. I've tried before. Aine, I'm exhausted. Can we just speak tomorrow?

A long pause. He felt her hurt even though she tried to keep her reply cheerful. *Aye, we can do this tomorrow. You might like to know, though . . . the baby is kicking. I can feel it from the outside now. Riordan felt his grandson move today.*

That's wonderful. He said the words in his head, but there was no real enthusiasm attached to it. He couldn't generate the emotion. *I'll be home soon to feel it myself.*

You will. Conor?

Aye?

Please, just . . . don't do anything drastic. I know you think you're being rational right now, but you've seen and experienced things no man should have to. At some point, you're going to have to talk—

At some point I will, just not now. There is a job to be done. Tomorrow, Aine. He slammed the door shut on his mind as she had taught him, though he suspected she could still find a way in if she tried. What had she seen that prompted the lecture? Was she just sensing his despair and weariness? Or had she seen the thing that he had kept hidden but unforgotten?

He took the vial from his pouch and set it on the stool beside the bed. Tiny. Innocuous. Dangerous. Yet it somehow made him feel better having it there while he rested. His body was too exhausted to pace the floor for another night, but his mind quailed at the idea of closing his eyes. He would just stretch out and ease his muscles for a bit before he found other occupations for the night.

The minute his body hit the horizontal, he was asleep.

+ + +

Pain. Blood. Screaming. All his own. A quiet voice that managed to be chilling instead of soothing. That was someone else's, even though he couldn't figure out who it belonged to. He strained against his bonds, blood and sweat chafing his skin beneath the ropes.

This is just a dream. This isn't real. You can wake up now.

Except he couldn't.

CHAPTER
TWENTY-FIVE

Aine gasped awake, curling around her belly to protect her baby from another blow. Only then did she realize that she was safe in her bed at Ard Dhaimhin.

It had only been a dream.

She pushed her wet hair away from her forehead and rolled onto her back, drawing in deep breaths to flush out the fear that remained. It had been a dream, but not her own. Conor's.

The memory of the things she had relived along with him hit her at the same time her stomach decided to give up its pretense of being settled, and she barely made it to the chamber pot. She'd thought she'd known what he'd been through.

She'd had absolutely no idea.

Aine slumped back against the wall, welcoming the cold of the stones as it seeped through her shift and cooled her feverish body. She'd left her mind open to Conor for this very reason, but she'd never thought she could get dragged into his dream. He'd even known it was a dream, but try as he might, he hadn't been able to break free. And tied to him as she was, neither had she.

Dear Comdiu, I pray Your peace upon us. No wonder Conor

was so edgy and irritable. He was trying to block out the memories of the sidhe's glamour while trying not to fall asleep. *Take these memories. Or make them livable.*

She finally pushed herself off the floor and walked in a cramped shuffle back to the bed, her muscles screaming from what must have been a clenched position most of the night. Then another pain hit her, a tightening in her belly.

Birth pains.

"No no no," she murmured, stretching out on the bed immediately. "It's too early." She was only five months along, much too early to be having labor pains. If the baby was born now, he or she had no chance of survival. She had assisted in too many early births, seen too many children born unformed before their time. It could not happen to her child.

She breathed deeply and counted in her mind so she knew how close the pains were coming. If they increased in intensity, she would worry. If they settled, they might just be a result of the night's terrifying experiences. Stress could induce this effect in pregnant women.

Just when she thought she was safe, another one hit her, weaker than the last, but still enough to make her shift uncomfortably on the mattress. As soon as it passed, she threw her shawl over her shoulders, thrust her feet into shoes, and peeked out into the hall.

It was still early enough that no one stirred on the upper floor of the keep, even though the light coming through the windows was already tinged the blue of early morning. As expected, two men still stood guard outside Morrigan's chamber. She nodded to them, trying to act as if her disheveled appearance were perfectly ordinary, and then knocked on the door.

After a few moments, a sleepy-eyed Morrigan answered. "My lady?"

"May I come in?"

"Of course, my lady." She stood aside and shut the door behind her. Aine noticed that instead of a shift, she was wearing her long man's shirt and boots. Did she sleep with shoes on? Why on earth would she do such a thing?

"My lady?" Morrigan prompted.

"Oh." Aine swallowed and focused her scattered thoughts. "I need a favor."

"Before sunrise?" Morrigan returned to her bed and sat on the edge. "Sounds like an illicit request."

"Not illicit. Just . . . secret. Surely you realize I wouldn't have come to you if—"

"If you weren't desperate. Aye, I guessed that much. What is it? I will help if I can."

"I need you to go to the healer's cottage and get some herbs from Murchadh. Cramp bark and blazing star, enough for a pot of tea."

Morrigan's eyebrows lifted and an expression of alarm appeared. "Are you having problems with the baby, my lady?"

"I don't want to take any chances. Morrigan, you can't tell anyone it's for me."

"There's nothing to be ashamed of here, my lady. Why hide it?"

"Because nothing remains secret here for long. If it's you, they'll ignore it as a matter of modesty. If it's me, they'll send a messenger to inform Conor that I'm ill. And he has far too much to worry about to be concerned with me and his child."

Morrigan seemed to be considering the matter. "Don't you think Conor has the right to know that there might be something wrong with his child?"

"And if there is, what could he possibly do about it? Worry along with me? If and when there is truly something to be concerned about, I will let him know. But for now, please . . .

just help me. And remain silent." Aine winced as another pain hit her, stronger this time. Even though she tried to hide it, Morrigan's eyes narrowed.

"That was another one, wasn't it? All right. I don't like it, but I'll help you."

"In return for my help someday?"

"I didn't say that. After all, this is, in a sense, my niece or nephew we're discussing." Morrigan gave her a tiny smile. "But, aye, some reciprocity is implied in my assistance."

"If I can without betraying my husband or my king. Will you go now, please? Before there are too many people about in the village?"

"All right, all right. Wait for me in your chamber. I'll bring it to you when I've gotten it. What do you suggest I tell the guards?"

"Don't worry about them. I'll take care of them." She gave Morrigan a little bow of her head. "Thank you."

"Aye, I know. Now go so I can get dressed."

Outside, Aine gave a vague explanation that seemed to satisfy the guards, then returned to her bed, where she lay on her side while she prayed. For herself and for the life of her unborn child. For Conor and his traumatized mind. For this whole convoluted war they were fighting, an island-sized game of King and Conqueror where they continually moved pieces around as threats. All of it, out of her control. All of it, a never-ending danger in the back of her mind.

It felt like hours, even though it was probably just a portion of one, before Morrigan knocked on her door. As soon as Aine let her in, Morrigan thrust out a small fabric sack. "Here."

Aine emptied the bag's contents onto the table to verify it contained only the blazing star and the cramp bark she had requested.

"Making sure I'm not trying to poison you?"

"Making sure a mistake wasn't made," Aine said, even though

that thought had crossed her mind. "If he'd taken down the wrong jar—"

"I stood and watched him. I read the labels. He put just those two in the sack that you requested." She gave her a rueful look. "You are not the only one who knows the value of herbs to women, my lady. I would not give you anything that would harm your child."

"Thank you, Morrigan. You don't know what your help means."

"I think I do." She gave Aine a little bow and a sad smile. "Rest, my lady. As will I, as there is little else for me to do."

Aine watched her go, a pang of sympathy for the other woman in her chest. She was trying to tell her something, even though Aine wasn't completely sure what. But she suspected that some of Morrigan's secrets remained buried not because they were signs of treachery but because she could not bear to bring them into the light of day.

✦   ✦   ✦

When a knock sounded at Aine's door later that afternoon, she almost expected it to be Morrigan. Instead Riordan stood in the corridor. A frown creased his forehead at her disheveled appearance. "My lady, are you well?"

"Well enough." At least the herbs seemed to have worked, and the pains had slowed if not completely subsided. She pushed a lock of tangled hair from her eyes. "Do you need me?"

"Forgive me, my lady. Eoghan wants you present when he speaks to the Conclave."

Aine just nodded her agreement and shut the door, even though lacing up her ever-more-snug-fitting dress and combing her hair was almost more effort than she could contemplate. She settled for lacing the gown loosely and tying back her hair in a single tail. Then she splashed water on her face before descending to the great hall.

Eoghan focused on her immediately, and the slight pinch of his brow told her that her efforts were not fooling him a bit. He merely gave her a slight bow, however, and gestured to her customary seat, a place of honor between him and Riordan.

"We've more reports from Faolán," Eoghan said without preamble. "Niall has seized two more keeps."

Aine drew in a breath of surprise. "Which ones?"

"Drumdubh and Cionnlath. Both old, both abandoned. It seems that the people got word of what happened at Bánduran and fled before he arrived."

"How does he even know of their existence?" she mused aloud.

"Remember," Eoghan said, "we don't even know how old Niall really is. The rolls of the brotherhood seem to indicate he's been hopping bodies for well over two centuries, if not longer. He's lived as a druid. He has access to arcane knowledge that we don't. And the likelihood of discovering everything he knows, being able to anticipate his movements, is small." Eoghan's glance fell on her significantly.

"You want me to contact Keondric."

"You know I wouldn't consider it were it not our best option."

Aine slowly scanned the table to judge the men's thoughts on the matter. She required only the lightest touch to see they agreed with Eoghan, though Riordan's thoughts in particular were tinged with regret. He knew what they asked of her.

"Very well, then. I will try later. I've made contact only during late-night or early-morning hours, so I suspect Niall's hold on him weakens when he's asleep." She hesitated. "You do realize that what you ask could have the opposite effect, don't you? If Niall becomes aware that Keondric is still present, it puts our only protection against him at risk."

"Not our only protection," Dal said. "Do you forget the two thousand warriors who man the city?"

"Do you forget how easily a woman with a sleeping potion breached Ard Dhaimhin?" Aine countered.

"Aine is right. We've defenses against his warriors, but our main advantage is in Niall's believing he can't take the shield rune." Eoghan directed his attention to Aine. "Would you know if he discovered you speaking to Keondric?"

"I couldn't begin to guess."

Eoghan pressed his folded hands to his lips as he considered. Perhaps he was speaking to Comdiu. "We can't afford not to try. I believe it's worth the risk. But you're taking on a large risk yourself, my lady. Are you willing?"

He was giving her a choice in the matter? She swallowed hard and nodded.

"Good. Now we must consider what to do with the refugees who have entered the city."

The report directly affected her, but she couldn't focus on the words through her jittery limbs and pounding heart. They were counting on her to do something she barely understood and for which she had little chance of success. How on earth could she live up to those expectations?

The meeting adjourned without her hearing another word. She rose with the men, but Eoghan drew her aside.

"Lady Aine, is there anything wrong? Is there something you'd like to tell me?"

"Nothing's wrong. I'm just tired. It's not unusual, considering." She waved a vague hand over her belly.

"Are you sure? Something I should know about Conor?"

Either Comdiu had told him that something was wrong or he was fishing. His questions were too directed. She forced an unconvincing smile. "No. There's nothing you should know."

Eoghan's slight smile said he knew how carefully she had phrased her answer, but he just bowed his head. "As you wish, my lady. With your permission, I'll have supper sent to your chamber so you can rest."

"Thank you, Eoghan . . . my lord." For some reason, she felt compelled to give him a little bow. Every day he slipped into his role as king more easily. It was strange to watch him change from a man avoiding responsibility to one who was more and more comfortable making hard decisions, taking risks.

Even though it was early, she searched for Conor's mind as soon as she returned to her chamber. *Are you there, my love?*

It took him some time to answer, and she wondered if he might already be asleep. *Aye. What is it, Aine?*

Her brow furrowed slightly at the weary sound of his voice in her head. He seemed unhappy to speak with her. *What is it, my love? Am I interrupting something?*

No, nothing. The day has been never-ending. I'm ready to sleep. Do you have news?

Aine pushed away her pang of hurt and filled him in about Niall's movements.

That's interesting. He's besieging fortresses of the old clan lords.

Aine frowned at the specificity of the comment. *How do you know that?*

You forget that my education was littered with what I thought were useless facts. Not so useless, after all, apparently.

Tell me.

The fortresses in questions are all ring forts. The dry-stacked stone ones, as well as those carved out of mountains, were built in Daimhin's time or later for the principal clan chiefs and later the four kings of Seare. But the older earthen ring forts predate the coming of Daimhin or Balianism to the isle.

So those sites had some significance to the druids. That's why they chose to hide the runes there?

I don't know much about that. Remember that the druids once followed Comdiu before the coming of Balus. The runes predate the coming of Balus, so there has to be some significance there; I just don't know what it is.

Perhaps Murchadh would know. I'll ask him. Aine wavered on the edge of her question. *Conor, is everything okay?*

Everything is fine, Aine.

He was lying to her now as surely as she had lied to Eoghan about there being nothing wrong. For a heartbeat, she was tempted to push her way into his mind and find out the truth, but at the last minute, she pulled back. Their physical distance made it harder to pick up stray thoughts; it took conscious effort to find them. That would be an invasion of his privacy he wouldn't forgive.

I just want to help you.

Some things are beyond your help, Aine. Give me time.

Stung, Aine pulled back and broke the connection between their minds. He was rarely so severe with her, but after what he'd been through, she couldn't criticize him too harshly.

Then several minutes later, his voice reached out to her. *Aine.*

Aye, Conor?

I'm sorry. I love you. Don't give up on me.

She let out a relieved breath. *I will love you always, no matter what.*

It was true. She might sometimes doubt the timing that had led them to marry and conceive a child only to be repeatedly separated and put in danger, but she knew they were meant to be together, that their love was somehow ordained. She had to trust that, even as he pulled further away from her each day, even as the image of another woman lingered in the back of her mind.

A brother arrived with her supper, just a bowl of soup and

a large piece of bread with honey. She lifted the first spoonful to her lips and realized that it was filled with chunks of meat. Hadn't that been one of things they talked about at the meeting, the scarcity of game and their dwindling supplies? She knew for certain there were no more active hives; this had to be the last of the honey.

She lowered the spoon back to the bowl. This was Eoghan's doing, whether it be from his own initiative or Conor's charge that he take care of her while he was gone. The pregnant women below, although they continued to receive full rations while the men got half, were not being served food like this. She couldn't reject the gift, but it didn't come without guilt.

Yet what kind of mother would she be if she didn't do whatever it took to ensure the health of her baby?

She finished the food and set the tray aside, then climbed under the blankets with the last volume of Shanna's journals. She could tell herself that she was killing time until she could reach Keondric, while Niall's consciousness was sleeping, but in truth she was scared—frightened of making a mistake, of tipping off the druid, of what he might do if he found out the truth.

Comdiu, give me strength for this, she prayed, burying her face in her hands. *This is more than I can handle. This is more than I am capable of.*

It didn't take long for the answering truth to fill her: it might be too much for her to handle, but nothing was too great to accomplish with Comdiu's help.

Before her fear could convince her to change her mind, she reached out and began searching for a mind that felt like Keondric's. She didn't dare call out to him lest she draw too much attention. And then, as unlikely as finding a sewing needle in a straw bale, she caught the thread of a thought that felt familiar.

Keondric, can you hear me? Keondric! Fight to the surface!

My lady? Is that you?

Aye, it's me. Listen to me very carefully. Do you know where you are?

No, I don't understand.

Keondric, your body was seized by the druid, but somehow your spirit did not flee. You must gain control. If you do it now, I know you can do it more frequently.

Very impressive, my lady. It's too bad you don't understand your gift more thoroughly.

Chills traced her skin, and her stomach dropped to her feet. Niall. She knew that voice, more by its arrogance and oiliness than by any resemblance to the voices he'd controlled while she'd known him. What had he done with Keondric? Had he heard what she'd said to him?

Oh, aye, my lady. I heard every word. Just as I hear every word you're thinking now.

Impossible. You're surely guessing.

Not impossible, clearly. You are a clever girl to have figured it out, though. And to try to use it against me, though obviously that will fail.

Why obviously?

Because I knew that Keondric was attempting to contact you all along. I wanted to speak to you.

Then why the charade? You knew where I was; you could have called to me.

Ah, but I did. It was only the familiarity of Keondric's voice that broke through the noise of all the other thoughts. That must be most inconvenient for you, my dear.

She bristled at the use of the endearment, at his attempt to establish rapport. He laughed, picking up on her feelings.

I suppose it would be a complete waste of time to convince you to come join me, wouldn't it?

You supposed correctly. I would never—

No need for theatrics, my lady. A no suffices. Of course, it would be helpful for you to fully understand the nature of your child's gifts.

Aine went cold. He couldn't have flattened her more thoroughly if he'd tried. *How do you—?*

Know about your child? You give me too little credit. Now, how I felt your child's gift, that is more impressive—just not as impressive as his gift. Do you really believe that your powers just spontaneously grew? You owe much to that tiny little spark of a life in you. It would be a shame to see it snuffed out.

Now the chill changed to a flush of fury. *You dare threaten my child? You underestimate* me *if you think that I would ever allow you—*

Calm yourself, little one. It was not a threat. Merely an observation of what happens to expecting women when they're under great deals of stress. You know that firsthand, don't you?

Aine gasped and slammed the door shut on her mind, closing him out before she could think through the action. He knew about her problems. He claimed to recognize her child's gifts, implied that her baby possessed abilities even greater than his own. Was it all manipulation, or was it truly meant as a warning?

Dizziness washed over her when she realized the depth of her mistake. This had nothing to do with her or Keondric. It was her baby he'd wanted to assess all along.

And she had just given him everything he needed to know.

+ + +

In two weeks, Eoghan had managed to undo all the safety that Ard Dhaimhin had enjoyed.

He paced the Ceannaire's office, his hands clasped behind his head, trying to think of a way around his failures, but there was none—at least none that wasn't worse than the very thing he was trying to fix. Aine had tried to warn him of the risks of contacting Keondric, and he'd thought they were more intelligent, safe enough to take the risk. And then exactly what she'd warned them of had happened.

"Aine herself said that he already knew of the existence of Keondric's soul." Riordan watched him from a chair, as calm as he'd been since Aine had notified them of what had happened.

"But now he knows about her child and its gifts. That's a concern." Eoghan stopped pacing when the door to the chamber opened, and he waved in the newcomer. "Iomhar, come, sit."

The young man looked surprised, but he obeyed and perched on the edge of the chair as if he were expecting a reprimand. "Is there a problem, sir?"

"No. Well, aye, but not with you. I'm reassigning you."

"Is there something wrong with my work, sir? My céad is operating as efficiently as ever."

"We've become aware of a threat to Lady Aine, and I'm assigning you to her as her guard. During daylight hours, you are not to leave her side, unless she's in her chamber, at which point you will stand watch outside. I have already assigned a night guard to her. Do you understand?"

"Aye, sir. It's an honor, sir."

"Good. Now get some sleep. You're expected at Carraigmór at dawn tomorrow."

Iomhar stood and bowed before exiting the room. Eoghan wiped a hand over his face. At least that was taken care of. He'd feel slightly better with Iomhar by her side.

"A bit of overkill, don't you think?"

Eoghan stopped and looked at Riordan. "She's your daughter by marriage. I'd think you would be as concerned as I am."

"I am concerned. But Iomhar is needed as a céad leader in the city. Taking him now puts his men at risk."

"And Aine is one of the greatest advantages we have. The men will fight under whomever we put in command. But she cannot come to any harm."

Riordan arched an eyebrow. "Are you sure that's what this is about?"

For a moment, shame and anger at Riordan's opinion of him welled up inside, but he stuffed the feelings back down where they belonged. "It doesn't matter what you think my motivations are. What is important is that I'm right."

Riordan stood and gave him an abbreviated bow. "Aye, sir, understood. Conor will be back in a fortnight, though. You might want to give some thought to how you're going to explain why his wife is Niall's newest target."

Eoghan watched the older man go, both baffled by and worried about his reaction. Did Riordan disagree with his actions? Or was he merely worried that Eoghan's concern for Aine was more than strictly tactical? Either way, his actions would be the same. She was an asset, his best friend's wife, and someone important to him. He would make sure she was protected.

CHAPTER
TWENTY-SIX

Perhaps it was defiance, or perhaps it was just the knowledge that there were preparations to be made before the city was hit with another wave of refugees, but Aine refused to hide in her chamber as Eoghan and Riordan seemed to believe she should. She rose early, washed and dressed, and opened the door of her chamber—only to nearly collide into a wall of solid muscle.

"My lady." The man standing outside her chamber gave her a short bow. "I'm Brother Iomhar."

"I know who you are, Iomhar." She recognized the young swordsman immediately. He was reputed to be one of Ard Dhaimhin's best fighters and commanded a céad of his own.

"Master Eoghan assigned me to you today."

Of course he had. She should have expected as much. "That's not necessary."

"He thought you'd say that." Iomhar's expression cracked into a good-natured smile. "But I suspect I'll be facing a flogging should I let you out of my sight."

Aine just shook her head, unsurprised. Eoghan was almost as bad as Conor. "Then breakfast first. I'm starving. Are you hungry?"

"No, my lady. We eat before sunrise."

Right. Even with the influx of kingdom citizens, those Fíréin-raised men stuck to the same rigid schedule they always had. When they reached the cookhouse, it was only women and children with a smattering of men in line. The Fíréin and the more able-bodied of the kingdom's men were already at their assignments for the day. Aine slammed down the boundaries of her mind before the hum of voices could grow into a head-splitting cacophony. The instinct had become automatic shortly after she'd arrived at Ard Dhaimhin, but having to keep herself open to both Conor and Keondric in the late hours had made it less and less natural.

Aine accepted a bowl of thin soup and a hunk of bread, then moved off to eat it away from the others, aware of Iomhar following two paces behind.

"I'm sorry you drew this duty," she said as she settled on a patch of reasonably dry grass.

"It's my honor."

She tilted her head to study him. "Why?"

"You don't remember?" When Aine shook her head, he pulled down the neck of his tunic to show a thick white scar. "You healed this when you first came. I'd suffered it in the attack on the city. It wasn't life-threatening, but it wouldn't heal properly. I could barely raise a sword."

She vaguely remembered the incident, but those early days in which she had been overwhelmed by both her gift and the sheer volume of work were just a blur in her memory.

"Is that why Eoghan chose you?"

Iomhar chuckled. "Eoghan chose me because next to him and your husband, I'm the best sword in the city. Besides, you'd be hard-pressed to find a man you haven't helped in some way, my lady."

Aine smiled. She liked this man. Confident but not cocky. Good-humored. And quick. "What do you think about all of this?"

Iomhar sobered. "About the danger you face, or about Ard Dhaimhin in general?"

"In general."

He thought for a long moment. "This is all temporary. Right now we're doing the best that we can with what we have. But the real fight is still to come."

Aine nodded slightly, sobered by his assessment. She wasn't the only one who felt they were just holding on. In order for them to have any hope of rebuilding Seare, they needed to stop with the small, stopgap measures and end the war once and for all. But as she looked around at the men, women, and children—fighters and non-fighters alike—she wondered what price they would pay to accomplish it.

Iomhar chatted with her while he walked her to the healers' cottages, so different from taciturn Ruarc and fierce Lorcan. She had been so taken in by the illusory safety of the city that she had forgotten the security she drew from a warrior's constant presence. Iomhar was pleasant, intelligent, and kind in his demeanor, but he was also ever watchful, his eyes assessing possible threats even as he told her stories about growing up in Ard Dhaimhin. She got a glimpse of the mischievous little boy, gradually shaped and molded into a man of duty and conscience. How easily he and others like him accepted that duty, how willing they were to die to discharge it. How could she think her life was worth the constant risk to theirs? Love, she understood. But this steadfast devotion to an idea . . .

Why do you think those two things are in opposition?

The thought pierced through her own, clearly from Comdiu. She nearly stumbled from the clarity of it.

*Why do you fight for people you don't know, if not for love? Love
of country, love of justice. Your knowledge that I love them and
know each one. Do you not risk all for an idea?*

"Lady Aine?"

Aine realized she'd stopped and shot Iomhar an embarrassed
smile. "Just thinking too deeply, I suppose. I'm fine."

But she couldn't shake the feeling that she'd been entrusted
with something important, something precious. Perhaps it was
simply an insight into the heart of Comdiu.

Or perhaps it was encouragement to persevere in the face of
the danger to come.

When they arrived at the healers' cottage, Iomhar took
up his post outside the door. Inside, Murchadh was already
hard at work. He glanced up and nodded in her direction.
"You're looking well today, Lady Aine. Had a good night's rest,
I hope?"

Hardly, she thought, but she just smiled. At least that was
proof they'd been successful in keeping Aine's activities quiet.
She perused the freshly washed roots laid out on the table before
him. "Are you making tinctures today?"

"Dandelion." He produced a heavy-bladed knife and began
to chop them into tiny, precise pieces. He nodded toward the
bucket of rendered lard in the corner. "If you want, we could
use a new batch of salve."

Aine retrieved the bucket and hefted it onto the bench.
They went through this salve most quickly of all their preparations. It was as good for treating blisters and skin ulcers as it
was for cuts and bruises. She selected a jar of marshmallow
root oil from the shelf and then added bottles of marigold and
arnica extract to her apron to bring over to the bench. She
quickly lost herself in the careful measurements of the recipe
Mistress Bearrach had taught her during her apprenticeship at

Lisdara, stirring the oils into the fat until her arms ached from the effort of plying the wooden spoon. Then she started the painstaking process of spooning it into jars to be distributed to the other healers.

When the last of the salve was in the jars, she carried them two by two to the wooden shelving opposite the bench. "I think I'm done here. I'm going to go walk the garden and make sure the rain didn't disturb the mulch before I go back to the fortress."

"I thought to do the same," he said. "I'll accompany you."

She looked askance at the healer. Ever since she had compelled him to tell his story to the Conclave, he'd been friendly but businesslike with her. He certainly hadn't shown any interest in her personal plantings before or in spending any time with her beyond the tasks that he set her in the cottage.

Still, she smiled at him. "I'll welcome the company."

The older man removed his apron and followed her out of the cottage silently. He lifted an eyebrow at Iomhar's presence, then frowned when the young man followed them into the garden. "Acquired a new shadow?"

"You know Eoghan," she said with a smile, hoping he'd leave it at that. But Murchadh seemed content to just walk beside her. Sure enough, the mulch that she'd mounded around the trimmed stalks of her chamomile plants had slid away in the overnight rain. She picked her way through the rows, brushing the mulch up where it belonged, pressing down earth that had begun to crumble from the hills.

"Your monk's collar is looking sickly," Murchadh said, moving to a row of bushy plants. He used his knife to dig down beside the roots of one of them. "See here?"

Aine knelt beside him. "A little pale perhaps, but it's late in the season. Were there a real problem in the soil, we'd see evidence on the—"

Before she could finish the thought, the healer's body slammed into her, his thin frame crashing her back into the dirt of her garden. She froze in shock as his knife hovered above her, too stunned to fight back. And then all of a sudden, his weight was gone and he was flying back to the turf. Iomhar straddled him on the ground, striking the weapon from his hand, and then flipped him onto his stomach in an armlock that made the old man cry out in pain.

"Are you hurt, my lady?" Iomhar's tone carried concern but not panic.

"I—I—what just happened? He tried to kill me!"

"My lady, are you hurt? You're bleeding."

Aine looked down at herself and saw the smear of blood on the front of her dress, then traced it to her palm. "I'm fine. I think I just sliced it open on one of the plant's canes. He didn't strike me."

"Good." Iomhar looked around, then raised his voice and shouted, "Rafer! Come here!"

A short, muscular brother caught Iomhar's eye and trotted to their side immediately. Concern passed through his expression when he took in the scene. "How may I be of service, sir?"

"Escort Lady Aine to Master Eoghan. Don't let anyone get within three feet of her. There's been an assassination attempt."

Another flash of unease surfaced on Rafer's face, but he bowed in acknowledgment. "Aye, sir. Lady Aine, if you would come with me."

"Go," Iomhar said. "Rafer will see you safely to the fortress. I'll be right behind you."

Numbly, she let the brother draw her to her feet, only now noticing that he had his sword free from his sheath. "Murchadh tried to kill me."

"Aye, my lady, it would seem so," Rafer said in a quiet voice. "Let us get you someplace more defensible, shall we?"

Iomhar gave her a reassuring nod before he hauled Murchadh to his feet. She expected to see hatred or fury in the healer's face, but it was only as placid as it ever was.

CHAPTER
TWENTY-SEVEN

"How could this happen?" Eoghan roared.

Aine cringed, even though she knew his fury was not directed toward her. She focused instead on the sting in her palm where she had sliced it open on the thorns of the monk's collar plant. Even beneath the numbing salve and the wrapping, it hurt.

Not as bad as a knife wound would have—or had. She had been cut before by an assassin's blade, and that had been someone she had trusted as well.

She had a terrible record of trusting people who secretly wanted to kill her.

"Eoghan," Riordan said gently, nodding in her direction.

Eoghan focused on her, and his demeanor softened. He came to kneel beside the chair in the Ceannaire's office where she sat and took her unwounded hand. "Aine, look at me. Are you all right? Are you hurt in any way?"

She shook her head numbly. "I suspect I'm in shock, though."

"We should get you to your chamber. But first, did he say anything? Did he give any indication why he tried to kill you?"

"No, none. I thought it was odd that he wanted to

accompany me to the garden, because the garden is not his responsibility. It never entered my mind he would do something like this."

"I don't understand why if he wanted to kill her he didn't do it inside the cottage," Iomhar wondered. "He was alone with her for hours. Instead he takes her outside where he can be seen and stopped? It doesn't make any sense."

Eoghan's eyes narrowed. "You left her alone? After your express orders were to not leave her side?"

Aine squeezed Eoghan's hand to stem the flow of his tirade. "Iomhar was doing as I asked. Would you have honestly believed that Murchadh was a threat? The fact is, he saved me, and I don't even know how he managed that. He was several feet away."

Eoghan's eyes returned to the guard. "How did you manage that?"

"I don't know, sir. Something felt wrong. I was already walking toward them when he turned the blade on her. I was there just in time."

"Or he didn't really want to kill me," Aine said softly.

The three men in the room stared disbelievingly at her.

"Think about it. He waited until we were outside, where Iomhar could stop him. He knocked me over and hesitated before he tried to stab me. That doesn't sound like a well-thought-out plan for assassination." It was certainly easier to believe that the healer with whom she'd worked for months hadn't truly wanted to kill her, even if his real motivations hadn't yet been explained.

"Then why do it at all?" Eoghan asked.

"Maybe he was compelled." The words spilled out before she could consider them, but they felt right. They felt possible. Hadn't she seen what a spell could do to a person's will? "What better way to get to me than through someone I trusted? After all, as soon as you thought there might be a threat against me, you assigned a guard. I can't move more than a handful of steps without someone watching over me. A stranger would never get within a dozen feet of me."

"Why do it at all? And how could he have been spelled? Murchadh isn't new here. I would have expected such a thing from a patient or one of the refugees. But not a sworn brother who has lived more of his life here than he has elsewhere."

"In the nemetons."

Again, all the men's attention fell on her.

"Murchadh was a druid. He spent the first thirty years of his life there. He himself said that he still considers himself a druid. Now Niall is trying to collect the runes his order scattered, and we are trying to stop him. Somehow I don't believe that's any coincidence."

"So you think he's loyal to the druidic order and they somehow want you dead?" Riordan said doubtfully.

"I'm not saying that. I'm just saying that there are too many coincidences here. It seems that I'm always being attacked by people I trust. First, Keondric ambushed and kidnapped me under Niall's direction. Then I was attacked by a man who had helped me reach Forrais safely. They'd both had the opportunity to harm me before then, but they hadn't taken it. And now Murchadh."

"But you yourself said you didn't think Niall had anything to do with the attack on you at your aunt's keep. You thought that was orchestrated by her or your cousin."

"Aye. But the sidhe . . . the druid . . . they all may be acting for their own purposes, but who pulls the strings?" The words flowed out of her as if she'd always known the answer, even if this was the first time she had ever truly articulated the idea. "Lord Balus told me that the storm of darkness must be stopped before it spread across the world. I don't think He meant mere physical oppression or even the control of the sidhe."

"You're saying this is all part of a larger plan by the Adversary," Riordan said.

"What else? Is that not how the story goes? That the Adversary hated the creation that Comdiu loved? That Comdiu gave him dominion over the earth, even as He gave us tools to fight him? And now we threaten that reign on earth, Conor and I especially. We have been targeted every step of the way, by evil men, by spirit, by magic."

"We need to question Murchadh," Eoghan said.

"Let me."

"My lady?"

"He didn't want to kill me. I'm almost sure of it. Let me question him. I'm more likely to get the answers we seek from him than you are."

"You were almost just killed!" Eoghan said. "No. I won't allow it."

Aine arched an eyebrow at him. "You won't allow it? Last time I checked, you were neither my husband nor my king."

Eoghan flinched, but he didn't budge. "I am the leader here and responsible for your safety."

"What do you think is going to happen with him restrained? Iomhar overpowered him without a struggle. He's not going to harm me. At least let me try. You question him too strenuously and he will tell us nothing. I'm sure of that."

Another round of doubtful looks. Aine sighed. "I promise, no harm is going to come to me."

After a long moment of deliberation, Eoghan nodded. "Fine. But only if we all are with you."

"Good. Thank you. All right, before we go down, we need some things. Where can I find ink and a brush?"

Eoghan called for one of the brothers on watch in the corridor to retrieve the implements. "Come, my lady. He's being held in the dungeons." He ushered her out the door with a light touch on her elbow.

"Carraigmór has a dungeon?"

"Aye. Not often used, but equipped for the task."

"Somehow I didn't take the Fíréin as proponents of torture." A shudder of horror skittered down her back, the mere word taking her back to what she had experienced through Conor's mind.

"It's nothing for you to be concerned about, my lady. Murchadh is one of us. He will be given the opportunity to confess. I don't anticipate any unpleasantness being necessary to get to the bottom of this."

Eoghan's careful dodge of the topic did nothing to ease the sick feeling in her stomach. Somehow she had thought of the brotherhood as being more civilized, more enlightened, than the kingdoms, but perhaps that was just a false conceit. Up until recently, they'd had no outsiders and relatively little crime. Interlopers who had no good reason to be in their forests were killed, and brothers who committed crimes were already held to a codified standard of discipline. Where did that leave Murchadh, she wondered, who had taken an oath as a brother and then attempted to kill someone under the Ceannaire's protection?

Eoghan led Aine down the stairs to a part of the keep she hadn't even known existed, beside the isolated Hall of Prophecies. Rather than the dark, dingy, foul-smelling lower level she'd expected, it was rather a warren of small chambers that looked like storerooms, each closed with a heavy iron-bound door. The brother on duty stepped aside from one in the middle of the hall.

"Are you sure you want to do this?" Eoghan asked, his hand on the latch. "He did just try to kill you."

"Which is why I must speak with him."

Eoghan exchanged a glance with Riordan, who nodded. Iomhar followed at her heels, his hand on the knife at his waist. Aine found it laughable. What danger did he think she would face?

Certainly not Murchadh. He had always struck her as hale and full of life when working in the cottage, but now, tied to a chair with heavy ropes, he looked like a withered husk.

Aine stopped several paces in front of him. He raised miserable eyes to hers and then dropped his gaze to the stones again. No, this was not a man who was proud of his actions. She reached out for his thoughts, but they were slippery, like trying to catch smoke with her hands. Still, she caught guilt, regret, anger. And among it, the distinctive, oily taint of sorcery.

"He's spelled," Aine murmured. "I'm sure of it."

She crouched down in front of him. "Brother Murchadh, why did you do it? I don't truly believe you want me dead."

He refused to meet her eyes, and he said nothing.

"Lady Aine, this is pointless," Riordan said. "Even if he does answer, I don't think you're going to like what he has to say."

The door creaked open behind them and a brother entered with a jar of ink and a brush in hand. Aine thanked him, and Eoghan dismissed him with a nod.

"Take off his shirt," she directed.

Iomhar came forward, slit the neckline of Murchadh's shirt with a knife, and pulled it open.

Something about the sight of the old man tied to a chair with the wrinkled, sagging flesh of his torso exposed struck her with a deep pang of pity. She knelt before him.

"Don't move, brother." Iomhar put the edge of his knife against Murchadh's throat to ensure he didn't try anything reckless while Aine was close to him. Her pity grew. She uncorked the inkwell and dipped in the brush.

At the first stroke of ink, Murchadh's breath hissed from between his teeth, but he didn't move. She worked quickly to draw the rest of the rune as precisely as she could. When the last stroke was complete, all the tension drained from his body.

"The rune blocks all magic," she said quietly. "You can speak freely now."

"Bless you, my lady." Tears trickled down his face. "Forgive me."

"You didn't really want to kill me, did you?"

He shook his head.

"Then why?"

"Some time ago, after I was a brother of Ard Dhaimhin, I swore an oath to another. I was stupid and shortsighted, and I didn't see the harm. But it bound me in ways I didn't expect."

"Through magic."

"Aye. He used my continued respect for my mentor in the nemetons to elicit a promise I never should have made. And when it came time for him to call in the favor, I found I couldn't refuse."

"You're speaking of Niall."

Murchadh bowed his head and nodded once.

"Which is why you came outside with me."

"Aye. Because I knew someone would likely stop me before I could be successful."

"And if they didn't?"

"Then I would have murdered you and your child, and I would have had to stand before Comdiu with the blood of innocents on my hands."

Aine jumped to her feet and moved away from him. What could she say to that? He'd known what he did was wrong, even if he was compelled by a foolish, ill-advised oath. He had done all within his power to make sure he would be stopped. Yet had Iomhar not acted on his instincts, Aine and her baby would be dead.

The realization of how close she had come began the trembling. She hugged her arms to herself.

"Iomhar, take Lady Aine to her chamber and stay there."

"No, wait. I have another question. Brother Murchadh, you spoke to us only once we applied the rune. Does that mean Niall has been watching you all this time?"

He nodded.

"So he's heard all our conversations. He already knew of the baby. He knew of the preparations we've been making."

"I would assume so."

Eoghan stepped forward, danger in his expression and his tone. "If you made the oath years ago, who or what told you to act now?"

Murchadh's throat worked, but he remained silent.

But Aine had the terrible, sinking suspicion that she knew.

✦ ✦ ✦

"You think Morrigan has something to do with this."

Aine huddled beneath the blanket in her chair, willing the shivers to subside. She looked between Eoghan and Riordan, who stood before her while Iomhar guarded the door. "I don't know what to think. It's all a bit too much of a coincidence."

"How could that even be possible? She's been under guard since she arrived. She's barely even left the fortress, and certainly not without supervision."

Aine cringed. "I asked her for help a few days ago. She went to Murchadh for me."

"I don't understand," Eoghan said.

"I needed herbs and I didn't want anyone to know. I sent her to Murchadh early in the morning."

"Why?"

She was going to have to make a full confession. Dodging

the issue wasn't going to work here. "I was beginning to have labor pains, and it's much too early. I asked her to go get a tea to stop them."

"Aine, you should have told someone!" Riordan said.

"And risk you telling Conor? He has enough on his mind without worrying about me. Trust me."

"So you think that Morrigan spoke with Murchadh. She was the one who gave the order to him?"

"It seems reasonable, doesn't it? It's been years since Murchadh swore his oath. Suddenly, Morrigan shows up with information that proves to be true but doesn't help us at all. Then days after I enlist her help with Murchadh, he tries to kill me."

"It still could be a coincidence," Riordan said. "All of that can be explained away by the fact that the war is escalating. It doesn't mean she's responsible for that, too."

Eoghan sighed. "I'd have to agree with Riordan. But, just in case, I'll change her guards."

It was a logical, measured response, even if deep down, Aine knew she was right. Morrigan had some part in all of this; she was sure of it. She just had no way to prove it. The rune branded into Morrigan's flesh prevented Aine from learning what she knew and what she had done. And despite the fact the dungeons had indeed been equipped for their intended purpose, she was sure Eoghan would never stoop to the painful and bloody step of removing the rune from her flesh.

Were it to be marred in some way though . . . Would a small cut, for example, negate the rune so Aine could find a way through to her mind?

She immediately dismissed the idea. To remove the rune would be to allow Niall to contact Morrigan. If she were innocent, they would be putting her at risk. If she were guilty, who knew what Niall could accomplish with unfettered access to her?

She kept the idea to herself, instead extracting a promise from the three men that they would not tell Conor. In return, she gave her word that she would notify them about any additional troubles, phrasing it in a way that left her as much flexibility as possible. Her father-in-law and her future king didn't need to know every detail about her pregnancy, even if they did treat her as though she were carrying the crown prince.

But she couldn't say that she was surprised by the news that awaited her when she awoke the next morning and was called to Eoghan's office.

"Brother Murchadh is dead."

CHAPTER
TWENTY-EIGHT

The temperature took a rapid dip, making Conor wonder if perhaps the sidhe were congregating en masse, despite the fact that the wards kept them at a harmless distance. Then he realized that among the concerns of magic and war and the movement of men, their late-coming fall had finally arrived. Frost misted the slate roofs of Ard Bealach's buildings in the morning, and the sun took longer and longer each day to burn off the night's chill.

Conor's life at Ard Bealach consisted of the same minutia as his life at Ard Dhaimhin: assessing their supplies, evaluating their defenses, setting up the routines on which the Fíréin-trained men thrived. Since Conor didn't have access to the rune that would seal the tunnels seamlessly again, he ordered his men to wall it back up with stones and mortar several feet thick. He knew full well this wouldn't stop someone who was truly determined to enter. But the miles of dark tunnel at least fed to their advantage.

He devised a plan to sleep as little as possible, which involved taking a watch with the men and allowing himself to doze only right before someone came to wake him for his turn. The cold night air kept him alert enough to discharge his duty until he could fall senseless into bed for the remaining pair of hours until dawn.

Even he recognized it wasn't the best solution, especially as his temper grew shorter and his tone more caustic with each passing day. It was better than reliving the nightmares each time he closed his eyes. In some ways, it might have been easier had he actually undergone physical torture; the body had much more reliable ways of anesthetizing pain and clouding memories than the mind.

He wasn't sure whether he felt relief or dread in stronger measure when the replacements finally arrived, exactly two weeks after the taking of Ard Bealach.

Conor ordered the gates opened to receive the party, fifty men and six packhorses. He picked out Nuada instantly, several inches taller than Conor with a rail-thin body. He reminded Conor of a war bow, stretched taut with anticipation even in movement.

Nuada came forward and gave him a respectful bow. "Sir, I'm reporting as ordered to take command of Ard Bealach."

"Aye. Welcome. Your men can unload your supplies in the courtyard and put the ponies in the stables beyond. Come, I'll give you a tour."

Conor led Nuada up the two stone steps into the hall, aware of the man's intense observation of him even though he didn't understand it.

"They said something about ensorcelled men in torture chambers," Nuada said finally.

"Aye, that's been taken care of. The fortress is warded just as Ard Dhaimhin and the corridors have been, so you will be safe from the sidhe as well. Just use caution if you venture out into the villages. The spirits still have influence there."

"Have you seen many of the villagers?"

"No. And, frankly, we've avoided it. As you'll see when I show you the storerooms, our resources are limited. We can't afford to be overrun with petitioners such as Ard Dhaimhin."

Nuada seemed startled by his words. "Isn't that the point of all this? To liberate the region?"

"The point of this was to establish a strategic outpost," Conor said. "If we want to help the local people, we're better off focusing on ending the threat to them altogether. Come, I'll show you the upper quarters before we tour the barracks and the catacombs."

Conor led the young commander up the stairs to the upper floor. Confusion poured off Nuada as they went. Had he ever been that green? Surely there had been a time he'd thought he could not only save the world but all the people in it as well. But that conceit had died a long time ago.

He threw open his chamber first. "These are currently my quarters. I chose them for the view of the courtyard, but you can do what you wish. There are a few other rooms up here, but the bulk of the men will need to be quartered below."

Conor didn't tarry in the tour of the upstairs but immediately led Nuada down two floors to the catacombs. When the other man faltered, Conor said, "You'll get used to the smell. It fades a bit more each day. You should have been here before we cleared the chambers."

Secretly, he felt a twinge of satisfaction at Nuada's weak stomach, though he didn't comment. He could hardly blame the young man for being accustomed to Ard Dhaimhin's cleanliness and sanitation. It took venturing out into the wider world to understand the wonder of what King Dhaimhin and Queen Shanna had accomplished.

Conor named off the chamber's purposes as they passed.

"Storeroom for dried goods. Root cellar. More storage. These are the dungeons. Only one cell is occupied at present. The rest of the prisoners met unfortunate ends."

"What is to be done with him?" Nuada asked.

Conor paused in front of Somhairle's cell. The man didn't open his eyes, but the rhythmic tapping of his foot told Conor he was awake and listening to every word. "I'm considering taking him back with me."

The tapping stopped, and Somhairle squinted through one open eye. "Take me back where?"

"Ard Dhaimhin. They're more creative with punishment. I haven't the time."

"All talk," Somhairle muttered.

"You think so?" Conor said. "You don't believe I'm capable of following through?"

Somhairle's other eye opened. He fixed Conor with a suddenly penetrating stare. "I meant them. You are capable of all that and more. And it terrifies you."

Conor swallowed, frozen in that knowing gaze for what felt like hours. Then he shrugged in his best imitation of nonchalance and turned back the way they'd come. "I'm beginning to think he's mad."

"Quite," Nuada murmured.

Conor showed the commander the tunnel that held the barracks, and then they climbed upward once more. Nuada sucked in a grateful breath of fresh air from the hall. "I have the tallies in my chamber. There are enough stores to get you through winter if you're frugal, which is more than I can say for Ard Dhaimhin, but we'll all be scrambling not to starve come spring. The Clanless will come trade meat and furs for coin. Any questions?"

"When are you leaving? When do I meet the rest of the men?"

"You mistake your orders. My men return with me. You're more or less on your own."

✦ ✦ ✦

Two weeks. It might as well have been one long day, as seamlessly as one sleepless night flowed into the next. Conor's group packed the ponies that had brought them to Ard Bealach with enough supplies to reach the High City. Conor personally put Somhairle into chains and assigned four men to watch him. The prisoner didn't even acknowledge their presence, just followed with a docility that made Conor wonder if he really was mad. The newness of the shield rune suggested he might have been subject to the sidhe's influence previously. Conor knew better than anyone what the spirits could do to a man's mind.

Conor kept an eye out for any sign of the Clanless, but Oenghus and his party never appeared. He couldn't say he was sorry. He didn't have the energy or the clarity of mind to spar with the man. Nor was he sure anymore that they were actually on the same side, though he was the first to admit that his judgment was hazy. He put Ferus in charge on the way back, trusting the man's steady demeanor to compensate for his exhaustion.

The only thing that he did continue to do was play his harp. It seemed to be the only thing that brought a measure of clarity to his thoughts. As soon as they made camp at night, he would put his fingers to the strings, heedless of who might be listening, and play whatever came to mind. Sometimes they were the old songs taught to him as a child by the traveling bards, things his fingers knew instinctively. Other times they would be completely new compositions, which he cut off midsong. Labhrás had once told him he gave away too much with his playing, and this time he knew it to be true. Even he could hear the anguish and confusion in the notes.

Once they crossed into Fíréin territory, the days seemed to stretch on even longer, knowing that they were within the city's boundaries but still had more than a week to travel. The last bits of grain had been harvested, leaving short stubs where there had once been golden fields. A fine layer of frost draped the country-side each morning, giving it all a slightly storybook appearance and adding to the unreality of the trip in his increasingly hazy state.

Then on the seventeenth night after they had left Ard Bealach, they entered the village proper, down to the last crumbs of food in their packs. Conor numbly removed his belongings from the pony while Ferus handed off the leads to the young men in charge of the animals. Just being back in the High City brought a little life to his limbs.

"Sir, will you be all right?" Ferus looked directly into Conor's eyes as if to make sure that he understood what he was asking.

Had he really been that insensible since they left Ard Bealach? He thought back and realized he could remember almost nothing of the preceding weeks. But he nodded. "Fine. I'm going to wash in the springhouse before I go to the fortress."

"Aye, sir." Ferus hesitated, as if he wanted to say more, and then just gave a little bow.

"Ferus?"

"Sir?"

"Well done. You have proven your fitness as a leader."

"With all due respect, sir, it was mostly due to you. Between the wards and your playing, trouble stayed far away from us."

What did his playing have to do with anything? It wasn't worth the time it would take to ask. "Even so. You've earned your rest."

"Thank you, sir. I hope you find some here as well."

Conor hiked his bag over one shoulder and wove his way

through the village toward the bathhouse that had been erected over the hot springs in the center of the city. He managed friendly responses to the men's greetings, though conversation was the last thing he felt like at the moment. He stepped inside the steam-filled structure, and immediately the warmth took the edge off the ever-present chill in his extremities. There were a few men bathing, and Conor just gave them polite nods while he dropped his bag and stripped off his clothing.

Conor had just managed to slide into a hot pool when a voice came from overhead. "Sir, you've returned from Ard Bealach?"

He winced and squinted up at the boy who was squatting by the edge of the pool. He couldn't have been more than fifteen, with the gangly, overeager demeanor of a young man desperate to make his mark on the world. Conor searched in vain for his name and came up empty. "Aye."

"We've all heard how you took the fortress bloodlessly. It must have been a glorious battle."

Conor closed his eyes and gave a pained, weary chuckle. Bloodlessly? In a sense. Glorious? Not even close. "The fortress is secure. It matters little how it happened."

"Aye, but they say the magic stretches all the way from here across half of Sliebhan."

"Is that what they're saying?" Apparently, he was becoming something of a legend. Too bad it wasn't even close to true.

"Aye, sir. I hope someday that I will have the chance to serve under you."

The innocent words struck him with such melancholy weight that he didn't know what to say. Had he been so naive at that age? How had he managed to become so cynical in a mere seven years? He cleared his throat. "Son, I appreciate that, but I hope you never have the need."

It was apparently good enough, because the boy gave him a

bow and hurried off. The other men followed suit, leaving Conor alone with his thoughts in a room full of steam. Only when he dozed off and slid up to his chin in the water did he finally rouse himself enough to get out and dress so he could go up to Aine.

The three hundred steps of the fortress might as well have been a thousand for how they felt to his aching muscles and his weary mind. When he reached the top, he accepted the greetings of the guards on duty with a nod. Inside, he snagged the first brother he found. "Let Master Eoghan know that I've returned and I'll speak with him in the morning. I'm going to see my wife."

But when he reached the upper corridor where his chamber lay, he stopped. Iomhar leaned casually against the wall opposite the door. Conor frowned. "What are you doing here?"

Iomhar straightened abruptly and bowed. "Sir, waiting for the night guard."

Conor just blinked at him.

"I'm sorry, I thought you knew. Master Eoghan assigned me to Lady Aine during the day. Given everything that's happened, he thought it best she have a dedicated guard. Another man stands watch in the evening."

There were things there that were important, but he couldn't fish them out from his swimming thoughts. "Aye. Well, you're dismissed for this evening. I trust you'll be back in the morning as expected."

"Sir, with all due respect, Master Eoghan would have me flogged if I shirked my duties for any reason."

Conor sighed. He was too tired to argue. Besides, given his current state, it probably wasn't the worst idea to have someone on watch outside. He gave Iomhar a weary nod and grabbed the latch, only to find the door locked.

A rap brought rustling and the scrape of the lock from the

other side. Aine yanked the door open, wearing her long shift and a quizzical look. "Iomhar, is something—" She stopped short when she saw Conor.

"May I come in?" he asked, a smile playing on his lips for the first time in weeks. "Or is your guard determined to protect your virtue from even your husband?"

Iomhar cleared his throat from behind, a sure sign that he was trying not to laugh. Aine's face eased into a grin, and she opened the door wider. "I think he might make an exception."

Conor let his bag drop to the floor, took her face in his hands, and kissed her before she could say another word, kicking the door closed behind them. She slid her arms around his neck and held him tight, refusing to break the kiss for several long moments. "Thank Comdiu you're back," she said with a sigh, kissing him again. "You have no idea how I've missed you."

"I think I have." He pulled back from her and took in the changes that had occurred in the month he was gone. There was a definite roundness beneath her clothing that hadn't been there before. "How is my son?"

"Oh, you're so certain it's a son?"

"Pretty certain. Though I won't complain if it's a daughter who looks just like my wife."

"I do rather like you when you've been gone for a while. You're very flattering."

He grinned as she unbuckled the harness that held his weapons and began to lay them aside. Just being in her presence made the last month feel like a bad dream. Maybe now that he was back, he could throw off the memories that plagued him, at least for a time. This had the feeling of a temporary reprieve before the other, more-difficult duties to be done. But he had earned it. They both had.

"Come to bed," she said. "I'm just going to stoke the brazier."

He started to make some comment about keeping her warm, but it got lost somewhere between his brain and his mouth. Instead, he undressed down to his long shirt and slid beneath the blankets. The instant his head touched the pillow, he was asleep.

✦ ✦ ✦

A cry awoke Conor sometime in the night. He sat bolt upright in the bed, panting and covered in sweat. It took him several moments to remember where he was and several more to register that the voice speaking to him was real and not just in his head.

"Shh, Conor, I'm here. It was just a dream." Aine's hands were touching him, making soothing motions that he could still scarcely reconcile with the pain he'd just experienced. "Come, lie back down."

He let her guide him down to the mattress and slid his arms around her, pulling her tight to his body. He'd hoped returning to Ard Dhaimhin would help him put that experience behind him. He buried his head against her neck and breathed in the lavender scent of her hair while his heartbeat returned to normal. She just held him and stroked his hair as she might a heartbroken child.

"I wish I could do something," she murmured, the anguish plain in her voice. "If I could make it stop, I would."

"It's not real. It was never real, yet I still lived it. How do you forget something that never happened?" He wasn't making any sense, but none of this made any sense. Her hair was wet against his face, dampening his skin. Except it was the other way around—his tears were dampening her hair and her shoulder and pouring out with big, gulping sobs.

But men did not weep from nightmares. He wrenched himself from her arms and dragged his sleeve across his face. "I'm sorry. I didn't mean . . . I'll be fine."

Aine pushed herself up on one elbow. "Why won't you let me help you?"

"How exactly can you help me? Did you find a rune that could block memory instead of magic? A spell to go back in time so I never let this happen? Because unless you have, I don't see how you can do anything to help."

He waited for her angry answer, welcomed it even, but she still just looked at him with that same sad, sympathetic expression. Then she kissed him.

What she could find lovable or desirable about him in that moment—angry, tearful, and terrified, not even half the man she thought she'd married—he couldn't fathom. But she seemed determined to make him believe that none of that mattered to her. And for a while, at least, he did.

✦ ✦ ✦

Aine crept out of bed while the light was still pale and gray, careful not to wake Conor, who seemed to have at last fallen into a dreamless slumber. She had hoped—prayed—that returning to Ard Dhaimhin might help him shake off those memories. She'd also believed she could erect a wall between their minds strong enough to separate her from the dreams. Yet the strength of his nightmares, or maybe the strength of their connection, had blasted straight through the barrier until she was as enmeshed in those horrible recollections as he was.

She splashed frigid water on her face from the basin, wishing she could wash away the memories as easily as the tracks her tears had left on her cheeks.

"I'm sorry, Aine."

She straightened to see him watching her from the bed. "For what? You have nothing left to apologize for."

He patted the bed next to him, and when she came to sit

by his side, he lifted her hand to his lips. "I'll ask to move to another chamber today."

"Why would you do that? What's wrong with this one?"

"Don't make this harder than it is. Believe me, I hate the fact it happens so often. I would never subject you to that every night. You need your rest."

For a moment, she thought he was talking about her ability to share his dreams, but then she realized he meant being awakened abruptly at night. She twisted her hand so they could interlace their fingers.

"No. I won't allow it."

"You won't *allow* it?"

"No. You claim you're doing this for me. And I say no. I need my husband by my side more than I need a full night's sleep. Do you realize that out of the time we've been married, we've spent only something like six weeks together?"

"What if I hurt you by accident? I couldn't live with myself—"

"You won't. You haven't. I'm not afraid of you, Conor. You are the gentlest man I've ever met."

The worried look on his face began to fade, and a playful look sparked in his eyes. "I'm not sure 'gentle' is a description a warrior wants to own."

"Oh, but he should." She climbed back in bed beside him. "It doesn't mean you're weak. It simply means you want peace more than glory. That is a very good trait for a father, in my opinion."

He smiled and placed his hand on her belly, then drew in a breath. "Was that the baby kicking?"

"It was. He must recognize his father's voice."

He sighed in what sounded like contentment and pulled her tighter to his side, though he didn't remove his hand from her belly. "I wish I could stay here, just like this, and pretend none of the other exists."

"What's stopping you?" she asked, her tone teasing.

"Unfortunately, duty calls. I came straight to you when I arrived last night, so Eoghan and the Conclave will expect my report first thing this morning." He leaned over and pressed a lingering kiss to her lips, then swung his legs over the side of the bed.

She watched him dress. It seemed as though every time they managed a moment of connection, he left her, either physically or mentally.

As if he heard her thoughts, he turned to her and gave her a smile. "I'll be back soon. I promise."

She returned the smile, even though she really didn't feel it. "I'm counting on it."

CHAPTER
TWENTY-NINE

Conor knocked on Eoghan's door, hoping he had caught him before he went below for morning devotions. After a moment, the door opened. Eoghan adjusted the strap on his baldric at the same time.

"Conor?" He clasped Conor's arm and pulled him into a hug, pounding the air from him with his customary enthusiasm. Then he stepped back and scowled. "You look terrible."

"Nice to see you, too." But he couldn't really argue when it was true. He stepped past Eoghan and nudged the door shut behind him. His friend lingered by the door, curiously uneasy.

"What was the situation when you left?" Eoghan asked finally.

"Stable. Quiet. Nuada had things in hand by the second day. He'll be fine. With the wards and the corridor established, I doubt he'll see any action."

Eoghan nodded thoughtfully. "And you?"

Conor knew what he was asking, but he wasn't about to delve into his feelings on the subject. "I'm fine. What about Ard Dhaimhin? I found Iomhar outside Aine's chamber last night."

"Conor, you have to understand, I had no inkling something like this could happen. Aine's safety has always been a top priority."

"What?" Conor frowned. "What about Aine's safety?"

Now Eoghan looked ill. "I was sure she would have told you. There was an attempt on her life. It failed, thanks to Iomhar's intervention."

"What?" Conor shouted. "Someone tried to kill my wife and no one told me?"

"On her orders." Eoghan gestured to a chair. "Please, sit. I need to back up to what precipitated this."

The story Eoghan told him about Keondric's soul being present alongside Niall's in one body would have been unbelievable had Conor not already witnessed unbelievable things. When Eoghan got to the part about Murchadh's halfhearted attempt to murder Aine, he felt like he was going to burst. He gritted his teeth so hard he thought they might crack.

"So essentially, Niall is trying to make his own version of the Rune Throne, which he can use only because of Keondric's presence. Aine is the sole one who can reach Keondric, so therefore Niall wants her dead. Did I get that correct?"

"That's what we believe, aye." Eoghan held out a hand in supplication. "There is no way we could have anticipated this."

"No, but Niall seems to have anticipated our actions fairly well. Especially if he had the foresight to plant Murchadh in Ard Dhaimhin years ago. I want to speak with Murchadh."

"You can't. He's dead."

"Suicide?"

"Aine suspects Morrigan, but the truth is we don't know."

"There seems to be much you don't know," Conor snapped, then tempered his voice. "I'm sorry. It's just . . . too much. I'm going to assemble the Conclave, and then I need you to get a couple of items from the library." He detailed the things he wanted and then made his way to the door.

"Conor? It's good to have you back."

"Thank you. Even if we both know I can't stay long."

Eoghan's expression showed he knew, had been thinking the same thing but had been afraid to broach the subject. "If I had any other choice—"

"Don't worry about it. It's exactly what I would do in your place."

Conor returned to Carraigmór's hall, already fighting a wave of bleary exhaustion. Focusing on Eoghan's words had taken far more of his energy than he wanted to admit. After giving the order to convene the Conclave, he wandered around the great hall, stopping before the Rune Throne. Somehow it managed to both dominate the room and repel observers, much like the warding on the Hall of Prophecies. Imagine if they knew what rune had been used for that. It would be worth the loss of their fading skills if they could bear a rune that made the enemy unconsciously stay away. Of course, that could always have unintended consequences. Magic, especially runic magic, usually did.

When the men began to trickle into the hall, Conor greeted them with a vague smile, though he still felt detached. It had been so long since he'd had a full night of sleep, everything had taken on a hazy, dreamlike cast. In some way, it made these difficult decisions easier.

Riordan was one of the last to enter the room, and instead of keeping his distance like the others, he immediately crushed Conor into a bone-breaking hug. It cracked his numbness for just a moment. "Welcome back, son."

Eoghan appeared with two rolled sheets of parchment under one arm and gave Conor a nod of affirmation. The other men stood as he entered. "Brothers, take a seat please."

"So, they've no doubt told you you're the talk of Ard Dhaimhin," Eoghan said with a grin.

Conor frowned. "I don't understand."

"You don't know?"

"I have no idea what you're talking about."

Eoghan exchanged a glance with Riordan that set a nervous shimmy in Conor's stomach. "Will someone tell me what's going on? What's wrong?"

"Nothing's wrong, Conor," Riordan said. "We were just under the impression that you'd done it intentionally. The corridor between the fortresses—"

"Aye, which was done intentionally—"

"Has expanded."

Conor blinked. "Expanded? I don't understand."

"Didn't you play your harp on the way back?"

He nodded, even though he no longer remembered what he had played.

"Whatever you did pushed the boundaries of the wards beyond the passage between the fortresses. It bled over into the mountains, liberated villages that had been isolated by the sidhe for months."

Conor still stared, uncomprehending.

"We had the first travelers arrive at Ard Dhaimhin from this side of the Sliebhanaigh mountains, looking for supplies," Eoghan said. "The sidhe had been keeping them corralled, essentially, starving them to death as they fed on their fears. Your wards somehow swallowed up their towns and liberated them."

"They're speaking of you as a hero," Riordan added.

How could he be a hero for something he hadn't even intended to do? It had been a happy accident, if anything. If they were hoping he could reproduce that action, they would be sadly disappointed.

He focused on the strategic implication. "That should restrict the movement of any ensorcelled men, at least. It will have killed anyone who was under the druid's direct influence."

"Aye, but the ensorcelled men aren't our biggest problem now," Gradaigh said. "The wards will keep out the army, but they are no longer a defense against Niall himself."

"Nor Niall's men inside Ard Dhaimhin." He could barely grit out the words.

"Aine told you?" Riordan asked.

"Eoghan told me. He's not going to stop now that he knows she can target his weakness."

"Maybe not." Eoghan exchanged a significant look with Riordan.

"What?"

"Niall made some telling comments to Aine about your baby. He seems to believe she's tapping into the child's powers."

Conor went cold when he understood what they were saying. Not only was Aine a target but his baby was too? "You think he wants the child?"

"It's a possibility," Eoghan said. "Which means they're both safe—relatively speaking—for a few more months. But it also means he has another reason to breach Ard Dhaimhin."

Nausea built inside him—his wife and child the target of a madman. But there was another possibility they weren't considering. "What if this is all a distraction?"

Perplexed looks circulated the table. "How?" Fechin asked.

Conor gestured for the scrolls Eoghan had brought and unrolled them on the table. "This is a map of the Old Kingdom, before the modern fortresses were built. You already know that the runes are contained on the standing stones, which were used as the foundations for the old dún. What if this is just a big game of misdirection? We throw our efforts into protecting

Carraigmór while he quietly takes the fortresses? And once he has all the runes, it matters very little what we do."

"What are you proposing, then?" Riordan asked.

"That depends. How confident are you in your ability to protect the Rune Throne?"

"Ard Dhaimhin is secure," Gradaigh said.

"Is it really? The last time the druid laid siege on Ard Dhaimhin, he was halfway up the steps before anyone noticed his presence. It was only because of Riordan's gift that he was stopped. If he knows he can slip beneath the wards now, there's nothing to stop him."

"Ah, but you're forgetting one thing," Eoghan said. "Keondric's presence allows him to take the shield rune without dying, which acts as a barrier between his sorcery and the wards. But it also suppresses his magic. He can't do both. If he comes to Ard Dhaimhin, he has to do so without his sorcery."

"Which would make him vulnerable. There's no reason he would do that."

"Exactly."

At least that was one thing he didn't have to worry about for now. "In that case, our best chance of stopping him is to prevent him from getting the remaining runes."

He removed a fistful of hand stones from his belt pouch and began to place them on various points of the map. "These are all his targets he has yet to strike."

"Twelve," Fechin said. "Plus the four that he's already taken. You think the runes have been scattered across sixteen fortresses?"

"So far, all the fortresses he's taken have been ring forts, the earthen ones that were erected by the ancient clans prior to Daimhin's arrival. All the stone fortresses, and those carved out by magic like Ard Dhaimhin and Ard Bealach, were done hundreds of years later. The druids must have found some significance in putting them in the places of the Old Kingdom."

"But some of them have been destroyed."

"Aye. Only nine of these are intact fortresses, but the stones are too large to be moved. I'd venture to say they're still there. Our best chance is to beat Niall to these fortresses and destroy the rune stones before he can collect them."

"As soon as he finds out about it, you will be a target too," Eoghan said.

"That's why it's going to have to be a coordinated effort. And we're going to need Aine to help."

Conor outlined the plan as it formed, the pieces falling into place almost as quickly as he could speak them. They would assign several groups of men to go to the locations of the other stones. Because there were locations that no longer had walls, those were the least likely to have people who needed to be persuaded. They would send other brothers to those. Conor would focus on those that were likely to have sidhe activity and erect wards around them at the same time.

"I will have to strike the fortress that's nearest the sorcerer's last known location," Conor said. "After that, he'll know what we're attempting to do, and he'll either try to crush us with numbers or beat us to the next fortress. I suspect, traveling light and fast, we'll be able to reach our destination first."

"It's a risk," Eoghan said. "A big risk."

"Aye. It's a risk. Do you see any alternative?"

The men looked at each other, resignation in their expressions. Eoghan shook his head. "No. We'll do it. Pick your men. We'll need to select only those who can see the runes. Otherwise they'll have no idea what they're looking for."

"I'll go," Riordan said.

"No," Conor and Eoghan said simultaneously.

"You're needed here," Eoghan continued. "Should something happen to me, Riordan, you are the next in command."

Riordan didn't look pleased, but he didn't argue.

"We need to do this quickly, before he has a chance to move on another fortress." Conor studied the map. "If I were to guess his next move, I'd say he's going to hit Glas Na Baile next."

"Why not Gorm Lis?" Dal asked. "It's closer to his last conquest than Glas Na Baile."

"It is, but the terrain is rougher and it's closer to our borders. If you look, he's moving from north to south in a relatively straight line. I'd guess it's because he can travel faster in the meadowlands."

The room fell silent as they all contemplated the impossible mission ahead of them. It was easy to say they could do something, but Conor knew better than any of them how the easiest missions—such as Ard Bealach—had unforeseen consequences. Had it not been for that bloodless victory, Daigh would be with them today, debating this issue with his usual blend of practicality and bile.

"There is one last thing to consider," Eoghan said. "If we succeed in this, Niall will be desperate. He will throw every last resource at Ard Dhaimhin to get the Rune Throne."

Conor nodded solemnly. "And it will be your job to be ready for him."

They talked over other matters affecting the city, but Conor just let them slide through his mind. Eoghan and Riordan had taken command of the city while he was gone, leaving no place for him in the conversation. He would be leaving again soon, had known it would become necessary ever since Larkin had questioned him at Ard Bealach. Now he just had to figure out how to break the news to Aine.

When the meeting dissolved, Eoghan drew Conor aside.

"I didn't want to discuss it before the Conclave, but there's still the matter of the prisoner."

Somhairle. Somehow, in his sleepless fog and his reunion with Aine, Conor had forgotten about him. "Is he in one of the lower chambers?"

"Aye. But so far he's not been cooperative. Hasn't said a word to any of the brothers who have tried to talk to him." Eoghan hesitated. "I think we should have Aine try."

"No. Not an option."

"Then short of applying methods the brotherhood doesn't officially condone, I don't think he's going to tell us anything of value."

Conor sighed. If Somhairle didn't have the shield rune, it would be easy. Aine could pluck the information they needed out of his head and be done with it. But the idea of letting her stand in the same chamber with the man, letting him toy with her mind as he had with Conor . . .

"What about Morrigan?" he asked suddenly.

"Do you think that's a good idea, considering what she's been through? If even a fraction of what she said about him is true, it would be unspeakably cruel."

"But we would know immediately if she were telling the truth. And I'm sure she is the last one Somhairle would expect to see."

Eoghan sighed. "I don't like it, and I wouldn't have expected you of all people to suggest it. But Aine is the one who has had the most contact with her. Get her opinion. If she agrees, I'll agree."

✦ ✦ ✦

"Absolutely not!" Aine stared at Conor as if he were mad. "It's cruel."

Conor blinked. He had thought it was a reasonable way to use their resources. "You said yourself that Morrigan isn't being honest."

"About what she's doing here. Not about what happened to her. In fact, that's the one thing I'd venture to say she's been totally honest about."

"Then we're out of options."

"Of course we're not. I'll talk to him."

"No." Conor shook his head vehemently. "You have no idea what kind of man he is. I would not subject you to his company for any reason."

Aine sighed and plopped down on their bed. "I'm fairly certain I do. I traveled with mercenaries in Aron. One of them tried to kill me."

"Exactly."

"And what do you think he's going to do while in bonds? He's got the shield rune, so even if he possessed magic, he wouldn't be able to use it."

"And because he has the shield rune, you won't have any more luck than we would."

"I don't need my mind-reading gifts. Once more, you underestimate me."

From her smirk, Conor thought that might be true.

✦ ✦ ✦

Despite her confident words, Aine's pulse raced as she descended the stairs to the lower confines of Carraigmór, followed by both Conor and Iomhar. The last time she'd been here, she'd questioned Murchadh, who had tried to kill her. Now she was to speak with a man who had tortured Morrigan and had tried to kill Conor.

Eoghan already waited for them in front of the same chamber that had once held the healer. He addressed Aine first. "Are you sure you want to do this?"

"Aye. He's bound, isn't he?"

"Of course."

"Then you must promise me you won't interfere, no matter what he says or does."

Eoghan exchanged a look with Conor that said he was no more pleased by the request than her husband had been. "I promise. *If* you keep your distance. We have no way of knowing exactly what he's capable of."

She nodded her agreement, and Eoghan unbarred the door.

The prisoner sat tied to a single chair in the center of the room, his arms and legs shackled to the stone. But for his filthy state, he looked to have been treated well. Apparently, the Fírein were serious about their rules for the treatment of prisoners.

An unsettling light gleamed in his eyes as soon as he saw her. "Brought me some entertainment, did you?"

Aine didn't show her repulsion. This was all just for show, to anger the men behind her, to unsettle her. She clasped her hands and stopped at arm's distance before him while Iomhar circled behind, his knife at the ready. "I have some questions for you."

Somhairle's mouth curved into a nasty smile. "Why should I answer them?"

Aine met his eyes squarely, unafraid. "Because I'm going to ask you nicely. And you will answer because my methods are much less painful than my husband's. You've already proven you have a taste for self-preservation. So could we just bypass the part where you refuse, and they threaten, and then you tell us anyway?"

He sized her up, his gaze riveting on her obviously pregnant belly. "Which one is your husband?"

"The one who wants to kill you for looking at me like that."

He grinned at her. "Dove, in this instance, that doesn't help much."

A quick glance over her shoulder showed Eoghan and Conor

wearing identical scowls. She almost laughed, but instead she just gestured for a chair to be brought for her. When she sat, she folded her hands in her lap and studied him for a minute.

"You're the last survivor of Ard Bealach. Why did Lord Keondric leave you alive when you had the potential to tell us about his plans?"

He glanced between her and the men. For a moment, she thought he wouldn't answer. "He had me spelled."

"Was that before or after you took the shield rune?"

His eyebrows lifted. "Before. He left me to care for the prisoner."

"Meallachán. The bard. Aye?" He nodded and she moved on. "Why did he give you the rune?"

"Survival, I'd think. Surely you know about the spirits by now. Had I been caught in one of their glamours, we would both be dead."

"But you killed him anyway, even after he helped you."

"Aye. It was my job. Should a rescue attempt come, he was to die." Somhairle delivered the statement as calmly as if he'd been talking about the weather. For the first time, a little curl of unease climbed up her spine. This man wasn't just cold; he was soulless.

Had he simply burned away his humanity in his pursuit of gold? Or was this some sort of side effect of the shield rune? The idea was almost as chilling as the emptiness in Somhairle's eyes.

"The woman, Morrigan—how did she escape the keep?"

Genuine surprise shifted into another of those nasty smiles. "She told you she escaped, did she? I've never met a woman who could lie as convincingly as that one. Told me she loved me. Almost made me believe it too. Women can be very persuasive. But I suppose you've learned that yourself or you wouldn't be here."

Aine didn't flinch. "So Morrigan didn't escape. She was allowed to leave."

"No, my innocent little dove, she was sent. Does that surprise you?"

"Not particularly. Sent to do what?"

"I couldn't tell you."

He was lying now, and from the grin he sent her way, she realized he'd just been toying with her. He wouldn't give her anything beyond what they already knew. He just wanted her to think he would, while he leered and made veiled innuendos. She pushed herself out of the chair. "We're done."

"No, we're not." Conor pulled the dagger from his waist and strode toward Somhairle. The determination on his face sent a chill through her.

"Conor, what are you doing?"

He ripped open the man's shirt to reveal the pink shield rune. In one swift movement, he sliced a line through the marking on the prisoner's chest, bringing up a bright swell of blood. "Read him. Now, before the druid can get to him."

Aine stared in shock for a moment and then obeyed. She knelt beside Somhairle and grabbed his hand. Now that the integrity of the rune had been broken, sensations and thoughts assailed her. Memories of the sick things he had done in service of Niall and others like him. Images of Morrigan—and others—screaming while he tormented them. Unspeakable acts she would never be able to wipe from her mind. And below it all, a familiar thread of sorcery, keeping his actions in check, his loyalty to the druid secure.

She let go of his hand and managed to stumble to the corner before she vomited. Tears slid down her face. "He can't be allowed to leave. Kill him," she whispered.

"Too late," Eoghan said.

She lifted her head and turned from the corner. Somhairle slumped in the chair, his shirt stained red. She looked to Conor, who simply shook his head to her unspoken question.

Then she understood. Niall never left traitors alive.

+ + +

They refrained from questioning her until she was seated in the Ceannaire's office, her hands wrapped around a cup of tea, a fur draped over her shoulders. Conor pulled up a chair beside her and took her hand. "Tell us what you saw."

Aine swallowed and shook her head. What she'd seen would torment her as surely as what she'd experienced through Conor's mind. Somehow she'd thought she understood depravity, but having seen a glimpse of the experiments with which Somhairle had assisted, the torments he'd devised for his own pleasure, she could no longer deny that Niall was not the only true evil in the world.

"Tell us the important bits," Eoghan said gently from his post by the door.

That she could manage. She shut the memories out and sifted through the information she'd gleaned from the flood of images. "He wasn't lying about Morrigan. She didn't escape. She was sent."

"Sent to do what?"

She looked between Conor and Eoghan. "To control the flow of information here. To limit what we could learn. I got the impression Niall is holding something over her."

Eoghan frowned. "I don't understand. If Morrigan didn't want us to know anything, why did she tell us about Ard Bealach? We wouldn't have learned about the shield rune had it not been for that."

"I don't think that was part of the plan."

"So she's been playing both sides," Conor said. "She might

not be helping Niall willingly, but we still don't know which side she would choose if forced."

"I can't answer that, because Somhairle didn't know."

"What else did you learn?" Conor prompted.

Aine shook her head. Most of what she had seen were just the memories of his own depraved acts. "Did you know that Niall was going to kill him when you removed the protection of the rune?"

Conor hesitated. "I suspected, aye. Thought it would save us the trouble. And now we know that the druid's reach extends through Ard Dhaimhin's wards."

"Only when he has some sort of connection, though," Eoghan said. "Somhairle was spelled. Aine initiated a mind link with him when she heard Keondric call for her. That tells me he has to have a way in first."

"So we really can't break Morrigan's rune," Aine said. "He will be able to contact her—maybe even kill her—from afar, and he'll potentially have access to anything she knows."

"I'm not sure she knows anything that can help us," Conor said. "I imagine Niall told her only what she needed to know to complete her mission."

"And we might never know what that is," Eoghan remarked.

"Maybe we should just ask her," Aine said.

"We already did," Conor said. "She's given us lies and half-truths from the start."

"Aye, but now we can give her something she truly wants," Aine said with a grim certainty.

It was decided that because Aine had the most established relationship with Morrigan, she should be the one to break the news. She instead retrieved the woman and her two guards from the upper chamber and led them two floors down.

"Where are we going?" Morrigan asked. "Did Master Eoghan finally decide it was safe to let me out?"

"Rather the opposite," Aine said. "But I thought you would want to see this."

Aine nodded to the brother on guard outside the chamber, and he opened the door for them. She waved for Morrigan to precede her.

The woman stopped, a hand flying to her mouth. "It's him."

"Aye. It's him."

"Did you kill him?"

"Your master did, to keep him from talking. But not before I pulled everything out of his mind. I know. I know what he did to you. And it wasn't just you."

Morrigan sank down to a crouch, stunned. "He's really dead."

"Aye. He can't hurt anyone else now."

She sat there, her face buried in her hands for several minutes, her shoulders shaking with silent sobs. Then she jerked her head up, her eyes panicked. "Did you bring him into the city blindfolded? Unconscious?"

Aine glanced at Conor, who waited in the doorway. He shook his head.

"No. Why?"

"Did you talk about me?"

Slowly, Aine nodded.

A hysterical-sounding laugh slipped out of Morrigan's mouth. "That was your last mistake. Everything Somhairle saw or knew, Lord Keondric now does as well. The city. Your defenses. My presence. You let him in."

She straightened from her crouch and visibly pulled the shreds of her emotions together, that hard, calculated expression sliding onto her face again. Then she leaned in close. "You gave me a gift, Lady Aine, so I'll give you one in return. Take the shield rune and flee, while you still can."

CHAPTER
THIRTY

For the next several days, Conor shirked his duties around Ard Dhaimhin unapologetically, skipping his morning practices and devotions, refusing to attend even Conclave meetings unless he was specifically summoned. Aine might pretend her experiences with Somhairle and Morrigan hadn't affected her, but he saw the sick look that crept over her face in unguarded moments. Nothing less than an emergency was going to pull him from her side.

And he found every reason he could think of not to tell Aine about his plans.

She sensed it, though, even if she didn't pull it outright from his brain. When he asked if she needed to go to the village to work, she merely shook her head and said that the healers could handle it without her. She knew. She had to. And she had to know, too, that his leaving again meant he would miss the birth of his child.

If he came back at all.

He wouldn't think about that, though. There was no reason to believe this mission was any more dangerous than any of the others from which he had returned. They had the advantage of speed and surprise. Ard Dhaimhin had gained more resources in the past several months, including a stable of fast horses, which they could use to hopefully stay ahead of Niall and his large parties of slow-moving foot soldiers.

But one night, when they lay in their bed with their limbs tangled together beneath the heavy blankets, Aine finally asked, "When do you leave?"

He didn't try to deny it. "Four days."

"For how long?"

"I don't know. A couple of months, I would think. You've heard the talk around Carraigmór?"

"I know you're going to try to destroy the runes before Niall reaches them, aye. Eoghan told me."

"You and Eoghan are close now."

She didn't even flinch. "He's been supportive while you were gone. He is a good friend to us, Conor."

"A better friend to you, I think." The words spilled out before he could consider how they sounded.

Aine pulled back from him. "I thought we settled this already."

"I thought we did too. But it seems clear to me that whatever he feels toward you was not brought on by your gift." He knew he should stop before he dug himself in too deeply to escape, but the part of his mind that prevented those words from leaving his lips seemed to be asleep. "And when I find out that you two have conspired to keep information from me, what am I supposed to think?"

She pushed herself off the bed and lit the torch from the small candle that still burned at the bedside. "You are supposed to trust me. You are supposed to trust *him*. Never have we given you reason to suspect us. Never have we done anything to earn this . . . insecurity. I don't know how many times I can tell you that I love you and only you before you will believe it!"

"Then why did I have to hear about the assassination attempt from Eoghan, weeks after it happened?"

She stopped. "Conor, I don't think you understand how not yourself you've been since Ard Bealach. We didn't want to add to your worries."

"'We' again."

Aine let out a cry of pure frustration. "Enough! Either you're going to believe me or you're not. I can't keep trying to convince you. Do you think it hasn't killed me to know there was someone else in Gwydden? Do you think it's easy to give you the benefit of the doubt when I have that image in my mind? No. But I don't question your love, Conor. I trusted that you would tell me when you were ready."

All the blood drained from Conor's face, leaving him light-headed. "You saw that?"

"Aye, I saw that. I was connected to your mind." She turned to him again, and he saw the traces of tears on her cheeks. "I saw everything."

He closed his eyes while he considered his words. He should have known this would come back to haunt him. His wife was a mind reader. How could he ever have thought he could keep this a secret? "Then you saw all there was. One kiss. Ill-advised, aye, but born out of the pain of thinking you were marrying another man. And I came to my senses." Because his gift had shown her for what she was. Had it not been for that . . .

"Who was she?"

"A sidhe."

Aine's startled expression showed that was the last thing she had expected. "The one who wove the glamour."

"Aye. Pretended to be the daughter Prince Talfryn never had. And I was taken in like the rest of them. Had I not kissed her, we might never have learned the truth." Conor held up his hand. "I'm not justifying my actions. I'm just saying what happened."

Aine wrapped her arms around herself, her expression forlorn. "But you don't deny that you wanted her. I can understand temptation. But the way you kissed her . . ."

A harsh laugh slipped out of Conor's mouth. "Is that what bothers you? That wasn't love, Aine, or desire. I wanted to hurt her for ruining my memory of you, for showing me things I didn't want to see." The slight look of horror in her eyes just pushed him on. "Like it or not, that's the man you married: someone who could torture a prisoner for information, someone who could hurt a woman. You might want to believe I'm still the person you knew at Lisdara, but I'm not."

"I don't believe that." She inched closer to him.

"You should. I have blood on my hands. I don't think you realize how much."

"And the fact you do tells me you're not nearly as cruel as you think you are." Now she was standing before him, between his knees, her hand on his shoulders. "If you tell me that nothing else happened with Briallu, nothing happened."

She combed her hands through his hair and bent to kiss him. "I still believe in you, even if you don't believe in yourself."

She couldn't have said anything to make him smaller, more unworthy. His arms went around her waist, his head pillowed on the roundness where his child grew. All that she had seen and endured, and she still believed in the goodness of the world. Still saw the best in everyone.

"I don't deserve you," he whispered.

In answer, she shifted to sit on his lap. Then her mouth

found his in earnest, and even though he knew for certain that her lips were otherwise occupied, he was sure he heard the echo of her voice in his mind.

Just come back to me.

CHAPTER
THIRTY-ONE

For the first time since he'd returned to Ard Dhaimhin,
Conor met Eoghan and Riordan in the practice yard at dawn
the day before his departure, eliciting raised eyebrows but no
questions. He took a wooden practice sword and faced Riordan
first.

"Sure you're up to this?" his father asked, settling into a balanced, comfortable stance.

"Best we find out now. I leave tomorrow."

And find out he did. Riordan put him through his paces, not
giving any quarter. Distracted, Conor lost his sword twice, having to pull out some fancy moves to retrieve it before his father
finished him. In the end, he had to admit that it hadn't been
pretty, but he'd managed not to get killed.

"Not bad." Riordan looked as fresh as he had when they'd
begun, even though Conor was sweating and panting like a
novice.

"If by 'not bad' you mean forgetting every single thing I
taught him over the course of two years." Eoghan shot Conor a
look that practically dared him to prove otherwise.

But Conor simply shrugged. "If you expect beautiful technique, I should just yield now."

"Huh. I hardly expected a philosophical answer from you. What happened to your competitive spirit?"

"I don't care about competition. Right now I mostly just care about getting home alive again."

A glint of satisfaction surfaced in Eoghan's face. "Good. Let's do that."

Conor noticed the shift in Eoghan's usual style immediately, but he didn't have any time to think about why before the man rushed with a flurry of thrusts and crossways strikes. Gone was the elegant fluidity that marked the Fíréin's sword work; in its place a direct, effective, almost brutally efficient method that had only one aim: to kill or maim. Instead of letting the pressure force him into foolishness, Conor found himself leaning more on his Fíréin training: proper technique, a fluid rhythm of defense and counterattack. And when Eoghan stepped back, Conor realized that never once had his friend's blade touched him, nor had his sword left his hand.

"Aye. That's the way you do it," Eoghan said with a nod. "Nothing to prove. It's merely a matter of keeping his sword from you and looking for your opening. When you relax, you win."

Conor waited until Eoghan's back was turned before he dropped his guard and turned away. He rolled his shoulders but found that without the tension he'd held while fighting Riordan, he actually felt less tired than before. "Where did you learn that style, by the way?"

"I've spent a lot of time in the yards, fighting the kingdom's men. Seemed like it might be helpful to know their style."

"Words I never thought I would hear." Conor worked the kink out of his neck and handed off his sword to his father.

"Considering how much you two have done to brutalize my self-worth, I'll leave you to it."

Eoghan and Riordan just grinned at him and took their places facing each other. The clack of wooden swords followed him up the path to the village.

He stopped at the cookhouse on his way to Carraigmór to pick up porridge for him and Aine, noting that the cook put an extra scoop of oats and a handful of dried fruit into one. Conor just smiled to himself. She might think it was her gift that caused people to love her, but it was more likely the fact that she gave of herself without asking anything in return. The people of Ard Dhaimhin reciprocated.

Conor nodded to the night guard still on watch while he pushed the door open. "Breakfast."

Aine pushed herself up on her elbow, bleary-eyed. "Let me guess. Porridge?"

He grinned, glad to see that her mood had improved. "Aye. What else? At least you've got the men in the cookhouse wrapped around your finger."

Aine took the bowl from him and smiled. "Must be Corrin at the porridge pot this morning. He always tells me that I need to eat more fruit to ensure that the child gets my sweet disposition."

"As compared to my salty one?"

She shrugged, though a mischievous smile played over her lips. "You'd have to ask him about that."

"Is there a man in the city who isn't half in love with you?"

"Aye."

"Who would that be?"

A wicked little smile. "You, of course. You are *all* the way in love with me."

"Well, you have that part right." Aine accepted his kiss and then sobered. "This is your last day at Ard Dhaimhin. What are you doing?"

"I'm going to go see Morrigan before I leave. Check on the supplies. All the things I've neglected."

"Then I should make a list of items for you to retrieve from the healers' cottage before you go." When he gave her a searching look, she said, "Because we agreed that I would stay up at Carraigmór for safety."

"Right. I'm glad." Even if it did concern him that she was being so agreeable to the restrictions. Conor took their bowls and leaned down to kiss her good-bye. "Rest. Think of yourself and the baby first. Promise?"

"I promise."

Oh, aye, there was definitely something up.

He returned his bowls to the small kitchen inside Carraigmór, where they would be washed and returned to the cookhouse down below, then found his way to Morrigan's door.

"I heard you were back," she said, standing aside for him to enter. "Come to visit the prisoner?"

"Prisoner? Hardly. Honored but not-completely-trusted guest would be more apt." He smiled at the face Morrigan made. It was almost like old times, growing up at Balurnan. She had been serious, but he could always get a rise out of her with his teasing.

"Right. Honored guest who isn't allowed to go anywhere. It seems I have developed amazing powers that allow me to kill people without setting foot outside my chamber."

"Have you?"

That face again. "Of course not. If that were possible, I wouldn't still be trapped in here, would I?"

"No, I suppose not." Conor wandered around the room, but there was nothing to look at as a distraction. She was wearing her men's clothing again, he noticed, with her borrowed dress hanging on a hook. Did that mean she had abandoned the pretense of her cooperative, ladylike attitude?

"Why are you here, Conor?"

"I came to say good-bye." He turned and watched her reaction to the words. "I'm leaving again tomorrow."

"I thought you might." She took a seat at the little table on one side of her chamber. "How is Aine taking it?"

"Aine understands the necessity. The sooner I go, the sooner I can be back. Hopefully in time for the birth of our baby."

"Right."

He narrowed his eyes. "What? Say what you're thinking, sister."

"Ah, so I'm your sister again? Fine. She's better off without you."

It was the last thing he'd expected her to say. "What?"

"Surely you've seen it, Conor. She doesn't look well. She's not sleeping because of you, and it's harming the baby. Did she tell you about the herbs?"

He frowned. "What herbs?"

"To stop her labor pains. The ones she asked me to get for her." Morrigan studied him. "She really didn't tell you. I wonder why that is."

Conor stared at her with mounting horror. Aine was having labor pains already, and she had kept it from him?

But of course she had kept many things from him, not just that.

He shook off that doubt. "I'm leaving, so it hardly matters. Without me around to disturb her sleep, she'll feel much better."

"And if it's not your physical presence that's the problem?"

"I don't understand."

A nasty little smile surfaced on Morrigan's face. "Come, Conor. I don't believe you're that daft. You've been at Ard

Bealach. Your wife reads minds. What do you think that kind of stress might do to a pregnant woman?"

Conor's stomach twisted with the sudden urge to vomit. Could what Morrigan hinted be true? Could Aine have been going through that terror and pain night after night with him? Why hadn't she told him?

Because she couldn't. Or she wouldn't. Knowing Aine, she'd been so concerned about his getting lost in the memories or doing something terrible to himself to make them stop, she'd left herself open to it. Naturally, she would never tell him, because she would never want him to feel the kind of guilt he was feeling now.

"You know, Morrigan, I never took you for malicious."

"Aine deserves some rest, some peace, away from the trouble you've brought her." She met his eyes, and the hatred there nearly knocked him off his feet. "The malice comes with the fact that I'm glad you get to experience a tiny portion of the pain we've felt."

His flash of anger dissolved immediately into a wave of sorrow. "I'm sorry, Morrigan, for what you've been through. And I know that you think you're looking out for Aine. The difference between you and her is that she can recognize when people truly love her. I'm not sure you can anymore."

He turned to the door but paused partway. "If you had just been honest with me from the start, I would have defended you to the ends of the earth. But you've lied to far too many people about far too many things for me to trust you, and trust is the one thing I'm not willing to risk anymore."

Conor stepped outside and pulled the door shut. He had no idea if that had been the right thing to say or do. But it was the truth. He couldn't trust her. He did have to thank her for one thing however: she'd shown him exactly what he had to do when he left.

CHAPTER
THIRTY-TWO

She would not cry. Aine repeated the directive to herself over
and over on Conor's last day at Ard Dhaimhin. While he went
about his final preparations below, she arranged for a simple supper, including a small jug of mead from the fortress's dwindling
stores. Her eyes stung from tiredness, not tears—and she told
herself that often enough that she began to believe it.

When Conor nudged her from sleep before first light,
though, fear and grief slammed into her, crushing her beneath
its unexpected weight. Still, she did not cry. Instead, she went
through the motions that had become their routine. She held his
clothes for him while he dressed. She buckled on his weapons.
And the whole time she prayed: for his safety, for his success,
that he would find some relief from his memories.

An eerie sense of sameness haunted her as she walked down
the stairs to the clearing below the fortress. This time instead of
ponies waiting, it was dozens of horses, packed with their individual supplies and kept calm by a clutch of young stable boys.
She held tight to Conor's hand, the baby's flips in her midsection
making her think the little one was as nervous as she was.

"Stay safe," Conor whispered before he pulled her close

enough to kiss her. She wrapped her arms around his neck and refused to let him go until they'd been clinging to each other for an embarrassing amount of time.

"I have faith in you," she said. "You may not be meant to be king, but you are the one about which Shanna's prophecy was written: the sword and the song. And I know in my heart that you were meant to use both to finally end the danger to Seare. Do your duty and then come back to me."

He lifted her hand to his lips, then crossed the clearing and mounted up with one easy motion, settling his weapons around him. The other men followed suit, clustering in their groups behind their respective leaders. Conor caught her gaze amid the activity and winked at her, his teasing grin giving a little lift to her heart.

Then he ordered his men forward, and the entire party churned into movement. Half of them went northwest out of the city and up the switchbacks through the burned forest. The other half moved south, where they would traverse the guarded pass into Sliebhan.

"He'll come back," Eoghan said lightly at her shoulder. "He always does. Usually after some dramatic spectacle he pretends not to understand."

It so perfectly described the outcome of Conor's missions, Aine laughed out loud. "He does tend to do that, doesn't he?"

"Aye. Come, I'll walk you back to the fortress. Iomhar is waiting for you at the top."

Aine climbed the long staircase, with several brief rests on the way, to where Iomhar indeed waited on the landing. He greeted them each with a bow. "Sir. My lady."

"See Lady Aine inside, please. I have responsibilities below."

"Aye, sir. My lady." Iomhar swept a hand ahead of him for her to precede him. "Where to today?"

"I think I'd just like to rest and read in my room," she said. She'd promised she would stay in the fortress, where it was safe and controlled, but she'd have to figure out some way to bring other work to her. If all she could do for the next several months was read and embroider, she would surely go mad.

But for today, reading suited her melancholy mood. She curled up in their bed, covers pulled to her waist beneath one of Shanna's journals, her mind divided between the writing and Conor's party's progress from Ard Dhaimhin. After several hours, she realized they had stopped. Conor was concentrating on something, but at this distance, she couldn't pick up what.

Then his presence vanished from her mind.

She gasped, searching through the surrounding minds, picking up stray thoughts but nothing that could explain what she was feeling. Surely if they were under attack, she would pick up urgency or fear from the other men. If he'd been killed or injured, they would be sending someone back to the city. So why couldn't she find him?

Her eyes fell on the small table that held all her possessions. Or at least it had. Her comb, mirror, and ribbons were still there. But the small jar of ink was gone, in its place a small vial.

She lifted the glass vial and turned it over, then uncapped the stopper. Just as quickly, she pulled it away. She recognized the distinctive, musty smell: hemlock. She had used it in small doses as a sedative, but there was enough here in this vial to kill a man. Why had Conor had it in his possession in the first place? Had he left it for her? Or was it something he'd been leaving behind? She almost reached out to him to ask before she understood the truth. He'd drawn the shield rune. He'd blocked her out.

Momentary panic welled up inside her before she could make herself think rationally. Why would he do that? On one hand, it would be that much more difficult for the druid to track him. On the other, he would be unable to reach her with updates as they'd planned. Why would he sever his one main link back to Ard Dhaimhin?

Morrigan.

She shoved the book aside, leapt out of bed, and stormed out of her chamber without acknowledging Iomhar. He hurried to catch up. "What's wrong, my lady?"

"I don't know. That's what I'm trying to find out." She pushed past Morrigan's guards and pounded on her door.

"Lady Aine?" Morrigan blinked innocently.

"Iomhar, with me." She shoved her way into the room, earning a shocked look from Conor's sister. She rounded on her. "What did you tell him?"

"I don't understand."

"You spoke with Conor last night. What did you tell him?"

"Ah. He took the rune, didn't he? I thought he might. I just thought he'd deliberate for longer." She sat on the edge of her bed, looking quite satisfied with herself.

"What did you tell him?"

"Nothing. He figured it out for himself—how your connection with him was harming you and the baby."

"Why would you do that?"

"Why do you think? Your love is blinding you, Lady Aine. He's using you. They are all using you. Do you think they have you under guard because they care about you? You are their most valuable tool. They are protecting you only because they need you."

"Then why on earth would you tell Conor that?"

"Because it was the right thing to do. Once you reflect on that, you'll see I'm right."

Aine paced a little path back and forth in front of Morrigan. "I don't understand you. Have your experiences twisted you so much that you trust no one? Have they completely skewed your perspective on humanity?"

"Skewed it? No. Made it clear to me." Morrigan stood and took Aine's hands to stop her pacing, her voice earnest. "Aine, you must understand, I did this for you. I know what it's like to be tormented. You don't deserve that. Your baby doesn't deserve that. You're finally free."

Aine just stared at Morrigan as if she'd never seen her before. She was either a master strategist or a little mad. "You have no idea what you've done."

She turned and marched out of the room, accompanied by Iomhar, who seemed confused by the whole exchange. "Where's Eoghan?"

"I don't know, my lady. He could still be down below."

"I need him now." She continued down the corridor, down the staircase, toward the Ceannaire's office. Iomhar caught another brother passing in the hall and whispered a few words before he hurried after her. The chamber was empty, as she expected it to be, but she plopped herself in a chair to wait. Less than ten minutes later, Eoghan appeared.

"My lady, you summoned me?"

Aine flushed, realizing how high-handed the gesture had been. Eoghan was just too gracious to acknowledge it. "Conor has taken the shield rune. I can't sense him anymore."

He blinked at her. "Why would he do that?"

"He knows I'm dreaming his nightmares."

Eoghan circled around and sat on the edge of the desk. "And so he thinks he's doing you a favor."

"Except now he's making it so we can't communicate in any way." She loaded irritation in her voice so she didn't have to acknowledge her very real fear.

"Well, let's think about this a moment. It has the effect of making him harder to track. And he probably knew you'd be upset if he told you ahead of time."

"I thought the same. But Morrigan basically admitted to manipulating the situation. She thinks I'm being used against my will and that I'm being protected only because I'm too valuable to Ard Dhaimhin to lose."

"Morrigan's partially right. We do need you."

"And the rest?"

"I won't even answer that question. You know I'd see you protected if you didn't have a single gift. You're Conor's wife, and even if you weren't—"

"I believe you," she said before he could elaborate further. "But the fact is, I am important to the war effort, and she used Conor's concern for me to make me basically ineffective."

"Perhaps that was the idea," Eoghan said grimly. "But she obviously doesn't know we planned for this. My lady, I know it's painful to be shut out, but as long as you can still monitor the other members of his party, there's no reason to be concerned. They have the doves if they need to convey anything of importance."

His measured demeanor only highlighted how emotional her reaction had been. If she were honest with herself, wasn't it more hurt over his pushing her away than real concern for the mission? She sighed. "How do you manage to be so calm about everything?"

"I'm not. I just know that some things are out of our control. Some things we just have to entrust to our Maker. And no, He hasn't shown me how this turns out. My decisions would be a lot easier if He actually did show me the future."

She pushed herself to her feet, feeling suddenly foolish. "I'm sorry to have disturbed you."

"It is my pleasure, my lady." He gave her a formal little bow and nodded to Iomhar to escort her from the room.

She felt a little foolish for her tirade as they climbed back up the stairs to her chamber. Somehow having faith seemed easier when she could assure herself that he was alive and well anytime she wished it. But if she could entrust him to Comdiu moment to moment, she could learn to trust Him without her involvement.

✦ ✦ ✦

Eoghan limited his interactions with Aine in Conor's absence, even if he kept an eye on her activities through the reports of her guards. It didn't take long for her to chafe at the necessary restrictions on her movements, wandering the halls at all hours with Iomhar by her side. Eoghan authorized her requests immediately—herbs for her healing concoctions, fabric for a baby's cap and gown, even the odd bit of embroidery thread— though he had a feeling they were all merely distractions.

After about a week of such reports from Iomhar, Eoghan couldn't stand it any longer. Aine must feel as if she were in a prison after having the freedom to roam the entire city. Despite his vow to leave her be while Conor was gone, despite the possibility he might have buried ulterior motives, he devised a way to get her into the fresh air while still keeping her safe.

Iomhar's eyebrows lifted when he showed up at Aine's door. Eoghan ignored the silent indictment and rapped softly. As soon as the door opened, before she could voice her surprise, he asked, "Would you care to join me for a game of King and Conqueror?"

Her eyes brightened for a moment and then her expression shuttered. "Thank you, Eoghan, but I think I will decline."

"Even if it means you'll get some fresh air?"

"How?"

He smiled and gestured for her to follow. "Come and see. You, too, Iomhar."

Curiosity apparently overtook her suspicion, because she followed him down the stairs toward the Ceannaire's office. Before he reached it, he made a quick turn and opened a door. They stepped into a blast of cold afternoon air from the balcony where Liam had always come to think. Eoghan had already set up a small table and two stools with a game board between them and a pile of furs on the ground beside them.

"Compromise," he said, sweeping his arm out. "You get out of the fortress, but you're practically guaranteed safety."

A smile lifted the corners of her mouth, and the answering twinge in his chest was immediately followed by a rush of guilt. He could pretend he would do the same for anyone else, but even he knew that for a lie. Too late now, though.

He waited for her to choose one of the stools before draping a fur around her shoulders and another across her lap. Then he sat across from her, forcing nonchalance. "Conor tells me you're a good player."

"I'm passable. Not like he is."

"Very few people play like he does," Eoghan said. At least this was a safe topic. "Did he ever tell you that was how he earned the respect of his céad mates when he first came to Ard Dhaimhin?"

She shook her head.

"No, he probably wouldn't. There's a fair bit of . . . initiation . . . that goes on with the older novices. A couple of the boys in our céad decided they were going to make life difficult for him, and as you've probably guessed, he's not the type to fight back unless he needs to. Plus, there was no way he could actually fight. So he spent every spare moment carving pieces for a King and Conqueror set and promptly destroyed each boy in the clochán on every game."

"And did that stop the initiation rites?"

"It slowed them. What stopped them is when everyone realized that Conor was making enough progress to destroy them in the practice yard as well."

Aine laughed. "He never told me that."

"He wouldn't. To be honest, he was never completely happy here. Always, in everything he did, there was the desire to get back to you. Had he not had that goal, I'm not sure whether he would have accomplished all that he did."

She stayed lost in that thought for a moment before alarm flashed in her eyes. "Wait. Something didn't happen to him, did it?"

"No!" Eoghan said. "Of course not. I wouldn't keep that from you." He reached into the pouch at his waist and produced a tiny cylinder of paper. "This did arrive today, though, with a dove."

Aine unrolled it and tilted it toward the dim light of the overcast sky. He'd already read it half a dozen times, making sure he wasn't missing anything in the tiny, cramped writing: *Arrived Glas Na Baile. Friendly. Entry tomorrow.*

Aine let the paper curl back in her palm. "'Friendly'? That means they don't expect any opposition, right?"

"He would have written 'hostile' had he thought they would need to fight. That's a good sign, Aine." Eoghan smiled at her, forcing all the reassurance he could muster, and then realized he might be overdoing it. He nodded toward the game board. "You get the opening move."

Aine selected a gray pawn and moved it forward in a traditional opening. Eoghan immediately moved his black piece to mirror hers.

"I can't decide if it's easier or more difficult for you," she said while she considered her next move.

"What do you mean?"

"Having Comdiu's voice in your head."

It was a surprisingly personal observation, considering how hard Aine seemed to work to keep things light and superficial. "I'm not sure I can answer that. I've never experienced its absence. I mean, there have been times when He chooses to be silent, but He's there all the same." Even now, when Eoghan wasn't sure if the warning he was feeling was from Comdiu or his own conscience.

Aine chose another pawn and moved it on the outside of the board. "Sometimes I wonder if I imagined His presence. Lord Balus appeared to me once, you know. He's sent his Companions multiple times. Yet when I sit here alone, it all seems very distant."

He didn't answer right away. She had hit on his biggest challenge. He considered how much to confide in her before he decided she deserved the truth. "You have no idea how long I questioned whether the voice I heard was real or a product of madness. I learned to keep it hidden, secret, as soon as I was old enough to understand I was different. Even now, when Comdiu won't give me specifics and just talks in hints, I wonder."

"What's the point, then?" Aine asked. "Why do you think He speaks to you if He won't tell you what to do?"

How many times had he asked that very question? He moved a piece and took one of her soldiers. "I suppose if He were always perfectly clear, I wouldn't have to have faith. Is this about Conor and the rune?"

She blinked, surprised, and he laughed. "I know you two better than you think. You've always been connected in a way. He could feel when you were in danger. Whether it was Comdiu telling him or it was some sort of magical link, you two have always had something unusual—something I confess I'm a little envious of. And now you're grieving the loss of that in a way, even though he's still there."

"And doubting my own faith," she muttered.

"Aye. Because so many of your fears are for him and not for yourself."

"Did Comdiu tell you that?"

"No. As I said, I know you two better than you think. Everything will work out as it must, Aine. You need to believe that. You also need to watch your queen, because she's in danger."

Aine stared down at the board, where he was poised to take the piece in four moves. "I never claimed to be great at this game, you know."

His heart beat a little too fast as he considered his next words, even if he weren't so clear on his own motivations. "I never claimed to be good at this"—he waved a hand vaguely between them—"but I'll give it a try. Do you think we could be friends, Aine? Just friends."

"I think we already are." She nudged a piece forward. "You might be a better friend if you ignored what a terrible move that was."

"We're not that close," he said, right before he put her king into check.

By the time they'd played two games—both of which Eoghan won, even though she made a far better showing the second time—her eyes shone and her cheeks were pink from the cold. She also looked more cheerful than she had since Conor left. Gradually, the awkwardness fell away and Aine relaxed in his presence. Even if he couldn't claim that his feelings were purely friendly, he'd convinced himself he could push them down where they wouldn't get in the way. She was his best friend's wife, and right now she needed his support. He would not do anything to jeopardize that trust, no matter how hard it might be.

✦ ✦ ✦

Iomhar escorted Aine from the balcony. Even though his face was expressionless, she thought she felt a vague wave of disapproval. Or maybe that was just her own guilt speaking.

I have nothing to feel guilty about. But accepting the company of a man who was clearly interested in more than friendship felt like a betrayal.

Beside her, Iomhar muttered something that she didn't catch. "Pardon me?" she asked, a touch crossly.

Iomhar gave her a bewildered look. "I'm sorry, my lady?"

"It must have been my imagination." She hugged her arms around herself against the cold breeze coming through the balcony door. But then she heard it again. A whisper. A man's voice.

Keondric? But no, it wasn't that kind of voice. It wasn't even familiar. It was distant, faded even.

Eoghan stepped through the doorway, game board tucked under his arm, and immediately picked up on her confusion. "Something the matter?"

"I thought I heard something."

"Keondric?"

"No." She shook her head. "Maybe I'm just tired. I haven't slept all that well lately." In fact, she'd slept fine since Conor had left, but admitting that aloud felt like another betrayal. Yet, that tickle, that whisper, returned. "I would swear it's coming from your office."

"It should be empty. But let's look."

Eoghan led them back toward the office and up the steps. He gave the door a little push open. Empty.

Aine pressed a hand to her forehead. She wandered around the chamber, ready to declare herself mistaken, when she heard it again: not a whisper but an echo. Dozens of echoes.

And they were coming from a flat wooden box.

"You have the sword here." She looked back at Eoghan for confirmation.

"Conor brought it up before he left. We thought it was a poor idea to have it locked away in the event we needed it and he was . . . unavailable."

In case he was dead and the password didn't pass to his successor like it was supposed to, you mean. But she couldn't bring herself to speak that thought.

Instead, she opened the box to reveal the sword, the shimmer of runes along the blade reflecting a light that had no appreciable source in the room. She glanced over her shoulder again. "This is what I'm hearing. The oaths. May I?"

Eoghan stood, mesmerized by the development. "Aye, of course."

Aine reached for the sword. The instant her hand closed around it, the hum of energy pulsed through her, that old bright magic she had always sensed in the wards. And then she heard the voices, thousands of them, echoing the same oath over and over again. She pulled in a shocked breath and dropped the sword back into the case.

"I heard them. The oaths. What does that mean?" She looked between the two men, feeling just as amazed as they looked.

"I don't know," Eoghan said. "The only people who have ever been able to hear them were Liam and Conor. And now you."

"Maybe that means we're supposed to have a High Queen," Iomhar quipped, then quickly sobered at Eoghan's sharp look.

"I doubt it," Aine said. "Conor heard the oaths when Liam was alive, so hearing them doesn't necessarily indicate leadership."

"Except Conor ended up being Liam's successor," Eoghan said.

"So does that mean that Aine is the next Ceannaire of the Fíréin brotherhood?" Iomhar asked, seriously this time.

Eoghan actually seemed to consider the question. "Queen Shanna was the one who formed the brotherhood in the first place. Stranger things have happened."

Aine let that remarkable thought wash over her. Things had changed much in the High City; that was true. She already had the respect of the men, and combined with her particular gifts, it would be easy for her to command. Could that even be a possibility? Was that why she suddenly was able to hear the oaths?

"I think maybe we're missing the bigger picture here," Aine said. "All this time, we've been trying to figure out how the sword was to be used to recall the men. Liam heard it. Conor heard it. Neither of them actually had the ability to speak to men's minds directly. I do."

"You think you heard these because it's time to recall the men's oaths."

"You tell me, Eoghan. You're the one who hears the voice of Comdiu."

Eoghan stared at her hard. She heard the echo of the question he asked of Comdiu: *What do You mean Aine to do with the sword? Guide us.*

Then he smiled and looked directly at her. "Not yet. But soon."

CHAPTER
THIRTY-THREE

Glas Na Baile lay nearly fifty miles beyond the border of Seanrós, an isolated earthen ring fort that was the only building visible for miles amongst the green pastureland. Had Conor not been so sure of the druid's strategy in hiding the rune stones, he never would have thought anything of import could lie inside the crumbling walls.

He stopped his party about half a mile away, just as the sun had passed its highest point and was creeping down to the opposite horizon. "Ailill, ride ahead and request shelter for a bard and his party. We'll be able to gauge our response from there."

"Aye, sir." Ailill gave a little bow on horseback and spurred the animal forward at a brisk clip. There weren't many bards traveling Seare at the moment, but Conor hoped the inhabitants would imagine their luck had changed. In these dark days, he didn't know a village that would not welcome the prospect of a little music to brighten the night.

After what seemed like hours but was probably only several minutes, Ailill came riding back out at a gallop. He pulled up his horse, breathless. "I think the charade might be useless at this point, sir."

"Why's that? Did they not believe you?"

Ailill laughed. "We are too readily recognized as Fíréin, and your acclaim is too great. I barely managed my request before word went out that Conor of Ard Dhaimhin had come to stay."

So the Conclave really hadn't been exaggerating. "Safe, you think?"

"They're just villagers and farmers. Armed, but not warriors. Safe as we'll get on this mission, I'd think."

"Very well, then. Let's not reject their hospitality." Conor cued his horse forward, and the other men fell in around him.

Conor had been through a number of villages and stayed at various keeps over his lifetime, but somehow he was still taken aback as they rode through the broken-down gates. Men, women, and children swarmed around them, their faces shining with hope. A woman reached out to touch his boot as if he were some sort of saint, then was swallowed back into the crowd. The tiny fort had been home to perhaps a hundred people at the height of its use a thousand years ago, fewer in modern times, but now it was packed full. Why had they congregated here when the earthen walls offered so little protection? Clearly, it wasn't because of abundance of supplies. The people looked emaciated, their clothing in rags.

An older man in a dirty yellow tunic emerged from the throng and stopped in front of them. "Welcome to Glas Na Baile. I am Lonn, the town father. We offer you our hospitality, such as it is."

Town father. It was such an archaic term that it took a second for Conor to remember the meaning. It was used in a place where the people did not all belong to one clan but needed a leader. Was this a gathering of Clanless? Or were they simply all who were left from the region's crofters?

"I'm Conor. These are my companions. We would be pleased to offer a gift of music in return for your hospitality."

Excited whispers rustled through the group, as if his words only confirmed what they already expected. Lonn smiled and spread his arms wide. "Please, join me. We will care for your animals."

In better times, he would have trusted the laws of hospitality, but he couldn't risk the loss of their supplies. "Blair, Ibor, stay with the horses," he murmured. "The rest with me."

Conor dismounted and then removed the strapping of his harp case from the horse's cinch. The other men took their weapons and followed close behind, their manner calm but alert.

Lonn led the way into one of three large clocháns with a thatched roof, similar to those that served as barracks in Ard Dhaimhin. This structure was divided into warrens of rooms, ostensibly to house families away from the elements. The center section had all the accoutrements of a typical hall on a much smaller scale, arranged around a central fire pit that sent curls of gray smoke to the sky. Conor took a seat at the table across from Lonn, his men filling in protectively around him.

Conor accepted the earthenware cup of water that was set before him, but he didn't drink. "This was once the seat of Clan Dalaigh, was it not?"

"Aye, it was. But the family was killed. Some of the people you see here were of Dalaigh's septs. Others were merely crofters whose livestock and crops were taken. Still others lost their livelihood to the plague."

"The plague," Conor repeated. "Disease?"

"Only of the animals. Entire flocks sickened and died, those that weren't already taken by the king's men. But without the animals—"

"There's nothing to live on."

"Exactly. So the people came here, where they have some

protection from the spirits and the elements and to take what safety there is in larger numbers." Lonn took a seat opposite him and studied him carefully. "You are younger than I thought, Conor of Ard Dhaimhin."

"I'm curious. How did you know me when my man came to the gates?"

"You've not heard the stories about you, then. The warrior with the bard's gift. The one who bears both the sword and the song. But because you ask our hospitality as a bard, I assume that your business has to do with the latter and not the former."

The whole exchange had the feeling of ritual, and despite the man's appearance and his claim of being the town father, Conor was certain Lonn must be one of the remaining members of the destroyed Clan Dalaigh. He would treat him as such, with the deference and formality due a clan lord. "We seek something that you might have."

"What is that?"

"A standing stone."

"You see for yourself, there are no standing stones here." Lonn waved a hand nonchalantly.

"Aye, but it may have been appropriated for other uses. Or hidden?"

Something quick and humorless lit Lonn's eyes. "So that's what Lord Keondric is after. The pattern stone."

"Is that what you call it? Where is it?"

Lonn rose. "Come and I'll show you."

Conor exchanged a look with the men and then followed their host from the clochán back into the earthen courtyard. Once more they were thronged by people, but Lonn waved them off as the party wound through the huts and tents pitched in what would have been the courtyard and training grounds. He led them behind a kitchen emanating smoke and cooking smells and pointed to a long rectangular piece of granite embedded in the earth.

"That's it?" Conor asked, noting the dark stains along the top surface.

"It's where we butcher animals. Hard to find a solid piece of granite like that."

Conor exchanged a wry glance with Ailill. "That's one way to put it to use. I doubt anyone would be looking for it there." He circled the stone, looking for the etched rune on its surface. He finally glimpsed a gouge in the stone where it disappeared into the ground. Centuries of dirt had built up around the base, obscuring it almost completely from sight. He removed his knife and began to excavate the space in front of it.

"That's not just one rune; that's several," Blair murmured from beside him. "How do we destroy them?"

"The same way they were made, I'd think. Chisel them off."

"I'm afraid I can't let you do that." Lonn stepped in front of them, a brave move considering that Conor had an unsheathed blade in hand. "Those markings are the only things keeping the spirits away from the fortress. You can't take them."

"You know of the runes' effect?" Conor asked.

"Oh, aye. It's well known in the area that the old magic is strong at the fort."

"What if I were to replace it with something better?"

Now interest sparked in his eyes. "As you've done with the High City? And Ard Bealach?"

Word really did travel fast. "Aye, just like."

"Do that first and you may do whatever you wish with the stone."

"Fair enough. After supper?"

Lonn grinned. "After supper."

They tramped back to the main clochán, where Lonn served

them small platters of fish and what Conor suspected was the last of their wine. It was a modest meal and yet one that Conor was sure stretched them beyond their usual limits of hospitality. He didn't refuse, however. The town father knew very well what they offered in return, just as he must suspect the importance of their mission. Still, they ate and drank modestly, taking only as much as they needed to sate their hunger and keep up their energy, knowing the leftovers would go to the others waiting outside. When the plates were cleared, Conor unbuckled the straps on his harp case and brought out the instrument. He put his fingers to the strings, expecting to find the echoes of magic from the rune pins, but they felt dull and lifeless. Unexceptional.

The rune. He'd completely forgotten about it. He dipped his finger into his water cup and smeared the ink on his chest.

This time when he touched the strings, a song immediately came to mind, but it wasn't the one he'd played at Ard Bealach, nor the one that had formed the runes at Ard Dhaimhin. Odd how he never consciously attempted to change the tune, yet each ward had its own melody. As the notes filled the room, so did the magic, spreading through the clochán and out through the fortress itself, arching overhead and creeping along the ground. Instinctively, he sent a thread from the confines of the dún across the countryside to Ard Dhaimhin's wards, where it joined with a great fountain of golden light. And then it was done, set-tling into a pleasant trickle of power. He lowered the harp.

"That's it?" Lonn asked, his eyes wide.

"That's it. It's more protection than the stone was. The sidhe will find more convenient locations to plague now."

"Bless you, sir," he murmured. "And now . . ."

Conor returned his harp to the case. Now they would see if it were really as simple to remove the rune as they thought.

He gave Ailill the honors of chipping away the symbols from

the stone, which broke off in finger-sized chunks. Blair then pulverized them into smaller pieces with a mallet. When they were finished, all that remained was an unevenly carved granite surface. He tried not to think of the fact that they were defacing thousand-year-old artifacts that had been around since before the coming of Balus. Right now, his job was strictly pragmatic: destroy all sources of runes that the druid could use to increase his power.

They slept in the hall of the clochán that night, aware they were likely displacing this patch of floor's usual occupants. Despite the fact they seemed to be among friends, Conor lay down with his hand on his knife, only dozing throughout the night. When they woke in the morning, they begged off Lonn's offer of breakfast and said their good-byes.

"I hope they're all that simple," Ailill said as they kicked their horses into a canter and headed southward toward the next fortress.

"Aye, and that easy to locate," Blair said. "What's to keep the next one from being the foundation stone for the entire fort?"

Conor kept quiet. He didn't want to dampen the men's enthusiasm for their first success, but he couldn't help but feel they were underestimating their opponent. Two days later, he looked to the north and knew why: a plume of smoke rose in the distance, too large to signal anything but total destruction.

He'd suspected Niall would somehow make them pay for their successes. Now he knew the price was no less than the lives of innocents.

✦　✦　✦

Aine felt the exact moment that Conor broke the integrity of the rune. His mind blazed bright in her consciousness, drawing her to it without any conscious thought. He was optimistic about their success, their hosts friendly and cooperative. She felt his triumph when the wards around the fortress joined with Ard Dhaimhin's, his satisfaction when they completed the task they'd set out to do.

Then all too quickly, she heard his determination to shut her out. But just before he repaired the rune on his skin, she thought she heard him whisper, *I love you.*

CHAPTER
THIRTY-FOUR

Aine took the stairs from the upper floor as quickly as she could, her heart feeling as though it had permanently lodged into her throat. She burst breathlessly into the Ceannaire's chamber, followed moments later by Iomhar. "What is it? Is it Conor?"

Eoghan gestured to the chair in front of him. "Sit down."

She sat, a numbness creeping into her legs. "Is it Conor? Have you heard something?" She hadn't been able to locate him since he redrew the rune, but she hadn't felt anything from the other men that would indicate bad news. Had she just missed it? Was her own worry blocking her abilities?"

"No, nothing like that," Eoghan said, and her breath whooshed out of her body. "Aine, you must believe me. If anything happened to Conor, I would not keep you in suspense. Please put that out of your mind."

She nodded, too enthusiastically. Anything else she could manage. "What is it, then?"

"We received a dove today from Conor. Glas Na Baile has been destroyed."

"What? I don't understand."

"By Niall. As reprisal, we think, for the destruction of the runes at the fortress."

Another wave of sickness washed over her. She'd sensed the presence of hundreds gathered around the safety of the ring fort. And now they were all dead? Because of our clan's actions? "What do we do now? Is he coming back?"

"Aine," Eoghan said gently. "This doesn't change anything. He can't stop. Those we lost at Glas Na Baile are minor compared to those who will die if Niall manages to collect the runes."

"Why are you telling me this if there's nothing we can do about it?"

"Because this was Conor's decision. He's determined to continue. But we both know he's going to feel like their blood is on his hands."

That was exactly how Conor would feel, and cut off from him as Aine was, she couldn't even offer him comfort or assess his mindset. "What do you want me to do?"

"For one thing, have the men convince him to get rid of the rune so we can communicate with him."

"He won't. He's doing it to protect me." She knew that once Conor was convinced he was causing her harm, nothing would be able to persuade him otherwise. "Can't we do something? Send men to protect the forts?"

"We don't have the men to spare, Aine. If Conor's successful, Niall has no choice but to turn his attention to Ard Dhaimhin. One way or another, we are going to have to fight. We need every man we can get."

"What about evacuating them? If there aren't any people there to kill—"

"Where would they go?"

"I don't know. Somewhere, anywhere!" She jumped from the chair, struck by the need to move, escape, but unable to get away from the news. "You can't tell me this and then say there's nothing we can do. How can you just make these decisions with so much certainty when there are lives at stake?"

Part of her welcomed Eoghan's anger, but he just regarded her with an expression of sympathy. "You know I don't make them lightly, nor does Conor. I'm sorry if I upset you. I thought you would want to know."

"I'm sorry. I do. It's just . . . there's been so much death already. I want it to be over."

"No more than I do. Perhaps you should rest for a bit. I'll let you know if there is any more news."

Aine nodded, even though the last thing she wanted to do was rest. She couldn't even hold the decision against them. Emotional as she might be, she knew Eoghan and Conor were making the choices that meant survival for the greatest number of people. They were looking at the big picture, even if she could think only of the men, women, and children who would be killed for no other reason than their location. The only thing she could do was wait for the next time Conor removed the rune and try to convince him that she would be fine without it.

✦ ✦ ✦

It was nearly two weeks' travel to the next fortress, a broken-down earth-and-stone ring fort named Fincashiel, located at the top of what seemed to be the only large hill in southern Faolán. Or it should have been two weeks; Conor nearly killed their horses to reach it in nine days, hoping to beat both the druid's army and word about the fate of Glas Na Baile.

"What do you think?" Ailill asked. "Same approach as before?"

"Aye, I think we need to try. But take Ibor and Lommán with you, just in case."

Ailill and the two other men bowed their obedience and

started off toward the fortress at a brisk clip. Blair situated his horse beside Conor. "What kind of reception do you think they'll get?"

"I couldn't begin to guess." The smoke was still heavy on the horizon from the destruction of Glas Na Baile, a reminder of the danger they brought with their presence.

Less than a half hour later, three horsemen descended the switchbacks leading from the ring fort more quickly than they had approached. When they came within shouting distance, Conor's heart sank. Their dampened, stained tunics spoke for the village's answer more strongly than words.

Ailill reined his horse and pulled his sticky tunic away from his body. Remnants of rotten vegetables dropped to the earth. "I don't know about you, but I would take this as a no."

"At least you still have your sense of humor," Conor muttered. "Go wash in the stream while I decide our next move."

"We're not just going to move on?" Lommán asked, surprised. He seemed to have taken the least of the brunt of their response, even though bits of rotten lettuce clung to his blond hair.

"Permission or not, there is still a rune stone inside that fortress, and we need to destroy it. Do you actually think they will be spared because we passed it by?"

The looks on the other men's faces shifted when they realized that the very existence of this mission meant people would die. The only question was whether they would be successful before that happened. Much sobered, Ailill, Ibor, and Lommán dismounted and trudged to the nearby spring to wash the remnants of the filth from their clothing.

Conor considered for a moment, then dismounted and removed his harp case.

"What are you doing?" Blair asked, moving to his side while he settled himself on the turf.

"An experiment." He took out the harp and spent a couple of minutes tuning the strings, which loosened from the constant jostling of the horse day after day. He scrubbed the inked shield rune from his chest and prepared to play.

Conor, thank Comdiu. I need to talk to you.

Conor sighed, even though part of him thrilled to hear his wife's voice in his head. Had she just been waiting for him? *Aine, love, I'm busy right now.*

Conor, I know what happened at Glas Na Baile. Please don't shut me out.

Why? The last thing you need are my thoughts inside your head. I know you feel guilty—

I feel pained. Distressed. Not guilty. Guilty implies that I've done something wrong, and I haven't.

Pushing everyone away isn't going to help matters.

I'm not pushing everyone away. I'm just pushing you away. The minute he thought the unkind words, he regretted them. Aine didn't deserve his cruelty. *I'm sorry. I didn't mean that. But you have to understand that what we are doing is critical. And I can't have any distractions right now. I am attempting to do things differently at Fincashiel.*

She said nothing in return. Maybe he'd offended her, or maybe she was just honoring his wishes, but she hadn't completely pulled away from him. He was still aware of her in the back of his mind, waiting. It would have to be good enough for his concentration. He settled the harp on the turf between his legs and began to play.

Once again, the tune that came to mind was only remotely related to the other ones. He didn't bother to weave a shield around the fortress and spread out as he usually did, though. In his mind's eye, it was simply a sheet of golden light: simple, direct, blanketing the area for as far as he could see. He stretched himself, hoping to meet the border of one of his other wards, but ten days' ride was too far from even his imagination. Instead, he pushed it to the west into the tree line of Seanrós, linking up once more to the wards who protected the entire central section of Seare. This time, the pulse of power beneath the wards was stronger, as if it were strengthened by the connection to Ard Dhaimhin. Was that why the wards had originally emanated from the High City? Had it been a point of connection through which all the wards shared power?

He set the harp back in his case, gradually becoming aware of the puzzled expressions of the men in his party.

"Isn't that just a beacon, telling Lord Keondric that we've been here?" Ferus asked.

"He'll know we've been here one way or another. But this will tell us whether the men he's using are ensorcelled or not. If they are, they won't be able to come within fifty miles of the fortress."

"And the rune stones?"

"We'll make entry after dark without their knowledge."

"How do you intend to do that?" Ailill asked.

"The same way we got into Ard Bealach. Through solid stone."

They waited until nightfall to implement the second phase of his plan. Conor led Ailill, Blair, and Muiris from their makeshift camp. They faded into the shadows and made stealthy progress across the meadow to the hill.

The mount upon which Fincashiel was built was made to repel armies, but no one had thought about the possibility of being taken by a handful. While it was impossible to bring horses and siege engines up its rocky face, the craggy surface provided the perfect handholds for a small group of climbers to slip in completely unnoticed.

Still, the going was slow in the dark, and they had to stop

frequently to rest their aching muscles. The rock scraped their fingertips until they bled, and the toes of their soft leather shoes shredded from constant contact with sharp edges. When they finally reached the top hours later, the moon was beginning to sink over the horizon, leaving only the faintest glow overhead. All the better for their plan.

Conor dug a charcoal stub wrapped in oilcloth from his pocket and approached the bit of the wall they'd chosen for their entry. It opened onto the back part of the courtyard behind an outbuilding, which should be deserted at this time of night. Once inside, the Fírein would be in their element, moving soundlessly through the shadows. Conor selected a spot several feet off the ground, where the wall's thick base had begun to narrow somewhat, and sent a pleading prayer upward. *Dear Comdiu, be with us. Please let it work.*

He began with the outer circle of the softening rune and then began to slowly draw the intersecting lines and squiggly marks that made up the rest of it. It was slow work in the dark, and the rough stone exterior of the wall meant he had to draw each line multiple times. When he was finished, he uttered one more silent prayer, then dug his battered fingertips into the wall. It crumbled in his hand like sand.

A relieved breath escaped him. Conor stepped aside and gestured to Blair, who immediately brought out the hand ax he had slung across his back. One swift stroke, and part of the wall vanished in a crumble of dust.

"It's working!" Ailill whispered, his eyes wide and glowing in the little light that remained.

"Aye. Keep at it."

Even so, it took several minutes for Blair to break completely through the wall, several more to widen it to the width of a man. Ailill stepped up, gestured for them to wait, and climbed through. A moment later, his face appeared in the opening and he waved them through.

Conor immediately saw he had misjudged the location. Instead of coming out behind a cookhouse or a storeroom, the hole opened onto an animal pen that held a single goat. It lifted its head from where it lay on a straggly patch of straw but seemed otherwise unconcerned by the emergence of four men into its home.

"I don't suppose you know where the stone is," he muttered to the goat, taking a moment to make sure he was still concealed in the shadows.

Unlike Glas Na Baile, these walls were stone, which meant that the rune stone easily could have been used as a pillar or the lintel of the front gates or . . . the front step of the elevated clochán that dominated the majority of the inner courtyard.

"There," he whispered to Ailill beside him.

"You mean right in front of where everyone is sleeping?" Ailill hissed back. Once more, he seemed more amused than annoyed. Conor just shook his head.

It *was* a problematic location, though, in full view of the watch at the front gate and right outside the sleeping area of a good portion of the fort's inhabitants. This wasn't going to be an operation that could be completed with a chisel and a mallet but rather a lump of charcoal and his bare fingertips. *Comdiu, protect me from view and turn their guards' eyes away from our position.*

"Stay here," he whispered. "And if they sound the alarm, escape the way we came."

"No," Ailill said, reaching for the charcoal in Conor's hand. "You're too valuable to lose. Let me."

It might have been for the best, though, because even watching for the man's presence, Conor lost him in the dark courtyard. Only the eventual soft scratch of the rune being drawn onto granite drew his eye back to the shadow crouched before the clochán. Conor could just make out the glint of a knife before Ailill started to shave away the chunks of softened rock.

"What's this—"came a startled voice from behind them.

Before Conor could even turn all the way around, Blair loomed up behind the man and landed a heavy blow against the back of his head with the haft of the ax. The Fíréin knelt beside him and felt for a pulse, then gave Conor a nod. He was still alive.

Conor gave the soft night-singer whistle, alerting Ailill that they were running out of time. Another minute, and the man appeared beside Conor in a crouch.

"Did you get them all?"

"I think so. All I could see at least. If you hadn't noticed, it's dark."

"It will have to do. Our time's run out." He inclined his head toward the man who was still laid out cold beside the goat pen. It was impossible to know how long he'd stay unconscious, but given the time it had taken to climb the hill, he figured someone would raise the alarm before they made it all the way to the meadow below.

Although it would have been easier to kill him, Conor wasn't sure he could handle the thought of more blood on his hands.

But Comdiu was on their side, it seemed. No alarm came from the fortress above, despite the fact that it took them almost as long to climb down the side of the great hill as it had to climb up it. They crossed the half mile to the camp at a jog, arriving out of breath but also out of range.

"We were discovered," Conor said. "We need to go now."

Instantly, the other men jumped into action, unhobbling the horses and packing their bedrolls. Within twenty minutes, they were riding south as quickly as they dared, leaving as little evidence in their wake as possible.

Did you do it? Aine's voice intruded into his mind, startling him from his focus on the uneven terrain in front of his horse.

Aye, we did it. It remains to be seen what Niall does in return. And now you know what I have to do.

Conor, I wish you wouldn't. I wish you would just trust me.

He signaled the men to pull up the horses while he dug the ink from his bag. He used the little bit of moonlight peeking through the clouds to redraw the rune on himself. Even without words, he could feel Aine's disappointment in his head, until the last line was drawn and the link between them winked out.

That night, he dreamed of blood and torture and battle for the first time in days, as if his resting mind were trying to tell him he was doing the right thing by shutting her out.

The next night, they got their answer from Niall, in the form of another black plume of smoke.

Conor hung his head and sloughed off the immediate feeling of failure. He'd done his best, and it hadn't been enough. That meant that not all Niall's men were ensorcelled or the druid's destructive magic possessed a much greater range than they thought. Either way, for them to succeed, many more would die.

CHAPTER
THIRTY-FIVE

Aine sat motionless on the balcony beneath a covering of furs, her forgotten sewing draped across her lap. She'd taken to sitting on this balcony down the corridor from the Ceannaire's office, not because she particularly wanted to think but because the stone walls of her chamber had begun closing in on her. Her confinement to the fortress might be voluntary, but that didn't make it feel any less like a prison.

She sensed Eoghan before he even stepped through the doorway, but she didn't turn her head. "Any news?"

"A dove came today. It's done."

Aine blinked up at Eoghan as he took his seat. "Done. Already? It's been scarcely a month."

"Conor didn't waste any time in Faolán, and the other groups didn't face opposition. We were lucky, I suppose."

Aine tossed around that word in her head. Lucky. She supposed they could look at it that way. They hadn't lost any of their men. "How many dead? The villagers, I mean."

Eoghan sighed heavily. He took a few moments before he could manage to answer. "Nine hundred, perhaps."

"So only the fortresses that Conor visited." She looked up at Eoghan, her eyes filling with tears. "Niall's tormenting him, isn't he? This wasn't meant as a deterrent. Conor proved he was going to go through with his mission regardless. Niall just wants to make sure he feels all the lives that have been lost because of it."

"I don't know. Niall has taken a special interest in Conor since he's thwarted his plans more than once. Maybe he's just toying with him."

"Why?"

"Because he delights in the pain of other people."

"While we sit by and do nothing."

Eoghan seemed to measure his words before he spoke. "Aine, I know that what I'm doing feels cruel, even unconscionable. But I can't discount the possibility that this is all a distraction. What happens if I divert men from Ard Dhaimhin and he chooses that moment to attack? Then we don't just have hundreds of people dead, we have thousands, and we've lost Seare in the process. I have a responsibility to more than just individual lives."

Eoghan was right. Aine knew he was right, but it didn't feel any better knowing that people were dying because of the Fírein's actions. "Conor would say that's why you were chosen to be king."

"He would, wouldn't he?" Eoghan shot her a smile. "At least this means he'll be back in time to see the birth of his son."

"Not you, too. It could still be a daughter." She rubbed her stomach, now unmistakably round beneath the pleats of her skirt.

"How long?"

"About eight weeks."

"Good." Eoghan rose and gave her a little bow. "Don't stay out here too long. The nights are getting colder now."

"Aye, I'll go in soon."

With a sad smile, she watched him go, until Iomhar stepped forward. "My lady, he's right. We should go in."

"Just a few more minutes."

Eoghan had said it was done, that Conor would be coming home. She wanted to hear that for herself. But other than a short period of time when he had played the wards around the last fortress, she hadn't been able to catch his thoughts. He was avoiding her when he should be celebrating a mission completed. That could mean only one thing.

He was hiding something.

+ + +

Sixteen.

The number had been bothering him for the last two fortresses. Sixteen old strongholds. Sixteen rune stones. A nice even number, divisible by four, the number of kingdoms in Seare. It all fit nicely, neatly, like the four major prophets, the four divisions of each book of the Holy Canon.

Except that was a Balian conceit. The druids did not think in even numbers. Three, five, seven, eleven, thirteen . . .

Seventeen. The holy number of the druidic order, even now. Had the druids truly wanted to divide up important information, they would have done it on seventeen stones in seventeen places.

Which meant there had to be one more stone out there still. How could they have missed one? He pictured the map in his mind's eye, counting off each fortress. Maybe there had been one destroyed that was no longer on the maps? The ancient Seareanns were too deliberate about their numbers for them to have stopped short of the holy number when planning their strongholds.

And then it came to him so abruptly he nearly fell off his horse. Dún Eavan.

He'd not even thought of it because it had been used as a Faolanaigh palace before Lisdara was built, but it dated back much further than that. Hadn't Aine always said she sensed an old, deep magic there? Of course she'd also encountered the sidhe, which might argue against the existence of a rune stone. Except he knew very well the runes merely dissuaded rather than prevented the presence of the sidhe.

"Halt," he called, and the group reined in around him. "Ailill, send a dove. We have one stop left."

CHAPTER
THIRTY-SIX

The next two weeks were the longest of Aine's life. Eoghan had said that Conor was coming home, but a mere day later, Conor had sent a message saying he thought there was one more stone located at Dún Eavan—less than a day's ride from Lisdara, where Niall had taken up residence, where he could very well be now.

"Conor knows what he's doing, Aine," Eoghan told her. "If he's sure there are seventeen stones, there are seventeen stones."

"I don't doubt his knowledge," she had said. "I just don't understand why he has to be the one who does it."

"Because he's the closest. And he's not a man to ask another to do his duty for him."

She couldn't disagree, but the waiting wore on her with each passing day. She had never been walled up in a fortress for this long. She'd been on the battlefield, actually participating in their efforts against the evil that threatened Seare. But they'd lost that battle, and now Aine felt she was waiting on the final battleground. Even Eoghan with his encouraging words seemed as on edge as she was, though he wouldn't admit it aloud. She wondered if he sensed it as she did: a storm on the horizon, simply waiting for the first thunderclap.

She left herself open when she slept, hoping Conor would try to contact her, hoping for some reassurance that he was all right. All she got were slivers and shreds of other people's thoughts and dreams—until one night, she found herself out in the cold, her breath puffing around her in clouds of steam.

She crept slowly into the darkened clochán, the buzz of snoring men hiding the scuff of her footsteps on the hardpacked floor. Despite the late hour, a fire still roared in the center pit, raising beads of sweat on her forehead. She signaled to the men behind her and slowly drew the sword from the sheath on her back.

Wait. Why did she have a sword? Why was she in the brothers' barracks? She tried to release the weapon, but her hands wouldn't obey her. She watched, a terrified prisoner in her own body as the men fanned out behind her with bared blades.

On her command, the men fell on the sleeping brothers, swords cutting silently into bodies, daggers slicing across windpipes to still screams before they could escape. Blood sprayed warm against her skin. Aine struggled against the urge to vomit.

She scrambled out of bed and hunched over the chamber pot before she realized she was back in her own body, back in her chamber at Carraigmór. For a moment, she imagined she heard Conor stirring in the bed behind her before she realized she was once again alone.

"A nightmare," she whispered shakily. But it wasn't a nightmare. Nor was it the way she usually experienced visions.

Horror surged through her as she made the connection.

Up to this point, she'd only picked up on others' thoughts and memories. Now she was linked with someone else's mind, experiencing what he experienced, through his eyes.

That meant that what she saw had been no dream. Her fingernails dug into her clenched palm. They had to know. They had to stop this, if it weren't already too late.

She threw her shawl around her shoulders and unbolted the chamber door, not bothering to put on her slippers before she flew into the passage. Peadar, her night guard, straightened from his lean against the wall. "My lady?"

"I need to speak with Eoghan now." She didn't wait for Peadar before rushing down the corridor to Eoghan's room. She pounded furiously on the door until it swung inward. Her words tumbled over each other. "They're going to die if we don't do something. You have to hurry."

"Slow down." Eoghan put his hands on her shoulders to still the frantic flow of words. "Stay right there while I get dressed."

Aine paced little circles in the hallway while she waited, aware of Peadar's furrowed brow, but the brother didn't question her.

When Eoghan emerged several minutes later, once again fully dressed and armed, he gave a nod for the guard to follow them and then guided Aine down to the staircase. It wasn't until he nudged her into a cushioned chair that she fully registered he had brought them to the Ceannaire's office.

"Now, start at the beginning and tell me what you saw."

Aine related the entire dream to him. He listened carefully, but as soon as she finished, he went to the window and peered down below. "I don't see any torches. Peadar, bar the front entrance, then go rouse the Conclave. Meet back here." He escorted the brother to the door and dropped the bar, then went directly toward the bookshelf, where he located a rolled-up sheet of parchment. He pushed the stacks of books and tablets aside and spread out a map of the city on the table.

"This is very important, Aine. The barracks you saw him enter, was it a cottage or a clochán?"

"Clochán. Very clearly."

"Good. Now, how many steps went down into the structure?"

Aine closed her eyes and recalled the sensation of entering, even though it made her shudder. "Three."

"Okay. That means it's one of the older ones on the east side of the compound. Here's the trickiest question. When you entered the door, where was the moon? Was it over your left shoulder or your right?"

She hadn't been paying any attention to the moon, as the man whose mind she was in hadn't been paying attention. But she distinctly remembered the slant of shadow to the right. "Left. It had to be the left."

"We're in luck. It's one of these two here." He looked up and gave her an encouraging smile. "That's good, Aine. You've done well."

"Good? Someone just killed dozens of men, if not more! How could that be good?"

"It's good because we know where to start looking. Had you not paid so much attention, it could have taken us all night. There are thousands of men here and dozens of clocháns."

Aine nodded numbly, but the shaking was beginning again. Eoghan looked around the room, and she couldn't figure out what he was trying to find. Instead, he ended up crouching down in front of her, one of her hands held between his like he was trying to rub some warmth into it. "It will be okay, Aine. You're safe here. You understand that, don't you?"

She nodded again, but before she could answer, a knock sounded at the door. Eoghan waited for the newcomers to identify themselves before opening the door. The Conclave members flooded in with Iomhar trailing behind, looking as if he'd been roused from a deep sleep.

"Peadar, Iomhar, take Aine to her chamber. Iomhar, stay

inside with her and bar the door. No one enters before daylight, not even me. Understood?"

"Aye, sir." Iomhar guided Aine from the chair and threaded their way back through the men in the room. As soon as they got into the corridor, he bent his head toward hers. "Are you feeling all right, my lady? You look as if you're going to faint."

She felt like she was going to vomit. The scene she'd witnessed played over and over in her head, sticking on the feel of warm blood on her skin. This wasn't a vision of the future; this was a vision of something that was happening right now. She knew it, just as she'd known it when she'd seen Niall and his men sack a village disguised as Sofarende, even though she was hundreds of miles away. She'd experienced death then, too.

"Whoa, Lady Aine." Iomhar caught her around the waist as she started to sway.

She pressed a hand against her clammy cheek. Why was there ringing in her ears? "I'm fine," she said. "I'm not the type to faint."

It was the last thing she could remember.

✦ ✦ ✦

Eoghan didn't question Aine's instincts. One look at her face was enough to tell him that she believed what she was saying, that it was happening now. One look out the window was enough to tell him that all was not as it should be. In the middle of the night, there should be torches burning at intervals around the village. The patches of darkness suggested people who didn't want to be noticed.

He quickly detailed the situation to the men gathered in the Ceannaire's office, his voice calm but certain. "It's one of the two south-facing clocháns, right here." He pointed to two round circles on the map. "But that doesn't mean that was the only céad attacked. Rouse the village; account for the guards. I'll want the prefects to report anyone missing from their quarters who shouldn't be."

"Are you sure this information is reliable?" Dal crossed his arms.

"Would you rather wait until morning and see who doesn't arrive at their posts? Better we find out now. And if it's something that hasn't happened yet, it might discourage the perpetrators from attempting it later."

"Aye, sir." A chorus of agreement went up from the men before they filed out.

Eoghan caught Riordan aside before he left. "Post two more men outside Aine's chamber. I won't take any chances."

Riordan gave a crisp nod. "It's beginning, you think?"

Eoghan hadn't wanted to give voice to the thought, but he wouldn't lie. "Aye. It's beginning."

✦ ✦ ✦

By dawn, it was clear that Aine's experience hadn't been a dream and that it wasn't an isolated incident. Two hundred thirty men, slaughtered in their sleep. When they were sure it wasn't the beginning of a larger siege, Eoghan came down and viewed the scene himself. Part of him wished he hadn't. The view of blood-soaked bodies, mattresses, earth . . . they would all stay with him even longer than the cleanup from the first battle at Ard Dhaimhin. That had been war. This was butchery.

Even worse, they had absolutely no idea who had done it. The prefects accounted for all the men. None was missing from his bed, none bloodstained, none wounded, though the latter was unlikely anyway considering the victims had been killed in their sleep. The one suspicious detail was the lack of guards on the clocháns that had been attacked. All men on guard duty could account for their whereabouts; it seemed that those posts had simply been forgotten.

Eoghan wearily climbed the stairs back to Carraigmór and went straight to Aine's room. The two men stationed outside her chamber bowed to him as he rapped on the door. "Aine, Iomhar. It's me. Open the door."

The bar and the latch scraped open to reveal Iomhar, his sword drawn. At least Eoghan had made a good selection for Aine's guard, who didn't stand down until verifying that the three men in the hall had reason to be there.

"How is she?" Eoghan murmured.

"Shockingly strong," Iomhar said.

"I heard that." Aine pushed herself up in bed, fully dressed even though her hair had come loose from her braid. She cradled her belly protectively. "What he means is stubborn. I must have asked him for an update a dozen times through the night."

"And well he didn't obey you, else I'd be finding you a new guardsman. Are you feeling well, my lady? The baby?"

"Well enough. What did you learn?"

He pulled up a chair beside the bed. "You were right. And unfortunately, it wasn't just that one clochán."

She paled to a sickly gray. "How many?"

"Two hundred thirty men."

"It could have been worse."

"Aye, it could have been much worse. Sounding the alarm may have interrupted their plans. You likely saved lives by reacting as you did."

"I've been hoping it was all just a vivid nightmare. What do we do now?"

He glanced at Iomhar, who wore the same dread that Eoghan felt. "I don't think this was an isolated incident. We're preparing for siege. While I know that Niall likes theatrics, I would also have expected him to strike fast and hard. I think we were fortunate we got a warning. He probably didn't intend to stop with two clocháns."

"So you're sure Niall is behind this?" Aine asked.

"Not entirely. It looks to have been done by someone familiar with our routines, our discipline. But that doesn't mean Niall isn't behind it." He hesitated. "Have you been able to reach Conor?"

"No. Why?"

"The timing feels suspicious." Eoghan knew he was giving her too much information, but it was concerning her husband. She had a right to know. It had been two weeks since Conor had set off for Dún Eavan, a trip he thought would take only a fortnight. He should be arriving at Loch Eirich now. Eoghan couldn't ignore the possibility that the attack had been timed to coincide with Conor's arrival at the fortress.

"Do you think he's in danger?"

"I think he's always in danger. But in special danger? I don't think so."

She nodded slowly and twisted her skirt in her lap, a sign of distress that her voice didn't betray. "We couldn't afford to lose those men, could we?"

"No. We need the numbers. And they were among the most experienced of our men, something else that points to the attack having been done by someone familiar with Ard Dhaimhin."

A knock sounded at the door right before it opened. One of the guards poked his head in. "Master Eoghan? You're needed outside."

Eoghan rose immediately. "I'll let you know if I find out any more. Stay here. You're safest with Iomhar. If you're concerned about appearances—"

"At this point, appearances are the least of my worries. But thank you."

No one could doubt her bravery; that was certain. "I'll let you know if we learn anything else of interest. And keep trying to reach Conor."

"Aye. Go with Comdiu, Eoghan."

He gave her a little bow, shoving away any thoughts but those that related to the situation in the city below.

Gradaigh was waiting for him outside Aine's door, and he fell into step beside him in the corridor. "Sir, we've received the first reports from our sentries. There are men massing on the outer edges of our territory."

"Niall's staging an attack on the city? Openly?"

"That's the thing, sir. It doesn't appear that they're trying to get in. It looks like they're there to keep people from getting *out*."

Eoghan blinked. Getting out? That didn't make any sense, unless the attack to which Aine had alerted them wasn't merely an isolated incident involving a few spies. His heart beat faster as he considered the possibilities, and his steps sped automatically.

"Riordan!" he called as soon as he set foot into the hall where the men were gathered. "How many fighting men are there in the city now? Ones who are not Fíréin?"

"I'd have to get the prefects' last census to be exact, but somewhere between seventeen hundred and two thousand. Clearly, we'll need them, but their numbers have already been included."

"But we've been thinking of them as our allies." He looked slowly around the table. "What if we're not being attacked from the outside because the men are already here?"

Looks of horror circulated around the table. There were almost as many men in Ard Dhaimhin who could be potential enemies as there were Fíréin.

"How is that possible?" Dal asked. "They couldn't be ensorcelled, as they wouldn't be able to sleep beneath the wards. And they couldn't bear the runes because they'd be dead."

"But they could be spelled."

Eoghan swiveled toward the doorway to find Aine standing there, Iomhar directly behind her. "What are you doing here?"

"I heard your conclusion." She gave him a wry smile that indicated it was his thoughts and not his words that had drawn her. "I have a suggestion."

Iomhar stepped forward with a flat wooden case: the oath-binding sword.

"No, it's too dangerous."

"No more dangerous than what we already face in the city. There have to be, what . . . one, two thousand men outside Ard Dhaimhin who are linked to the sword? If even a portion of those men respond, those are valuable reinforcements."

He sighed. She was right. And if they had been infiltrated from within, their best bet was to call reinforcements from the outside. But to his knowledge, no one had ever attempted it. Who knew what the ramifications could be of having Aine try to connect with so many minds at once?

"What other choice do we have?" she asked softly. "I don't believe it's an accident that the sword responded to me. It's a gift, Eoghan."

He studied her face, so assured even though he had to believe she harbored doubts of her own. "Very well. But first we need to secure the men we do have. Riordan, Gradaigh, I want you to go below and speak to the céad leaders. Let them know we might be facing opposition from within. Speak also to the kingdom men and tell them to expect battle from outside. They'll need to be on alert, but I don't mind a little misdirection, either."

The two men hastened to obey him, and Eoghan turned to Aine. "You're sure about this? You know Conor would do everything he could to dissuade you from putting yourself at risk."

"Aye, and he'd give up in the end when he realized it was my risk to take."

Eoghan sighed. She was exactly right. "Then let's do it." And pray that Comdiu protect her, for all their sakes.

CHAPTER
THIRTY-SEVEN

Aine waited until Riordan and Gradaigh returned to the hall
before she attempted to recall the men with the sword, even
though the weapon pulsed with an unseen energy, calling to her.
It was as if the magic somehow knew she was the one who was
meant to use it and waited in anticipation. But that was odd,
wasn't it? Magic wasn't sentient.

"You look deep in thought." Iomhar settled in the chair beside
her, deceptively casual considering she knew he was on alert to any
threat, even here. The Fíréin's dedication was truly remarkable.
She was counting on that dedication to ensure their response.

"There is so much we don't know," she said finally. "I imagine that linking with the minds of the men still living will be
straightforward. But what about the fact that there are generations of Fíréin brothers who have passed?"

"I don't think that's a concern, my lady. Our oath to the
brotherhood is for our mortal service. It isn't as if we pledge our
souls. Those belong to Comdiu alone, and I don't believe He
would grant the power to reach across the boundaries of eternity.
He knows that's a responsibility humanity couldn't shoulder."

"You're right." Her respect for Iomhar inched upward. Once more he was proving himself to be mature beyond his years, and once more she was immensely grateful for his presence.

The hall's main door opened and Iomhar tensed beside her before they recognized Gradaigh and Riordan. "They've been notified," Riordan said to Eoghan as he circled the table to his seat.

Eoghan turned to her. "Let's discuss this before you make the attempt. What are you going to say?"

"I don't know yet. Can you trust me to follow Comdiu's leading and speak what comes to my mind?"

Eoghan paused, his eyes averted as if he were listening to Him. Perhaps he was. "Aye. The sword called to you, for whatever reason. In my mind, that means you are meant to use it. I will trust you." He glanced around the table. "What say you?"

Slowly, the other men voiced their agreement.

"It's decided, then," Aine said, her voice trembling a little. "Eoghan, would you say a prayer before we begin?"

He gave her a little smile and bowed his head. "Merciful Comdiu, we pray Your blessing on this endeavor. Give Lady Aine strength and wisdom. Your will be done. So may it be."

"So may it be," the table echoed.

Eoghan pulled the case from the center of the table and turned it to face her, then gave her an encouraging nod.

Aine took a deep breath before she flipped the latches on the case and lifted the lid. Magic hummed through her as her hand hovered over the sword. The runes seemed to glisten in the lamplight.

Please, Comdiu, guide my words and actions.

Before she could change her mind, she gripped the sword like a weapon and lifted it from the case. Power surged through her, whipping her consciousness like a maelstrom. She gasped, her fingers curling involuntarily around the sword's grip.

Then the whispers began—first just a few, some she recognized as belonging to men who sat in this chamber. The sounds rippled outward like concentric rings from a raindrop in a puddle, ever widening until they were like the wind in the trees, the rush of the ocean. She couldn't tell who was in control, she or the power of the sword, but as the collective strength of the oaths rushed through her, she knew what had to be said.

She spoke only in her mind, but the words echoed through her as strongly as if she'd shouted them aloud.

Brothers, I call on you today on behalf of Seare. I am Aine, healer of Ard Dhaimhin and wife to Conor, Ceannaire of the Firéin brotherhood.

Since the fall of the Great Kingdom, the Firéin have stood fast, ever faithful in their oath to protect the High City. The city has now been breached and the brotherhood disbanded. Seare has fallen, and the evil spirits from the first days have been loosed on the island.

It is now time for you to fulfill your oaths. It is time to relinquish the old ways and embrace the new. Those who have defended the city from the kingdoms must now defend the kingdoms themselves from a greater evil. The age of the brotherhood is over, but a new one shall begin.

Seare has seen the flames of disaster and trial. But like Ard Dhaimhin, she will rise again, not burned away but refined by her trials into a purity of purpose.

All of you who call yourselves faithful, I beg of you, fulfill your oaths. Return to Ard Dhaimhin. Join with us, and we will throw off the tyranny of sorcery in favor of peace—not beneath a regime of fear but in unity beneath the One God who unites all.

Then slowly the hum of power ebbed from the sword. Coherent thought crept back. She realized she was breathing heavily, her whole body trembling, but she still gripped the sword. She waited for the whispers to fade, but they only continued to grow stronger, tumbling over each other, jumbling together into a nonsensical, deafening rush. And beneath it all, she felt it. Their conviction to return. Their obedience to their oath.

Their devotion to her.

"They're coming," she whispered, just before she swayed sideways in the chair.

A pair of strong arms caught her, but she didn't know whom they belonged to. Someone called for a healer. She tried to tell them that she was all right, just tired, but the words wouldn't come from her suddenly thick tongue. And then the room slipped away.

+ + +

She awoke to silence.

Had she been struck deaf? No. Even through the fogginess in her mind, she knew that wasn't right. This was a different kind of silence, a deep and penetrating quiet that felt suspiciously like loneliness.

She tried to push herself up, but her limbs wouldn't obey. Even her head felt too heavy to lift from where it lay on something soft. A pallet? No, her bed in her chamber at Carraigmór. She opened her eyes enough to let in a thin stream of light and then squeezed them tightly shut again as the pounding started between her ears.

Murmurs at the edge of her consciousness. Then the squeak of hinges, the soft thud of a door closing, heavy footsteps.

"Aine."

That voice was familiar. Conor? No, not Conor. He wasn't here. She pried her eyes open again, this time enough to resolve the speaker's face. Eoghan. Their friend. The king. His expression was enough to shoot a jolt of wakefulness through her:

tense, concerned, even fearful. When she tried to speak, her mouth felt dry and her voice raspy. "What happened?"

"You collapsed after you recalled the brothers." He seated himself in the chair beside the bed, his hands clasped tightly together. "We brought you back to your chamber."

"How long have I been unconscious?"

"A day and a night. Do you want to try to sit up?" He slid a hand behind her shoulders, but the slightest upward motion sent the room spinning around her. She managed a weak shake of her head, and he laid her back down again.

"Aine, there's something else you should know."

Another voice, seemingly loud in the stark quiet. She focused with difficulty on the man across the room. His identity came back more quickly to her. Riordan, her father-in-law.

"We called one of the healers to help when you collapsed," Eoghan said. "He thought you might be overcome by the connection to so many minds at once."

Aye, that sounded right. So many of them. But they were gone now. Why were they gone?

"We had to draw the shield rune on you, my lady."

Aine yanked her shift forward, shocked by the black ink drawn over her heart. That explained why she couldn't hear anything, not even the thoughts of Eoghan and Riordan. "You have to take it off. I can't communicate with Conor or his men if this is here."

"Aine, you must rest for a bit." Eoghan again. She focused on him, blinking so that this time his face fully resolved in her vision. "We don't know how the connection to so many will affect you. It's possible that if you remove the rune, you might be overwhelmed and slip away from us. Next time you might not wake up."

It was too much to think about. Instead, she focused on her most pressing need. "I'm thirsty."

Riordan poured water from a pitcher into an earthenware cup and handed to it to Eoghan. He helped her sit up enough to press the cup to her lips. She was suddenly glad she couldn't hear his thoughts. Given their history, this felt far too intimate, but she was too weak to protest. She sipped cautiously and managed to push the cup away when she was finished. A sudden tightening in her middle reminded her of what she had forgotten: the baby.

She had been asleep for almost two days with no food and very little water, though she suspected the healer would have forced as much down her throat as he could manage. Had the deprivation harmed the child? She hadn't felt any movement since she had awoken.

She rolled to her side and stayed as still as possible, barely even breathing, while she prayed for a sign her child was still alive. And then it came, a roll and a heavy kick, as if the baby were irritated to have been awoken. She nearly wept with relief.

The door opened then, and Caemgen, one of the elder healers, entered. "Ah, you're awake. We were concerned."

Eoghan rose wordlessly and moved out of the healer's way.

"Have you felt the child yet?"

"Just now."

"Good." Caemgen made a show of examining her, studying her eyes, checking her pulse, but she had a feeling it was simply a way to make himself useful.

"What went wrong?"

The healer paused. "Perhaps nothing. The human mind is not made to channel so many thoughts and voices, my lady. Not even yours."

He had called her "my lady." The healers never called her

anything but Lady Aine or occasionally "girl" when they forgot themselves. What had changed?

And then she remembered what she had felt after she'd summoned the men. Devotion, obedience to her. Her face flushed. How had she not thought of that? How had it not occurred to her that if she were speaking directly to the minds of thousands of men, she might inadvertently use her powers to compel them to return? Was that why she had been given this gift? So that she could get their attention and ensure their return? And if that were true, why did she feel so guilty about it?

"My best advice now, my lady, is to rest. Drink as much as you can. Begin eating slowly again. We'll have food brought to you. You need to think of both the child and yourself."

She surveyed the concerned faces of the three men in the room and realized there was one question they hadn't yet answered.

"Did it work?"

They exchanged glances that held far more than she could unravel in her weakened—and blocked—state.

"Aye," Eoghan said. "It worked. The men of Ard Dhaimhin heard you, and the ones outside the city have been amassing beyond the druid's forces for the past two days."

She heaved a sigh of relief. "Thank Comdiu. Their oaths still hold."

"Aye, their oaths still hold." Eoghan hesitated. "But not just to Ard Dhaimhin. To you as well."

✦ ✦ ✦

Eoghan left Aine's chamber, troubled. It wasn't the fact that the men she'd recalled were loyal to her. That actually might work in their favor if she were able to command them. The real problem was that, according to the healer, the attempt might kill her.

"Sir?" Iomhar stood watch with another man opposite Aine's door. He looked to Eoghan, waiting for orders.

"Make sure she doesn't leave. No one but me, Riordan, or Caemgen."

"Aye, sir." Iomhar nodded as Riordan and the healer exited the room. Riordan and Eoghan moved down the corridor and descended the steps to the first floor.

"What now?" Riordan asked. "It feels like the calm before the storm."

Eoghan felt that sense of expectancy as well, but Comdiu was being silent on the matter. He took that to mean they had done all they could do. The returning Fíréin had not yet attempted to fight through Niall's ranks, lacking the numbers for victory, but it was only a matter of time. He found himself going to Liam's balcony, the one Aine had used, hoping the fresh air would clear his head.

Below, everything looked as it should in the late evening. Calm, orderly. Torches burning.

Yet Eoghan felt the vague sense that something was amiss. As a cool wind stirred up, he shivered.

You didn't really think you could command the city, did you? Look at you. You don't even know what to do next.

Fear slammed into him, making him gasp aloud.

"I feel it too," Riordan murmured. "I just don't understand how it's possible."

"The sidhe?"

"I expect so. But they've never encroached on Ard Dhaimhin before."

"They never had a reason to." A growing dread took Eoghan, and this time he recognized it as his own feelings, not the sidhe's influence. There were men on the borders to keep them in . . . why was that, exactly?

A distant scream broke the silence just as a man burst onto the balcony—one of the sentries, Casidhe. "There's fighting on the south side of the city, sir."

He snapped to attention. "Who's on the attack? The kingdom men?"

Casidhe shook his head. "No, sir. It's Keondric's army. They've somehow breached the wards."

CHAPTER
THIRTY-EIGHT

Aine lay in her chamber, her stomach knotting, anxiety rising in her chest. Surely she had no reason to feel this way. She couldn't even be picking up on someone else's emotions, considering the shield rune that marked her skin.

Or maybe that was the reason for those feelings. Without the voices of countless others in her head, she felt as though she were the last person on earth, her world shrinking to the expanse of one room. Even when she'd blocked out the other voices, she'd still had the impression of the others around her, vague echoes of thoughts and movement. That was all gone.

Yet she had the distinct feeling that something was wrong.

Despite the strict orders that she stay in bed, Aine pushed herself to a sitting position and swung her feet over the side. She tested her sense of balance, pleased to find she was no longer dizzy. The porridge sent up to her had done much to restore her energy, even though she still felt desperately thirsty.

"Stay with me, little one," she murmured, rubbing her stomach.

Her heart beat a little too fast as she made her way unsteadily to the water-filled basin and took up the rag lying beside it.

Comdiu, protect me, she murmured, a fervent prayer just before she swiped the cloth across the inked rune.

Voices rushed in, nearly knocking her to her knees before she slammed down the protections on her mind. Even so, it felt like holding a door closed against twenty men trying to batter it down. Her thoughts grew fuzzy around the edges.

Breathe. You can do this. You're just out of practice because you've had the rune for two days.

Gradually, she built her resistance against the voices, imagining herself strengthening her barrier against them like building a wall brick by brick, until she heard the others as a pleasant, distant hum.

And with that distance, she could make out whispers and echoes of what was happening beyond.

They were terrified.

Aine rushed to the window and peered out. It still looked peaceful in the twilight, nothing to indicate trouble. Until she felt them herself.

The sidhe.

Cold rippled across her skin, and her knees turned to water. She managed to make it onto the bed before she collapsed and dropped her head between her knees. Despite all the wards, they were here. And from what she sensed, there were a lot of them.

This wasn't just a coincidence. This was an attack.

Her heart rose into her throat. Conor. He needed to know what was happening at Ard Dhaimhin. He might be walking into a trap. She reached for his mind out of reflex before realizing he must still be shielded.

She scanned for the other men in his party. Keallach's mind burned brightest. He was a young, quiet brother who'd helped her with settling some of the refugees during her early days at Ard Dhaimhin. She touched his mind as gently as possible.

Keallach.

There was no mistaking the fright in his thoughts. Even though they'd planned for this contingency, it still must be a shock to one unused to her communications.

It's Lady Aine. I need to speak with my husband. He needs to mar his rune.

After a long pause, Keallach came back. *Aye, my lady. I will tell him.*

Aine let out a deep breath of relief. Thank Comdiu Conor was still alive and the only distress she sensed was from her popping into the young brother's thoughts unannounced. She focused her attention on the place where she had found Keallach until she recognized the bright flare of Conor's thoughts.

Joy flooded her at the first sound of his voice. *I'm here, Aine.*

✦ ✦ ✦

They left their horses a full two miles away from Loch Eirich and continued toward the old crannog fortress on foot. The clumpy stands of trees that surrounded the lake were beginning to change to colors of brown and orange and red beneath a now-constant covering of hoarfrost. That posed a challenge for two reasons: one, the sparse foliage left them less cover than they might have had earlier in the year; and two, the fallen leaves underfoot made it nearly impossible to travel silently.

Still, Conor counted on his party's stealth, even if their care did mean that their progress slowed to a crawl. Their breath puffed out around them, telltale signs of their passage even when they blended in with the sparse foliage around them. It seemed that fall had passed immediately into winter in the northern reaches of Seare, if this misty evening with its rapidly falling temperature were any indication.

And then the forest began to thin, not on the edge of the lake as all the maps showed but a full quarter mile from the water. The churned brown earth and piles of logs suggested that it had been cleared recently.

"That's not something one does to protect an old rune stone," Ailill observed near Conor's ear as they surveyed the land before them.

"No, I don't think so either." He remained crouched in the evergreen underbrush, watching for the motions of guards on the crannog or sentries on the perimeter of the shore. After several minutes, everything remained as still and quiet as death. Clearly, the druid's men had been here, and they'd increased the defensibility of the island, never mind the fact that it never had lent itself to an easy siege. So why go to the trouble if they weren't going to station men there?

"We'll check the perimeter and wait until dark before making our move," Conor whispered. "Just because it looks deserted doesn't mean it is."

They backed away from the forest's edge and split to circle the lake in opposite directions. Conor kept his eyes peeled for any indication of human presence: tracks in the forest, animal sounds, metal glinting in the light that seeped through the overcast sky. It wasn't until he noticed that he and his group were shivering that he realized he should have been watching out for signs of inhuman presence as well.

"Steady, men," he whispered. "This cold isn't entirely natural."

Sure enough, as dark fell, the mist thickened. Was that evidence of the sidhe gathering? Why now?

When they met up with the other half of the party, Ailill confirmed his thinking. "The dread is strong here. Even I feel it, and I like nothing better than besieging an unbreachable fortress in the freezing cold."

Conor grinned at the man's wry tone. The sidhe were indeed

here, but it didn't appear that any soldiers were. As he gathered
the men in a circle to discuss their options, Keallach leapt backward away from the group.

Hands immediately went to weapons, eyes scanning their
surroundings.

"Sorry, sorry," Keallach muttered. "You might tell your wife
not to scare the daylights from me if she wants to talk to you."

Conor looked quizzically at the young man, who just tapped
his forehead with two fingers. "Lady Aine just took five years off
my life."

The group grinned at him, but Conor's stomach lurched.
He'd shut her out for weeks. If it hadn't been for his men's nearly
abandoning him two days ago, he wouldn't even have known
she'd figured out how to use the sword. Every one of them
had heard her call, but this was the first time she'd ever used
them to contact him. That meant something dire. He smeared
the ink from the rune and opened his mind. *I'm here, Aine.
What's wrong?*

Thank Comdiu, Conor. Where are you?

We just arrived at Dún Eavan. Why?

*Ard Dhaimhin is under siege. Or it's about to be. We were
attacked from within, and Niall has moved ensorcelled men around
the perimeter of the forests. The sidhe are here.*

He followed her thinking immediately. *You think it's somehow
related to our attack on Dún Eavan?*

*I don't know, Conor, but it seems terribly coincidental that it's
happening now. Why attack us at the very moment you've arrived
there?*

She was right, it was coincidental, and the druid rarely did
things out of anything but deliberate planning. *Aine, when
you were here at Dún Eavan, do you remember any large stone?
Something that could be a rune stone?*

I don't remember seeing anything like that. But I wasn't looking for it either.

That's what I was afraid of. The sidhe are here as well.

A long pause. *The sidhe have always been present at Dún Eavan. But they generally avoid the runes.*

Aye. Unless there's a greater source of power there.

It was exactly what he had been thinking, except they had seen no sign of humans. So why would the sidhe congregate in a place that had a rune stone but no humans on which to feed?

Unless, like at Ard Bealach, they were guarding something.

I need to go, Aine.

Please, Conor, don't block me out.

I'm going to be entering a fortress that is thick with spirits. I need to replace the rune.

And how are you going to cross?

He'd been wondering about that himself. The only way to reach the crannog stealthily was to swim, which would almost immediately mar the ink. He would have to rely on the power of the rune charm, despite the fact it had only limited power against the sidhe. It might prevent them from seizing him completely but wouldn't stop them from communicating with him. As he well knew, the sidhe could be convincing.

Let me stay with you, Conor. Together we can be sure you are able to resist their lies.

He looked out onto the crannog, only then becoming aware of the men staring at him. He glanced down at his shaking hands. Whether it was the sidhe's influence or his own fear, he hoped they would dismiss it as cold instead of cowardice.

Aine, is someone with you?

Iomhar. He'll make sure I don't get pulled in too deep.

Conor realized then that if the rune charm failed, if the sidhe attacked him, he didn't want to face it alone.

Please, Conor. All you've ever done is protect me. Let me help protect you for once.

That made his decision for him. *Aye. But not yet. I'll let you know when we're going to enter. We need to stay free of their influence for as long as we can.*

I love you, Conor.

Those four words warmed him against the unnatural chill better than any other reassurance could. *I love you, too, Aine. Always.*

✦ ✦ ✦

"Sir, you can't go down there."

Eoghan ignored Gradaigh as he checked his sword and shouldered his spear. The reports coming in from sentries and céad leaders were nearly unbelievable: thousands of men pouring across Ard Dhaimhin's borders, far more men than they'd thought Niall had at his disposal. If the Fíréin were breaking rank like untrained novices, Eoghan had to see this threat for himself.

"Where's Riordan?" he asked.

"Here." The man appeared at the door, his sword on his back and a bow in hand. "Are you sure you want to do this?"

"I must. I have to see for myself, rally our men. Just keep any archers within range from picking us off on the stairs."

"Aye, sir."

Comdiu protect us. He strode toward the hall's main entrance and drew his sword. Shouts, screams, all the sounds of battle met him as he stepped onto the balcony and looked down through the arrow slits. Men fought in clusters below, mere hundreds scattered across the expanse of Ard Dhaimhin. Where was this army? Eoghan exchanged a confused look with Riordan and started down the steps.

The older brother followed close behind, an arrow nocked as he scanned the area below for threats. Eoghan's unease grew with every step. So far, he saw only Fíréin and kingdom men locked in small-scale skirmishes.

And then he lifted his eyes to the dark horizon and saw them: a shadowy expanse on the edge of the tree line, their numbers punctuated by torches. Hundreds of brothers fought them back, struggling to keep the attacking forces from breaking into the village proper.

The trembling began in Eoghan's knees and spread through his entire body. He might be the leader of the city, the future High King, but he was untried in battle. How was he to even begin to fight off a horde that made his thousands look like specks of sand on a beach? He wasn't prepared for this. The last time Ard Dhaimhin had seen battle, he'd cowered in the Hall of Prophecies until the danger was past.

The last time Ard Dhaimhin had seen battle. There was something important in that phrase.

The last time, the druid had burned the forests.

The forests. When had they grown back? How could he not have noticed that?

Eoghan focused on the tree line and blinked away the odd shimmer in his vision rising from the ground like steam. For an instant, the image wavered and he caught a glimpse of the trees' black carapaces stretching skeletal fingers to the sky. And then the green forests melted away, taking the men with it.

"It's all a glamour!" He shuddered, realizing for the first time that his shivering was due to the cold and not cowardice. He gripped Riordan and shook him hard. "It's not real. Look."

Riordan blinked too, and the fear fell away from his expression. "We need the shield rune," he said. "And then we need Aine."

Eoghan turned to meet a sword thrust coming his direction. Dread struck deep as he saw the flood of men headed their way. The sidhe had noticed their presence, and now the spirits were determined they wouldn't make it out alive.

CHAPTER
THIRTY-NINE

Aine walked her chamber from end to end, gripped by the simultaneous urges to block out everything that was happening down below and the desperate need to contact Conor. Neither were advisable. She needed to be aware of any danger, and she couldn't afford to interrupt Conor while he was planning his entry to Dún Eavan, which left her nothing to do but pace, pray, and worry.

Comdiu, protect us. Comdiu, watch over us.

She started into the old prayer without thinking, felt a bit of her anxiety ease, both a result of her confidence in Comdiu's power and the prayer's effect on the sidhe that now surrounded the fortress. Why they hadn't yet attacked her directly, she couldn't say. Perhaps it was simply a function of Comdiu's providence. Whatever it was, she was not about to complain.

She winced as another pain tightened her stomach. She should be lying down, but that only made her feel as though she were suffocating. She glanced at the pot of tea steeping next to the brazier. She'd brewed it a little stronger than usual, even though she was sure this was false labor like the rest. Stress and dehydration were simply making her body irritable. The herbs would soothe it.

A knock sounded at the door. "Lady Aine? You have a visitor."

Iomhar's voice. She lifted the door's heavy bar, then undid the metal latch before opening the door to her guard. He stood with two other warriors, Morrigan in the middle.

"It's all right, Iomhar. Let her in." Aine stood aside and waited for Conor's sister to enter, even though her senses screamed warning. Morrigan's face was completely placid, but anxiety seeped from every pore.

"What's wrong?" Aine asked, shutting the door behind them.

Morrigan immediately went over to the window and peered out. "It's time to go, my lady. Now, while you still can."

"Go?" Aine's pulse jolted into action. There was something disturbingly familiar about this situation. "Go where?"

"Out of Ard Dhaimhin. If you take the rune now, he won't be able to locate you. But we haven't much time."

Aine stared dumbly. "Who?"

"Niall."

The name turned the blood in her veins to ice. Aine sank down onto the bed, stunned, even though they'd known it was a possibility. "How do you know?"

Morrigan gave her a reproving look. "Come now, my lady. I don't believe you're that stupid. How do you think?"

"You've been working for him all along," Aine whispered. Somehow she hadn't expected being proven right to be so painful.

"Aye, but you knew that." Morrigan sighed, and her expression softened. "I can see why my brother is so taken with you. You really are impossibly good, which is why I don't want to see you and your baby in Niall's grasp. I may have agreed to help him get the Rune Throne, but I never agreed to this." She straightened, her manner growing hard. "Now, come here.

This is going to hurt, but a lot less than what Niall will do if he gets you."

Morrigan removed a knife from her boot. With a wash of horror, Aine realized that she meant to carve the rune into her skin. She recoiled. "No. I can't." If she gave up her healing gift and her baby came early, she would have condemned it to death. That was something she couldn't live with.

"My lady, I know you're frightened. But it's the only way. He won't be able to ever find you, and even if he does, you'll be useless to him." Morrigan's eyes pleaded for her to understand. "If he controls you, you will never be free."

Aine recognized the truth of those words, just as she recognized the familiarity of the situation. Once before, in Forrais, she'd used magic to save herself from what seemed certain death, and that choice had killed someone loyal to her. She was being given a chance to show if she had learned anything about trusting Comdiu.

She raised her head and looked Morrigan straight in the eye. "No. I won't do it."

Horror and distress flashed over Morrigan's face before settling into resignation. She didn't put the knife away. "Then you're coming with me."

Aine swallowed and nodded, only her convictions keeping the strength in her trembling limbs. *I throw myself on your mercy, my Lord. Protect me.* She focused on the other woman. "Just tell me why."

Morrigan paused. "The fact that I'm here at all should tell you I'm not completely heartless. I simply had to . . . prioritize. I know you can understand that. The lives of my sisters are worth more to me than anything else on this island, and I made a vow to protect them with my life. I will not break that vow."

Morrigan's expression hardened, and she clamped a hand

around Aine's arm. She was far stronger than she looked. Even
her demeanor had changed. She'd played the demure lady and
projected the bravado of a woman unsure of her place in the
world, but now she exuded only cold, calculated determination.

"Make it look friendlier," Aine murmured. "I don't want my
guards dying on my behalf."

Morrigan looked surprised, but she adjusted her grip so it
appeared she was helping Aine rather than compelling her.

As soon as they emerged into the corridor, Iomhar's hand
went to his sword. Aine shook her head. "We're just taking a
walk. Stay here. That's an order."

Iomhar looked as though he would protest, but Aine spoke to
his mind before the words left his lips. *Play along. Find Eoghan
and the others. Let them know the druid is at Ard Dhaimhin. And
above all, stay alive. I will need you.*

Iomhar bowed his head, as if responding to her verbal order.
"Aye, my lady. As you command."

As soon as they were out of earshot, Morrigan said, "That
was nicely done, my lady. You just saved their lives."

"What's going to be done to me?"

Morrigan faltered. "If you cooperate, probably nothing. I would
urge you to cooperate, my lady. The penalties for resistance . . ."

"Your sisters are his hostages," Aine said, finally putting
all the pieces together. She should have known. That part of
Morrigan's story—the indignities she'd suffered—had always
rung true. They'd already known that Niall was a master of using
loved ones against people.

Did that mean Conor was leverage for her, or vice versa? Or
even worse, was it her baby he intended to use against her?

As soon as they reached the bottom floor, she realized that
her hopes of having Iomhar reach Eoghan were futile. The bodies of Fíréin brothers littered the corridor, evidence that the

fighting had reached Carraigmór already. She refused to look at their faces, couldn't, lest it weaken her resolve and unleash the panic hiding just below the surface.

But as Morrigan propelled her into the hall, there was no way to suppress the wave of terror that welled up inside her, especially when the man standing by the Rune Throne turned and smiled at her. "Good evening, Lady Aine."

Niall was already here.

+ + +

Almost immediately, Eoghan put up his sword. These men were not his enemies, even if they were attacking him. He swiveled to meet an oncoming sword with his staff, disarmed the man, and dropped him to the ground with a blow to the solar plexus. He wouldn't die, even if for a minute or two he would think he would. But the men just kept coming, driven by fear and the illusion. He caught Riordan out of the corner of his eye, saw Dal and Gradaigh had joined them. They'd resorted to nonlethal means as well, attempting not to kill the men who rushed piecemeal into the melee.

This wasn't even a proper siege. It was just . . .

. . . a distraction.

Eoghan cast a gaze toward Carraigmór in the distance and the truth of the matter seeped into him. Comdiu's voice echoed in his head. *Go.*

He took off at a run, dodging oncoming men the best he could, but he still got caught up in the tangle of bodies, the sheer numbers of men fighting. He found himself being less careful, striking too hard, in his desperation to get to the fortress, but if he didn't get there soon, it wouldn't matter. Niall could not be allowed to take the Rune Throne.

And he could not be allowed to take Aine.

CHAPTER
FORTY

Conor and his men stayed at their posts as night fell, the temperature plummeting with it. They'd watched for hours from every angle, but they'd seen no indication of warriors or watchmen on the crannog, nothing but the cold structure of earth and stone that made up the old keep. Had Niall perhaps prepared the location for a fallback position or designated it for some other use? Or were they missing something important?

Of his nine companions, only seven could swim. That left two men on the shore as lookouts to alert them of approaching enemy with the Fíréin's birdcall signals. Conor was all too aware of how vulnerable they would be on the approach, precisely the point of the fortress's design. Less vulnerable, of course, than had the boat still been attached to the pulley between the two docks. Someone must have decided that offered far too much access. Another indication there was something inside worth protecting.

Conor wrapped the ink and brush inside a square of waxed canvas and tucked it into the top edge of his sword's sheath, hoping it was enough to keep the ink dry. So far they had experienced little from the sidhe but a vague sense of unrest, which could have just as easily come from their own worries. Ideally, Conor would simply play the shield around the fortress, but when stealth was their only advantage, he couldn't afford to give up their position that easily. They would instead have to face their opponent blind. The harp was too delicate to risk getting wet and far too heavy to hold over his head as he swam. If the boat that belonged to the pulley system had been stored somewhere on the crannog as he hoped, he could send it back across and have the remaining two members of the party bring his harp with them.

"Ready?" Conor pitched his voice low and waited for the answering nods from the other seven. Concentrating on fading into the surroundings, he led the party at a swift run across the open space to the edge of the loch.

He'd chosen the back edge of the lake for the crossing. It had the least amount of open space and the most amount of concealment from the probable watchpoints on the island. Still, he imagined he felt archers sighting him down arrows as he darted across the field in the dim sliver of moonlight overhead. As he reached the edge of the lake, he pulled the sword harness over his head and plunged into the water.

The lake water—colder than it should be even at this time of year—slid over his skin and immediately started an unpleasant numbness in his limbs. He ignored it and trudged deeper into the water, the mud at the shoreline sticking around his boots and hampering his forward motion. Finally, he was deep enough to push off into a slow, one-armed breaststroke, keeping his weapon just barely above water.

Only the faint sounds of movement around him said his companions were making the same slow progress across the lake to the crannog. He tried to breathe evenly, measuring each inhalation and exhalation so he didn't fatigue, but by the time his feet hit solid ground a handful of yards from the shoreline, his breath was coming in gasps. He emerged from the water just enough to slide his sword back on and free his hands, then climbed the bank in a crouch.

Despite his fears, no shout of alarm came. In fact, there was no indication anyone had noticed their presence.

The air had felt cold before, but soaked to the skin, it felt downright arctic. The uncontrollable shivering began, so much worse than Conor had expected. Maybe the fortress didn't have watchmen. If the temperature kept falling, anyone who crossed with this method would die of exposure within an hour.

Water sloshed behind him as the rest of his men emerged from the lake. He signaled for them to fan out as they'd planned, dividing into four pairs to check each corner of the seemingly deserted fortress. Ailill took up his assigned position to his left. Conor drew his own blade and led the way forward directly to the fort itself.

The sensation of cold subsided a little as they moved through the open space, senses tuned to the signs of impending battle. And yet none came. In fact, there was no sign of life anywhere on the island. No torches, no glimmer of light from the arrow slits in the fort. No guards on battlements, at doors, or on the dock. Nothing to indicate there was anything here but silent stone.

Except the sidhe. The first wave of dread hit him, so over-whelmingly repellant even with the charm that he could barely stay on his feet. Why were they even here? They would die here. That's why there were no guards. They needed no guards. If they didn't leave now—

No. That was the sidhe's influence. He had to resist it.

"Comdiu, protect us," he murmured, his words barely audible. "Comdiu, watch over us."

The sidhe's oppression eased a bit, though he still had to

brace himself against the emotions their presence dredged up. The urge to stop and draw the rune on his skin was nearly irresistible, but that would take more time than he had, not to mention the fact he was still dripping wet from the swim. He'd planned to enter with the softening rune through one of the side chambers Aine had told him about, but because there didn't seem to be anyone watching, that would be more dangerous than simply going through the front door.

He signaled to Ailill before fading into the shadows by the wall. Four other men joined them, the remaining two taking up watch positions on the edge of the crannog. His partner moved forward, his hand on the latch, shoulder to the door. Conor expected Ailill's shove to be useless—surely it was locked. Instead, the door swung inward, letting out a dim red light, like the low glow of coals.

Ambush, his mind screamed in warning, *turn back now!* That might or might not have been the sidhe, but he was once again aware of his exposed position as they flowed through the door, weapons ready. But the only thing that greeted them was silence.

Only then did Conor understand the reason for the quiet, the lack of warriors. What remained at Dún Eavan needed no guard.

Bodies.

CHAPTER
FORTY-ONE

"You look shocked to see me, my dear. I'm disappointed. I thought you'd have figured this out much earlier."

Morrigan pushed Aine forward and forced her into a chair. She sat willingly, her hands clasped in her lap. "Figured what out? We knew you would come eventually. I just don't understand why."

"Don't you? I would have thought that was obvious." Niall moved forward and pulled a chair out across the table from Aine. He looked exactly like Keondric, but there was a wrongness there she would have recognized instantly. The mannerisms old-fashioned, the expressions calculated.

"You're here for the runes."

"Aye, I'm here for the runes. And for you."

"Then why did you try to have me killed?"

"That was a bit shortsighted, I admit. But that was before I realized the full extent of what your child could do. I assume Conor is the father, hmmm?"

She recoiled at the mention of the baby, unsure whether to be insulted that he questioned its parentage or fearful about what he was implying. "I don't understand."

He cocked his head, another mannerism that didn't quite fit Keondric's body. "You really don't know? All this knowledge, all these so-called scholars around you, and you still can't see the truth?"

Her heart knocked loudly in her chest, her breath coming too quickly. What was he talking about? What truth?

Niall flashed a calculated little smile and rounded the table to kneel beside her. His hand hovered over her belly, not touching her, but she was sickened all the same. "Do you not wonder why your abilities were so far amplified, my dear? Oh, aye, I know all about those. Your ability to heal in Aron, the miraculous works you did there. The fact that you recalled all the brothers here, in fact *compelled* them to come back? You didn't think I could hear you, did you? But I, too, swore an oath on that sword. I knew about your abilities, and I could still barely resist returning to you. Of course, in a way, I suppose I did." He leaned forward to murmur in her ear, his breath brushing her neck. "Your baby is gifted."

She pulled away from him with a dismissive laugh that she didn't feel. "That's your big secret? That my baby is gifted? Of course he is. He—or she—is a product of two gifted parents."

"Aye. But his power is not in his own abilities. It's in his ability to amplify the gifts in others."

Aine's eyes widened. Even Riordan had said he'd noticed something strange about her magic. Could what Niall said be true? Did her child have an intrinsic ability to amplify the gifts in others?

"Of course what makes him so very special and valuable is what makes him so dangerous. If I don't control him, I can't leave him alive for anyone else to do so. After all, with him by your side, you alone could rule the world. It's almost a pity that you won't ever do such a thing." He waved a hand. "So you understand now, there are only two ways that this can end. Either you swear to serve me or I kill you."

Aine's thoughts spun, searching for holes in his logic, searching for ways out. "What do you want?"

"It is very simple, my lady. First I am going to copy the runes from the throne, and then you and I are going to walk out of here. Together."

"It will never work. There are hundreds of men outside who would die to stop that."

Niall gave her a nasty little smile. "I think they're otherwise occupied. And in case you're thinking about being heroic, just remember the child is the one I want. I have no compunction about cutting it out of you." Niall pulled a knife from his belt and ran the flat along the curve of her belly to emphasize his threat.

The words turned her stomach, made her vision go soft around the edges as she tried to catch her breath. She had to choose between letting the druid have the runes and her child, or dying and losing them both anyway? If it were just her, it would be an easy decision. She would turn the blade on herself. But now . . .

She grasped at whatever straw was within reach. "You can't kill me, and you can't take my child if I'm dead."

"Oh? And why is that?"

"Because without me, it will never survive. It will be born six weeks early, too weak. But I can heal it when it's born. So you see, if you lose me, you lose us both."

Niall stared at her as if he were trying to decide if she were being truthful. Then he smiled. "I never seem to account for the depth of a mother's love. Or a sister's, in Morrigan's case. Very well, my lady. If you want to ensure your child's survival, then I suggest you do nothing to jeopardize my decision to keep you alive. In fact, since Morrigan tells me you can read the runes, I'll let you copy them for me."

Aine bowed her head in acknowledgment, though her heart still thudded frantically. If she didn't think he would verify her work, she would draw them incorrectly. For now, agreeing to his demands was merely a stall tactic while she decided what to do next.

One of Niall's men brought forward parchment and ink. Aine knelt before the throne with the writing supplies. No matter what, he could not be allowed to leave with the runes.

"You're making the right decision," Morrigan whispered from her post beside her.

"Am I?" Aine shot back. "I'm not so sure." But she dipped the quill into the ink and forced herself to focus on one of the ever-shifting runes.

"What's taking so long?" Niall demanded. "Begin."

"It's complicated. There's some sort of protection on the throne. It's hard to focus on a particular rune." The lines and squiggles seemed to squirm before her eyes.

Niall looked surprised, and only then did she understand he had enlisted her because he was having the same difficulty. He probably thought it was a function of the shield rune he bore.

The shield rune. She almost laughed out loud. Of course. That's why he was making these threats. Because inside Ard Dhaimhin with the rune, he was simply an ordinary man. And she could exploit that.

She winced and clutched her belly as a labor pain hit her. It was mild, but she played it up. "It's even harder to concentrate when these keep coming. I need my tea."

Niall looked suspicious, but he nodded to Morrigan, who immediately turned and left the hall. Aine took advantage of the situation by slumping forward over her rounded belly. Inwardly, she was casting her mind beyond Ard Dhaimhin's walls. There were hundreds—thousands—of men out there who would respond to her call.

She eased the barriers in her mind slowly, at first letting in only a handful, then dozens, then a few hundred. Her brain buzzed with all the fear and distress, but she managed to hold on anyway.

What you are doing now, the images that you're seeing, the fighting—this is all an illusion. This is all the sidhe's doing to distract you. Lord Keondric has infiltrated the city and captured me. Find Eoghan! Defend Carraigmór and the Rune Throne!

Another pain squeezed her entire abdomen, and this time she didn't need to feign a groan. She opened her eyes. "It's difficult to concentrate."

Niall's eyes were cold. "You're stalling, Lady Aine."

Morrigan arrived with the teapot and poured a cup, which Aine took gratefully, even cold. She pretended to sigh in relief and bent over the throne again, feigning that she was studying the markings. But this time she cast for Conor's thoughts. Somewhere inside her, call it instinct or Comdiu's leading, she knew he needed her. Whatever he was doing was important enough to risk Niall's wrath.

Conor, where are you? I'm here.

✦ ✦ ✦

Dozens of bodies stretched out on the hall's earthen floor, laid lifelessly on pallets in neat rows, their hands folded on their chests as if they were about to be prepared for burial. Conor stared for several moments, paralyzed by the morbid sight. Yet the horror that should be there was not because there were no signs of death and decay upon them. Had they been somehow spelled to keep them frozen in death?

"They're alive," Blair whispered. "Look."

Conor focused on where Blair pointed. There it was, the barely perceptible rise and fall of the nearest man's chest. Were these souls locked in the sidhe's glamour? How long had they been here? And why?

"Conor." Ailill's warning whisper drew his attention to movement on the opposite side of the fortress. Conor raised his sword automatically, anticipating a threat. Instead, he saw an old couple sitting in chairs against the wall, their sightless eyes staring uncomprehending at the group.

"They're ensorcelled," Conor said. "They probably don't see us as a threat because they haven't been told to guard against this kind of threat."

"They're just here to tend to the bodies?" Blair said, Conor's repulsion reflected in his voice. "Like . . . gardeners?"

Conor shuddered at the analogy, but that was exactly what it seemed like. "I don't understand. Why go to the trouble? For what purpose?"

He put up his sword. The caretakers would not resist them, and even if they did, they posed no threat. Slowly, Conor walked between the rows of motionless bodies, looking for a clue, some common trait that would give a hint as to why they were there. A young boy and an old woman. Two men who looked like farmers. A woman whose ripped and dirty clothes still suggested nobility, back when that meant something.

And then as he stepped between two girls, his heart nearly stopped. It couldn't be. Surely his imagination was playing tricks on him. But as he knelt to brush aside a lock of dirty hair from the younger girl, he could not mistake the round scar on her collarbone. A burning brand from the fireplace had flown up and gotten trapped in her dress. He remembered it as if it were yesterday, how he'd fished the wood out, burning his fingertips in the process. His foster sister Liadan. That meant that the dirty, slightly battered form of the girl beside him had to be another of his foster sisters, Etaoin.

He just stared at their senseless forms, wondering what the sidhe were showing them and sickened by the possibilities. How long had they been trapped here? If Morrigan knew . . .

And then all the pieces fell into place: the reason for the sidhe, the motley collection of people without a connection. They weren't here because of their importance to Niall; they were here because of their importance to someone Niall wanted to control. They were hostages in the truest sense of the word, blackmail to ensure the compliance of his spies.

Conor, where are you? I'm here.

Aine's voice jolted him out of his dazed state. *Aine, Niall has imprisoned my sisters Liadan and Etaoin at Dún Eavan. I think Morrigan—*

Searing pain pierced him, squeezing every last thought from his mind. He fell to his knees with a cry, clawing at his head as if he could make it stop. And then he was back in the chamber in Ard Bealach, strapped to a table, wriggling and screaming beneath the slow, agonizing sweep of a knife.

No, that couldn't be right. He couldn't be back in Ard Bealach. He was at Dún Eavan. He was in the great hall, amidst the druid's collection of bodies. None of this was real.

None of this is real, Conor. Fight it. You must fight.

He realized then that the thoughts were not his own but Aine's. He grasped onto that voice, used it as a lifeline to pull himself out of the illusion that had taken him so quickly, even with the charm around his neck. Dún Eavan's hall appeared around him. The hardpacked earthen floor, the bodies. "Comdiu, stand between us and the harm of this world and banish the darkness with the light of Your Son, Balus." He picked up the prayer where he had left off, repeating it over and over as he pushed himself back to his feet. And then he saw that he was not the only one who had been attacked. His men were on the ground as well, moaning, screaming within whatever horrific illusion they had found themselves in. He looked around for a way to release them. His harp. No, the harp was back on shore. He knew too well from Daigh's example what could happen if he waited until he could retrieve it.

The rune. Of course. He pulled the ink from his scabbard and unwrapped the cloth. The brush was wet, but the lake water hadn't made it into the stoppered jar. It would have to do. Murmuring the prayer to himself the whole time, he knelt by Ailill first. The man fought and screamed the moment Conor touched him. That would make the task difficult. He had to brace one knee on his neck and the other on his chest to keep Ailill still enough to open his shirt. He uncorked the bottle with his teeth and, after wiping the wet brush on his trousers, dipped the bristles. Even pinning him down, Conor had to stop and start half a dozen times before he managed to draw the last line. And then abruptly, Ailill's movements stilled.

It was a full minute more before the man opened his eyes, which were flooded with terror and confusion. When he finally recognized Conor, he relaxed a little. "Where am I? What happened?"

"The sidhe," Conor said simply. "You have the rune now. But I need your help to put it on the others."

Ailill pushed himself shakily to a sitting position and then lumbered to his feet, swaying. "I had no idea."

"They are desperate to keep us from sending word back to Ard Dhaimhin. They will do whatever's possible to keep us here."

Ailill just nodded, wide-eyed, and followed Conor to the next man. Together they managed to draw the runes on the other four members of their party, even though it took both of them and all their strength to accomplish it. When the men were finally roused from their sleep, shaky and confused, Conor called them close.

"The sidhe are not going to stop attacking us until I can play the wards around this place strongly enough to dissuade them. To do that, we need to find the boat and bring the harp from shore. Expect opposition. Work in pairs. We'll need to put the runes on the lookouts as well."

"What about you?" Blair asked. "You don't have the rune."

"So you'll need to keep an eye on me. I can't take the shield because it will keep me from playing the wards. Blair and Tomey, stay here and keep watch over the hostages. Make sure the caretakers don't harm them. We don't know the extent of their orders or how they've been ensorcelled to respond."

"Aye, sir." The two men took up positions on opposite sides of the door, their swords in hand. Conor nodded to the other three men and gestured toward the door.

Outside the hall, the crannog was as still as ever. Too still. A niggling sense of disquiet began in the back of Conor's mind, but nothing was out of place: no guards, no noise, not even any illusion from the sidhe.

His first indication that something was truly wrong was the impact of the arrow as it slammed into him.

✦ ✦ ✦

Aine jerked as the connection between her and Conor fractured. Tears sprang to her eyes. Surely it couldn't be true. Surely she couldn't have understood that correctly. It had to be another part of the sidhe's illusion, another way to entrap him so he couldn't finish his mission.

"What is it?" Niall's scowling face broke into her vision.

Then a labor pain hit her, so strong that she could no longer deny the truth. But it also provided her the opening she needed.

"My baby," she gasped. "It's coming."

That drew Niall to her side. He knelt and hovered his hand over her belly, a chilling smile coming onto his face. "We're in luck, Lady Aine. I might not need your services after all." He switched his focus to Morrigan. "Help her."

"I don't know what help I'm going to be," Morrigan said. "I've never delivered a baby. She needs a midwife."

"No midwife," he said. "You'll have to do."

Aine ignored the conversation and breathed through another pain. They were coming more rhythmically now, a sure sign that this wasn't false labor but the real thing. She forced away her rising panic over the fact that she was still weeks from when she should be delivering. She might have one chance, and she couldn't waste it.

"Help me upstairs," she said, gripping Morrigan's arm. The other woman hauled her to her feet.

"No," Niall said. "She stays here."

Horror pierced her pain. He expected her to birth her child here? On the floor of the hall, in front of a dozen men?

"At least get her something to lie on," Morrigan snapped. "Do you expect me to put the baby on cold stone?"

Niall nodded to one of the men, who disappeared down the corridor. Morrigan helped Aine to the corner, where she lowered herself to the ground again. The pains were not so bad that she couldn't think through them still, but the men didn't need to know that. She cried out and dragged Morrigan down to her knees beside her.

"Conor found your sisters," she whispered. "They're at Dún Eavan. The Fíréin will liberate them."

Morrigan's eyes went wide with shock. "That's impossible."

"No, not impossible. I know you're just helping him because he has hostages, but your sisters are safe now. You have to help me."

"I don't believe you. You're lying."

Tears flooded Aine's eyes. "I'm not. Conor is hurt. I need time to find out how badly. You have to give me time."

"How?"

"I don't know. Just tell him I'm in hard labor. He won't expect me to do anything else." Aine winced again at the tightening in her abdomen.

"You really are going to have your child, aren't you?"

"Aye, but it's my first. It might be a while. Now go."

Morrigan pulled away, but she didn't give any indication whether she would help or not. All Aine could do was hope she'd been convincing enough.

She at last found Eoghan's mind in the crowd, but she didn't dare call for him while he was engaged in battle. Instead, she opened her mind as wide as she could manage, taking in the blast of thoughts, fears, and desires of thousands of people at once. She gasped at the rush of information, but somehow she still managed to filter it—only the Fíréin she'd contacted through the sword, only the ones she recognized as vaguely north of them.

All oath-bound brothers who are near the fortress of Dún Eavan, your aid is needed there now! Make haste!

This time when the next labor pain hit her, she didn't need to pretend to cry out.

✦   ✦   ✦

Aine's call echoed in Eoghan's head, laced with a compulsion he couldn't resist. Focused so strongly on reaching Carraigmór, it took him several minutes to realize he was no longer fighting against the flow of men but rather getting swept up in waves going the same direction.

"Sir!" A young man, barely old enough to have taken his oath, fell into stride alongside him. "Lady Aine is being held against her will at Carraigmór. What are your orders?"

His orders? He needed to know what they faced first. *Aine? Are you there?*

Eoghan, the baby is coming.

The pronouncement jolted him, but not as much as the rambling briefing that followed. *Conor is hurt at Dún Eavan. I sent men from the area to go help him. Keondric thinks I'm incapacitated. Morrigan is only helping him because he's holding her sisters. I don't know if she's on our side or his now.*

What do you want me to do?

He's completely mortal, Eoghan. Ordinary. As long as he has the rune, he doesn't have any powers. But I don't think he knows we know that.

Instantly Eoghan's mind clicked through the possibilities. *How many guards on the hall?*

Aine was gone long enough to make his heart rise into his throat. *Aine?*

I don't think it will be as long as I thought.

Aine, tell me. How many men?

Twelve, perhaps? Others scattered throughout the fortress, I'm sure.

A dozen men. Not so many, especially if Aine really had managed to turn Morrigan to their side. If he was wrong, though, or she had miscounted, he could easily be serving himself up to someone who wanted him dead.

He didn't even hesitate as he broke into a run toward the fortress.

CHAPTER
FORTY-TWO

Conor hit the ground hard, knocked to his back by the impact of the arrow. For a moment, he was unable to comprehend the reason for the shaft sticking out from his middle. And then the pain came, a searing, burning feeling that made him think he'd been stuck in the gut with a hot poker.

Ailill was saying something to him, but he couldn't make out the words. The other man lifted him by the arms and dragged him back through the open door of the fortress as arrows continued to fly around them. Then they laid him down on his side against the wall. Somewhere in the back of his mind, Conor thought it was strange that none of the other men had been hit even though they had preceded him out of the hall.

"Sir, you need to hold this here." Ailill wadded up the hem of Conor's tunic and stuffed it against the spot where the arrow shaft protruded. "You're bleeding."

"I was shot by an arrow. Of course I'm bleeding." His attempted laugh came out more like a moan. Blast, getting shot by an arrow hurt. Almost as much as what he'd experienced in the sidhe's illusion. Except this was real blood darkening the fabric of his tunic, a real arrow sticking out of his body, a real expression of concern on Ailill's face. When he'd talked about opposition, this hadn't even registered as a possibility.

"Who shot me?" he remembered to ask. "Are there guards after all? Warriors?"

"Shh, stop trying to talk, Conor."

"Tell me."

Ailill's expression darkened. "It was Keallach. I'd never have taken him for a traitor."

"It's . . . the . . . sidhe." Conor groaned and stifled a curse at the burning pain that was spreading through his whole midsection. The sidhe had taken their guards before they could get to them, convinced them to shoot Conor. The men probably didn't even comprehend what they had done. They were just being used for the spirits' purposes.

The spirits. The bodies. He'd never told Aine what he needed to tell her.

Comdiu, protect us. Comdiu, watch over us. He didn't know if he whispered it aloud or not, but Ailill took up the refrain. "Keep doing that," he said. "Just . . . a while . . . longer."

Aine—

I'm here. Oh, dear Comdiu, Conor, what happened?

The panic in Aine's voice was the first indication that he might have reason to worry. *Listen to me, Aine. Morrigan is a traitor. She is being used by the druid. The sidhe are holding Etaoin and Liadan hostage. But tell her we have them. We are going to get them out.*

I know, Conor. I know Morrigan is working for him.

Not of her own will. There are others.

Do you know who?

He realized she was not asking the identities of the hostages but rather whom they might belong to at Ard Dhaimhin. But he had no way of knowing when they were unconscious. *No.*

No one else I recognized. Tell Morrigan. I promise, Aine, we will get them out. We will get them all out.

Blair darted inside the hall and barred the door behind him. "We have a problem."

"Is it an arrow sort of problem?" The pain and now the resulting numbness was making Conor feel giddy. He looked down and realized the blood had soaked into more of his tunic than just the bit he had pressed around the arrow shaft. That probably wasn't a good sign.

"It's a warrior sort of problem. Men in boats, crossing the crannog."

Aine, we are under attack.

They're here to help, Conor. They're Fírein. Stand down.

How do you—

I sent them. Ask them. They'll tell you.

Conor conveyed the message to Blair, who looked doubtful. "She sent more men? What's to keep the sidhe from taking them as well?"

Aine, do they have the rune?

A long pause, and then Aine's distressed voice. *No. They don't.*

"I need my harp," Conor said weakly. "Get me my harp!"

"It's on the shore. We can't get it."

Blair was right. They couldn't risk the men's coming to shore under the sidhe's glamour, but they didn't have time to return for the harp without the boat—assuming the men didn't turn on them before they reached it.

For the first time, Conor realized he might have promised far more to Aine than he could deliver. And as Ailill knelt before him, his expression grim, Conor wondered if he would make it from Dún Eavan alive.

Conor, don't say that. Don't give up. You can't give up. We're depending on you.

Aine, I love you.

Conor, listen to me! You have to pull yourself together. You cannot die. All those people are depending on you. Etaoin and Liadan, they are depending on you. Now what are you going to do?

Outside the fortress, the first sounds of battle began, the clash of swords, the shouts of men, all unaware that they were fighting—killing—their allies.

He needed the harp. He needed to set up the shield, connect it to Ard Dhaimhin, share the magic that seemed to grow stronger with each ward he established. But he was feeling so tired, even the pain didn't serve to keep him awake.

✦ ✦ ✦

It took six men to escort Eoghan into the great hall from the balcony. He supposed he should be flattered. They had taken his weapons—his sword, his staff, and his knives—yet they still treated him as if he were a great danger.

If he thought it would get him anywhere, he might be.

But that would give away his play, and it would tell Niall they knew he was powerless beneath the rune and the wards of Ard Dhaimhin. It was a mark of desperation that the sorcerer would come here without his magic, or maybe a mark of arrogance. All of the havoc that he had wreaked across their land, yet now he stood here as an ordinary man.

Eoghan stumbled forward, scowling at the men holding his arms, while he took in the scene. Half a dozen warriors stood by a man who could only be Niall, surprisingly young and handsome in his host body. Beyond, in the corner of the hall behind the Rune Throne, stood Morrigan and, he realized a moment later, Aine. She didn't seem to notice him, her face twisted in pain and concentration, gripping Morrigan's hand. Niall was forcing her to deliver her baby here?

"The uncrowned king," Niall said quietly, a smile on his face. He paced forward, his hands linked behind his back. Add theatrics to his list of vices. "Yet you come as a prisoner, a penitent. Tell me why."

Eoghan nodded in the women's direction. "Release Lady Aine. I want her escorted to someplace safe."

"You are hardly in a position to make demands. What will you give me in return?"

Eoghan infused all the sincerity he could manage into his voice. "Me."

"You? You, proclaimed king of Seare, would give up your throne and your life for another man's woman? Come now, I don't believe you are that selfless." Niall's eyes narrowed as he studied him. "Unless, *King* Eoghan, that child she carries is really yours."

"How dare you suggest—"

The druid waved him off. "Enough, enough. I don't truly suggest. But you just told me what I needed to know. You're certainly not worried about your own reputation. Tell me, how does it feel to love a woman and know you can never have her?"

Eoghan knew he was just being mocked, knew Niall was trying to cloud his thinking with anger, but the question hit its mark anyway. He prayed Aine's focus was too divided to have heard. "Unlike you, I accept there are some things in life that are not meant for me. But I'm not willing to lie and kill for them."

"Aren't you? Didn't you send Conor off on his mission, knowing that he might not return? And somewhere deep in your heart, didn't you wonder if—after he was out of the way—you might have your chance with his wife?"

"No."

"And now you are lying, which you said you would not do." Niall smiled an ugly smile, twice as disturbing on Keondric's face. "And right now, Conor is lying in a pool of his own blood, hundreds of miles from here, sent by your command. Within hours, if not minutes, you will be the murderer you accuse me of being."

Eoghan stared, stunned. That couldn't be true. Aine would have told him. Wouldn't she have? Unless she didn't know.

Or she didn't want to distract him from his purpose.

Or maybe she isn't as loyal as she claims to be. After all, you and she have become . . . close. Do you think, knowing how Conor feels about it, she would have accepted your friendship had she not felt something more?

They sounded like his own thoughts, but they weren't. He knew they couldn't be. Even though he hadn't been able to get his unruly emotions in check, he'd never truly contemplated the things running through his mind now.

Can you live with yourself? How will it be to look her in the face and tell her you are responsible for the fact she's a widow? How can you tell her you are the reason her child has no father? Do you really think you could step in and fill that role?

The voices in his head grew to a volume he could no longer shut out. "Stop. I don't believe them. I never intended that. I'm not responsible. I didn't even send him on this mission."

He realized he was on his knees. That was significant some-how, but beneath the barrage of ugliness and doubt, he couldn't think why.

"Do you think I would really come here unprepared?" Niall asked, satisfaction thick in his voice. "Your weakness is enough to break you. If you'd just owned up to your desires, accepted them, you wouldn't be susceptible to the whispers."

"No." Eoghan pushed away the voices with effort and struggled to his feet. "That's the one thing you could never understand, and the one thing that will be your downfall."

"What's that?" Niall smirked.

"Loyalty can be neither earned nor broken by threats."

Niall stared at Eoghan in confusion. Then he looked down in shock at his own body.

A blade protruded from Niall's chest.

And then it slid back out with barely a whisper, bright with blood and held in shaking hands.

Morrigan.

✦ ✦ ✦

Aine felt rather than heard the activity going on around her, the competing voices in her head growing to a nauseating clamor. The fighting below. Conor and his men. Eoghan's distress. And above it all, the insistent demands of her own body. She barely noticed when Morrigan left her side and glided around the back edge of the hall, her intentions just another thread of consciousness in the back of her mind.

Yet she felt the instant the blade pierced Niall's body, as if some invisible thread had been cut. The spirits of the two men rushed out—one angry, shrieking beneath the runic magic that tore it apart, the other like a breath of wind. For that single moment, she felt Keondric's soul surround her.

You're free.

And then they were gone like a puff of smoke, only a whisper and the oily taint of sorcery remaining as it burned away beneath the city's wards.

Aine gathered her strength, mustering her will even through her growing exhaustion. Conor needed her. She couldn't let him down now.

✦ ✦ ✦

Conor, are you there? Stay with me.

Aine's voice cut through the fog, bringing Conor temporarily back to the present. *I'm here.* His eyelids drifted halfway shut. The magic. There was something about magic that he had been thinking about.

It was all interconnected.

Of course it was interconnected; *he'd* interconnected it. If he concentrated, he could feel it, those golden pools, woven together in places with fine threads, in others with corridors, great floods of magic. They felt so close he could almost touch them. But he was completely useless if he didn't have the harp.

Are you sure about that?

He wasn't sure if that thought came from Aine or himself, but it spooled his mind down impossible paths. Hadn't he once said that he had the ability to manipulate magic? Isn't that what he had done within the sidhe's construct in Gwydden? Wasn't that essentially what he did each time he played the harp?

"Conor, stay awake." A stinging on his face made his eyes pop open. Ailill had slapped him. Why had he slapped him?

Right, he needed to stay awake. He refocused his thoughts. "Join the fight, Ailill. Those are our allies. Don't let them kill each other."

"But you—"

"I'll be fine. Go."

He barely noticed Ailill stand and leave the room with Blair, already reaching for the magic that lingered in the distant reaches of his consciousness. There was a fortress with a shield fifty miles away. That wasn't so far. He reached out, mentally grasping at the edges, imagining stretching it his way. But he might as well be trying to catch moonbeams. He could feel them, see them, but he couldn't take hold of them.

The magic. Focus on the magic. In his mind's eye, he had been trying to capture it physically. But that was ridiculous, considering that it existed on another plane completely. If he could really manipulate it, couldn't he just command it?

This time he thrust away the pain and thought of himself as a lodestone that drew metal to itself, except he wasn't attracting metal; he was drawing magic. Slowly, the golden light began to shudder and stretch toward him.

Why do you think you can do this? You're useless. You've always been useless, a disappointment since the day you were born. Your own father left you to be raised by a man who hated you. That's why he sent you away.

Aine's voice penetrated the whispers. *Conor, listen to me. You must block out those thoughts.*

How many men have died on missions you were supposed to be leading? How many have been lost today while you cower inside the keep's safety? Some leader you are. It's a good thing another is meant to be king.

The light slowly receded, solidifying to its original form.

See, it was a useless conceit. You are nothing without the harp. Nothing without your woman.

It was the mention of Aine that broke through the fog. The statement might have been meant as an insult, but it turned his attention back to the quiet, calm voice in his head.

Conor, you may not believe in yourself, but I do. And more important, Comdiu does. He has provided you with all you need to accomplish His purpose. Nothing anyone or anything else does can change that. Now build the shield!

He sucked in a breath, which turned into a hissing sob. Why did it hurt so much? Wasn't he supposed to go numb from shock already?

Conor, focus. You must do this! You must do it now!

Maybe Aine did have the power of command over him, because he called the magic to him before he fully comprehended what he was doing. It shot toward him like a great tidal wave, spreading out the distance between the fortress and Dún Eavan, a flood of magic consuming all in its wake. He bent it up and over the lake, the crannog, twisting it in his mind into a great shining dome that spilled down around them. But it didn't stop there. He pushed it out until it picked up the thread of another ward, bare filaments left over from the original wards like cobwebs hanging from the abandoned covering of an old fortress. That arced the magic in a jagged line like a lightning strike where it collided with the edge of Ard Dhaimhin's wards in a flash of light.

Conor just stared blankly, transfixed by the images in his mind, no longer able to tell whether he merely felt the magic or controlled it. It burst out from Ard Dhaimhin into a starburst pattern, connecting all the other warded fortresses and then spreading in the gaps like warm honey, reaching out . . . out . . . out until the shield of gold extended from one edge of the island to the other.

And then the screaming started.

Not just from the ensorcelled caretakers at Dún Eavan but across the land. He felt their agony, somehow, heard their cries as the magic in them clawed away from the pure golden light. He was connected to the shield now, aware of every place it touched, every swirl and eddy of magic, living, quixotic like the ocean.

A laugh bubbled up inside him. He had done it. Comdiu only knew how, away from the harp, commanding magic he barely understood. And it had been easy. All it took was his wife yelling at him in his mind.

The laugh turned to a cough and then just as quickly to a moan. He still had an arrow in him, and the wound was still bleeding. He needed to get help. He needed to reach the door.

Conor tried to roll onto his hands and knees, but he

collapsed before he got his limbs beneath him. It was futile. He was too immobilized by the arrow. But surely now that the shield had been erected, the fighting would stop and someone would come to him.

And then he heard it: a low, keening wail so horrifying he was sure he'd hear it in his sleep. Even without Aine's description he would recognize that sound—the bean-sidhe, the herald of death.

He might have erected the shields, but he'd forgotten one important thing: the wards didn't bar the sidhe; they simply dissuaded them. And from the sounds of the fighting still raging outside, they had plenty here at Dún Eavan on which to feed.

CHAPTER
FORTY-THREE

Pain. Why was there so much pain? It wound around Aine, through her link with Conor and back, shooting through her body. But that wasn't right. She wasn't feeling his pain, was she? It was her own pain.

The baby.

Panic ripped through her. She was alone. She'd delivered other women's children but never her own. What if something went wrong? What if she couldn't take the pain?

This wasn't the way it was supposed to be.

And then she felt it, the wash of golden light over her, the bright vibration of the wards around them. Conor. It had to be. She felt the influence of the sidhe recede momentarily, the confused awakening of countless men below.

You're doing it, Conor. Don't give up!

In the distance began the screaming. But as the next pain hit, she couldn't be sure if it were coming from outside the fortress or within.

✦ ✦ ✦

Aine's scream echoed through Carraigmór's great hall as they stared at the lifeless body of the man who had held them all in thrall through fear and sorcery. In that moment, the air seemed to freeze, crystallizing in the moment of decision as the men around them contemplated what to do.

As if of one mind, they sheathed their weapons.

Eoghan let out a breath of relief, his eyes drifting to Morrigan, who still stood over the body with the bloody sword. The fight visibly drained from her as the weapon clattered to the ground. She nodded in Aine's direction. "Help her."

✦ ✦ ✦

She couldn't handle the pain. Surely this was the sign of something wrong. Or maybe it was Conor's pain. She couldn't tell the difference, hanging suspended in the minutes between one clench of agony and the next.

"Aine, I'm here." A strong hand clamped over hers, and she forced her eyes open.

Eoghan.

"I think Conor's dying," she whispered. "I think we both are."

"You are not dying." Eoghan scooped her up in his arms like a child and infused his voice with every bit of authority he could muster. "You have to hold on. Both of you have to hold on."

✦ ✦ ✦

As the fight raged on, the whispers began again.

You thought you could defeat us so easily?

Your weak God gave us this earth. Why would you believe you could contain us?

You're going to die. Alone. A failure. Unremembered.

Conor tried to block them out, but their words, false as they were, wormed into his heart and mind. *Aine, it didn't work. The wards are completed, but it didn't work. The sidhe . . .*

I know. They're here, too.

That got his attention. Ard Dhaimhin? They had stayed away from the fortress all this time, he thought due to the wards and the presence of so many believers. *Are you all right? What's happening?*

The baby's coming. And you're hurt. You need to get to some help.

I'm fine. This time he gritted his teeth and forced himself to his knees. He would not lie here on the ground and bleed to death. He still had work to do. They hadn't found anything resembling a standing stone here. The others had been easy to find, prominent but overlooked because the observers weren't expecting to see anything but a slab of stone. But there was nothing like that here. The entire fortress was built from earth and small chunks of quarried rocks. The yard was hardpacked dirt, the outbuildings timber. If there were once a stone here, it was here no longer, had been buried, or had been sunk in the loch. Much good any of that did them now.

Aine, how many runes are there on the throne?

I don't know.

Find out.

He didn't know how long he sat there, propped up against a wall, waiting for Aine's answer. But it was not her voice that came into his mind.

Forty-nine? I can't be certain.

Eoghan? What are you doing there?

Conor, I'm here with Aine. The baby is coming. Please, let me help. What are you thinking?

Forty-nine. The calculation made his head hurt. Sixteen for-tresses so far, and all of them seemed to have had three runes per stone. Praise Comdiu for the druids' methodical natures. That meant they were missing one. It could be only here. *Did the other men tell you which runes were destroyed?*

No. We didn't think about it. We were so sure there were only sixteen fortresses.

It was too late now. He didn't have time to think about what they should have done. Without anywhere else to congregate, the sidhe would go for the largest concentration of souls, the most amount of unrest they could find, feeding off the fear and pain of those involved to compensate for the discomfort the magic inflicted. That was Ard Dhaimhin. *I need to know that rune.*

Eoghan's voice answered again. *We have no way of knowing. How can you be sure there is even one there? Maybe you were wrong. Or maybe Ard Dhaimhin is the seventeenth fortress. After all, Dún Eavan was the last to be built of all the places you've visited.*

What?

Aye, it may be old-style construction, but it barely predates King Faolán. I know it wasn't there on the old maps at Ard Dhaimhin. It was just a building.

What kind of building?

Eoghan paused, giving him the impression that he was looking something up or asking a question. *It was a nemeton. A temple.*

Conor's mind spun out of control, his fast-forming thoughts seemingly impossible. The seventeenth location, but no rune stone. Originally a nemeton.

He eased his knife from his sheath and drew a circle on the packed-earth ground with the tip. The island itself. He closed his eyes, orienting himself, and then drew a smaller circle in the center for the fortress. Dots for the location of each outbuilding, even the ones that were crumbling and out of use, the ones that should have been demolished long ago. When he opened his eyes, he had two concentric circles and a constellation of dots between them.

Dear Comdiu, give me Your vision for this. Show me how this goes together. Tell me if I've lost my mind.

As he stared at the drawing from beneath lowered lids, he saw it. These were not marks but rather points of intersection. The runes were formed with circles and crossed lines. Slowly, painstakingly, he drew the lines through the points, four of them crossing at oblique angles to the circle and to each other. And when the last one was completed, the word came to him, like a breath, like the whisper of the password that protected the Hall of Prophecies.

Seal.

He let out a moaning laugh and leaned his head back against the wall. *I have it, Aine. The last rune. The seal. It was too important to commit to a stone, so they made the entire crannog a rune. I know what I have to d—*

The shriek of the bean-sidhe shattered his ears before he finished the thought. He opened his eyes to a swirl of shadows. Hundreds of them: inky black, vaguely human forms, coalescing like the formation of thunderheads, churning in the space overhead. His heart started pumping in earnest again, bringing another gush of warm blood from his midsection. His dread over the significance got lost in a sudden surge of panic, stark, visceral fear. The malevolence poured off the sidhe, the thoughts being sent his way too numerous and vicious to process, but he felt every one of them impact his soul like invisible arrows.

Worthless. Weak. Unloved. Abandoned. Stupid. Helpless. All the things he had attributed to himself, all the reasons why he knew he wasn't worthy. Each one of them beat him a little further down until all he wanted to do was to curl within himself and weep. He couldn't do this. He was foolish to think he could ever leave a mark on the world, that he could ever live up to the expectations of those around him. He was worthless. Worthless and alone.

And then a quiet voice in his head. Not Aine's, but it filled him with the same sort of warmth, just amplified.

You are not alone. I am with you.

He grabbed on to the voice as he had with Aine's, let it pull him up through the mire of his own criticism. *What must I do? I don't understand.*

By blood you were redeemed. By blood you will be remembered.

The runes weren't enough. The sidhe had been liberated through blood magic, and through blood magic they had to be returned. Except the Red Druid had brought them forth with the blood of others, the pain and fear and loss that surrounded a human life taken unjustly—the things that the sidhe fed on, the things that allowed them to thrive.

To seal them back again, it would take the blood of sacrifice, freely given in love and compassion.

Do not be afraid.

Tears filled his eyes when he realized what he was being asked to do. He closed his fingers around the shaft of the arrow and brought them away wet and red. The decision had already been laid out before him, the first step taken. All he had to do was finish it.

Aine, are you there?

Aine's voice, weak and fearful, came into his head. *I'm here. Conor, what's going on? Why . . . what . . . ?*

Clearly she understood his thoughts. The only thing he wanted to do now was console her.

It's okay, Aine. I finally know what has to be done. Please don't be afraid. I'm not.

Conor, I don't know what you're doing, but stop and think for a minute. The sidhe—

They can't hurt me anymore. I see through their lies. Comdiu has shown me the truth.

Conor, no—

Please, listen to me. There are two things you must know. The first is that the runes need to be destroyed. All of them. The harp, the throne, the sword. Let them fall into the oblivion of history, where they can't be resurrected. It's the only way.

Aye, Conor, I understand. What is the second?

I love you. Tell my son that I loved him as well.

A tearful-sounding laugh rang in his head. *Still insisting it's a son, are you?*

It is a son. And his name must be Siochain. Promise me.

No! I won't! You need to be here to name him yourself!

It's all right, Aine. Let me go. I always knew I wasn't the hero of this story anyway.

He didn't know whether her long pause was her weeping or if she were fighting through another birth pang, but when she spoke again, her voice managed to be strong. *I'm here, Conor. I'm here with you until the end.*

It was time. He took both hands and pulled the arrow free from his body with a wrenching scream that started the flow of blood draining into the earth that was the rune, mingling life and magic around him. Then he reached for the bright, golden light that surrounded him. He didn't think; he just wove them together, through, over, beneath into a shining prison. The sidhe screamed in an inhuman mixture of pain and outrage, yet they couldn't resist the magic that twined around them and pulled them toward Dun Eavan. In his mind's eye, their dark forms blotted out the moonlight, writhing beneath the fingers of light as they were sucked back into their eternal prison.

And then the screaming stopped as abruptly as it had begun, leaving stillness in its wake.

No fighting outside.

No whispers.

He let himself slide down the wall, shivering now from exertion and cold, enwrapped in the costly silence of victory.

It's done, Aine.

Conor, please, don't go.

He smiled suddenly as the silence was broken by a familiar sound. *They were right all along, Aine. I hear music.*

Everything else slid away. The fortress, the magic, Aine's voice in his head whispering that she loved him—all enveloped in a melody that resonated down to his very soul. Nothing left but light. Love. Music.

CHAPTER
FORTY-FOUR

Eoghan stumbled away from Aine's bedside, blinded by the
tears streaming unrestrained down his face. He couldn't think
about what he'd just witnessed, couldn't think about the sacrifice
that had just been made.

"Hold on," he whispered to Aine. "I'll be right back."

She sobbed silently in the bed, arms wrapped around herself
while her body shook with grief. But he couldn't think about
that, either. There was one more task to be finished, one more
duty to ensure that Conor's sacrifice had not been in vain.

He raced down the corridor blindly, squelching the sobs
that wanted to well up from his own chest. When he reached
the hall, he barely registered the men still standing there, staring at the dead body of the druid as if they were sure it would
rise again.

"Sword! I need my sword."

One of his former captors handed him his sheathed weapon.
Eoghan drew the sword from it and threw the scabbard on the
ground. The runes of the oath-binding sword glistened in the
torchlight.

Morrigan caught his eye. Somehow she seemed to understand what he meant to do. "Do it."

He strode toward the throne, the blade upraised over his head, and brought it down with all his force.

The impossibly hard edge of the sword met the equally hard marble slab with a flash of light and the sound of shattering glass. The sword broke in his hands, disintegrating into the pile of dust. And somewhere in his mind, the magic around them—the wards, the dome—all fell like the shards of a great window, sparkling like newly fallen snow.

In their place, he felt it: a weight and yet a freedom.

His wonder didn't last long. Freedom, aye, but one bought with a heavy price, bought with blood and sorrow. He sank to his knees and wept.

CHAPTER
FORTY-FIVE

Two hours later, in the dark of night, Conor's son entered the world—tiny, pink, and mewling more like a newborn kitten than a human child. Aine cradled him to her body, staring down into alert blue eyes that already held so much wonder.

She'd never thought she could be capable of such joy and such sorrow at the same time. Her son. She pressed her lips to his forehead as tears slid down her face and dampened his skin. His father would never see him take his first steps, ride his first horse, grow to manhood. But thanks to Conor's sacrifice, there would be a future for him, for them all. Conor's magic encased them now, woven indelibly into the fabric of Seare. The sidhe had been bound, the key to their prison destroyed.

And no matter how shattered her heart might be, she would go on. She owed Conor that much. She owed Siochain.

The door opened softly, and she looked up from her bed to the newcomers. Eoghan and Riordan stepped inside, tear-stained and somber.

"Your grandson," Aine said hoarsely. "I think he looks like Conor."

She offered him up to Riordan and he took him with a tenderness that made her wonder if he'd done the same with Conor, even while pretending to be his uncle and not his father. And then the man's expression shifted, plummeting her heart into her stomach.

"What is it? What's wrong?"

Riordan forced a smile. "Nothing's wrong. I just didn't expect . . ." He swallowed hard. "I don't know if it's a matter of your gifts and Conor's together, or something else entirely, but he has power. I can feel it."

"Of course he does," Eoghan said, peering into the baby's face. "They're both gifted."

"You don't understand." Riordan met Aine's gaze, a serious look overtaking him. "I've never felt so much in one person, let alone a child. Those gifts are usually just a glimmer."

Aine took the baby back from his grandfather, clutching him to her chest as if she could protect the boy from the significance of the words. "Niall said something about my baby's powers, that he could amplify the gifts of those around him?"

"Perhaps. But I wouldn't be surprised if it were more. We have absolutely no idea what he's capable of, Aine. It's no wonder Niall wanted him. He won't be the last."

She began trembling again. It was too much. After all that had happened—the losses, the victory—she could barely comprehend what Riordan was saying. And then Eoghan was kneeling beside the bed, his expression kind. "What's his name, Aine?"

"Siochain," she whispered, her voice wavering. "He—Conor—chose it."

Eoghan's eyes widened. Then he began to laugh. First a chuckle, then a bellow that reverberated off the stone chamber, until tears ran down his face. He bent his head toward the mattress, his shoulders shaking, though she couldn't tell if it was from laughter or sobs.

Siochain let out a wail at the noise. Aine murmured soothingly to him, then asked Eoghan, "What on earth are you laughing about?"

Eoghan wiped his red eyes. "Conor figured it out in the end."

"Explain yourself," Riordan said tightly.

"The prophecy that we've twisted ourselves into knots over. We know it refers to the High King, and we know the many ways we've interpreted it already. 'In that hour alone, the son of Daimhin shall come; wielding the sword and the song, he shall stand against the Kinslayer, binding the power of the sidhe, and, for a time, bringing peace.'

"Siochain means 'peaceful descendant.' Peace, Aine. Literally."

She looked down at her child: innocent, serene, ordinary. "It can't be."

"Oh, it can. Comdiu confirms it. All our wrangling over the meaning, talking about which one of us it referred to, and we were all wrong."

Aine just stared wide-eyed at Eoghan, the man she'd already accepted in her mind as her monarch. But if what Eoghan said was correct and Comdiu had confirmed it, then the prophecy belonged to her son.

Epilogue

The wind whipped Aine's heavy wool cloak around her body, bringing a distinct chill despite the fact that the sun still shone brightly overhead. Fall was coming slowly this year, which was good. She still had plenty of lessons to teach before her students would be given leave to return to their villages in the spring.

"Look carefully," Aine said, pitching her voice above the whisper of the wind and the crunch of her boots in the field's drying foliage. "This late in the season, the yellow dock leaves have mostly died back. If you didn't take detailed notes when we came through in the summer, you're likely to go back empty-handed."

Her dozen students, mostly young women, with the exception of three older boys, hurriedly consulted the small, hand-sewn books that contained their sketches, maps, and notes on the herbs that grew wild in the meadows south of Carraigmór. Out here, in the places that had once been charred by unnatural sorcerous fire, the medicinal plants had been the first to come back. Over time, the fields had once again been planted with crops, but Aine had asked that the small one nearest the city be reserved for wildcrafting and cultivating herbs that wouldn't grow within the small walled gardens of the healers' quarter. Eoghan hadn't objected. He wasn't inclined to deny Aine much, even if she tried hard not to take advantage of that fact.

"I'm not even sure *I* remember where it was," Liadan murmured from where she tramped through the long grasses beside Aine. "And this was my idea."

Aine chuckled and Liadan returned the smile. It was hard to believe that this poised young woman was the same frightened and traumatized girl who had come to Ard Dhaimhin after being rescued from Dún Eavan. Etaoin, the elder sister, had taken the situation in stride and married a young Fíréin apprentice within the year, but Liadan hadn't spoken for months, following Aine around like a shadow. Only when she'd found interest in healing had she finally begun to come out of her shell.

In the end, Morrigan's actions, abhorrent as they had been, had saved both her sisters. Aine could only hope she was finding some measure of peace in the Aronan convent to which she'd exiled herself.

"Here!" A young woman named Dealla raised her book in the air triumphantly as she spotted a cluster of the brown stalks, almost stripped bare of their red-brown leaves by the wind. Aine pulled herself out of her musings and waved for the others' attention.

"Very good. That is indeed yellow dock." Aine raised her voice so the others could hear and removed a small hand trowel from her belt. "Yellow dock, like its cousins burdock and dandelion, has a single taproot. If you try to pull them directly out of the ground, they will break. Rather, they must be dug up whole from beneath." She shoved the spade into the ground and pulled up a clump of mature brown roots, then hacked a bit off the end to show the yellow inside.

"Now spread out," she said. "I know for a fact an entire

section of this field was covered with yellow dock earlier this summer. We'll see how keen your eyes and your memories are."

She stood back and watched her students comb the grassy meadow in search of today's lesson, a smile coming to her face. The truth was, she didn't need to teach anymore. In the nearly thirteen years since they had retaken Seare from Niall, Ard Dhaimhin had flourished, and with it had come the dozens of healers required to take care of the blossoming city population. Each one of those men and women—Liadan included—had both their own permanent apprentices and a constant stream of new students. But she enjoyed watching the gleam of discovery on their young faces, took satisfaction in the knowledge that she had a hand in equipping the rest of united Seare to take care of their own clans and villages. And it eased a bit of the natural ache that came with knowing that each passing year took Siochain a little further away from her and a little closer to assuming the throne.

The sound of galloping hooves made her pull her attention away from the plants, her heart rising briefly into her throat. Even after years of peace, she hadn't quite thrown off the dread that fast-approaching riders always brought. But even before the man reined in at the edge of the field, leading a second horse behind him, she knew what this was about. Siochain had talked of almost nothing else for two weeks.

"Liadan will supervise while I go back to the city," Aine called. "I'll expect you all to have your roots cleaned and laid out on your workbenches when I get back."

"Aye, my lady," a dozen voices said in near unison. Aine smiled warmly at them and made her way over to the man atop the gray gelding.

"The Lord Regent summons you, my lady," Iomhar said, but there was a hint of a smile in his voice.

"He does, does he?" Aine fit her foot into the Gwynn-style stirrup and threw her leg over the back of the horse. She straightened her dress and nodded to the man. "Lead on, then."

Iomhar cued his horse into an easy canter, and Aine followed automatically. It wasn't that she hadn't known this day would come. Siochain was almost thirteen, and up to this time, he'd been trained and educated in private, most often by the regent himself. But the idea of another skilled man coming at her only son with a dangerous weapon . . . How did women ever send their children off to war when she couldn't even imagine letting her son fight in a public practice match?

Their arrival back in the city caused barely a ripple in the bustling activity that went on around them, but those who recognized Aine dropped bows and curtsies in deference as they passed. She held no official title, but the fact that her son was the future king of Seare gave her unofficial status as queen mother. The oath-bound brothers who remained in the city showed a particular devotion. They may have sworn fealty to the throne of Seare, but their ties to her through the sword remained.

She smiled and nodded back, feeling her heart expand at the warmth she felt pouring from them. Could she ever have imagined this place? After years of strife and pain, could she have envisioned that Ard Dhaimhin would become this cheerful, busy center of trade, herself as an unofficial symbol of what had brought it about?

Iomhar led her to the new training compound nearest the fortress, where the king's guard drilled. There was already a crowd gathered around the central yard, low conversation buzzing in speculation over whether the king-elect was ready, whether even the Lord Regent could have trained him well enough in the past seven years to warrant a public spectacle. The fluttering in her stomach took up a similar refrain.

As soon as they reined in, the crowd parted for the dark-haired man striding toward her. He was dressed simply but richly, fully armed as he always remained in public. Eoghan held out his hands to help her from her horse. As soon as her feet touched the ground, he said formally, "My lady, I'm so pleased you were able to leave your work to join us."

She inclined her head and took his arm to be escorted to the practice yard—some traditions had carried over from the kingdoms after all—but beneath her breath, she murmured, "If he's not ready or he gets hurt, you are in mortal danger."

Eoghan chuckled. "Duly noted, my lady. You'll be pleased, I promise. Haven't I been telling you as much for the past year?"

Aye, he had, but despite being Siochain's foster father and mentor, Eoghan could never understand how difficult it was for a mother to see her son trained for war, especially when the child's father had been lost in that manner. She gripped a handful of skirt in her free hand and forced herself to take a deep breath.

As if understanding her thoughts, he squeezed her hand where it gripped his arm. She let out the breath. No, she trusted him. She was just being overprotective.

She rethought that decision when she saw her son with the weighted practice sword in his hand, standing a full foot shorter than his opponent. "He's fighting Breann?"

"Aye. Breann's larger, but he'd rather die than hurt Siochain. You know that." Eoghan had trained the young man personally since his first battle at Ard Dhaimhin thirteen years ago, and he had chosen him only three years ago to be Siochain's companion. Naturally, that meant both sparring partner and personal guard.

"I wouldn't worry about Siochain," Iomhar said. "I've seen him fight. Sometimes it's as if he knows what his opponent is going to do before he does it."

Aine and Eoghan exchanged a look, barely repressing their smiles.

"Let me get this match started." Eoghan nodded at Iomhar in a way that felt like an order, and the man slipped in next to Aine.

Aine watched as Eoghan stepped up to speak with both Breann and Siochain, her heart again thumping too hard in her chest. She was being far too protective. But in his simple, kingdom-styled clothing, his long blond-brown hair tied back in a queue, Siochain looked heartbreakingly like Conor. Tall for his age, he had that lanky, rawboned look that meant he hadn't quite yet grown into himself. When Eoghan finished with the instructions, though, Siochain threw a grin over his shoulder at her. Despite herself, she smiled back.

Eoghan came back to her side as both young men assumed their guard positions, and the conversation died down, anticipation heavy. The Lord Regent bent his head toward hers and murmured, "You know, Conor was nineteen when I tried him against his first opponent."

"Is that supposed to make me feel any better?" she whispered back.

"Aye. Just watch."

So she watched, breath held until she felt dizzy, as Breann took Siochain through his paces. By now, Aine was a good-enough judge of skill to recognize that both men's technique was near flawless, a result of Eoghan's exacting standards. Siochain knew exactly what his opponent was going to do, and he knew exactly how to avoid it. The other man's practice sword didn't come within inches of his body. Eventually, the reason why would emerge. For now, she was satisfied to let everyone believe that it was merely skill and not his ever-evolving gifts.

Then Siochain looked toward them. Eoghan gave a barely

perceptible nod. Three more swift moves, and Breann's sword was sailing across the practice yard, Siochain's wooden weapon pressed to his heart.

"I yield." Breann's words drifted across the yard, and then a broad smile illuminated his face as he yanked Siochain toward him in a victory embrace, one arm slung around his neck. Siochain pretended not to be pleased, but Aine could practically feel the satisfaction radiate from her son like heat from the hot springs.

"I told you," Eoghan said smugly.

"Aye, you did." She hesitated and then asked, "Gifts aside, he's really quite good, isn't he?"

"He's exceptional. And that's coming from someone who has seen some of the best swordsmen to ever come from here." He cut off his words as if he knew this wasn't the direction she wanted to take with the conversation. "Do you have a few minutes? I want to talk to you about preparations for Siochain's name-day celebration."

"Aye." She cast a last look at her son, but Eoghan said quickly, "Breann and Iomhar will look after him."

She let Eoghan escort her to the steps to Carraigmór, dropping his arm to precede him up. She followed him silently through the hall to the room that had once been the Ceannaire's office and now served as the Lord Regent's personal meeting room and study.

"I thought we'd agreed not to make too big of a fuss over this," Aine said as soon as they were alone.

"It's an important occasion. The thirteenth name day of our future king? It would be unseemly not to celebrate. The people would think we were hiding something."

He was right, and the country was thriving, so there was no reason to spare expense. It might have taken more than a decade to get to this point, but it seemed that the last marks of the revolution—the economic ones—were finally disappearing from the face of Seare. And yet . . .

"I know this is hard for you," Eoghan said, his eyes softening. He took a seat across from her at the large table. "Will this be a very difficult thing to celebrate?"

She chewed her lip, debating diplomatic answers. But after all Eoghan had done for her and Siochain, he deserved the truth.

"Some days I wake up and I miss Conor as if he died yesterday," she said. "And other days I barely even think about him. It's been nearly thirteen years and I still feel—"

"Like it's wrong to be happy without him?"

She gave him a twist of a smile. Once more, he proved he knew her better than anyone else in her life. "Something like that."

He just nodded. "I know that Conor would be proud of the life you've made here and the son you've raised. I think he would be pleased by this celebration. He sacrificed for you and for Siochain and for the future of Seare. None of this would be possible without that. It seems only right to honor both him and our future king in a joyous way."

She turned over his words in her head, and gradually the fingers of anxiety relaxed. He was right: Conor had died, aye, but his death had ensured that the kingdom their son would inherit could never be terrorized by the sidhe or seized by the runes again. It was time to throw off this indefinite sense of mourning and embrace the life she and Siochain had made here.

She studied Eoghan from across the table, taking in the shadow tracing his jaw, the barely visible lines at the corners of his eyes. She'd expected him to marry and have his own children by now, but he'd shown no interest in that. Instead, he'd waited more patiently than any woman had a right to expect, never wavering in his devotion to her and Siochain, never pressuring even though she knew his feelings toward her had not changed. For the first time since Conor's death, the barriers on Aine's heart cracked open.

Perhaps it really was time to move on.

Too late, she realized she was staring, and heat rose to her cheeks. Eoghan cleared his throat. "Something arrived for Siochain last week, in honor of his name day."

"Oh? From whom?"

Eoghan didn't immediately answer, just rose and retrieved a carved wooden box from the shelf. When he handed it to her, she immediately noted the royal crest of Gwydden inlaid in gold on the surface.

"From Prince Talfryn?"

Eoghan nodded. "According to his letter, it's a family heirloom meant to give protection to the wearer. It seems that he owed Conor a boon for his assistance at Cwmmaen, and he wishes to extend that same promise to Conor's son."

Slowly Aine lifted the lid, then gasped. Nestled on a field of velvet lay a medallion of ivory, inset with gold and rubies. Yet there was something very familiar about it. Twin tendrils of fascination and horror spiraled through her as she lifted it from the case.

It may have been far fancier than the one they had destroyed, fit for a king and not for a priest, but there was no mistaking the nature of the medallion that Talfryn had sent to her son.

A rune charm.

Discussion Questions

1. Why do you think sorcery and the runic magic can't coexist? How is the druid's intrinsic fear of the runic magic both symbolic and practical in the book?

2. Somhairle believes that Meallachán gave him the shield rune in order to ensure his own survival. What other motivations might Meallachán have had? What do Somhairle's assumptions reveal about himself?

3. Larkin asks Conor why he hasn't played wards around the other fortresses in Seare. Conor says it's because the risks are too great and he is needed elsewhere. Do you think a leader has a responsibility to help the individual wherever possible, even at the risk of his own life, or do the needs of the whole outweigh the safety of a few?

4. Conor allows certain fears to guide his actions, which makes him vulnerable to the sidhe's influence at Ard Bealach. How do our own fears sometimes guide us into bad decisions? Contrast this with the fact that while in the tunnel, Conor cannot sense his own magic and must trust the abilities Comdiu has given him (see 2 Corinthians 5:7).

5. When Conor questions Somhairle, Larkin is willing to set aside his oath of obedience to his commander in favor of his own conscience, even if that means punishment. In what situations is disobedience or insubordination preferable to violating your personal beliefs? When do the consequences become less important than the need to stand up for what you believe is right?

6. At one point, Aine and Riordan discuss the possibility that their struggles may be in vain, that the odds are too great and the war against Niall impossible to win. How do you decide when to fight a losing battle and when to surrender?

7. It takes Aine thirteen years before she is ready to completely put aside her mourning and look to the future with hope of renewed life. Conor battled guilt for every life lost as a result of his actions, even those willingly sacrificed for him. What does the Bible teach about sacrifice? How have people sacrificed for you? What should our response be in the way we live our lives?

Glossary

Abban (OB-bawn) – former commander of southern Faolanaigh forces; whereabouts unknown

Adversary, the – Arkiel, the leader of the fallen Companions (the sidhe)

Ailill (AYE-lill) – Fíréin brother; member of Conor's contingents to Ard Bealach and eastern Seare

Aine Nic Tamhais (ON-yuh nik TAV-ish) – the "lady healer of Lisdara"; married to Conor Mac Nir

Ard Bealach (ard BE-lah) – fortress in mountains of Sliebhan

Ard Dhaimhin (ard DAV-in) – former High City of Seare; home of the Fíréin brotherhood

Aron (ah-RUN) – Aine's birthplace, across the Amantine Sea

Balian (BAH-lee-an) – the faith of those who follow Balus; a follower of Balus

Balurnan – Timhaigh manor; former home of Lord Labhrás, Conor, and Morrigan

Balus (BAH-lus) – son of Comdiu; savior of mankind

Bánduran (BAHN-dur-ahn) – Faolanaigh fortress seized by Niall

Banndara (bahn-DAR-uh) – location of the druidic nemetons in Sliebhan

Bearrach (BEAR-uhk) – healer at Lisdara; Aine's former instructor

Bersi (BER-si) – mercenary working for Niall; Morrigan's former lover

Blair (blair) – Fíréin brother; member of Conor's contingents to Ard Bealach and eastern Seare

Breann (BREE-ahn) – novice of the Fíréin brotherhood

Briallu (bree-AHL-lu) – sidhe who had masqueraded as Prince Talfryn's daughter

Caemgen (CAM-gen) – healer of Ard Dhaimhin

Calhoun Mac Cuillinn (cal-HOON mok CUL-in) – former King of Faolán, assumed deceased; Aine's half brother

Carraigmór (CAIR-ig-mor) – fortress of the High King and the Fíréin brotherhood

céad (ked) – a company of men; literally, one hundred

Ceannaire (KAN-na-ahr) – leader of the Fíréin brotherhood

Cill Rhí (kill ree) – Balian monastery

Cionnlath (KYUN-lath) – fortress seized by Niall

Cira/Ciraen (seer-AH) (seer-AY-ahn) – largest empire in history, now reduced to a small portion of the continent

Clanless – a group of Seareanns who claim no allegiance to clan, lord, or king

Comdiu (COM-dyoo) – God

Companions – the spirit warriors of Comdiu; angels

Conclave – the ruling body of the Fíréin brotherhood

Conor Mac Nir (CON-ner mok NEER) – Timhaigh warrior and musician; former Fíréin apprentice; married to Aine

Cwmmaen (coom-MINE) – a former Ciraen fortress in Gwydden; seat of Prince Talfryn

Daigh (dy) – senior member of the Fíréin brotherhood

Daimhin (DAV-in) – the first High King of Seare

Dal (dahl) – senior member of the Fíréin brotherhood

Diocail (dyuh-KEL) – master of Forrais's house guard; now deceased

druid – priests of the pagan religion that predated Balian beliefs in Seare

Drumdubh (drum-DOOV) – fortress seized by Niall

Dún Eavan (doon EE-van) – crannog fortress; original seat of the king of Faolán

ensorcelled – possessed by sorcery; ensorcelled individuals are unable to exert their free will

Eoghan (OH-in) – Fíréin brother, believed to be the prophesied High King; Conor's best friend

Etaoin (ee-TAO-in) – middle daughter of Lord Lahbrás; Conor's foster sister; Morrigan's younger sister

Faolán/Faolanaigh (FEY-lahn) (FEY-lahn-aye) – northeastern kingdom in Seare, formerly ruled by Clan Cuillinn/their language and people

Fechin (feh-KEEN) – senior member of the Fíréin brotherhood

Fergus Mac Nir (FAYR-gus mok NEER) – former king of Tigh; Conor's uncle

Ferus (FAYR-us) – Fíréin brother; member of Conor's contingent to Ard Bealach

Fincashiel (finn-CASH-el) – fortress in eastern Seare; destroyed by Niall

Fíréin (FEER-een) brotherhood – ancient brotherhood dedicated to the reinstatement of the High King

Forrais (FOR-rahs) – Aine's birthplace in the Aronan Highlands

Galbraith Mac Nir (GOL-breth mok NEER) – king of Tigh; Conor's stepfather, now deceased

Glas Na Baile (GLAHS na BAH-leh) – fortress in Faolán; destroyed by Niall

Glenmallaig (glen-MAL-ag) – seat of the king of Tigh; Conor's birthplace

Gorm Lis (gorm LEES) – fortress in Faolán

Gradaigh (GRAH-duh) – senior member of the Fíréin brotherhood

Great Kingdom – the formerly united isle of Seare, under King Daimhin's rule

Gwydden/Gwynn (GWIH-duhn) (gwin) – a country across the Amantine Sea/ their people

Hall of Prophecies – magically concealed chamber in Carraigmór that contains the Fíréin brotherhood's ancient writings

Hesperides/Hesperidian (hes-PAIR-uh-dees)/(hes-PAIR-id-ee-an) – country within the Ciraean empire/their language and people

High City – Ard Dhaimhin

Holy Canon – the Balian holy scriptures

Ibor (EE-bor) – Fíréin brother; member of Conor's contingent to eastern Seare

Iomhar (EE-ver) – Fíréin brother; Aine's principal bodyguard

Keallach (CAL-lah) – Fíréin brother; member of Conor's contingent to eastern Seare

Keondric Mac Eirhinin (KEN-drick mok AYR-nin) – Faolanaigh battle captain; killed and identity stolen by the druid Niall

Labhrás Ó Maonagh (LAV-raws oh-MOY-nah) – Conor's foster father; now deceased

Lachtna (lukh-NA) – Fíréin brother; member of Conor's contingent to Ard Bealach

Larkin (LAR-kin) – Fíréin brother; member of Conor's contingent to Ard Bealach

Liadan (LEE-uh-den) – youngest daughter of Lord Labhrás; Conor's foster sister; Morrigan's youngest sister

Liam Mac Cuillinn (LEE-um mok CUL-in) – Ceannaire, leader of the Fíréin brotherhood; Aine's half brother; now deceased

Lisdara (lis-DAR-ah) – seat of the king of Faolán

Loch Ceo (lok kyo) – lake within Ard Dhaimhin

Loch Eirich (lok AYE-rick) – lake at which Dún Eavan is located

Lommán (lom-MAHN) – Fíréin brother; member of Conor's contingent to eastern
    Seare

Lonn (lon) – town father of Glas Na Baile

Lorcan (LUR-cawn) – Aine's previous bodyguard, presumed deceased

Macha (mah-HUH) – chief of Clan Tamhais; lady of Forrais

Meallachán (MOL-luck-on) – bard

Morrigan (MOHR-ree-gan) – eldest daughter of Lord Labhrás; Conor's foster sister;
    suspected to be a spy in Niall's service

Muiris (MYOOR-ees) – Fíréin brother; member of Conor's contingent to eastern
    Seare

Murchadh (MOOR-hah) – senior healer of Ard Dhaimhin

Nuada (NOO-uh-duh) – Fíréin brother; assigned to command of Ard Bealach

Niall (NEE-ahl) – former Ceannaire of the Fíréin brotherhood; also known as
    Diarmuid; currently occupies the body/identity of Lord Keondric Mac Eirhinin

Oath-Binding Sword – the sword on which generations of Fíréin oaths were sworn;
    an object of runic power

Old Kingdom – the formerly united isle of Seare, under King Daimhin's rule; see also
    "Great Kingdom"

Oscar (OS-car) – Clanless warrior under the command of Oenghus

Oenghus (EN-gus) – leader of a band of Clanless in the Sliebhanaigh mountains

Peadar (PAH-derh) – Fíréin brother; Aine's night guard

Red Druids – druids who have accumulated power through blood magic and the
    sidhe, which is forbidden by the druidic order

Regent – one who rules in the stead of an underage, disabled, or absent king

Riocárd (rih-CARD) – captain of Glenmallaig's guard; killed by Conor

Riordan Mac Nir (REER-uh-dawn mok NEER) – Conor's father; senior member
    of the Fíréin brotherhood

Roark (roark) – a young boy; one of two survivors of the siege on Bánduran

Ruarc (ROO-ark) – Aine's previous bodyguard, now deceased

Rune Throne – the original rune-carved throne of King Dhaimhin

Seanán (shuh-NAHN) – Fíréin brother; member of Conor's contingent to Ard Bealach

Seanrós (SHAWN-ross) – old forest bordering Faolán

Seare/Seareann (SHAR-uh)(SHAR-uhn) – island housing the four kingdoms/its
    language and people

sidhe (shee) – the evil spirits of the underworld; demons

Siochain (SHE-oh-hahn) – Aine's and Conor's son

Siomar/Siomaigh (SHO-mar) (SHO-my) – Southeastern kingdom in Seare/their language and people

Shanna (SHA-nah) – first queen of Seare; wife of King Daimhin

Sliebhan/Sliebhanaigh (SLEEV-ahn) (SLEEV-ahn-eye) – Southwestern kingdom in Seare/their language and people

Sofarende (soeh-FUR-end-uh) – seafarers from the Northern Isles (Norin)

Somhairle (SO-mar-lee) – commander of Ard Bealach under Niall

Sorcha (SOAR-kah) – a refugee woman from Ard Dhaimhin's village

spelled – under the influence of a spell, which is limited to a particular function; spelled people may otherwise exert free will

Tadhg (tyg) –captain of Balurnan's house guard; now deceased

Talfryn (TAL-frin) – prince of Gwydden; lord of Cwmmaen

Tigh/Timhaigh (ty) (TIH-vy) – northwestern kingdom in Seare/their language and people

Tomey (TOH-mee) – Fíréin brother; member of Conor's contingent to Ard Bealach

Uallas (WAL-luhs) – Aronan lord of Eilean Buidhe

Acknowledgments

The conclusion of this series is bittersweet. While I'm happy to pass the final chapter of this story on to my readers, it's hard to say good-bye to characters who have been with me for years. Thank you to all of you who have embraced Conor, Aine, and Eoghan in their journeys.

A special thank-you goes to all those who helped this series make its way into the world:

My original NavPress team, including Meg Wallin and Rebekah Guzman, who saw the potential of Conor's story at the start.

My current NavPress team—Don Pape, Caitlyn Carlson, Melissa Myers, Dave Zimmerman, Pat Reinheimer, and Stephanie Chalfant—who have been utterly gracious to this writer and this series they inherited. I am a very small deal, but you make me feel like a very big one.

My Tyndale group—Valerie Austin, Noel Birkey, Amie Carlson, Patty Caruso, Raquel Corbin, Caroline Hutchison, Annie Kim, Dean Renninger, Jeff Rustemeyer, Adam Sabados, Caleb Sjogren, Barry Smith, Sue Thompson, and Linda Vergara—thank you for all your hard work in getting this book into the hands of readers.

My amazing editor, Reagen Reed, who labored over this book as lovingly as if it were her own work. You deserve more than a little credit for how this one turned out.

Cover designer par excellence, Kirk DouPonce—you really outdid yourself on this one.

Steve Laube, who is always there with a reality check, a well-timed metaphor, and half a dozen stories when I need them. I'm grateful to have you on my side.

My soul sisters and partners in crime, Evangeline Denmark and Brandy Vallance, who kept me going even when the clocks ticked down and the caffeine ran out (perish the thought!).

Elizabeth Younts, who talked me through my characters, my story, and my doubts as I set out to rewrite this one yet again. Seriously, I wouldn't have made it to The End without your encouragement.

Laurie Tomlinson, my ever-enthusiastic barometer of awesome. Thanks for letting me ruin the surprise over and over again.

Halee Matthews, my secret weapon. You give me a little bit of my sanity back. Thank you, thank you.

My family—Rey, N., P., Dad, and Mom—who now know what it's like to live with a writer on deadline and have decided to keep me anyway. I love you guys.

About the Author

C. E. Laureano's love of fantasy began with a trip through a magical wardrobe, and she has never looked back. She's happiest when her day involves martial arts, swords, and a well-choreographed fight scene, though when pressed, she'll admit to a love of theater and travel as well. Appropriately, she's the wife to a martial arts master and mom to two boys who spend most of their time jumping off things and finding objects to turn into lightsabers. They live in Denver, Colorado, with a menagerie of small pets. Visit her on the web at www.CELaureano.com, or e-mail her at connect@CELaureano.com.

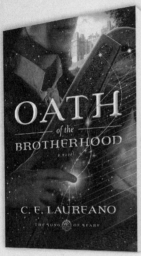